Since these episodes are necessary, indeed form a central part of any historical account, we have included the execution of one hundred citizens hanged in the public square, two friars burned alive, and the appearance of a comet – all descriptions which are worth a hundred tournaments and have the merit of diverting the reader's mind as much as possible from the principal action.

(Carlo Tenca, *La ca' dei cani*, 1840)

CONTENTS

1

A PASSERBY ON THAT GREY MORNING

A passerby on that grey morning in March 1897, crossing, at his own risk and peril, place Maubert or the Maub, as it was known in criminal circles (formerly a centre of university life in the Middle Ages when students flocked there from the Faculty of Arts in *Vicus Stramineus* or rue du Fouarre, and later a place of execution for apostles of free thought such as Étienne Dolet), would have found himself in one of the few spots in Paris spared from Baron Haussmann's devastations, amidst a tangle of malodorous alleys, sliced in two by the course of the Bièvre which still emerged here, flowing out from the bowels of the metropolis, where it had long been confined, before emptying feverish, gasping and verminous into the nearby Seine. From place Maubert, already scarred by boulevard Saint-Germain, a web of narrow lanes still branched off, such as rue Maître-Albert, rue Saint-Séverin, rue Galande, rue de la Bûcherie, rue Saint-Julien-le-Pauvre, as far as rue de la Huchette, littered with filthy hotels generally run by Auvergnat hoteliers of legendary cupidity, who demanded one franc for the first night and forty centimes thereafter (plus twenty sous if you wanted a sheet).

If he were then to turn into what was later to become rue Sauton but was then still rue d'Amboise, about halfway along the street, between a brothel masquerading as a brasserie and a tavern which served dinner with foul wine for two sous (cheap even then, but all that was affordable to students from the nearby Sorbonne), he would have found an impasse or blind alley which already by that time was called impasse Maubert, but up to 1865 had been called cul-de-sac d'Amboise, and years earlier had housed a *tapis-franc* (in underworld slang, a tavern, a hostelry of ill fame, generally run by an ex-convict, and the haunt of felons just released from gaol), and was also notorious because in the eighteenth century there had stood here the laboratory of three celebrated women poisoners, found one day asphyxiated by the deadly substances they were distilling on their stoves.

At the end of that alleyway, quite inconspicuous, was the window of a junk shop which a faded sign extolled as *Brocantage de Qualité* – a window whose glass was now covered by such a thick layer of dust that it was hard to see the goods on display or the interior, each pane being little more than twenty centimetres square, all held together by a wooden frame. Beside the window he would have seen a door, always shut, and a notice beside the bell-pull announcing that the proprietor was temporarily absent.

But if, as rarely happened, the door was open, anyone entering would have been able to make out in the half-light illuminating that dingy hovel, arranged on a few precarious shelves and several equally unsteady tables, a jumble of objects which, though attractive at first sight, would on closer inspection have turned out to be totally unsuitable for any honest commercial trade, even if they were to be offered at knock-down prices. They included a pair of fire dogs that would have disgraced any hearth, a pendulum clock in flaking blue enamel, cushions once perhaps embroidered in bright colours, vase stands with chipped ceramic putti, small wobbly tables of indeterminate style, a rusty iron visiting-card holder, indefinable pokerwork boxes, hideous mother-of-pearl fans decorated with Chinese designs, a necklace that might have been amber, two white felt slippers with buckles encrusted with Irish diamante, a chipped bust of Napoleon, butterflies under crazed glass, multicoloured marble fruit under a once-transparent bell, coconut shells, old albums with mediocre watercolours of flowers, a framed daguerreotype (which even then hardly seemed old) – so that if someone, taking a perverse fancy to one of those shameful remnants of past distraints on the possessions of destitute families, and finding himself in front of the highly suspicious proprietor, had asked the price, he would have heard a figure that would have deterred even the most eccentric collector of antiquarial teratology.

And if the visitor, by virtue of some special permission, had continued on through a second door separating the inside of the shop from the upper floors of the building, and had climbed one of those rickety spiral staircases typical of those Parisian houses whose frontages are as wide as their entrance doors (cramped together sidelong, one against the next), he would have entered a spacious room which, unlike the ground-floor collection of bric-a-brac, appeared to be furnished with objects of quite a different quality: a small three-legged Empire table decorated with eagle heads, a console table supported by a winged sphinx, a seventeenth-century wardrobe, a mahogany bookcase displaying a hundred or so books well bound in morocco leather, one of those so-called American-style

3

desks with a roll top and plenty of small drawers like a secretaire. And if he had passed into the adjoining room, he would have found a luxurious four-poster bed, a rustic *étagère* laden with Sèvres porcelain, a Turkish hookah, a large alabaster cup, a crystal vase and, on the far wall, panels painted with mythological scenes, two large canvases representing the Muses of History and Comedy and, hung variously upon the walls, Arab barracans, other oriental cashmere robes, an ancient pilgrim's flask; and then a washstand with a shelf filled with toiletry articles of the finest quality – in short, a bizarre collection of costly and curious objects which perhaps indicated not so much a consistency and refinement of taste as a desire for ostentatious opulence.

Returning to the first room, the visitor would have made out an elderly figure wrapped in a dressing gown, sitting at a table in front of the only window, through which filtered what little light illuminated the alleyway, who, from what he would have been able to glimpse over that man's shoulders, was writing what we are about to read, and which the Narrator will summarise from time to time, so as not to unduly bore the Reader.

Nor should the Reader expect the Narrator to reveal, to his surprise, that this figure is someone already named, since (this being the very beginning of the story) no one has yet been named. And the Narrator himself does not yet know who the mysterious writer is, proposing to find this out (together with the Reader) while both of us look on inquisitively and follow what he is noting down on those sheets of paper.

. . . I dreamt about Jews every night,
for years and years. . . .

[PAGE 7]

2

WHO AM I?

24th March 1897

I feel a certain embarrassment as I settle down here to write, as if I were baring my soul, at the command of – no, by God! Let us say on the advice of – a German Jew (or Austrian, though it's all the same). Who am I? Perhaps it is better to ask me about my passions, rather than what I've done in my life. Whom do I love? No one comes to mind. I know I love good food: just the name *Tour d'Argent* makes me quiver all over. Is that love?

Whom do I hate? I could say the Jews, but the fact that I am yielding so compliantly to the suggestions of that Austrian (or German) doctor suggests I have nothing against the damned Jews.

All I know about the Jews is what my grandfather taught me. "They are the most godless people," he used to say. "They start off from the idea that good must happen here, not beyond the grave. Therefore they work only for the conquest of this world."

My childhood years were soured by their spectre. My grandfather described those eyes that spy on you, so false as to turn you pale, those unctuous smiles, those hyena lips over bared teeth, those heavy, polluted, brutish looks, those restless creases between nose and lips, wrinkled by hatred, that nose of theirs like the beak of a southern bird . . . And those eyes, oh those eyes . . . They roll feverishly, their pupils the colour of toasted bread, indicating a diseased liver, corrupted by the secretions produced by eighteen centuries of hatred, framed by a thousand tiny wrinkles that deepen with age, and already at twenty the Jew seems shrivelled like an old man. When he smiles, my grandfather explained, his swollen eyelids half close to the point of leaving no more than an imperceptible line, a sign of cunning, some say of lechery . . . And when I was old enough to understand, he reminded me that the Jew, as well as being as vain as a Spaniard, ignorant as a Croat, greedy as a Levantine, ungrateful as a Maltese, insolent as a gypsy, dirty as an Englishman, unctuous as a Kalmuck, imperious as a Prussian and as slanderous as anyone from Asti, is adulterous through uncontrollable lust – the result of circumcision, which makes them more erectile, with a monstrous disproportion between their dwarfish build and the thickness of their semi-mutilated protuberance.

I dreamt about Jews every night for years and years.

Fortunately I have never met one, except for the whore from the Turin ghetto when I was a boy (though we exchanged only a few words) and the Austrian doctor (or German, though it's all the same).

I have known Germans, and even worked for them: the lowest conceivable level of humanity. A German produces on average twice the faeces of a Frenchman. Hyperactivity of the bowel at the expense of the brain, which demonstrates their physiological inferiority. During times of barbarian invasion, the Germanic hordes strewed their route with great masses of faecal material. Even in recent centuries, French travellers knew immediately when they had crossed the Alsace frontier by the abnormal size of the turds left lying along the roads. And if that were not enough, the typical German suffers from bromidrosis – foul-smelling sweat – and it's been shown that the urine of a German contains twenty per cent nitrogen while that of other races has only fifteen.

The German lives in a state of perpetual intestinal embarrassment due to an excess of beer and those pork sausages on which he gorges himself. I saw them one evening, during my only visit to Munich, in those species of deconsecrated cathedrals, as smoky as an English port, stinking of suet and lard, even sitting in couples, him and her, hands clasped around those tankards of beer which would alone be enough to quench the thirst of a herd of pachyderms, nose to nose in bestial love-talk, like two dogs sniffing each other, with their loud ungainly laughter, their murky guttural hilarity, translucent with a perpetual layer of grease smeared over their faces and limbs, like oil over the skin of athletes from an ancient arena.

They fill their mouths with their *Geist*, which means spirit, but it's the spirit of the ale, which stultifies them from their youth and explains why, beyond the Rhine, nothing interesting has ever been produced in art, except for a few paintings of repugnant faces, and poems of deadly tedium. Not to mention their music: I'm not talking about that funereal noise-monger Wagner who now sends even the French half crazy, but from the little I have heard of them, the compositions of their Bach too are totally lacking in musicality, cold as a winter's night, and the symphonies of that man Beethoven are an orgy of boorishness.

Their abuse of beer makes them incapable of having the slightest notion of their vulgarity, and the height of this vulgarity is that they feel no shame at being German. They only took a gluttonous and lecherous monk like Luther seriously (can you *really* marry a nun?) because he ruined the Bible by translating it into their own language. Who was it said that they've abused Europe's two great drugs, Alcohol and Christianity?

They think themselves profound because their language is vague – it does not have the clarity of French, and never says exactly what it should, so that no German ever knows what he meant to say, and mistakes this uncertainty for depth. With Germans, as with women, you never get to the point. Unfortunately, when I was a child, my grandfather (not surprisingly, with his Austrian sympathies) made me learn this inexpressive language, with verbs you have to search out carefully as you read since they are never where they ought to be. And so I hated this language, as much as I hated the Jesuit who came to teach it to me, caning my knuckles as he did so.

Since the time when that man Gobineau wrote about the inequality of the human races, it seems that if someone speaks ill of another race it is because he regards his own to be better. I have no bias. As soon as I became French (and I was already half French through my mother) I realised that my new compatriots were lazy, swindling, resentful, jealous, proud beyond all measure, to the point of thinking that anyone who is not French is a savage, and incapable of accepting criticism. But I have also understood that to induce

. . . They only took a gluttonous and
lecherous monk like Luther seriously
(can you really marry a nun?)
because he ruined the Bible translating
it into their own language. . . .

[PAGE 9]

a Frenchman to recognise a flaw in his own breed it is enough to speak ill of another, like saying, "We Poles have such-and-such a defect," and, since they do not want to be second to anyone, even in wrong, they react with, "Oh no, here in France we are worse," and they start running down the French until they realise they've been caught out.

They do not like their own kind, even when advantage is to be gained from it. No one is as rude as a French innkeeper. He seems to hate his clients (perhaps he does) and to wish they weren't there (and that's certainly not so, because the Frenchman is most avaricious). *Ils grognent toujours.* Try asking him something: "*Sais pas, moi*", and he'll pout as if he's about to blow a raspberry.

They are vicious. They kill out of boredom. They are the only people who kept their citizens busy for several years cutting each other's heads off, and it was a good thing that Napoleon diverted their anger onto those of another race, marching them off to destroy Europe.

They are proud to have a state they describe as powerful but they spend their time trying to bring it down: no one is as good as the Frenchman at putting up barricades for whatever reason and every time the wind changes, often without knowing why, allowing himself to get carried onto the streets by the worst kind of rabble. The Frenchman doesn't really know what he wants, but knows perfectly well that he doesn't want what he has. And the only way he knows of saying it is by singing songs.

They think the whole world speaks French. That's what happened a few decades ago with that fellow Lucas, a genius who forged thirty thousand documents, stealing antique paper by cutting the endpapers out of old books at the *Bibliothèque Nationale*, and imitating various kinds of handwriting, though not as well as me. . . . I don't know how many he sold at an outrageous price to that fool Chasles (a great mathematician, they say, and a member of the Academy of Sciences, but a blockhead). And not just him, but many of his fellow academicians took it for granted that Caligula, Cleopatra or Julius Caesar would have written their letters in French, and Pascal, Newton and Galileo would have written to each other in French, when every child knows that educated men in those days wrote to each other in Latin. French scholars had no idea that other people spoke anything other than French. And what's more, the false letters told how Pascal had discovered universal gravitation twenty years before Newton, and that was enough to trick those Sorbonnards who were so eaten up by national self-importance.

Perhaps their ignorance is a result of their meanness – the national vice which they take to be a virtue and call thrift. Only in this country has a whole comedy been devised around a miser. Not to mention Père Grandet.

You can see their meanness in their dusty apartments, in their threadbare upholstery, bathtubs handed down from their forebears, those rickety wooden spiral staircases constructed to ensure that no space is left unused. Graft together a Frenchman and a Jew (perhaps of German origin), as you do with plants, and you end up with what we have now, the Third Republic. . . .

If I have become French it's because I couldn't bear being Italian. Being Piedmontese (by birth) I felt I was only the caricature of a Gaul, but more narrow-minded. The people of Piedmont flinch at the idea of anything new, they are terrorised by the unexpected – to get them to move as far as the Kingdom of the Two Sicilies (though very few of Garibaldi's men were Piedmontese) it needed two Ligurians, a hothead like Garibaldi and an evil character like Mazzini. And let's not mention what I discovered when I was sent to Palermo (when was it? I'd have to work it out). Only that conceited fool Dumas loved those people, perhaps because they adored him more than the French, who always regarded him as a half-caste. He was liked by the Neapolitans and Sicilians, who are mulattoes themselves, not through the fault of a strumpet mother but through generations of history, born from the interbreeding of faithless Levantines, sweaty Arabs and degenerate Ostrogoths, who took the worst of each of their hybrid forebears – laziness from the Saracens, savagery from the Swabians, and from the Greeks, indecision and the taste for losing themselves in idle talk until they have split a hair into four. In any event, it's quite enough to see the guttersnipes in Naples who fascinate foreigners by gulping down spaghetti which they stuff into their gullets with their fingers, spattering themselves with rancid tomato. I've never seen them do it, but I know.

The Italian is an untrustworthy, lying, contemptible traitor, finds himself more at ease with a dagger than a sword, better with poison than medicine, a slippery bargainer, consistent only in changing sides with the wind – and I saw what happened to those Bourbon generals the moment Garibaldi's adventurers and Piedmontese generals appeared.

The fact is that the Italians have modelled themselves on the clergy, the only true government they've had since the time that pervert the last Roman emperor was buggered by the barbarians, because Christianity wore down the pride of the ancient race.

Priests . . . How did I come to know them? At my grandfather's house, I think. I have a vague memory of shifty looks, decaying teeth, bad breath, and sweaty hands trying to caress the back of my neck. Disgusting. They are idle, and belong to a class as dangerous as thieves and vagrants. They become priests or friars only to live a life of idleness, and idleness is guaranteed by their number. If there were, let us say, one priest in a thousand people then they'd have so much to do that they couldn't laze about eating capons. And from the most unworthy priests the government chooses the stupidest, and appoints them bishops.

You have them around as soon as you are born, when they baptise you; you have them at school, if your parents have been so fervent as to send you to them; then first communion, catechism, confirmation; there's a priest on the day of your wedding to tell you what to do in bed, and the day after at confession to ask you how many times you did it, so that he can arouse himself behind the grille. They talk with horror about sex but every day you see them getting out of an incestuous bed without even washing their hands, and they eat and drink their Lord, then shit and piss him out.

They keep saying that their kingdom is not of this world, then take everything they can lay their hands on. Civilisation will never reach perfection until the last stone of the last church has fallen on the last priest, and the earth is rid of that evil lot.

The communists have spread the idea that religion is the opium of the people. That's correct, because it is used to keep a hold on people's temptations, and without religion there would be twice the number of people on the barricades, whereas during the days of the Commune there weren't enough, and they could be gunned down without much trouble. But, after hearing that Austrian doctor talk about the advantages of the Colombian drug, I would say religion is also the cocaine of the people, because religion has always led to wars and the massacre of infidels, and this is true of Christians, Muslims and other idolaters. And while the negroes of Africa confined themselves to massacring each other, the missionaries converted them and made them into colonial troops, ideally suited to dying on the front line, and raping white women when they reached a city. People are never so completely and enthusiastically evil as when they act out of religious conviction.

Worst of all, without a doubt, are the Jesuits. I have the feeling I have played a few tricks on them, or perhaps it's they who have done me wrong, I'm not sure which. Or perhaps it was their blood brothers, the Masons. They're like the Jesuits, only more confused. The Jesuits at least have their theology and know how to use it, but the Masons have too much of it and lose their heads. My grandfather told me about the Masons. Along with the Jews, they had cut off the king's head. And they created the Carbonari, who are rather more stupid than the Masons – once they got

. . . Jesuits are Masons dressed up as women. . . .

[PAGE 17]

themselves shot, and later on they had their heads cut off for making a mistake in producing a bomb, or became social- ists, communists and Communards. All up against the wall. Well done, Thiers!

Masons and Jesuits. Jesuits are Masons dressed up as women.

I hate women, from what little I know of them. For years I was obsessed by those *brasseries à femmes,* the haunts of delinquents of every kind. They are worse than brothels, which are hard to set up because the neighbours object. Brasseries, on the other hand, can be opened anywhere because, as they say, they are just places for drinking. But you drink downstairs and the prostitution goes on upstairs. Each brasserie has a theme, and the girls are dressed accord- ingly: in one place you have German barmaids; the waitresses opposite the law courts wear lawyers' gowns. Elsewhere the names are enough, like the *Brasserie du Tire-cul,* the *Brasserie des Belles Marocaines* or the *Brasserie des Quatorze Fesses,* not far from the Sorbonne. They're nearly always run by Germans – here's a way of undermining French morality. There are at least sixty of them between the fifth and sixth *arrondissements,* but almost two hundred throughout Paris, and all are open even to the very youngest. Youths go there first of all out of curiosity, then out of habit, and finally they get the clap – if not worse. When the brasserie is near a school, the pupils go there after classes to spy on the girls through the door. I go there to drink . . . and to spy from inside, through the door, at the pupils who are spying in through the door. And not just at the pupils – you learn a great deal about the customs and habits of adults, and that can always be useful.

What I most enjoy is spotting the various kinds of pimps hanging around the tables; some are husbands living off the charms of their wives: they hang about, well-dressed, smoking and playing cards, and the landlord or the girls refer to them as the cuckolds' table. But in the Latin quarter many are failed ex-students, always worried that someone is going to make off with their source of income, and they often draw knives. Calmest of them all are the thieves and cut-throats, who come and go because they need to keep a low profile and know the girls won't betray them, otherwise they'd end up next day floating in the Bièvre.

There are also the inverts, busy looking for perverts of either sex for the most lurid services. They pick up clients at the Palais-Royal or the Champs-Élysées and attract them using a coded sign language. They often get their accomplices to turn up at their room dressed as policemen, threatening to arrest the client in his underpants, who then begs for mercy and pulls out a handful of coins.

When I enter these whorehouses I do so with caution, because I know what might happen to me. If the client looks as though he's wealthy, the landlord makes a sign, a girl introduces herself and gradually persuades him to invite all the other girls to the table and to order the most expensive things (but they drink *anisette superfine* or *cassis fin* so as not to get drunk, coloured water for which the client pays dearly). Or they get you to play cards, and of course they exchange signs so that you lose and have to buy dinner for everyone, including the landlord and his wife. And if you try to stop, they invite you to play not for money but so that for every hand you win a girl takes off a piece of clothing. . . . And each item of lace that falls reveals that disgusting white flesh, those swollen breasts, those dark sweaty armpits that unnerve you . . . .

I've never been upstairs. Someone said that women are just a substitute for the solitary vice, except that you need more imagination. So I return home and dream about them at night – I'm certainly not made of iron – and then it is they who've led me on.

I've read Dr Tissot and I know they harm you even from a distance. We do not know whether animal spirits and genital fluid are the same thing, but it is certain that these two fluids have a certain similarity and, after long nocturnal pollutions, people not only lose energy but the body grows thinner, the face turns pallid, memory becomes blurred, eyesight misty, the voice hoarse; sleep is disturbed by restless dreams, the eyes ache and red blotches appear on the face. Some people spit out a limy matter, feel palpitations, choking, fainting, while others complain of constipation or increasingly foul-smelling emissions. In the end, blindness.

Perhaps these are exaggerations. As a boy I had a pimply face, but that seems normal at such an age, or perhaps all boys indulge in such pleasures – some excessively, touching themselves day and night. Now I know how to pace myself. My dreams are disturbed only after I have spent an evening in a brasserie and I don't get an erection every time I see a skirt in the street, as many do. Work keeps me from moral laxity.

But why philosophise instead of piecing together events? Perhaps because I need to know not only what I did before yesterday, but also what I'm like inside – that is, assuming there is something inside me. They say that the soul is simply what a person does. But if I hate someone and I cultivate this grudge then, by God, that means there is something inside! What does the philosopher say? *Odi ergo sum*. I hate, therefore I am.

A while ago the bell rang downstairs. I thought maybe it was someone fool enough to want to buy something, but the fellow told me straight away that Tissot had sent him – why did I ever choose that password? He wanted a handwritten will, signed by a certain Bonnefoy in favour of someone called Guillot (which was certainly him). He had the writing paper that Bonnefoy uses, or used to use, and an example of his handwriting. I invited Guillot up into my office, I chose a pen and the right ink and wrote out the document perfectly without making a draft. Guillot handed me a payment proportionate to the legacy, as if he knew my rates.

So is this my trade? It's a marvellous thing, creating a legal deed out of nothing, forging a letter which looks genuine, drafting a compromising confession, creating a document that will lead someone to ruin. The power of art . . . to be rewarded by a visit to the *Café Anglais*.

My memory must be in my nose, yet I have the impression that centuries have passed since I last savoured the aroma of that menu: *soufflés à la reine, filets de sole à la vénitienne, escalopes de turbot au gratin, selle de mouton purée bretonne* . . . And as an *entrée*: *poulet à la portugaise*, or *pâté chaud de cailles*, or *homard à la parisienne*, or all of them, and as the *plat de résistance*, perhaps *canetons à la rouennaise* or *ortolans sur canapés*, and for *entremet, aubergines à l'espagnole, asperges en branches, cassolettes princesse* . . . For wine, I don't know, perhaps a Château Margaux, or Château Latour, or Château Lafite, depending on the vintage. And to finish, a *bombe glacée.*

I have always found more pleasure in food than sex – perhaps a mark left upon me by priests.

I feel as if my mind is in a continual cloud which prevents me from looking back. Why, all of a sudden, do memories resurface about my visits to *Bicerin* in Father Bergamaschi's robes? I had quite forgotten about Father Bergamaschi. Who was he? I'm enjoying letting my pen wander where my instinct takes it. According to the Austrian doctor, I ought to reach a point where my memory feels true pain, which would explain why I have suddenly blotted out so many things.

Yesterday, which I thought was Tuesday the 22nd of March, I woke up thinking I knew perfectly well who I was – Captain Simonini, sixty-seven years old, but carrying them well (I'm fat enough to be described as a fine-looking man). I assumed the title of Captain in France, in remembrance of my grandfather, making vague references to a military past in the ranks of Garibaldi's Thousand, which in this country, where Garibaldi is esteemed more highly than in Italy, carries a certain prestige. Simone Simonini, born in Turin, father from Turin, mother French (a Savoyard, but when she was born Savoy had been invaded by the French).

I was still in bed, allowing my thoughts to wander. . . . With the problems I'd been having with the Russians (the Russians?) it was better not to be seen around at my favourite

21

restaurants. I could cook something for myself. I find it relaxing to labour away for a few hours preparing some delicacy. For example, *côtes de veau Foyot*: meat at least four centimetres thick – a quantity for two, of course – two medium-sized onions, fifty grammes of bread without the crust, seventy-five of grated Gruyère, fifty of butter. Grate the bread into breadcrumbs and mix with the Gruyère, then peel and chop the onions and melt forty grammes of the butter in a small pan. Meanwhile, in another pan, gently melt the onions in the remaining butter. Cover the bottom of a dish with half the onions, season the meat with salt and pepper, arrange it on the dish and add the rest of the onions. Cover with a first layer of breadcrumbs and cheese, making sure that the meat sticks well to the bottom of the dish, allowing the melted butter to drain to the bottom and gently pressing by hand. Add another layer of breadcrumbs to form a sort of dome, and the last of the melted butter. Sprinkle with white wine and stock, up to no more than half the height of the meat. Put it all in the oven for around half an hour, continuing to baste with wine and stock. Serve with sautéed cauliflower.

It takes a little time, but the pleasures of cooking begin before the pleasures of the palate, and preparing means anticipating, which was what I was doing as I still luxuriated in my bed. Only fools need to keep a woman, or a young boy, under their bedcovers not to feel alone. They don't understand that a watering mouth is better than an erection.

I had almost everything in the house, except for the Gruyère and the meat. For the meat, on any other day there was the butcher in place Maubert – goodness knows why he closes on Tuesday. But I knew another one, two hundred metres away on boulevard Saint-Germain, and a short walk would do me no harm. I dressed and, before leaving, stuck on my usual black moustache and fine beard at the mirror over the washstand. I then put on my wig and combed it with a central parting, slightly wetting the comb. I slipped on my frock coat and placed the silver watch into my waistcoat pocket with its chain well visible. While I'm talking, in order to give the appearance of a retired captain, I like to fiddle with a tortoiseshell box of liquorice lozenges, a portrait of an ugly but well-dressed woman on the inside lid, no doubt a deceased loved one. Every now and then I pop a lozenge into my mouth and pass it with my tongue from one side to the other. This allows me to talk more slowly – and the listener follows the movement of your lips and doesn't hear what you're saying. The problem is trying to keep up the appearance of someone of less than average intelligence.

I went down to the street, turned the corner, trying not to stop in front of the brasserie, where the raucous voices of its fallen women could be heard from early morning.

Place Maubert is no longer the court of miracles it was when I arrived here thirty-five years ago. Then it teemed with sellers of recycled tobacco, the coarser variety obtained from cigar stubs and pipe ash and the finer variety from cigarette butts – coarse tobacco at one franc twenty centimes a pound, fine at between one franc fifty and one franc sixty (though the industry had hardly ever been profitable and, once they'd drunk away most of their profits in some wine cellar, none of those industrious recyclers had anywhere to sleep the night). It teemed with pimps who, having lazed about until at least two in the afternoon, spent the rest of the day smoking, propped against a wall like respectable pensioners, then going into action at dusk, like shepherd dogs. It teemed with thieves reduced to stealing from each other because no decent person (except for the occasional idler up from the countryside) would have dared to cross the square, and I would have been easy prey if it were not for my military step and the way I twirled my stick. And, in any event, the pickpockets of the area knew me, and one or other of them would greet me, even addressing me as Captain. Apart from that, they thought I belonged in some way to their underworld, and dog does not eat dog. It teemed with prostitutes whose beauty had faded – for those who were still attractive would have been working in the *brasseries à femmes* – and they therefore had no choice but to offer themselves to rag-and-bone men, petty thieves and foul-smelling sellers of second-hand tobacco. But on seeing a respectably dressed gentleman with a well-brushed top hat, they might dare to sidle up to you, or even take you by the arm, coming so close that you could smell their terrible cheap perfume mixed with sweat, and this would have been too appalling an experience (I had no wish to dream of them at night) so when I saw one of them approaching I would whirl my stick full circle, as if to form an inaccessible area of protection around me, and they understood at once, since they were used to being ordered about and knew how to respect a stick.

And last of all, it teemed with police spies who were there to recruit their *mouchards* or informers, or to gather highly valuable information about villainies that were being hatched and which someone was whispering too loudly to someone else, imagining his voice would be lost in the general din. They were immediately recognisable by their exaggeratedly sinister manner. No true villain looks like a villain, but they do.

Nowadays, tramways pass through the square and it no longer feels like home, though there are still some useful people around, if you know how to spot them, leaning in a corner, at the entrance to *Café Maître-Albert* or in one of the adjacent passageways. But Paris, all in all, isn't what it used to be, ever since that pencil sharpener, the Eiffel Tower, has been sticking up in the distance, visible from every angle.

Enough. I'm no sentimentalist, and there are plenty of other places where I can find what I need. Yesterday morning I wanted meat and cheese, and place Maubert still served my purpose.

Having bought the cheese, I passed the usual butcher and saw he was open.

"Open on Tuesday? How come?" I asked as I went in.

"But today is Wednesday, Captain," he answered with a laugh. I felt confused, and apologised, saying that you lose your memory with age. I was still a young lad, he said, and it's easy for anyone to lose track of what day it is when you get up in a hurry. I chose my meat and paid without asking for a discount (the only way of gaining respect from tradesmen).

I returned home, still wondering what day it was. I removed my moustache and beard, as I do when I am by myself, and went into the bedroom. Only then was I struck by something that seemed out of place. A piece of clothing was hanging from a hook by the chest of drawers, a cassock that undoubtedly belonged to a priest. Moving closer, I saw on top of the chest of drawers a light brown, almost blondish wig.

I was wondering what third-rate actor I might have given accommodation to over the past few days when I realised that I too had been in disguise, since the moustache and beard I'd been wearing were not my own. Was I someone, then, who dressed alternately as a respectable gentleman and as a priest? But how had I blotted out all recollection of this second part of me? Or maybe for some reason (perhaps to avoid an arrest warrant) I had disguised myself in moustache and beard but at the same time had given hospitality to a person dressed as an abbé? And if this fake abbé (a true abbé would not have worn a wig) had been staying with me, where did he sleep, considering there was only one bed in the house? Or perhaps he wasn't living here and, for some reason, had taken shelter here the day before, then ridding himself of his disguise to go God knows where to do God knows what?

My mind was a blank. It was as if I knew there was something I ought to recall but couldn't – I mean, something which was part of someone else's recollections. Talking about someone else's recollections is, I believe, the right expression. At that moment I felt I was another person who was watching, from the outside – someone watching Simonini who, all of a sudden, did not know exactly who he was.

Calm down, I told myself, let's think. For someone who forges documents under the pretext of selling bric-a-brac, and who has chosen to live in one of the less desirable districts of Paris, it was not improbable that I had given protection to an individual caught up in some shady machinations. But not to remember to whom I had given protection didn't seem normal.

I looked around, and suddenly my own house seemed strange, as if it were someone else's house, as if perhaps it held other secrets. Leaving the kitchen, to the right was the bedroom, to the left the living room with its usual furniture. I opened the drawers of the writing desk containing the tools of my trade – pens, bottles of various inks, sheets of paper from different periods, white or yellowing. On the shelves, in addition to books, there were boxes holding my papers and an old walnut tabernacle. I was trying to recall what purpose this served, when I heard the doorbell ring. I went downstairs to turn away any unwelcome visitor, and saw an old woman whom I seemed to recognise. "Tissot sent me," she said, and so I had to let her in. Goodness knows why I chose that password.

She came in and unwrapped a cloth she was clutching to her chest, showing me twenty hosts.

"Abbé Dalla Piccola told me you'd be interested."

"Certainly," I replied, puzzled by my own response, and asked how much.

"Ten francs each," said the old woman.

"You're mad," I said, out of tradesman's instinct.

"It's you who are mad – you and your black masses. You think it's easy going into twenty churches in three days to take communion, trying to keep my mouth dry, kneeling with my head in my hands, trying to get the hosts out of my mouth without wetting them, putting them into a purse I carry in my breast, and without the curate or anyone else noticing? Not to mention the sacrilege, and hell that awaits me. So if you please, two hundred francs, or I'll go to Abbé Boullan."

"Abbé Boullan's dead. Evidently you haven't been getting hosts for some time," I replied almost automatically. Then, confused, I decided to follow my instinct without much further thought.

"Never mind, I'll take them," I said, and paid her. I realised I had to place the consecrated wafers in the tabernacle, awaiting the arrival of some regular customer. A job like any other.

In short, everything seemed normal, familiar. And yet I sensed there was something sinister happening around me which I couldn't identify.

I went back up to my office and noticed a door at the far end, covered by a curtain. I opened it, knowing that I would enter a corridor so dark I would need a lamp to walk along it. The corridor was like a store for theatrical props, or the back room of a junk dealer in the Temple quarter. Hanging from the walls were clothes of all kinds – for farmer, coal merchant, delivery man, beggar, a soldier's jacket and trousers – and beside each costume the headgear to complete it. On a dozen stands, carefully arranged along a wooden shelf, were as many wigs. At the far end, a *coiffeuse*, similar to those in an actor's dressing room, covered with jars of whitener and rouge, black and dark-blue pencils, hare's feet, powder puffs, brushes, hairbrushes.

At a certain point the corridor turned a corner, and at the far end was another door leading into a room that was more brightly lit than mine, since it overlooked a street which was not the narrow impasse Maubert. In fact, looking out from one of the windows, I could see rue Maître-Albert below.

There was a stairway leading from the room down to the street, but nothing else. It was a one-room apartment, somewhere between an office and a bedroom, with plain dark furniture, a table, a prie-dieu and a bed. There was a small kitchen by the entrance and, on the stairway, a lavatory with washbasin.

It was obviously the pied-à-terre of a clergyman with whom I must have been acquainted, since our apartments were connected. And though it all seemed familiar, I felt I was visiting the room for the first time.

I approached the table and saw a bundle of letters in their envelopes, all addressed to the same person: the Most Reverend, or the Very Reverend, Abbé Dalla Piccola. Next to the envelopes were several handwritten sheets of paper, penned in a fine, graceful, almost feminine hand, very different from mine. Drafts of letters of no particular import-ance, expressing thanks for a gift, confirming an appointment. The sheet on top of these was written carelessly, as if the writer were making notes of points for further consideration. I read it with some difficulty:

Everything seems unreal. It is as though someone is watching me. Write it down to make sure it's true.

Today is the 22nd of March.

Where is my cassock, my wig?

What happened last night? My mind is confused.

I couldn't remember where that door at the end of the room led.

I found a corridor (never seen?) full of clothes, wigs, creams and greasepaint as used by actors.

A good cassock was hanging from a peg, and on a shelf I found not only a good wig but also fake eyebrows. With a foundation of ochre, a little rouge on both cheeks, I have returned to how I think I am, pallid and slightly feverish in appearance. Ascetic. This is me. But who am I?

I know I am Abbé Dalla Piccola. Or rather, the person everyone knows as Abbé Dalla Piccola. But clearly I am not, given that I have to dress up to look like him.

Where does that corridor lead? I'm frightened to go as far as the end.

Reread the above notes. If what is written is written, then it has actually happened. Believe in what is written.

Has someone drugged me? Boullan? He's perfectly capable of it. Or the Jesuits? Or the Freemasons? What have I to do with them?

The Jews! That's who it must have been.

I don't feel safe here. Someone could have broken in during the night, stolen my clothes and, worse still, rummaged through my papers. Perhaps someone's wandering around Paris making people think he is Abbé Dalla Piccola.

I must hide at Auteuil. Maybe Diana will know. Who is Diana?

Abbé Dalla Piccola's notes stopped here, and it was strange he hadn't taken with him a document as confidential as this – a clear indication of his state of anxiety. And all I could find out about him ended here.

I returned to the apartment in impasse Maubert and sat at my desk. In what way did Abbé Dalla Piccola's life cross with mine?

Naturally I was unable to avoid making the most obvious conjecture: that Abbé Dalla Piccola and I were the same person. If that were so, then it would explain everything – the two connecting apartments, how I had returned dressed as Dalla Piccola into the apartment of Simonini and how I had left the cassock and wig there and then fallen asleep. Except for one small detail: if Simonini was Dalla Piccola, why did I know nothing at all about Dalla Piccola? And why didn't I feel I was Dalla Piccola, who knew nothing at all about Simonini (in fact, to find out about Dalla Piccola's thoughts and feelings I had to read of them in his notes)? And if I had been Dalla Piccola as well, I should have been at Auteuil, in the house about which he seemed to know everything, and I (Simonini) knew nothing. And who was Diana?

Unless I was sometimes Simonini who had forgotten Dalla Piccola, and sometimes Dalla Piccola who had forgotten Simonini. That would be nothing new. Who was the person who told me about cases of double personality? Isn't this what happens to Diana? But who is Diana?

I decided to go stage by stage. I knew that I kept an appointments book, which is where I found the following notes:

21st March, mass
22nd March, Taxil
23rd March, Guillot for Bonnefoy will
24th March, to Drumont?

I have no idea why I had to go to mass on the 21st. I don't think I'm a believer. A believer believes in something. Do I believe in something? I don't think so. Therefore I'm not a believer. This is logical. Besides, sometimes you go to mass for all sorts of reasons, and faith has nothing to do with it.

What I felt more sure of was that the day, which I thought was Tuesday, was in fact Wednesday the 23rd of March, and that Guillot did in fact come for me to draw up the Bonnefoy will. It was the 23rd and I thought it was the 22nd. So what happened on the 22nd? And who or what was Taxil?

The idea of having to see that fellow Drumont on Thursday was now out of the question. Not knowing who I was, how could I meet someone? I had to hide until I had worked it all out. Drumont . . . I thought I knew perfectly well who he was, yet if I tried to think about him it was as if my mind was clouded by wine.

Let's consider other possibilities, I told myself. First: Dalla Piccola is someone else, who for whatever mysterious reasons often comes to my apartment which is linked to his by a more or less secret corridor. On the evening of the 21st of March he returned to my place in impasse Maubert, left his coat (why?), then went to sleep in his own apartment, where he woke the following morning, having lost his memory. And I woke two mornings later, also having lost my memory. In that case, what could I have done on Tuesday the 22nd, if I had woken on the morning of the 23rd with no memory? And why did Dalla Piccola have to undress here, then with no cassock go to his place – and at what time? I was struck with dread at the thought that he had passed the first part of the night in my bed . . . my God, it's true that women fill me with horror, but with a priest it would be much worse. I am celibate but not a pervert. . . .

Otherwise Dalla Piccola and I are the same person. Since I found the cassock in my bedroom, after the day of the mass (the 21st) I would have been able to return to impasse Maubert dressed as Dalla Piccola (if I'd had to go to a mass it is more credible that I'd have gone as an abbé), before then taking off the cassock and wig, then later on going to sleep in the abbé's apartment (and forgetting that I had left the cassock at Simonini's). The morning after, Tuesday the 22nd of March, waking up as Dalla Piccola, not only would I have found myself with no memory but I wouldn't have been able to find the cassock at the foot of the bed. As Dalla Piccola, with no memory, I would have found a spare cassock in the corridor and would have had as much time as I needed to escape the same day to Auteuil, only to change my mind by the end of the day, steel myself and return to Paris later that evening into the apartment at impasse Maubert, hanging the cassock on the hook in the bedroom, and waking up with no memory once again, but as Simonini, on the Wednesday, believing it was still Tuesday. Therefore, I reasoned, Dalla Piccola loses his memory on the 22nd of March, and remains amnesiac the whole day, finding himself on the 23rd as an amnesiac Simonini. Nothing exceptional after what I had learned from – what's his name? – that doctor at the clinic in Vincennes.

Except for a small problem. I reread my notes. If that was how things had happened, Simonini would have found in his bedroom, on the morning of the 23rd, not one but two cassocks – the one he had left on the night of the 21st and the other he had left on the night of the 22nd. And yet there was only one.

But no, what a fool I am. Dalla Piccola had returned from Auteuil to rue Maître-Albert on the evening of the 22nd, had put down his cassock, then gone to the apartment in impasse Maubert and slept there, waking the following morning (the 23rd) as Simonini, to find only one cassock on the rack. It is true that, if events had taken that course, when I entered Dalla Piccola's apartment on the morning of the 23rd, I should have found the cassock that he left there on the evening of the 22nd, but he could have hung it back up in the corridor where he had found it. All I had to do was check.

I went along the corridor, with lighted lamp, feeling a certain trepidation. If Dalla Piccola and I were not the same person, I told myself, I might have seen him appear at the other end of that passageway, he too perhaps carrying a lamp in front of him. . . . Fortunately that didn't happen. And I found the cassock hanging at the far end of the corridor.

And yet, and yet . . . if Dalla Piccola had returned from Auteuil and, on leaving the cassock, had walked the whole length of the corridor to my apartment and had happily gone to sleep in my bed, it was because at that point he knew who I was, and knew that he could sleep here just as well as in his own place, seeing that we were the same person. Dalla Piccola had therefore gone to bed knowing he was Simonini whereas, the morning after, Simonini had woken not knowing he was Dalla Piccola. In other words, Dalla Piccola first loses his memory, then regains it, then goes to sleep and passes his loss of memory on to Simonini.

Loss of memory . . . this word, meaning non-recollection, opens a gap in the mist of time which I had quite forgotten. I remember talking about people with memory loss at *Chez Magny*, more than ten years ago, with Bourru and Burot, with Du Maurier and with the Austrian doctor.

*. . . In the past it was regarded as an
exclusively female phenomenon caused by
disturbances in uterine function. . . .*

[PAGE 39]

3

CHEZ MAGNY

25th March 1897, at dawn

Chez Magny . . . so far as I recall, it used to cost no more than ten francs a head at that restaurant in rue de la Contrescarpe-Dauphine, and the quality matched the price. I'm a lover of good food, I know, but you can't eat at *Foyot* every day. In years gone by, many used to go to *Magny* just to catch a glimpse of famous writers like Gautier or Flaubert or, earlier still, that consumptive Polish pianist kept by a degenerate woman who went about in trousers. I looked in there one evening and left straight away. Artists are insufferable, even from afar, looking around to see whether we have recognised them.

The "great men" then stopped going to *Magny*, and moved on to *Brébant-Vachette*, in boulevard Poissonnière, where you ate better and paid more, but evidently *carmina dant panem* – poetry *does* give you bread. And once *Magny* had been purged, so to speak, I started going occasionally from the early eighties.

I saw men of science there, including eminent chemists such as Berthelot and many doctors from the Salpêtrière. The hospital isn't exactly close by, but perhaps the clinicians find pleasure in taking a short walk in the Latin Quarter, rather than eating at the filthy *gargottes* where the patients' families go. Medical discussions are interesting as they invariably relate to the infirmities of someone else, and at *Magny*,

37

to compete with the noise, everyone talks loudly, so that a trained ear can always pick up something interesting. Listening doesn't mean trying to understand. Anything, however trifling, may be of use one day. What matters is to know something that others don't know you know.

While the writers and artists always used to sit together at long tables, the men of science dined alone, as I did. But after we had sat at neighbouring tables on several occasions, a familiarity would begin. My first acquaintance was Dr Du Maurier, a man so loathsome that I wondered how a psychiatrist (which he was) could inspire the trust of his patients with such an unpleasant face. It was the pale envious face of one who thinks he is destined always to remain in second place. He was, in fact, the director of a small clinic for nervous illnesses at Vincennes, but knew full well that his institute would never enjoy the fame and prosperity of the clinic run by the more renowned Dr Blanche – though Du Maurier used to mutter sarcastically that one of Blanche's patients thirty years before had been a certain Nerval (according to him a poet of some merit) who had been driven to suicide after being treated at his famous clinic.

Another two table companions with whom I became familiar were Drs Bourru and Burot, unusual fellows who looked like twin brothers, both dressed in black with almost the same cut of coat, the same long black moustaches and clean-shaven chin, with collars always slightly grubby, inevitably as they were in Paris as travellers, since they practised at the *École de Médecine* at Rochefort and came to the capital for only a few days each month to follow Charcot's experiments.

"What, no leeks today?" Bourru asked one day, irritated. And Burot, scandalised, "No leeks?"

While the waiter apologised, I interposed from the next table, "But they have excellent wild salsify. I prefer it to leeks." Then, with a smile, I softly sang, "*Tous les légumes, / au clair de lune / étaient en train de s'amuser / et les passants les regardaient. / Les cornichons / dansaient en rond, / les salsifis / dansaient sans bruit . . .*"

Persuaded, the two table companions chose *salsifis*. And from there began a cordial acquaintance, on two days each month.

"You see, Monsieur Simonini," Bourru explained, "Dr Charcot is studying hysteria, a form of neurosis which manifests itself with various psychomotorial, sensorial and vegetative symptoms. In the past it was regarded as an exclusively female phenomenon caused by disturbances in uterine function, but Charcot has formed the view that hysterical manifestations are to be found equally in both sexes, and may include paralysis, epilepsy, blindness or deafness, and difficulties in breathing, speaking or swallowing."

"My colleague," Burot interrupted, "has not yet mentioned that Charcot claims to have developed a treatment that alleviates the symptoms."

"I was just about to get there," responded Bourru, exasperated. "Charcot has chosen the path of hypnotism, until recently an occupation for charlatans like Mesmer. Under hypnosis, patients ought to be able to recall traumatic episodes which are the origin of the hysteria, and be cured through awareness of them."

"And are they cured?"

"That is the point, Monsieur Simonini," said Bourru. "For us, what goes on at the Salpêtrière often feels more like the theatre than clinical psychiatry. Let us be clear, we wouldn't want to dispute the infallible diagnostic abilities of the Master. . . ."

"Not to question them at all," confirmed Burot. "It's the technique of hypnotism itself which . . ."

Bourru and Burot told me about the various systems for hypnotising, from the quackish methods of a certain Abbé Faria (my ears pricked up at that Dumasian name, though it is well known that Dumas plundered real stories) to the scientific approach of Dr Braid, a true pioneer.

"The best magnetisers," said Burot, "now follow procedures that are much simpler."

"And more effective," added Bourru. "A medallion or a key is waved before the patient, who is told to watch it closely: within the space of one to three minutes the subject's pupils develop an oscillatory movement, the pulse slows down, the eyes close, the face relaxes, and drowsiness may last for up to twenty minutes."

"It has to be said," Burot observed, "that much depends on the subject, since magnetisation does not rely upon the transmission of mysterious fluids (as that buffoon Mesmer suggested) but upon phenomena of autosuggestion. Indian gurus obtain the same result by focusing on the point of their nose, the monks of Mount Athos by staring at their navel."

"We do not much believe in these forms of autosuggestion," Burot added, "though we ourselves are only putting into practice ideas developed by Charcot himself, before he began to place so much trust in hypnotism. We are dealing

———

. . . "Charcot has chosen the path of hypnotism,
until recently an occupation for
charlatans like Mesmer." . . .

[PAGE 39]

———

with cases of personality variation, in other words with patients who think they are one person one day and someone else another, and the two personalities know nothing of each other. Last year a certain Louis came to our hospital."

"An interesting case," said Bourru. "He complained of paralysis, anaesthesia, contractions, muscular spasms, hyperesthesia, skin irritation, haemorrhaging, coughing, vomiting, epileptic fits, catatonia, sleepwalking, St Vitus's dance, speech impediments . . ."

"Sometimes he thought he was a dog," said Burot, "or a steam locomotive. And then he had persecutory delusions, restricted vision, gustatory, olfactory and visual hallucinations, pseudo-tubercular pulmonary congestion, headaches, stomach ache, constipation, anorexia, bulimia and lethargy, kleptomania . . ."

"In short," concluded Bourru, "a normal picture. But instead of resorting to hypnosis, we applied a steel bar to the patient's right arm and there, as if by magic, he appeared before us like a new man. Paralysis and insensitivity had disappeared from the right side and had moved to the left."

"In front of us was another person," continued Burot, "who remembered nothing of what had happened a moment earlier. Louis, in one of his states, was teetotal; in the other he had a tendency to drunkenness."

"Note," said Bourru, "that the magnetic force of a substance acts even from a distance. For example, a small bottle containing an alcoholic substance is placed under the subject's chair without his knowledge. In this state of somnambulism the subject will display all the symptoms of drunkenness."

"You understand that our practices respect the mental integrity of the patient," concluded Burot. "Hypnotism makes the subject lose consciousness whereas, with magnetism, there is no violent impact upon an organ but a progressive charging of the nervous plexus."

From that conversation I formed the view that Bourru and Burot were two imbeciles who tormented poor lunatics with injurious substances, and I felt confirmed in my opinion when I saw Dr Du Maurier, who was following the conversation from a nearby table, shaking his head several times.

"My dear friend," he said to me two days later, "Charcot and our two from Rochefort, instead of analysing the past history of their patients, and asking themselves what it means to have two states of consciousness, spend their time worrying about whether it's better to work on them with hypnosis or with metal bars. The problem is that in many patients the passage from one personality to another occurs spontaneously, without us being able to predict how and when. We might talk of self-hypnosis. In my view Charcot and his disciples have not given sufficient consideration to the experiences of Dr Azam and the Félida case. We still know very little about these phenomena. Memory disturbance may be caused by a reduction in the blood flow to a still-unknown part of the brain, and the momentary constriction of the vessels could be provoked by a state of hysteria. But where in the brain is the lack of blood flow that causes memory loss?"

"Where?"

"That is the point. You know that our brain has two hemispheres. There may be people who think sometimes

43

with a complete hemisphere and sometimes with one that is incomplete, in which the memory faculty is missing. In my clinic I have found a very similar case to that of Félida. A young woman a little over twenty called Diana."

Du Maurier stopped for a moment, as if anxious about revealing a confidential matter.

"A relative left her with me for treatment two years ago, and then died. The payments obviously stopped, but what could I do, turn the patient out onto the street? I know little of her past. It seems, according to what she has told me, that during her adolescence, every five or six days, she would feel pain in her temples after some excitement, and then collapse as if asleep. What she calls sleep is, in fact, an attack of hysteria; when she wakes up, or calms down, she is quite different from what she was before, in other words she has entered what Dr Azam described as the *second state*. In the state which we shall call normal, Diana behaves as the disciple of a Masonic sect. . . . Don't misunderstand me, I too belong to the Grand Orient, by which I mean the Freemasonry of respectable people, but perhaps you know that there exist various 'obediences' in the Templar tradition with peculiar propensities for the occult sciences, and some of them (which are, of course, fortunately very much on the fringe) incline towards satanic rites. In what must alas be defined as her *normal* state, Diana considers herself to be a disciple of Lucifer or something of that kind. She makes licentious remarks, talks about lewd incidents, tries to seduce members of the male nursing staff and even me. I am sorry to be so indelicate, especially as Diana is, one might say, a charming woman. In my view, in this state, she is suffering the effects of traumas inflicted upon her during her adolescence, and tries to escape those memories by entering periodically into her second state. In this state Diana appears as a mild, innocent creature; she is a good Christian, asks for her prayer book and to be allowed to go to mass. But the strange aspect, which also happened with Félida, is that Diana, in her second state, when she is the virtuous Diana, clearly remembers how she was in her normal state, and is distressed, and asks how she could have been so bad, and punishes herself with a hair shirt, to such a point that she calls the second state her *rational state*, and refers to her normal state as a period when she was prey to hallucinations. In her normal state, however, Diana remembers nothing of what she does in her second state. The two conditions alternate at unpredictable intervals, and sometimes she remains in one or other state for several days. I would agree with Dr Azam when it comes to *perfect somnambulism*. It is not just somnambulists, in fact, but also those who take drugs – hashish, belladonna, opium – or abuse alcohol, who do things they cannot remember when they wake up again."

I don't know why the account of Diana's illness intrigued me so much, but I remember saying to Du Maurier, "I will mention it to an acquaintance of mine who deals with sad cases such as this, and knows where an orphan girl might be best looked after. I will send Abbé Dalla Piccola to you; he has much influence among charitable institutions."

At least I knew the name Dalla Piccola when I spoke with Du Maurier. But why was I so concerned about this woman Diana?

*   *   *

45

I have been writing for hours, my thumb is aching, and I have eaten at my desk, spreading pâté and butter on bread, with a few glasses of Château Latour to stimulate the memory.

I would have liked to reward myself with, I don't know, perhaps a visit to *Brébant-Vachette*, but until I have understood who I am I can't be seen around. Sooner or later, though, I'll have to venture into place Maubert to bring back something else to eat.

Let us think no more about it, for the moment, and return to our writing.

During those years (I think it was 'eighty-five or 'eighty-six) I became acquainted with that man at *Magny* whom I still call the Austrian (or German) doctor. His name now comes back to me – he was called Froïde (I think that's how it's written), a doctor aged around thirty who most certainly came to *Magny* only because he couldn't afford better, and was doing an apprenticeship with Charcot. He sat alone at a nearby table, and at first we limited ourselves to exchanging a polite nod. I judged him to be gloomy by nature, ill at ease, timidly eager for someone to confide in, to unburden his anxieties. On two or three occasions he had found a pretext for exchanging a few words, but I had always remained aloof.

Even though the name Froïde did not have the same ring as Steiner or Rosenberg, I nevertheless knew that all Jews who live and make money in Paris have German names and, my suspicions having been raised by his hooked nose, one day I asked Du Maurier, who made a vague gesture, adding, "I'm not sure, but in any event I prefer to keep my distance – Jew and German are a mix I don't much like."

"Is he not Austrian?" I asked.

"It's the same, is it not? Same language, same way of thinking. I haven't forgotten the Prussians who marched along the Champs-Élysées."

"I am told that medicine is among the professions most often followed by Jews, as much as usury. It's a good thing never to be in need of money, and never to fall ill."

"But there are Christian doctors too," Du Maurier replied with an icy smile.

I had made a faux pas.

There are Paris intellectuals who, before expressing their distaste for Jews, concede that some of their best friends are Jews. Hypocrisy. I have no Jewish friends (God forbid). All my life I've avoided Jews. Perhaps I have instinctively avoided them, because the Jew (like the German) can be identified by his smell (as Victor Hugo put it – *fetor judaica*). This and other signs help them to recognise each other, as pederasts do. My grandfather used to say that their smell is due to the excessive use of garlic and onion, and perhaps mutton and goose, coated with sticky sugars which make them splenetic. But it must also be the race itself – their infected blood, their feeble loins. They are all communists – look at Marx and Lassalle. In this respect, my Jesuits were right for once.

I've also managed to avoid Jews because I keep an eye on names. Austrian Jews, as they grew rich, bought fancy names, of flowers, precious stones or noble metals, becoming

Silbermann or Goldstein. The poorer ones acquired names such as Grünspan (verdigris). In France, as well as Italy, they disguised themselves by adopting the names of cities or places such as Ravenna, Modena, Picard, Flamand, or sometimes they were inspired by the revolutionary calendar (Froment, Avoine, Laurier) – quite rightly, seeing that their fathers had been the hidden authors of the regicide. But you also have to be careful about first names which sometimes conceal Jewish names – Maurice comes from Moses, Isidore from Isaac, Edouard from Aaron, Jacques from Jacob and Alphonse from Adam. . . .

Is Sigmund a Jewish name? Instinctively I had decided to keep a distance from the mountebank, but one day Froïde knocked over the salt cellar as he went to pick it up. Certain rules of courtesy have to be respected between neighbouring tables and I offered him mine, observing that in some countries knocking over the salt was considered bad luck, and he laughed, saying that he was not superstitious. From that day on we began to exchange a few words. He apologised for his French, which he described as patchy, but which was easy to understand. They are nomadic by habit and have to cope with all languages. I said politely, "It's just a matter of getting used to the sound," and he smiled at me with gratitude. Slimy.

As a Jew Froïde was also deceitful. I had always heard it said that those of his race must eat only special food, cooked in a particular way, and for this reason they always live in ghettos, whereas Froïde tucked into all that *Magny* had to offer, and was not averse to a glass of beer with his meal.

One evening, it seemed he wanted to let himself go. He had already ordered two beers and, after dessert, while he was smoking nervously, he asked for a third. At a certain point, as he was talking and waving his hands, he knocked the salt over for the second time.

"It's not that I'm clumsy," he apologised, "but I'm rather anxious. It's three days since I last received a letter from my fiancée. I don't expect her to write as I do almost every day, but this silence worries me. She is in delicate health; it upsets me terribly not to be with her. And then I need her approval, for whatever I do. I would like to hear what she thinks about my dinner with Charcot. Because you know, Monsieur Simonini, I was invited to dinner at the great man's house a few evenings ago. It doesn't happen to every young visiting doctor, and a foreigner at that."

There, I thought, the little Semite parvenu, working his way into respectable families to advance in his career. And did his concern about his fiancée not betray the sensual and lascivious nature of the Jew, always thinking about sex? You think about her at night, don't you? And maybe you touch yourself fantasising about her – you too should read Tissot. But I let him go on.

"The guests were men of quality: Daudet's son, Dr Strauss, Pasteur's assistant, Professor Beck from the Institute and the great Italian painter Emilio Toffano. An evening that cost me fourteen francs – a fine black Hamburg cravat, white gloves, a new shirt, and a dress coat for the first time in my life. And for the first time in my life I had my beard trimmed, in the French style. As for my shyness, a little cocaine helps to loosen the tongue."

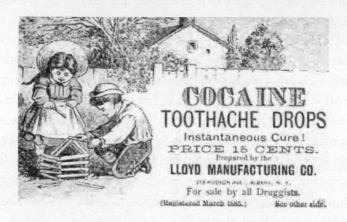

COCAINE
TOOTHACHE DROPS
Instantaneous Cure!
PRICE 15 CENTS.
Prepared by the
LLOYD MANUFACTURING CO.
219 HUDSON AVE., ALBANY, N. Y.
For sale by all Druggists.
(Registered March 1885.)   See other side.

. . . *"in cases of serious tooth decay
insert a wad of cotton into the cavity
soaked in a four per cent solution and
the pain subsides immediately."* . . .

[PAGE 51]

"Cocaine? Is it not a poison?"

"Everything is poisonous, if taken in excessive doses, even wine. But I have been studying this remarkable substance for two years. Cocaine, you see, is an alkaloid taken from a plant which is chewed by the natives of America to resist the Andean altitudes. Unlike opium and alcohol, it provokes mental states of excitement without producing negative effects. It is excellent for relieving pain, principally in ophthalmology, or for the cure of asthma, useful in treating alcoholism and drug addiction, perfect against seasickness and valuable in treating diabetes; it suppresses hunger, drowsiness and fatigue like magic, is a good substitute for tobacco, cures dyspepsia, flatulence, liver attacks, stomach cramps, hypochondria, spinal irritation, hay fever, is a valuable restorative in consumption and cures migraine; in cases of serious tooth decay insert a wad of cotton into the cavity soaked in a four per cent solution and the pain subsides immediately. And, above all, it is marvellous for depressives – in restoring their confidence, raising their spirits, making them more active and optimistic."

The doctor was by now on his fourth glass and had clearly reached a state of gloomy intoxication. He leaned forward, as if to make a confession.

"Cocaine, as I always say to my beloved Martha, is excellent for someone like me who doesn't consider himself particularly attractive, who in his youth had never been young and now at thirty is unable to grow up. There was a time when I was full of ambition and desperate to learn, and day after day I felt discouraged by the fact that mother nature had not, in one of her moments of compassion, stamped me with that mark of genius which she grants to people every now and then."

All of a sudden he stopped, with the air of one who realises he has laid bare his soul. Whingeing little Jew, I thought to myself. And I decided to embarrass him.

"Is cocaine not said to be an aphrodisiac as well?" I asked.

Froïde blushed: "It also has that virtue, so I understand . . . but I have no experience in that respect. As a man I am not inclined to such itches. And as a doctor, sex is not a matter that much interests me; though sex is beginning to be much discussed at the Salpêtrière. Charcot discovered that one of his patients, a certain Augustine, during an advanced phase of her hysterical manifestations, revealed that her earliest trauma had been sexual violence inflicted in early childhood. Naturally I don't deny that among the traumas provoking hysteria there may also be phenomena linked to sex, that is quite clear. But I think it is simply too much to reduce everything to sex. Perhaps, though, it is my bourgeois prudery that distances me from these problems."

No, I thought, it isn't your prudery, it's because like all the circumcised men of your race you're obsessed by sex but try to forget it. I'd just like to see, when you put your smutty hands on that Martha of yours, if you don't produce a long line of little Jews and don't make her consumptive from the exertion. . . .

Froïde meanwhile continued, "My problem, unfortunately, is another. I have finished my supply of cocaine and am plunging into melancholy. Doctors in ancient times would have said that I have an excess of black bile. I used to be able to find the compound at Merck & Gehe, but they have had to stop making it as they can only find poor-quality raw material now. The fresh leaves can be processed only in America and the best production is that of Parke & Davis of Detroit, a more soluble variety, pure white in colour and with an aromatic odour. I had a modest supply but here in Paris I don't know whom to ask."

Music to the ears of one who is well informed on all the secrets of place Maubert and its neighbourhood. I knew certain people to whom it was enough to mention not just cocaine, but a diamond, a stuffed lion or a carboy of vitriol, and the following day they would deliver it to you, so long as you didn't ask where they'd found it. For me cocaine is a poison, I thought, and I don't mind contributing towards poisoning a Jew. So I told Doctor Froïde that within a few days I would obtain a good supply of his alkaloid. Froïde, of course, didn't imagine my ways were anything less than irreproachable. "You know," I told him, "we antiquarians get to meet all kinds of people."

All of this has nothing to do with my problem, but helps to explain how, in the end, we became acquainted and spoke about all manner of things. Froïde was eloquent and witty. Perhaps I'd been mistaken – maybe he wasn't Jewish. It was easier to talk to him than to Bourru and Burot, and our conversation turned to the experiments of those two, and from there I mentioned Du Maurier's patient.

"Do you believe," I asked him, "a woman that sick could be cured with Bourru and Burot's magnets?"

"My dear friend," replied Froïde, "in many of the cases we examine, too much importance is placed upon physical aspects, forgetting that if sickness develops, its origins are most probably psychic. And if the origins are psychic, it is the mind that has to be treated, not the body. In a traumatic neurosis, the true cause of the illness is not the lesion, which in itself is generally modest, but the original psychic trauma. Do people not faint when they experience a powerful emotion? And therefore, for those concerned with nervous illnesses, the problem is not how they lose their senses, but what emotion caused it."

"But how can you know what this emotion was?"

"You see, my friend, when the symptoms are clearly hysterical, as in the case of Du Maurier's patient, then hypnosis can artificially reproduce those same symptoms, and it is indeed possible to go back to the initial trauma. But other patients have had an experience so unbearable that they have sought to erase it – it is as if they had hidden it in some inaccessible part of their mind so remote that you could not reach it even under hypnosis. Then again, why under hypnosis ought we to have greater psychic capacities than when we are awake?"

"And therefore we will never know . . ."

"Don't ask me for a clear and definitive answer. I'm expressing ideas not yet fully formed. Sometimes I am tempted to think we reach that deep area only when we dream. The ancients understood just how revealing dreams can be. My sense is that if a sick person could speak, and speak for a long period, for days on end, with someone who knew how to listen, perhaps by simply describing what he had dreamt, the original trauma might suddenly emerge, and become clear. In English you might use the expression 'talking cures'. You will have noticed when talking to someone about distant events, that while describing them you remember details you had forgotten, or rather, *thought* you had forgotten, but which in fact your brain was storing in some secret recess. I believe the more detailed this reconstruction is, the more likely it is for an episode to re-emerge. This, I would say, includes even an insignificant fact, a subtle detail which has had such an unbearably disturbing effect as to provoke a . . . how do you say, an *Abtrennung*, a *Beseitigung* . . . I cannot find the right word. In English I would say *removal*. What do you say in French when an organ is cut out . . . *une ablation*? Yes, perhaps the correct term in German would be *Entfernung*."

Here is the Jew emerging, I thought. At that time I was, I think, already interested in the various Jewish plots and that race's ambitions for their sons to become doctors and pharmacists in order to control Christian bodies as well as minds. If I were ill, would you want me to hand myself over to you, telling you things even I don't know about myself, so that you could become master of my soul? Worse than the Jesuit father confessor, because at least, talking to him, I would be protected by a grille and wouldn't tell him what I really thought but rather the things that everyone does, so that everything is described in the same almost technical terms – I have stolen, I have fornicated, I have not honoured my father and mother. Your very language betrays you. You talk of removal as if you wish to circumcise my brain. . . .

Meanwhile Froïde had begun to laugh and ordered yet another beer.

"But do not regard my pronouncements as fact. They are the imaginings of a dreamer. When I return to Austria I will marry and then, to look after my family, I'll have to set up in medical practice. And I'll use hypnosis wisely as Charcot has taught me, and will not go prying into my patients' dreams. I'm no oracle. I wonder whether Du Maurier's patient might not benefit from taking a little cocaine."

That was how the conversation ended. At the time it left little impression upon me, but now it all comes back to mind perhaps because I'm in the situation, not of someone like Diana, but of an almost normal person who has lost part of his memory. Apart from the fact that I have no idea where Froïde has ended up, nothing in the world would persuade me to retell my life story even to a good Christian, let alone to a Jew. With the work I do (whatever it is) I have to talk about other people's business, for payment, but must refrain at all costs from talking about my own. But perhaps I can retell my own story to myself. I remembered now how Bourru (or Burot) told me that holy men used to hypnotise themselves by staring at their navels.

That is why I have decided, with some reluctance, to keep this diary, writing down my past as I gradually bring it back to mind, including the most insignificant details, until (what did he say?) the traumatising element re-emerges. But I will do it by myself. And I want to recover by myself, not end up in the hands of doctors who treat lunatics.

Before beginning (though, in reality, I did so yesterday), I would have enjoyed a visit to *Chez Philippe* in rue

Montorgueil to put myself into the appropriate frame of mind for this form of self-hypnosis. I would have sat down quietly, taken my time in studying the menu – the one served from six to midnight – and would have ordered *potage à la Crécy*, turbot with caper sauce, fillet of beef and *langue de veau au jus*, finishing with a maraschino sorbet and petits fours, washed down with two bottles of vintage burgundy.

By then, midnight would have passed and I would have had a look at the night menu. I would have allowed myself a turtle soup (a delicious one comes to mind, made by Dumas – so did I know Dumas?), salmon with spring onions and artichokes with Javanese pepper, with a rum sorbet and English spiced cakes to follow. Further into the night I would have treated myself to some delicacy from the morning menu, perhaps the *soupe aux oignons* which the porters at Les Halles would also be tucking into at that moment, happy to demean myself with their company. Then, to prepare myself for a busy morning, a very strong coffee and a *pousse-café* of cognac and kirsch.

To tell the truth, I would have felt a little heavy, but my mind would have been rested.

Alas, I could not permit myself such sweet licence. I have no memory, I told myself. If you were to meet someone at the restaurant who recognises you, you may not recognise him. What would you do?

I also wondered what I would do if someone were to come and see me at the shop. It went well with the fellow who came about the Bonnefoy will and the old woman selling hosts, but it could have gone worse. So I've put a notice outside saying, "The owner will be away for a month," without any indication as to when the month starts or ends. And now I realise something else. I'll have to shut myself in here, going out only occasionally to buy food. Perhaps the abstinence will do me good – who's to say that what has happened is not the result of overindulgence . . . but when? The infamous evening of the 21st?

Then again, perhaps I ought to begin re-examining my past by contemplating my navel, as Burot (or Bourru?) described; and on a full stomach, since now I'm as heavy as my age demands, I'd have to start off by looking at myself in the mirror.

Instead, I began yesterday, seated at this desk, writing without a pause, without distraction, confining myself to nibbling something every now and then, and drinking – yes, drinking without restraint. What's best about this house is a fine cellar.

4

IN MY GRANDFATHER'S DAY

26th March 1897

My childhood. Turin . . . A hillside on the other bank of the Po, me on a balcony with my mother. Then she was gone, and my father was crying, sitting on the balcony overlooking the hills at dusk. My grandfather said it was God's will.

With my mother I spoke French, like every well-bred Piedmontese (when I speak it here in Paris it sounds as if I've learned it in Grenoble, where the purest French is spoken, not like the Parisian *babil*). Since I was a boy I've always felt more French than Italian, as everyone in Piedmont does. That's why I find the French unbearable.

Childhood for me was my grandfather, more than my father and mother. I hated my mother who had gone without telling me, I hated my father who had done nothing to stop her, I hated God because he had willed such a thing to happen, and I hated my grandfather because he thought it normal for God to will such things. My father was always somewhere else – making Italy, he used to say. Then Italy unmade him.

My grandfather. Giovan Battista Simonini, former officer in the Savoy army – I think he left it at the time of the

Napoleonic invasion, enlisting under the Bourbons in Florence and then, when Tuscany had also come under the control of a Bonaparte, he returned to Turin, a retired captain, nursing his disappointments.

A warty nose – when he held me close, all I could see was his nose. And I used to feel his saliva spluttering my face. He was what the French called *ci-devant,* one who looked back nostalgically on the *ancien régime,* who had not forgiven the crimes of the Revolution. He hadn't stopped wearing *culottes* – he still had fine calves – fastened with a gold buckle beneath the knee; and the buckles on his patent-leather shoes were of gold. His waistcoat, jacket and black cravat gave him a rather priestly air. The rules of bygone style also suggested the wearing of a powdered wig but he refused to do so because, he said, even ogres like Robespierre had dressed themselves up in powdered wigs.

I never understood whether he was rich, but he didn't stint when it came to good food. Of my grandfather and my childhood I remember above all the *bagna caöda*: a terracotta pot of boiling oil, flavoured with anchovies, garlic and butter, is kept hot on a charcoal burner, and into it are dipped cardoons (which have been left to soak in cold water and lemon juice – or some said milk, but not my grandfather), raw or grilled peppers, white leaves of Savoy cabbage, Jerusalem artichokes and tender cauliflower – or boiled vegetables, onions, beetroot, potatoes or carrots (but as my grandfather used to say, this was stuff for paupers). I liked eating, and my grandfather enjoyed seeing me fatten up like a little piglet (as he used to say affectionately).

Spraying me with saliva, my grandfather would instruct me upon his principles: "The Revolution, my boy, has made us the slaves of a godless state, more unequal than before and fraternal enemies, each a Cain to the other. It's no good being too free, nor is it good to have all we need. Our fathers were poorer and happier because they remained in touch with nature. The modern world has given us steam, which poisons the countryside, and mechanical looms, that have taken work from so many wretched souls, and don't produce fabrics as they once did. Man, left to himself, is too wicked to be free. What little freedom we need must be guaranteed by a sovereign."

But his favourite theme was Abbé Barruel. Thinking back to my childhood I can almost see Abbé Barruel, who seemed to inhabit our house, even though he must have been dead for quite some time.

"You see, my boy," I can hear my grandfather saying, "once the madness of the Revolution had shaken every European nation, word began to spread that the Revolution was none other than the last or latest chapter in a universal conspiracy led by the Templars against the throne and the altar, in other words against kings – in particular the kings of France – and our most Holy Mother Church. . . . This was the opinion of Abbé Barruel who, towards the end of the last century, had written his *Mémoires pour servir à l'histoire du jacobinisme* . . ."

———

*. . . "I can almost see Abbé Barruel,
who seemed to inhabit our house,
even though he must have been
dead for quite some time." . . .*

[PAGE 61]

———

"But Grandpapa," I then asked, "what had the Templars to do with it?" I already knew the story by heart but wanted to allow my grandfather to return to his favourite subject.

"The Templars, my boy, were an extremely powerful order of knights whom the king of France destroyed so as to seize their property, sending most of them to the stake. But the survivors set up a secret order to take revenge on the kings of France. And, sure enough, when King Louis was beheaded on the guillotine, a stranger climbed onto the block and held up that poor head, shouting, 'Jacques de Molay, you are avenged!' And Molay had been the Grand Master of the Templars whom the king had had burned at the stake on the furthest point of the Île de la Cité in Paris."

"When was this Molay burned?"

"In 1314."

"Let me work it out, Grandpapa . . . that was almost five hundred years before the Revolution. And how did the Templars manage to stay hidden for five hundred years?"

"They infiltrated the corporations of the ancient cathedral builders, and from those corporations English Freemasonry was born, called by that name because its members considered themselves *free masons*."

"And why did the Masons have to start the Revolution?"

"Barruel had understood that the original Templars and the free masons had been taken over and corrupted by the Illuminati of Bavaria! This was a dreadful sect, founded by a certain Weishaupt, where every member knew only his immediate superior and nothing about those higher up and their plans; its purpose was not only to destroy the throne and the altar, but also to create a society without laws and without morality, where personal belongings and even women were to be held in common – God forgive me if I say such things to a child, but Satan's designs must be exposed. And in league with the Bavarian Illuminati were those deniers of every faith who had brought the infamous *Encyclopédie* into being, by which I mean Voltaire, d'Alembert, Diderot and all that evil breed who, copying the Illuminati, spoke in France of the *Siècle des Lumières* and in Germany of *Aufklärung* or Enlightenment and who, meeting secretly to plot the downfall of the monarchy, set up the club known as the Jacobins, named after Jacques de Molay himself. And these are the very people who plotted the French Revolution!"

"Barruel had understood everything . . ."

"He hadn't understood how a group of Christian knights could grow into a sect hostile to Christ. It is like yeast in dough – without flour and water it doesn't grow, it doesn't rise, and you cannot make bread. And what was the yeast that someone, or fate, or the Devil introduced into the still-healthy body of the secret societies of the Templars and free masons to make them the most diabolic sect of all times?"

Here my grandfather stopped, placed his hands together as if to focus his mind, gave a wily smile, and revealed with calculated and triumphant modesty: "The person who had the courage first to say it, my dear boy, was your grandfather. As soon as I was able to read Barruel's book, I wrote to him. Go down there, my boy, fetch that casket."

I followed his instructions. My grandfather opened the small casket with a gold key that hung from his neck and took out a sheet of paper which had yellowed after forty years. "This is the original letter from which I made a fair copy to send to Barruel."

I can still see my grandfather reading it with dramatic pauses.

"Please accept, Sir, the most sincere congratulations of a soldier, ignorant though I am, on your book, which may rightly be described as the supreme work of the last century. Ah! how well have you unmasked those abominable sects preparing the way for the Antichrist, and who are the implacable foes, not only of the Christian religion but of every faith, of every society, of every idea of order. One of them, however, you have mentioned only in passing. Perhaps you have done so intentionally as it is the best known and consequently the least to be feared. But, in my view, it is the most formidable power today if we consider its great wealth and the protection it enjoys in almost every European state. You understand, Sir, that I am referring to the Hebrew sect. It seems entirely separate from and hostile to the other sects; but in truth it is not. Any of these sects need only show themselves as enemies to the name of Christ and it will encourage them, finance them, protect them. And have we not seen it, and do we not see it lavishing its gold and silver to support and guide the modern sophists, the Freemasons, the Jacobins, the Illuminati? The Jews, therefore, with all the other sectaries, are but a single faction seeking to destroy the name of Christ wherever possible. And do not think, Sir, that all of this is exaggeration on my part. I do not relate anything other than what has been told me by the Jews themselves. . . ."

"And how did you learn these things from the Jews?"

"I was just over twenty and a young officer in the Savoy

army when Napoleon invaded the Kingdom of Piedmont. We were defeated at Millesimo, and Piedmont was annexed to France. It was a victory for the godless Bonapartists, who began hunting out us officers of the king to string us up by the neck. And word spread that it was better not to go around any longer in uniform, nor even to be seen. My father was in trade, and had had dealings with a Jewish moneylender who owed him some kind of favour. So through his good offices I lodged for several weeks (at a high price, of course) in a small room in the ghetto, which at that time was right next to where we lived, between via San Filippo and via delle Rosine, until the dust had settled and I could leave the city and go to stay with relatives in Florence. I was hardly pleased to be mixed up with that kind of people, but it was the only place where no one ever dreamt of setting foot – the Jews could not leave there, and decent people kept well away."

My grandfather then put his hands to his eyes, as if to blot out an unbearable image: "And so, waiting for the storm to pass, I lived in those filthy backstreets, where sometimes as many as eight people lived in a single room with cooking stove, bed and slop bucket, worn down with anaemia, their skin waxy, imperceptibly blue like Sèvres china, always seeking out the darkest corners, illuminated by only the light of a candle. Not a drop of blood, yellowish hue, hair the colour of gelatine, their beards of an indefinable redness and, when black, seeming the colour of a faded frock coat . . . I could not bear the stink of my lodgings and wandered around the five courtyards. I remember them well – Cortile Grande, Cortile dei Preti, Cortile della Vite, Cortile della Taverna and Cortile della Terrazza, linked together by fearsome covered passageways, the Portici Oscuri. Now you find Jews even in piazza Carlina – in fact you find them everywhere because the Savoys are getting soft – but at that time they were crammed one on top of the other in those sunless lanes and (had it not been for fear of the Bonapartists) I would never have stomached it amidst that greasy, filthy crowd. . . ."

My grandfather paused, moistening his lips with a handkerchief, as if to remove a nasty taste from his mouth: "And thanks to them I was saved. What humiliation. But if we Christians despised them, they certainly weren't kind to us, indeed they hated us, in the same way as they still hate us today. And so I started telling them I was born in Livorno of a Jewish family, that while still a child I was brought up by relatives who unfortunately baptised me, but that I still remained a Jew at heart. These confidences didn't seem to impress them very much since, they explained, many of them were in the same situation as me and they no longer took much notice of such things. But my words had won me the trust of an old man who lived in Cortile della Terrazza next to an oven used for baking unleavened bread."

Here my grandfather became more animated as he recounted that meeting and, with rolling eyes and hand gestures, imitated the Jew he was describing. It seems this Mordechai was from Syria, and had been involved in a sad episode in Damascus. An Arab boy disappeared in the city and no one thought of the Jews at first because it was said that Jews killed only Christian children for their rituals. But then, in the bottom of a ditch, the remains of a young corpse were found which must have been cut into a thousand pieces and pounded in a mortar. The marks of the crime were so similar to those attributed to the Jews that the police began to think that, with Passover approaching, the Jews must have needed Christian blood to make their bread and, finding no Christian boy, had taken the Arab, baptised him and then slain him.

"You know," my grandfather explained, "that a baptism is always valid, whoever does it, provided that the person who baptises means to baptise according to the precepts of the Holy Roman Church. This is something the perfidious Jews know all too well and they have no shame in saying, 'I baptise you as would a Christian, in whose idolatry I do not believe, but which he performs fully believing it.' So the poor little martyr had, at least, the good fortune to end up in heaven, though thanks only to the Devil."

Mordechai was immediately suspected. To make him talk, they tied his wrists behind his back, put weights on his feet, and a dozen times they lifted him up with a pulley and let him fall to the ground. They put sulphur under his nose and then dropped him into icy water, and when he lifted his head they pushed him under, until he confessed. In short, to put an end to it, it was said the poor man gave the names of five of his brethren who had nothing to do with it; and they were sentenced to death, while he was set free, with dislocated limbs; but by now he had lost his wits, and some kind soul loaded him on a merchant ship departing for Genoa, otherwise the other Jews would have stoned him to death. Indeed, it was said that on the ship he had been lured by a Barnabite priest into being baptised and had accepted so he could find help when he landed in the Kingdom of Piedmont, though he remained faithful at heart to the religion of his fathers. He would therefore have been what the Christians call a Marrano, except that once he'd arrived at Turin he sought refuge in the ghetto and denied ever having been converted; many thought he was a false Jew who remained true to his new Christian faith – and therefore, you might say, a Marrano twice over. But as no one could prove all the rumours that came from abroad, out of pity for the insane he was kept alive by the meagre charity of all, and confined to a hole where not even an occupant of the ghetto would have dared to live.

Whatever he might have done in Damascus, my grandfather claimed that the old man hadn't really gone mad. He was quite simply filled with an unquenchable hatred towards Christians and, in that windowless hovel, his trembling hand clenching my grandfather by the wrist, his glistening eyes staring at him in the darkness, he declared that from then on he had dedicated his life to revenge. He told him how their Talmud preached hatred of the Christian race and how, in order to corrupt the Christians, they, the Jews, had invented Freemasonry, of which he had become one of their nameless superiors, and that he commanded lodges from Naples to London, except that he had to remain hidden, living in secret, segregated from the world, so as not to get knifed by the Jesuits, who were hunting for him everywhere.

He looked around as he spoke, as if some Jesuit armed with a dagger might appear from a dark corner. Then he would blow his nose loudly, sometimes lamenting his sad condition, sometimes giving a sly vengeful smile, enjoying the fact that the whole world was unaware of his terrible power. He unctuously fondled Simonini's hand and continued to let his imagination wander. And he told him that, if Simonini so wished, their sect would have welcomed him with open arms, and he would have him admitted into the most secret of the Masonic lodges.

And he revealed to him that both Mani, the prophet of the Manichean sect, as well as the infamous Old Man of the Mountain, who drugged his Assassins before sending them off to murder Christian princes, were Jewish by race. He told him that the Freemasons and the Illuminati had been founded by two Jews, and that Jews had founded all the Antichristian sects, which were now so numerous around the world as to include many millions of people, men and women of every position, class and status, including many men of the Church and even several cardinals, and before long they were not unhopeful of having a pope on their side (and, as my grandfather would later say, as soon as a dubious character like Pius IX had risen to the Throne of St Peter the idea no longer seemed quite so improbable); and he told me that they themselves often pretended to be Christians so as to deceive the Christians more effectively, travelling and moving about from one country to the other with false baptism certificates purchased from corrupt curates; and that with money and deception they hoped to gain civil recognition from every government, as they were already doing in many countries; and that once they had obtained rights of citizenship like everybody else they would start to buy houses and land; and that through moneylending they would strip the Christians of their estates and their wealth; and that they had vowed to become rulers of the world in less than a century, to abolish all other sects so that theirs would reign supreme, to build as many synagogues as Christian churches, and reduce everyone else to slavery.

"This," my grandfather concluded, "was what I told Barruel. Perhaps I exaggerated a little, saying that I had learned from all of them what, in fact, I had heard from one man alone, but I was and still am convinced the old man was telling the truth. And that is what I wrote, if you'll let me finish reading."

And my grandfather resumed:

"These, Sir, are the perfidious plans for the Hebrew nation, which I heard with my own ears. . . . It would therefore be most desirable that a persuasive and distinguished pen such as yours should open the eyes of the aforesaid governments, and direct them to return these people to the abjection which is properly theirs, and in which our more prudent and judicious forefathers had always endeavoured to keep them. This, Sir, I invite you to do on my behalf, asking you to forgive an Italian, a soldier, for any errors that you may find in this letter. I wish you by God's hand the most bounteous reward for the illuminating writings which you have bestowed on His Church, and that He may inspire, in those who read them, the highest and most profound esteem for you, to whom I am honoured to be, Sir, your most humble and obedient servant, Giovanni Battista Simonini."

At this point, on each occasion, my grandfather returned the letter to the chest and I asked, "And what did Abbé Barruel say?"

"He did not deign to reply. But I had some good friends in the Roman Curia, and so discovered that this coward was afraid that if such truths were to spread, it would trigger off a massacre of the Jews, which he did not wish to provoke since he believed there were innocent people among them. And what is more, when Napoleon decided to meet representatives of the Grand Sanhedrin to obtain their support for his ambitions, certain threats from the French Jews of the time must have had an effect – and someone must have informed the abbé that it was better not to stir up trouble. But at the same time Barruel felt unable to remain silent and this is why he sent my original letter to the Supreme Pontiff Pius VII, and copies to a large number of bishops. Nor did the matter finish there, because he also conveyed the letter to Cardinal Fesch, Primate of the Gauls at the time, so that he could inform Napoleon. And he did the same with the chief of police in Paris. And the Paris police, I am told, carried out an investigation at the Roman Curia to find out whether I was a reliable witness. And by the Devil I was – the cardinals could hardly deny it! In short, Barruel was attacking from undercover: he did not want to stir up any more trouble than his book had already caused but, while appearing silent, he was sending my revelations halfway round the world. You should know that Barruel was educated by the Jesuits until Louis XV drove them out of France, and then took orders as a lay priest, except that he became a Jesuit once again when Pius VII restored full rights to the order. Now, as you know, I am a fervent Catholic and profess the highest respect for any man of the cloth, but a Jesuit is surely always a Jesuit – he says one thing and does another, does one thing and says another – and Barruel behaved no differently. . . ."

And my grandfather chuckled, spluttering spit through his few remaining teeth, amused by that sulphurous impertinence of his. "So there it is, my dear Simonino. I am old, it is not for me to be the lone voice in the wilderness. If they didn't want to listen to me, they will answer for it before God Almighty, but I pass the flame of witness on to you young people, now that those most damnable Jews are becoming increasingly powerful, and our cowardly sovereign Carlo Alberto is proving ever more indulgent towards them. But he will be overthrown by their conspiracy. . . ."

"Are they also plotting here in Turin?" I asked.

My grandfather looked around him, as if someone were listening to his words, while the shadows of dusk darkened the room: "Here and everywhere else," he said. "They are an accursed race, and their Talmud says – as anyone who can read it will confirm – that the Jews must curse the Christians three times a day and ask God that they be exterminated and destroyed, and if one of them meets a Christian on a precipice he must push him over. You know why you are called Simonino? I wanted your parents to baptise you in memory of St Simonino, a child martyr who, back in the fifteenth century near Trent, was kidnapped by Jews who killed him and chopped him up to use his blood in their rituals."

"If you don't behave yourself and go straight to sleep, the horrible Mordechai will come to visit you tonight." That is how my grandfather threatens me. And it's hard to get to

73

sleep, in my small attic room, straining my ear each time the old house creaks, almost hearing the terrible old man's footsteps on the wooden staircase, coming to get me, to drag me off to his infernal den, to feed me unleavened bread made with the blood of infant martyrs. Confusing this with other stories I hear from Mamma Teresa, the old servant who had been my father's wet-nurse and still shuffles about the house, I imagine Mordechai dribbling lubriciously, muttering, "Fee-fi-fo-fum, I smell the blood of a Christian boy."

I am almost fourteen, and several times I've been tempted to go into the ghetto, which now oozes out beyond its old confines, since many restrictions are to be removed in Piedmont. Perhaps I'll come across a few Jews while I wander almost to the frontier of that forbidden world, but I've heard it said that many have abandoned their centuries-old ways. "They disguise themselves," my grandfather says, "they disguise themselves, pass us in the street without us even realising." While wandering its limits, I meet a girl with black hair who crosses piazza Carlina each morning carrying some kind of basket covered with a cloth to a nearby shop. Fiery gaze, velvet eyes, dark complexion . . . Impossible that she's a Jewess, that those men my grandfather has described, with rapacious features and venomous eyes, could produce women like her. And yet she can only have come from the ghetto.

. . . almost hearing the terrible old man's
footsteps on the wooden staircase, coming
to get me, to drag me off to his infernal
den, to feed me unleavened bread made
with the blood of infant martyrs. . . .

[PAGE 74]

This is the first time I have looked at a woman other than Mamma Teresa. I go backwards and forwards each morning and my heart begins to pound as soon as I see her in the distance. On those mornings when I do not see her, I wander around the square as if I'm trying to find an escape route and reject each one of them, and I'm still there when my grandfather expects me back home, sitting furious at the table, nibbling crumbs of bread.

One morning I dare to stop the girl and, eyes lowered, ask her if I can help carry her basket. She replies haughtily, in dialect, that she can manage perfectly well by herself. But she doesn't call me *monssü*, but *gagnu*, boy. I've stopped looking out for her. I haven't seen her since. I've been humiliated by a daughter of Zion. Is it perhaps because I'm fat? This, in fact, marks the beginning of my war against the daughters of Eve.

Throughout my childhood my grandfather refused to send me to the government school because he said the teachers were all Carbonari and republicans. I spent all those years alone at home, watching resentfully for hours as the other children played by the river, as if they were taking something away from me that was mine. The rest of the time I spent closed up in a room studying with a Jesuit father whom my grandfather always chose, according to my age, from among the black crows who flocked about the area. I hated the teacher of the moment, not just because his way of teaching was by rapping my knuckles, but also because my father (the few times he spent distractedly with me) had instilled in me a hatred of priests.

"But my teachers are not priests, they are Jesuit fathers," I used to say.

"Even worse," retorted my father. "Never trust Jesuits. Do you know what a holy priest has written (a priest, I say, and not a Mason or a Carbonaro or one of Satan's Illuminati – as they think I am – but a priest of saintly kindness, Father Gioberti)? It is Jesuitism that undermines, torments, afflicts, vilifies, persecutes, destroys men of free spirit; it is Jesuitism that drives good and valiant men out of public positions and replaces them with others who are base and contemptible; it is Jesuitism that slackens, obstructs, torments, harasses, confuses, weakens, corrupts public and private education in a thousand ways, which sows bitterness, mistrust, animosity, hatred, unrest, open and covert discord among individuals, families, classes, states, governments and peoples; it is Jesuitism that weakens minds, tames hearts and desires, reducing them to a state of sloth, that debilitates young people through feeble discipline, that corrupts adults through acquiescent, hypocritical morality, that combats, weakens and stifles friendship, domestic relationships, filial piety and the sacred love which most people feel for their country. . . . No sect in the world is so gutless (he said), so hard and ruthless when its own interests are at stake, as the Company of Jesus. Behind that soothing and alluring face, those sweet and honeyed words, that kind and most affable manner, the Jesuit who responds worthily to the discipline of the order and the instructions of his superiors has a heart of iron, impenetrable to higher feelings and nobler sentiments. He firmly puts into practice Machiavelli's precept that where the well-being of the state is in question, no consideration should be given to right or wrong, to compassion or cruelty. And for this reason they are taught as young seminarians not to cultivate family affections, not to have friends, but to be ready to reveal to their superiors every slightest shortcoming in even their closest companion, to control every impulse of the heart and to offer absolute obedience, *perinde ac cadaver*. Gioberti said that whereas the Indian Phansigars, or stranglers, sacrifice the bodies of their enemies to their deity, killing them with a garrotte or a knife, the Jesuits of Italy kill the soul with their tongues, like reptiles, or with their pen.

"But I have always been amused," my father concluded, "that Gioberti took some of these ideas second-hand from *The Wandering Jew*, a novel by Eugène Sue, published the year before."

My father. The black sheep of the family. My grandfather said he was mixed up with the Carbonari but when I mentioned this to my father, he told me quietly not to listen to such ramblings. He avoided talking to me about his own ideals, perhaps out of shame, or respect for his father's views, or disinterest towards me. But it was enough for me to over-hear my grandfather in conversation with his Jesuit fathers, or to catch the gossip between Mamma Teresa and the caretaker, to realise my father was among those who not only approved of the Revolution and Napoleon, but even talked about an Italy that would shake off the power of the Austrian empire, the Bourbons and the Pope, to become a Nation (a word never to be uttered in my grandfather's presence).

I learned my basic education from Father Pertuso, who had a face like a weasel. Father Pertuso was the first to instruct me in the history of our present times (while my grandfather taught me about the past).

Later, the first rumours began to circulate about the activities of the Carbonari – I found news about them in the journals that arrived addressed to my absent father, seizing them before my grandfather could have them destroyed. And I remember having to follow the Latin and German lessons given by Father Bergamaschi, who was such a close friend of my grandfather that a small room in the house was reserved for him, not far from my own. Father Bergamaschi . . . Unlike Father Pertuso, he was a fine-looking young man with curly hair, a well-proportioned face, and a charming manner of speech; and, at home at least, he wore his neat cassock with dignity. I remember his white hands with tapered fingers, and nails rather longer than might have been expected for a churchman.

Often, when he saw me bent over my studies, he would sit behind me stroking my head, and would warn me of the many dangers that threatened an unwary young man, and tell me how the Carbonari were no more than a cover for that greater scourge, communism.

"The communists," he said, "seemed to pose no danger until recently but now, after the manifesto of that Marsch (or so he seemed to pronounce it), we must expose their conspiracies. You know nothing about Babette of Interlaken – worthy great-niece of Weishaupt, she who was called the Great Virgin of Swiss Communism."

Who knows why Father Bergamaschi seemed more obsessed by religious conflicts between Catholics and Protestants in Switzerland than the insurrections in Milan or Vienna that were so much discussed at that time.

"Babette was born into crime and led a life of debauchery, thieving, kidnapping and bloodshed. She did not know God, apart from being heard continually cursing him. In the skirmishes below Lucerne, when the radicals had killed various Catholics in the oldest cantons, it was Babette whom they got to tear out their victims' hearts and eyes. Babette, her blonde hair blowing in the wind, like the whore of Babylon, concealed beneath her mantle of charms the fact that she was the herald of secret societies, the demon who orchestrated all the tricks and intrigues of those mysterious confraternities; she appeared and disappeared in a flash like a hobgoblin, she knew unfathomable secrets, intercepted diplomatic messages without interfering with their seals, slithered like an asp around the most private government chambers in Vienna, Berlin and even St Petersburg, forged cheques and altered the details on passports. Even as a child she had learned the art of poisoning, and knew how to practise it as the sect demanded. She seemed possessed by Satan, such was her restless energy and the allure of her gaze."

I was startled, I tried not to listen, but at night I dreamt of Babette of Interlaken. Half-asleep, I wanted to block out the picture of that blonde demon whose hair flowed down

*. . . I was startled, I tried not to listen,
but at night I dreamt of Babette of
Interlaken. . . .*

[PAGE 80]

her shoulders, most surely naked, that demonic, fragrant hobgoblin, her breast heaving rapturously with godless, sinful pride. Yet I dreamt of her as a model to imitate – or rather, filled with horror just at the thought of brushing her with my fingers, I felt a desire to be like her, a secret and all-powerful agent who forged passports and led victims of the other sex to perdition.

My teachers liked to eat well, and this vice must also have remained with me into adulthood. I remember mealtimes, sombre rather than lively gatherings, where the good fathers would discuss the excellence of a *bollito misto*, prepared as my grandfather had instructed.

It required at least half a kilo of shin of beef, an oxtail, a piece of rump, a small salami, a calf's tongue and head, *cotechino* sausage, a boiling fowl, an onion, two carrots, two sticks of celery and a handful of parsley. All left to cook for various lengths of time, according to the type of meat. But, as my grandfather insisted and Father Bergamaschi confirmed with emphatic nods of the head, once the boiled meat had been arranged on the serving dish, you had to sprinkle a few pinches of coarse salt and pour several spoonfuls of boiling broth over the meat to bring out the flavour. Not much vegetable, except for a few potatoes, but plenty of condiments – *mostarda d'uva, mostarda alla senape di frutta*, horseradish sauce, but above all (on this my grandfather was firm) *bagnetto verde*: a handful of parsley, a few anchovy fillets, fresh breadcrumbs, a teaspoonful of capers, a clove of garlic, the yolk of a hard-boiled egg, all finely chopped, with olive oil and vinegar.

These were, I remember, the pleasures of my childhood and adolescence. What more could I want?

A sultry afternoon. I am studying. Father Bergamaschi is sitting quietly behind me. His hand clasps the back of my neck and he whispers to me – to a boy so devout, so well disposed, who wishes to avoid the enticements of the opposite sex, he could offer not only paternal friendship but the warmth and affection that a mature man can give.

From then on, I've never let a priest touch me again. Am I perhaps dressing up as Abbé Dalla Piccola so that I can go touching others?

When I reached eighteen, my grandfather, who wanted me to be a lawyer (in Piedmont anyone who has studied law is called a lawyer) resigned himself to letting me out of the house and sending me to university. This was my first chance to mix with boys my own age, but it was too late, and I felt suspicious of them. I failed to understand their stifled laughs and meaningful looks when they talked about women and passed around French books with repulsive engravings. I preferred to keep my own company, reading. My father received *Le Constitutionnel* on subscription from Paris, in which Sue's *The Wandering Jew* was serialised, and of course

I read each instalment avidly. It was here that I learned how the infamous Society of Jesus had managed to plot the most abominable crimes to seize an inheritance, trampling on the rights of poor good people. As well as confirming my suspicions about the Jesuits, this experience initiated me into the delights of the *feuilleton*: in the attic I found a case of books which my father had evidently kept out of my grandfather's sight and (seeking likewise to conceal this solitary vice from my grandfather) I spent whole afternoons until my eyes were worn out on *The Mysteries of Paris*, *The Three Musketeers*, *The Count of Monte Cristo* . . .

It was now that marvellous year of 1848. Every student was delighted with the accession to the papacy of Cardinal Mastai Ferretti – Pius IX – who had granted an amnesty for political crimes two years earlier. The year had begun with the first protests in Milan against the Austrians, where citizens had stopped smoking to damage the revenues of the imperial government (those Milanese comrades, who stood firm when soldiers and police provoked them by blowing clouds of sweet-scented cigar smoke at them, were seen by my Turin companions as heroes). That same month, revolutionary disorder had broken out in the Kingdom of the Two Sicilies and Ferdinando II had promised a constitution. In February, popular insurrection in Paris had dethroned Louis Philippe, and the Republic was (once and for all!) proclaimed, slavery was abolished as well as the death penalty for political crimes, and universal suffrage established. By March the Pope had granted not only a constitution but also freedom of the press, and had released the Jews in the ghetto from many humiliating rituals and obligations. During the same period the Grand Duke of Tuscany also granted a constitution, while Carlo Alberto introduced the Albertine Statute in the Kingdom of Piedmont. Finally, there were the revolutionary protests in Vienna, in Bohemia and in Hungary, and those five days of insurrection in Milan which would lead to the Austrians being driven out, with the Piedmont army going to war so that liberated Milan was annexed to Piedmont. There were also rumours among my comrades that the communists had produced a manifesto, which brought rejoicing not only among students but also workers and men of poor circumstances, all convinced that the last priest would soon be hanged using the guts of the last king.

Not all the news was good: Carlo Alberto had suffered several defeats and was regarded as a traitor by the people of Milan, and in general by every patriot; Pius IX, frightened by the assassination of one of his ministers, had taken refuge at Gaeta with the King of the Two Sicilies and, after under-hand attempts to stir up trouble, proved to be less liberal than he had seemed at first; and many of the constitutions that had been granted were withdrawn. . . . But Garibaldi and Mazzini's patriots had arrived in the meantime in Rome – early the following year the Roman Republic would be proclaimed.

My father left home for good in March, and Mamma Teresa said she was sure he had gone to join the Milanese rebels, except that towards December one of the Jesuits living with us received news that he had joined up with Mazzini's supporters who were running to defend the Roman Republic. My grandfather was devastated, and tormented me with dreadful prophecies that transformed this *annus mirabilis* into an *annus horribilis*. During those same months, the Piedmont government suppressed the Jesuit order, confiscating its property and, in order to destroy everything around them, also suppressed orders sympathetic to the Jesuits such as the Oblates of San Carlo and of Maria Santissima, and the Redemptorists.

"This is the advent of the Antichrist," my grandfather mourned. He naturally blamed every event on Jewish intrigue, seeing Mordechai's darkest prophecies as being fulfilled.

My grandfather provided shelter for Jesuit fathers trying to escape the fury of the people, as they waited to be reinstated in some way among the lay clergy. In early 1849 many arrived secretly from Rome with appalling stories of what was happening down there.

Father Pacchi. After reading Sue's *The Wandering Jew*, I saw him as the incarnation of Father Rodin, the wicked Jesuit who moved about in the shadows, sacrificing every moral principle to the interests of the Society, perhaps because (like Father Rodin) he concealed his membership of the order by dressing in secular clothes, wearing a scruffy topcoat caked in old sweat and covered with dandruff, a neckerchief instead of a cravat, a black threadbare waistcoat and heavy shoes always encrusted with mud which he trampled inconsiderately into our fine carpets. He had a thin, pale, chiselled face, oily grey hair plastered over his temples, turtle eyes and thin purplish lips.

Not satisfied with the revulsion inspired by his simple presence at table, he ruined everyone's appetite by recounting terrifying stories, uttered in sermonising tones: "My friends," he said with tremulous voice, "I have to tell you . . . the leprosy has spread from Paris. Louis Philippe was certainly no saint, but he was a bulwark against anarchy. I have seen the Roman people these last few days! Yet were they indeed the people of Rome? They were ragged and dishevelled, thugs who would turn their backs upon heaven for a glass of wine. They are not people, they are a rabble, mixed with the vilest dregs from the cities of Italy and abroad, followers of Garibaldi and Mazzini, blind instruments for every evil. You know not how iniquitous are the abominations committed by the republicans. They enter churches and break open the reliquaries of martyrs, they scatter their ashes to the wind and use the urns as chamber pots. They rip out the altar stones and smear them with excrement, they deface the statues of the Virgin with their daggers, they cut the eyes out of the images of saints, and with charcoal they scrawl obscenities upon them. When a priest spoke out against the Republic, they dragged him into a doorway, stabbed him, gouged out his eyes and tore out his tongue and, after disembowelling him, they wrapped his guts around his neck and strangled him. And do not imagine, even if Rome is liberated (already there is talk of help arriving from France), that Mazzini's followers will be defeated. They have spewed out from every province of Italy; they are shrewd and crafty, fraudsters and deceivers; they are daring, patient and determined. They will continue to congregate in the city's most secret haunts, their falsity and hypocrisy allows them into the secrets of government offices, into the police, into the army, into the navy, into the city strongholds."

. . . *"When a priest spoke out against*
the Republic, they dragged him into a
doorway, stabbed him, gouged out his
eyes and tore out his tongue." . . .

[PAGE 87]

"And my son is among them," cried my grandfather, crushed in body and spirit.

Excellent beef braised in Barolo then arrived at table.

"My son will never understand the beauty of such a thing," he said. "Beef with onion, carrot, celery, sage, rosemary, bay leaf, cloves, cinnamon, juniper, salt, pepper, butter, olive oil and, of course, a bottle of Barolo wine, served with polenta or puréed potato. Go on, fight the Revolution. . . . All taste for life is gone. You people want to be rid of the Pope, and we'll end up being forced by that fisherman Garibaldi to eat *bouillabaisse niçoise*. . . . What is the world coming to!"

Father Bergamaschi often went off, dressed in secular clothing, saying he would be away for a few days, without explaining where or why. Then I would go into his room, take out his cassock, dress myself up in it, and admire myself in a mirror, moving about as if dancing – as if I were, heaven forbid, a woman . . . or as if I were imitating him. If it turns out I am Abbé Dalla Piccola, then I have discovered here the distant origins of these theatrical tastes of mine.

In the pockets of the cassock I found some money (which the priest had obviously forgotten), and I decided to afford myself a little gluttonous transgression and to explore certain places in the city which I had often heard praised.

Thus dressed – and without realising that in those days it was already a provocation – I headed off into the labyrinth of Balôn, that part of Porta Palazzo then inhabited by the dregs of Turin's population, where the worst band of miscreants to infest the city were recruited. But on feast days Porta Palazzo market offered extraordinary entertainment. The people jostled and shoved, pressing around the stalls; servant girls flocked into the butchers' shops; children stood spellbound in front of the nougat makers; gourmands purchased their poultry, game and charcuterie; and in the restaurants not a single table was free. In my cassock, I brushed past women's flapping dresses, and from the corner of my eye, which I kept ecclesiastically fixed upon my crossed hands, I saw the faces of women wearing hats, bonnets, veils or headscarves, and felt bewildered by the bustle of carriages and carts, by the shouts, the cries, the uproar.

Excited by the exuberance, from which my grandfather and my father had until then kept me hidden, though for different reasons, I pushed my way to one of Turin's legendary places at that time. Dressed as a Jesuit, and mischievously enjoying the curiosity I aroused, I arrived at *Caffè al Bicerin*, close to the Sanctuary of the Consolata, to taste their milk, fragrant with cocoa, coffee and other flavours, served in a glass with metal holder and handle. I was not to know that one of my heroes, Alexandre Dumas, would write about *bicerin* a few years later, but during the course of only two or three visits to that magical place I learned all about that nectar. It originated from *bavareisa* except that, whereas the milk, coffee and chocolate are mixed together in the *bavareisa*, in a *bicerin* they stay separated in three layers (which remain hot), so that you can order a *bicerin pur e fiur*, made with coffee and milk, *pur e barba*, with coffee and chocolate, or *'n poc'd tut*, meaning a little of everything.

It was a magnificent place, with its wrought-iron frontage edged by advertising panels, its cast-iron columns and capitals

. . . But, pleasures of coffee and chocolate apart, what I most enjoyed was appearing to be someone else . . .

[PAGE 92]

and, inside, wooden *boiseries* decorated with mirrors, marble-topped tables and, behind the counter, almond-scented jars with forty different types of confectionery. I enjoyed standing there watching, particularly on Sundays, when this drink was nectar for those who had fasted in preparation for communion and needed some sustenance on leaving the Consolata – and a *bicerin* was also much prized during the Lenten fast since hot chocolate was not regarded as food. What hypocrites.

But, pleasures of coffee and chocolate apart, what I most enjoyed was appearing to be someone else: the thought that people had no idea who I really was gave me a sense of superiority. I had a secret.

But I had to limit and then finally halt these adventures – I was frightened of bumping into my comrades who certainly didn't think of me as a religious zealot and believed that I too was fired by their enthusiasm for the Carbonari.

These aspiring national liberators generally gathered at the *Osteria del Gambero d'Oro*. In a dark narrow street, over a still darker doorway, a sign with a golden prawn read, 'Osteria del Gambero d'Oro, good wine & good food'. Inside was a room that also served as kitchen and wine cellar. Amid smells of salami and onions, customers drank and sometimes played *morra*. More often than not we passed the night, conspirators without a plot, dreaming of imminent insurrections. I had learned to enjoy good food at my grandfather's house and all that could be said about the *Gambero d'Oro* was that you could satisfy your hunger, provided you were not too fussy. But I needed to get out into society and escape from our Jesuit guests, and so the *Gambero*'s greasy food and my jovial friends were preferable to sombre dinners at home.

We would leave towards dawn, our breath heavy with garlic and our hearts filled with patriotic ardour, losing ourselves in a comforting mantle of fog, excellent for avoiding the attention of police spies. Sometimes we crossed the Po and climbed up to look back over the roofs and bell towers floating on the mist that covered the plain, while the faraway Basilica of Superga, already glinting in the sun, seemed like a lighthouse in the middle of the sea.

But we students didn't just talk about the Nation to come. We talked, as happens at that age, about women. Each in turn, eyes gleaming, recalled looking up towards a balcony and catching a smile, touching a hand while passing down a staircase, a dried flower dropped from a missal and picked up (the braggart claimed) while it still held the perfume of the hand that had placed it between those sacred pages. I feigned annoyance, and acquired the reputation of being a Mazzinian of strict and upright morals.

Except that one evening the most licentious of our companions announced that he had found in a chest in his attic, well hidden by his shameless, dissipated father, several of those volumes which in Turin were known (in French) as *cochons*, and not daring to lay them out on the greasy table of the *Gambero d'Oro*, he had decided to lend them to each of us in turn. When it came to me I could hardly refuse.

Late one night, I leafed through those volumes which must have been precious and valuable, bound as they were in morocco leather, spines with raised cords and red title label, gilt page edges, gilt *fleurons* on the covers and some with coats of arms. They had titles such as *Une veillée de jeune fille* or *Ah! monseigneur, si Thomas nous voyait!* and I shuddered as I turned the pages and found engravings which sent streams of sweat trickling from my hair down my cheeks and neck: young women who lifted their skirts to reveal buttocks of dazzling whiteness, offered for the abuse of lascivious men – nor did I know whether to be more disturbed by their brazen rotundity or by the almost virginal smile of the young girl, whose head was turned immodestly towards her violator, her face illuminated with mischievous eyes and a chaste smile, framed by jet-black hair parted into two side-knots; or still more terrifying, three girls on a couch with their legs open to display what should have been the natural defence of their virginal pudenda, one of them offering it to the right hand of a man with ruffled hair, who at the same time was penetrating the girl lying shamelessly beside her, while the third girl had her crotch nonchalantly exposed and with her left hand was parting her cleavage with subtle prurience through her ruffled corset. And then I found the curious caricature of a priest with a wart-covered face which, on closer inspection, was made up of naked men and women variously entwined, and penetrated by enormous male members, many of which hung in a line over the nape of the neck as if to form, with their testicles, a thick head of hair that ended in heavy ringlets.

I do not remember how that turbulent night ended,

when sex was presented to me at its most dreadful (in the biblical sense of the word, like the crash of thunder which arouses a sense of the sublime as well as fear of devilry and sacrilege). I remember only that I emerged from that disturbing experience mumbling repeatedly to myself, like a litany, the phrase of some writer or other of sacred texts which Father Pertuso had made me learn by heart many years earlier: "The beauty of the body is only skin-deep. If men could only see what is beneath the flesh, they would be nauseated just to look at women: all this feminine charm is nothing but phlegm, blood, humours, bile. Consider all that is hidden in the nostrils, in the throat, in the stomach . . . And we who are repelled by the very thought of touching vomit or ordure with the tips of our fingers, how can we ever want to embrace a sack of excrement?"

Perhaps at that age I still believed in divine justice, and attributed what happened the following day to holy vengeance for that tempestuous night. I found my grandfather sprawled gasping in his chair, holding a crumpled sheet of paper between his hands. We called the doctor, I took the letter from him and read that my father had been fatally shot by a French shell while defending the Roman Republic, in that June of 1849 when General Oudinot had been sent by Louis-Napoleon to free the papal throne from Mazzini and Garibaldi's army.

My grandfather was not dead, though he was already over eighty, but he shut himself up for days in a resentful silence, and no one knew whether this was out of hatred of the

French, or of the papal troops who had killed his son, or of his son for having dared so irresponsibly to challenge them, or of all the patriots who had corrupted him. From time to time he let out plaintive sighs, alluding to the responsibility of the Jews in the events that were shaking Italy, just as they had devastated France fifty years earlier.

Perhaps to feel closer to my father, I spent many long hours in the attic on the novels he had left behind, and I managed to intercept Dumas' *Joseph Balsamo* which arrived by post when he could no longer read it.

This wonderful book, as everyone knows, recounts the adventures of Cagliostro, and how he had plotted the affair of the queen's necklace, managing in a single stroke to morally and financially ruin Cardinal de Rohan, compromise the sovereign, and expose the entire court to ridicule, so that many believed that Cagliostro's fraud had so contributed towards undermining the prestige of the monarchy as to prepare the climate of disgrace which led to the Revolution of 'eighty-nine.

Dumas goes further, and sees Cagliostro, alias Joseph Balsamo, as someone who intentionally organised not just a fraud but a political plot under the protection of universal Freemasonry.

I was fascinated by the *ouverture*. Scene: Mont Tonnerre – Thunder Mountain. On the left bank of the Rhine, a few leagues from Worms, a range of desolate mountains begins – the King's Chair, Falcons' Rock, Serpent's Crest and, highest of all, Thunder Mountain. It was here, on the 6th of May 1770 (almost twenty years before the outbreak of the fateful Revolution), as the sun was setting behind the spire of Strasbourg Cathedral almost dividing it into two hemispheres of fire, that a Stranger from Mainz climbed the slopes of the mountain, abandoning his horse at a certain point, until he was seized by several masked beings. After blindfolding him, they led him through the forest to a clearing where three hundred phantoms awaited him, wrapped in shrouds and armed with swords. They began to question him most carefully.

What do you wish? To see the light. Are you ready to swear an oath? And a series of tests began, such as drinking the blood of a traitor who had just been killed, pointing a pistol to his head and pulling the trigger to prove his obedience, and nonsense of that kind, reminiscent of Masonic rituals of the lowest order well known to regular readers of Dumas, until the traveller decided to cut things short and turned disdainfully to the gathering, making it clear that he knew all their rituals and tricks, and that they should therefore stop play-acting with him, because he was something more than all of them, and was by divine right head of that universal Masonic congregation.

And he called for the members of the Masonic lodges of Stockholm, London, New York, Zurich, Madrid, Warsaw and various Asiatic countries, all of course already assembled on Thunder Mountain, to bow to his command.

Why were Masons from throughout the world gathered there? The Stranger then explained. He asked for the hand of iron, the sword of fire, the scales of diamond to banish the Impure from the earth, in other words to humiliate and destroy the two great enemies of humanity, the throne and the altar (my grandfather had indeed told me that the motto of that despicable man Voltaire was *écrasez l'infâme*). The Stranger then described how he, like all good necromancers of the time, had been alive for thousands of generations, since before the time of Moses and perhaps even Assurbanipal, and had come from the Orient to proclaim that the hour had arrived. The peoples of all countries form one vast phalanx which is marching relentlessly towards the light, and France was the advance guard of this phalanx – let the true torch be placed in her hands on this march and let her bring new light into the world. An old and corrupt king reigns in France, who still has a few years to live. One of those present (who was Lavater, the great physiognomist) tried to suggest that the faces of his two young successors (the future Louis XVI and his wife Marie Antoinette) revealed a kind and charitable disposition, but the Stranger (whom the readers would probably have recognised by now as Joseph Balsamo, whom Dumas had not yet named) reminded him that there could be no concern for human pity when advancement of the torch of progress was at stake. Within twenty years the French monarchy had to be wiped off the face of the earth.

At this point each representative of each lodge from each country came forward offering men or wealth for the victory of the republican and Masonic cause, under the banner of *lilia pedibus destrue* – tread under foot and destroy the lilies of France.

It didn't occur to me that a conspiracy of five continents

was perhaps rather an excessive way of changing the consti-
tutional rule in France. Anyone from Piedmont at that time
would, in fact, have said the only powers existing in the
world were France, certainly Austria, and perhaps Cochinchina
far far away, but no other country was worthy of note, except
of course the Papal States. From the picture created by Dumas
(in reverence to that great writer) I wondered whether the
Bard had not discovered, in describing one single conspiracy,
the Universal Form of every possible conspiracy.

Let us forget Thunder Mountain, the left bank of the
Rhine and those events, I said to myself. Let us imagine
conspirators who come from every part of the world and
represent the tentacles of their sect spread throughout every
country. Let us assemble them together in a forest clearing,
a cave, a castle, a cemetery or a crypt, provided it is reasonably dark. Let us get one of them to pronounce a discourse
which clearly sets out the plan, and the intention to conquer
the world. . . . I have known many people who feared the
conspiracy of some hidden enemy – for my grandfather it
was the Jews, for the Jesuits it was the Masons, for my
Garibaldian father it was the Jesuits, for the kings of half
Europe it was the Carbonari, for my Mazzinian companions
it was the king backed by the clergy, for the police throughout
half the world it was the Bavarian Illuminati, and so forth.
Who knows how many other people in this world still think
they are being threatened by some conspiracy. Here's a form
to be filled out at will, by each person with their own
conspiracy.

Dumas had truly a clear understanding of the human
mind. What does everyone desire, and desire more fervently

the more wretched and unfortunate they are? To earn money easily, to have power (the enormous pleasure in commanding and humiliating your fellow man) and to avenge every wrong suffered (everyone in life has suffered at least one wrong, however small it might be). And that is why in *Monte Cristo* he shows how to amass great wealth, enough to give you superhuman power, and how to make your enemies pay back every debt. But why, everybody asks, am I not blessed by fortune (or at least not as blessed as I would like to be)? Why have I not been favoured like others who are less deserving? As no one believes their misfortunes are attributable to any shortcoming of their own, that is why they must find a culprit. Dumas offers, to the frustration of everyone (individuals as well as countries), the explanation for their failure. It was someone else, on Thunder Mountain, who planned your ruin. . . .

On reflection, Dumas had invented nothing. He had simply put into story form what, according to my grandfather, Abbé Barruel had already shown. This led me to think, even then, that if I wanted to sell the story of a conspiracy, I didn't have to offer the buyer anything original, but simply something he already knew or could have found out more easily in other ways. People only believe what they already know, and this is the beauty of the Universal Form of Conspiracy.

It was 1855. I was already twenty-five. I had graduated in law and still did not know what to do with my life. I spent my time in the company of my old friends without feeling much enthusiasm for their revolutionary zeal, always expecting, sceptically, that they would be disappointed within a few months. Here once again was Rome re-captured by the Pope, and Pius IX, from being a reformer, had become even more reactionary than his predecessors. Here all hope was fading, through misfortune or cowardice, of Carlo Alberto becoming the harbinger of Italian unity. Here was the Empire re-established in France after violent socialist revolts which had set all hearts alight. Here was the new Piedmont government sending soldiers off to fight a useless war in Crimea instead of liberating Italy. . . .

I could no longer even read those novels that had taught me more than my Jesuits had ever managed to do – in France a supreme council of the university, which (for some reason or other) included a bishop and three archbishops, had passed the so-called Riancey Amendment imposing a five-cent tax on each copy of every newspaper that published a *feuilleton* in instalments. This news was of little importance for anyone who knew nothing about the publishing business, but my friends and I immediately realised its implication: the tax was too punitive and French newspapers were forced to stop publishing novels. The voices of those who had condemned the evils of society, such as Sue and Dumas, were silenced for ever.

My grandfather, who was becoming increasingly confused, though at times quite aware of what was going on around him, complained that the government of Piedmont, which had been taken over by such Masons as

... *"And when our Archbishop
Fransoni invited the clergy of Turin to
disobey these measures, he was arrested
as a common criminal and sentenced to
a month's imprisonment!"* ...

[PAGE 103]

d'Azeglio and Cavour, had been transformed into a synagogue of Satan.

"You realise, my boy," he said, "the laws of that man Siccardi have abolished the so-called privileges of the clergy. Why abolish the right of asylum in holy places? Does a church have fewer rights than a police station? Why abolish the ecclesiastical court for priests accused of common crimes? Does the Church not have the right to judge its own? Why abolish prior religious censure on publications? Can anyone now say whatever they please, without moderation and without respect for faith and morality? And when our Archbishop Fransoni invited the clergy of Turin to disobey these measures, he was arrested as a common criminal and sentenced to a month's imprisonment! And now we have arrived at the dissolution of the mendicant and contemplative orders, almost six thousand monks. The State confiscates their property, and says it will be used to pay parish stipends, but if you put together all the property from all these orders you reach a figure that is ten . . . I'd say a hundred times as much as all the stipends throughout the kingdom, and the government will spend the money on schools to give humble folk an education they don't need, or it will be used for paving the ghettos! And all under the motto of 'a free Church in a free State', where the only one who is truly free to abuse its power is the State. True freedom is man's right to follow the law of God, to be worthy of heaven or hell. And now instead, freedom means you can choose whatever beliefs and opinions you please, where one is the same as the other – and for the State it is all the same whether you are Mason, Christian, Jew or follower of the Great Turk. And no one cares about Truth."

"And there it is, my son," he cried one evening, no longer able in his senility to distinguish me from my father, and now he panted and groaned as he spoke. "They are all disappearing: the Canons of the Lateran, Canons Regular of Sant'Egidio, Calced and Discalced Carmelites, Carthusians, Cassinese Benedictines, Cistercians, Olivetans, Minims, Friars Minor Conventual, Observant, Reformed and Capuchin, Oblates of Saint Mary, Passionists, Domenicans, Mercedarians, Servants of Mary, Oratorian Fathers, and the Poor Clares, Crucified Sisters, Celestines or Turchines, and the Baptistines."

And having recited the list like a rosary, becoming increasingly agitated, and ending as if he had forgotten to take a breath, he ordered the *civet* to be served, made with belly pork, butter, flour, parsley, half a litre of Barbera wine, a hare cut into pieces the size of an egg (including heart and liver), small onions, salt, pepper, spices and sugar.

He was almost consoled, but at a certain point his eyes opened wide, and he passed away with a light belch.

The clock strikes midnight and I realise I have been writing almost without interruption for far too long. However hard I try, I can remember nothing more about the years following my grandfather's death.

My head reels.

5

SIMONINO THE CARBONARO

Night of 27th March 1897

Excuse me, Captain Simonini, if I intrude upon your diary, which I couldn't avoid reading. But it's through no wish of mine that I awoke this morning in your bed. You will have realised that I am (or at least believe myself to be) Abbé Dalla Piccola.

I awoke in a bed that is not my own, in a strange apartment, with no trace of my cassock or my wig. Only a false beard beside the bed. A false beard?

The same thing happened to me a few days ago, when I awoke with no idea who I was. But that occurred in my own place, whereas this morning I was in someone else's. My eyes felt rheumy. My tongue hurt, as if I had bitten it.

Standing by a window, I realised the apartment overlooks impasse Maubert, right on the corner of rue Maître-Albert, where I live.

I began to search the rooms, which seem to be occupied by a layman, obviously the wearer of a false beard, and therefore (if you'll allow me) a man of dubious morals. I went into an office, furnished with a certain ostentation. At the far end, behind a curtain, I found a small door and entered a corridor. It seemed like the backstage of a theatre, full of costumes and wigs. A few days ago, I found a cassock there. But this time I was going in the opposite direction, towards my lodgings.

On my table I found a series of notes which, judging from your reconstructions, I must have written on the 22nd of March

105

when, like this morning, I awoke with no memory. And what, I asked myself, is the meaning of the last note I made that day, referring to Auteuil and Diana? Who is Diana?

It is curious. You suspect we are the same person. You remember a great deal about your life and yet I remember very little about mine. On the other hand, as your diary shows, you know nothing about me, while I am beginning to realise I remember other things, by no means few of them, about what happened to you and – as chance would have it – exactly those things you seem unable to recall. If I can remember so many things about you, should I then say I am you?

Perhaps not. Perhaps we are different people who, for some mysterious reason, are involved in a sort of shared life. I am, after all, a clergyman and perhaps you've told me what I know under the seal of confession. Or have I taken the place of Dr Froïde and, without you knowing it, extracted from deep within what you were trying to keep buried?

Whatever the case, it is my priestly duty to remind you of what happened after your grandfather's death – may God have granted his soul the peace of the just. Rest assured that if you were to die right now, the Lord would not grant you such peace, since you haven't, it seems, behaved justly towards your fellow men, and perhaps that is why your memory refuses to recall matters which do you no honour.

Dalla Piccola left, in fact, only a scant series of notes for Simonini, written in a minuscule hand quite different from his own; but those short comments seemed to act as props for Simonini, on which to hang a series of images and words that suddenly flooded back. The Narrator will now attempt to summarise them, or rather to carry out the proper amplification, so that this game of cues and responses becomes more coherent, and in order not to burden the reader with the sanctimonious tone the abbé employed, in his account, to censure the past errors of his alter ego with excessive unction.

Simone was not, it seems, unduly upset by the abolition of the Discalced Carmelites, nor indeed by the death of his grandfather. Perhaps he felt a certain affection towards him but, after a childhood and adolescence spent shut up in a household which appeared to have been designed to stifle him, in which his grandfather as well as his black-habited tutors had always inspired mistrust, bitterness and resentment towards the world, Simonino had become increasingly incapable of nourishing feelings other than morbid self-love which had gradually assumed the calm serenity of a philosophical conviction.

After dealing with the funeral, attended by the ecclesiastical hierarchy and leading members of the Piedmont nobility close to the *ancien régime*, he went to meet a certain Rebaudengo, the old family notary, who read out the will in which his grandfather left him all his estate. Except, the notary informed him (and he seemed to take pleasure in doing so), that due to the many mortgages the old man had signed and the various bad investments he had made, none of his assets remained, not even the house with all its contents, which would have to go as soon as possible to the creditors, who had been holding back until then, out of respect for that esteemed gentleman, but would have no such qualms with the grandson.

"My dear Avvocato Simonini," said the notary, "these may just be the ways of modern times, which are not as they were, but sometimes even the sons of respectable families are obliged to seek work. Should you feel inclined, sir, towards such a humiliating choice, I can offer you a position in my office, where a young man with some legal knowledge would be useful. And let it be clear that I cannot fully remunerate you to the measure of your intelligence, but the little I could give you should enable you to find other lodgings and live with modest dignity."

Simone immediately suspected the notary of appropriating much of the wealth his grandfather had believed lost in unwise investments, but he had no proof and, in any event, he had to survive. By working for the notary, he told himself, he would one day be able to settle the score by recovering what he was sure the man had wrongly taken. And so he adapted to living in two rooms in via Barbaroux, skimped on visits to the taverns where his companions met, and began to work for the miserly, authoritarian, and mistrustful Notaio Rebaudengo, who immediately stopped addressing him as "Avvocato" and "sir", dropped all other formalities, and referred to him simply as Simonini, to make it clear who was master. After several years working as a scrivener (as they used to call it) he became legally qualified. He realised, as he gradually gained the cautious trust of his master, that his main business did not consist so much of what a notary normally does, such as proving wills, gifts, property transactions and other contracts, but rather of testifying gifts, transactions, wills and contracts which had never taken place. In other words, Notaio Rebaudengo drafted false documents for substantial sums of money, imitating where necessary the handwriting of others and providing witnesses whom he recruited in the neighbouring taverns.

"Let it be clear, my boy," he explained, all formality now gone, "that what I produce are not forgeries but new copies of genuine documents which have been lost or, by simple oversight, have never been produced, and which could and should have been produced. It would be forgery if I were to draw up a certificate of baptism from which it appeared – forgive the example – that you were the son of a prostitute, born near Odalengo Piccolo," and he chuckled with amusement at such a shameful idea. "I would never dream of committing such a crime because I am an honourable man. But if you had an enemy, so to speak, who sought to get hold of your inheritance, and you knew he was certainly not the child of your mother or your father but of a whore from Odalengo Piccolo, and that he had conveniently lost his certificate of baptism in order to obtain your inheritance, and if you were to ask me to produce that missing certificate in order to confound that rogue, I would assist, so to speak, the truth by proving what we know to be true, and I would have no remorse."

"Yes, but how would you know the true parentage of this person?"

"You would have told me yourself! You know the facts perfectly well."

———

. . ."Let it be clear, my boy," he explained, all formality now gone, "that what I produce are not forgeries but new copies of genuine documents which have been lost or, by simple oversight, have never been produced, and which could and should have been produced." . . .

[PAGE 109]

———

"And you would trust me?"

"I always trust my clients, because I serve only honourable people."

"But if by chance the client had lied to you?"

"Then it is he who has sinned, not me. If I had to start worrying whether the client might be lying, then I would no longer be in this profession, which is based on trust."

Simone was not entirely convinced that Rebaudengo's profession would have been regarded by others as honest but, from the moment of his initiation into the secrets of the office, he had became party to the forgeries, quickly overtaking his master and discovering that he himself had remarkable handwriting skills.

The notary, almost by way of apology for what he had said – or perhaps having identified his assistant's weak point – occasionally used to invite Simonino to such lavish restaurants as *Il Cambio* (frequented by Cavour himself), initiating him into the mysteries of the *Finanziera*, a symphony of cockscombs, sweetbreads, brains and veal testicles, fillet of beef, cep mushrooms, half a glass of Marsala wine, flour, salt, olive oil and butter, all of it sharpened with an alchemical dose of vinegar – to enjoy it properly one had to dress, as the dish's name suggested, in a frock coat, or *stiffelius* as it was otherwise called.

Simonino's education, despite his father's exhortations, may not have been heroic and self-sacrificing, but for those evenings he was ready to serve Rebaudengo to the death – at least to his, Rebaudengo's, if not his own . . . as we shall see.

His salary had now been increased, even if not by much – not least because the notary was ageing fast, his sight had become poor and his hand shook. Simone had in short become indispensable. But precisely because he could allow himself a little extra comfort, and was no longer able to avoid the pleasures of Turin's most renowned restaurants (ah, the delights of *agnolotti alla piemontese* – with their stuffing of roast white and red meats, boiled beef, boned boiled fowl, Savoy cabbage cooked with the roast meat, four eggs, Parmesan cheese, nutmeg, salt and pepper; and for the sauce, the juices from the roast, butter, a clove of garlic, a sprig of rosemary), the young Simonini could hardly frequent such places, and satisfy what was becoming his deepest sensual passion, wearing threadbare clothes. As his means increased, so did his needs.

Working for the notary, Simone discovered that Rebaudengo not only conducted confidential transactions for private clients but also provided services for those involved in public policing, perhaps to cover himself in the event of the authorities finding out about his not entirely lawful activities. Sometimes, he explained, in order properly to convict a suspect, some documentary proof had to be presented to the judges so as to persuade them that the police allegations were not without substance. In this way, Simone encountered mysterious characters who visited the office from time to time, and were what the lawyer described as "gentlemen from the Department". What this department and its representatives did was hardly difficult to guess: they were concerned with secret government business.

One of these gentlemen was Cavalier Bianco, who declared one day that he was most satisfied by the way Simone had produced a certain incontestable document. His responsibilities must have included gathering reliable information on people before they were approached because, drawing Simone aside one day, Bianco asked whether he still went to the *Caffè al Bicerin* and suggested meeting there for what he described as a private chat.

"My dear Avvocato Simonini," he said, "we are well aware that you were the grandson of one of His Majesty's most devoted subjects, and were therefore soundly educated. We also know that your father paid with his life for things we too consider to be just, even though he did it, shall we say, with excessive haste. We therefore confide in your loyalty and your willingness to collaborate, considering also that we have been most indulgent towards you. We could have incriminated you and Notaio Rebaudengo some time ago for your not wholly commendable activities. We know you have friends, associates, comrades in spirit, shall we say – Mazzinians, Garibaldians, Carbonari. That is natural. It would seem to be the fashion among the younger generations. But our problem is this: we do not want these young people to lose their heads, at least not until it is reasonable and helpful to do so. Our government has been most concerned about the mad antics of that man Pisacane who landed by boat on the island of Ponza several months ago waving the tricolour flag, along with another twenty-four subversives, then liberated three hundred prisoners and sailed for Sapri, thinking that the local people would be waiting to support him with arms. The more charitable say that Pisacane was a generous soul, the sceptical say he was a fool, but the truth is he was deluded. He and his supporters ended up being massacred by the scoundrels he wanted to liberate, and so you see where good intentions can lead when they take no account of the facts."

"I understand," Simone said, "but what do you want from me?"

"Well, if we need to stop these young men making mistakes, the best way is to put them behind bars for a while, accusing them of attacking the authorities, and release them when there's a real need for zealous spirits. We must therefore surprise them in some clear act of conspiracy. You surely know who their trusted leaders are. All you have to do is send a message to someone in charge, get him to call a meeting in a particular place, everyone armed from head to foot, with cockades and flags and other bits-and-pieces to make them look like Carbonari bearing arms. The police arrive, arrest them, and that'll be that."

"But if I'm with them, I'll be arrested too. And if I'm not, they'd immediately realise it was I who'd betrayed them."

"Of course, my good sir, we are not so naive as not to have thought of that."

As we shall see, Bianco had planned it well. But our Simone was also an excellent strategist and, having listened carefully to the plan that was being proposed to him, devised an extraordinary form of payment, and told Bianco what he expected from His Majesty's munificence.

"My employer, you see, committed many crimes before I became his assistant. It would be enough for me to point out two or three of these cases where sufficient documentary evidence exists, involving no one of any real importance – perhaps someone who has died in the meantime – and for me to present the evidence anonymously, through your kind mediation, to the public prosecutor. You would have enough to convict Notaio Rebaudengo for forgery of public deeds and to put him behind bars for a sufficient number of years, enough to let nature run its course – certainly not very long, given the old man's present state."

"And then?"

"And then, as soon as Notaio Rebaudengo is in prison, I will produce a contract, dated just a few days before his arrest, showing that I have completed the payment of a series of instalments on the purchase of his office and am therefore the owner. As for the money, it will appear that I have paid him in full. Everyone thinks I ought to have inherited a considerable estate from my grandfather and the only person who knows the truth is Rebaudengo himself."

"Interesting," said Bianco, "but the judge will want to know what happened to the money you are supposed to have paid him."

"Rebaudengo doesn't trust banks and keeps everything in a safe in his office. I know how to open it, of course, because he imagines that all he has to do is turn his back and, as he can't see me, he's convinced I can't see what he's doing. The police will surely open the safe somehow or other, and they'll find it empty. I could testify that Rebaudengo's offer was quite unexpected and that I myself was so astonished by the smallness of the sum he was asking that I suspected he had some reason for abandoning his business affairs. In fact, they'll find, along with the empty safe, the ashes of some mysterious documents in the fireplace, and in the drawer of his desk a letter from a hotel in Naples confirming his booking for a room. It will then be clear that Rebaudengo thought he was already being watched by the law and had decided to flee the nest, going off to enjoy his riches under Bourbon rule, where perhaps he had already sent his money."

"But if he's told about your contract in front of the judge, he'll deny it. . . ."

"Who knows what other things he'll be denying. The judge is hardly likely to believe him."

"A shrewd plan. I like you, Avvocato Simonini. You are brighter, more motivated, more decisive than Rebaudengo and, shall we say, more versatile. Very well then. You hand that group of Carbonari over to us, and we'll then deal with Rebaudengo."

The arrest of the Carbonari seemed like child's play, not least because those enthusiasts really were little more than children, and Carbonari only in their most fervent dreams. Simone, initially out of pure vanity, had been feeding the Carbonari for some time with certain bits of nonsense he had been told by Father Bergamaschi,

———

... *"All Carbonari owe allegiance to the*
Alta Vendita, *which has forty members,*
most of them (dreadful to say) the cream
of the Roman aristocracy – plus, of
course, several Jews." ...

[PAGE 118]

———

knowing that they would take each revelation to be news he had received from his heroic father. The Jesuit had continually warned him against the plots of the Carbonari, Freemasons, Mazzinians, republicans and Jews disguised as patriots, who hid themselves from the police around the world by pretending to be charcoal traders and met secretly on the pretext of carrying out their business dealings.

"All Carbonari owe allegiance to the *Alta Vendita*, which has forty members, most of them (dreadful to say) the cream of the Roman aristocracy – plus, of course, several Jews. Their leader was Nubius, a fine gentleman, as corrupt as the day is long, but who had created a position for himself in Rome that was beyond suspicion thanks to his name and wealth. From Paris, Buonarroti, General Lafayette and Saint-Simon consulted him as if he were the oracle of Delphi. From Munich, Dresden, Berlin, Vienna and St Petersburg, the heads of the main lodges, Tscharner, Heymann, Jacobi, Chodzko, Lieven, Mouravieff, Strauss, Pallavicini, Driesten, Bem, Bathyani, Oppenheim, Klauss and Carolus sought his advice. Nubius remained at the helm of the highest Vendita until 1844, when someone poisoned him with Aqua Tofana. Don't imagine it was we Jesuits who did it. The author of the killing is thought to have been Mazzini, who sought (and still seeks) to become head of the Carbonari, with the help of the Jews. Nubius's successor is now Little Tiger, a Jew who, like Nubius, never stops running around stirring up enemies of Calvary. But the members and meeting place of the *Alta Vendita* are secret. Everything must remain unknown to the lodges who receive their direction and impetus from it. Even those forty members of the *Alta Vendita* have no knowledge about the origin of the orders to be given or carried out. And they say that the Jesuits are slaves to their superiors. It is the Carbonari who are slaves to a master who keeps himself well hidden, perhaps a Great Old Man who directs this underground Europe."

Simone had transformed Nubius into a personal hero, almost a male counterpart of Babette of Interlaken. And he mesmerised his companions by turning into an epic poem what Father Bergamaschi had told him in the form of a Gothic tale . . . though concealing the small detail that Nubius was now dead.

Until one day he produced a letter which had not been difficult to fabricate, in which Nubius proclaimed an imminent insurrection across Piedmont, town by town. The group, led by Simone, would play a dangerous and exciting part. They were to meet on a particular morning in the courtyard of the *Osteria del Gambero d'Oro*, where they would find sabres and rifles, and four cartloads of old furniture and mattresses. Thus armed they had to make their way to the junction of via Barbaroux and build a barricade to block entry from piazza Castello. And there they should await orders.

That was more than enough to stir the hearts of the twenty or so students who met on that fateful morning in the innkeeper's courtyard and found the weapons they had been promised in several empty barrels. While they were looking around for the carts of furniture, without even thinking to load their rifles, the courtyard was invaded by fifty or so policemen with guns poised. Powerless to resist, the boys surrendered and were disarmed, taken out and lined up facing the wall on either side of the entrance gate. "Come on you rabble, hands up, silence!" an officer in plain clothes shouted with a scowl.

Although the rebels appeared to have been rounded up more or less at random, two policemen had positioned Simone at the very end of the line, right by the corner of an alleyway. At a certain moment, they were called away by their sergeant and went off towards the courtyard entrance. This was the (agreed) moment. Simone turned to his nearest companion and whispered something. Seeing that the police were a fair distance away, the two darted off around the corner in a flash and began running.

"To arms, they're escaping!" someone shouted. The two heard footsteps as they fled, and the shouts of policemen who had pursued them round the corner. Simone heard two shots. One hit his friend, though Simone was hardly concerned whether it was fatal or not. It was enough for him that the second shot was fired into the air, as agreed.

He turned into another street, then yet another. Far off, he could hear the shouts of his pursuers who, following their orders, had taken the wrong route. Before long he was crossing piazza Castello on his way home, like any other citizen. His companions – who in the meantime had been taken away – all assumed he had escaped, and since they had been arrested together and immediately lined up facing the wall, none of the police officers could remember his face. There was obviously no need, therefore, for him to leave Turin; he could return to work, and could even go to comfort the families of his arrested friends.

All that remained was to deal with the disposal of Notaio Rebaudengo, which took place according to plan. The old man died of a broken heart a year later in prison, but Simonini felt no guilt about that. The score had been settled – the notary had given him a job and he had been his slave for several years; the notary had ruined his grandfather and Simone had ruined him.

This, then, was what Abbé Dalla Piccola had been describing to Simonini. And that he too felt exhausted after all these recollections was proven by the fact that his contribution to the diary stopped halfway through a sentence as if, while he was writing, he had fallen into a state of slumber.

6

SERVING THE SECRET SERVICE

28th March 1897

Monsieur Abbé,

How curious that what is supposed to be a diary (to be read by its author alone) is turning into an exchange of messages. But here I am, writing you a letter, almost certain that one day, passing here, you will read it.

You know too much about me. You are a most disagreeable witness. And far too severe.

Yes, I admit it. In my conduct towards my would-be Carbonari comrades, and to Rebaudengo, I did not act in accordance with the morals you are supposed to preach. But let us be frank: Rebaudengo was a rogue and, when I think of all I have done since then, I seem to have practised my roguery only on rogues. As for those boys, they were fanatics, and fanatics are the scum of the earth because it's through them, and the vague principles they espouse, that wars and revolutions happen. And since I had come to realise that the number of fanatics in this world will never diminish, I decided I might as well profit from their fanaticism.

So I'll resume my *own* recollections, if you'll allow me. I was now in charge of what had been Rebaudengo's office – and since I had been falsifying legal deeds back in Rebaudengo's day, it should come as no surprise that I am still doing exactly the same here in Paris.

Now I also well remember Cavalier Bianco. One day he said to me, "You see, Avvocato Simonini, the Jesuits have been banished from the Kingdom of Piedmont, but everyone knows they continue their scheming and recruit followers under false guises. It happens in every country from which they have been expelled. I saw an amusing caricature in a foreign newspaper. It showed several Jesuits who every year pretend they want to return to their country of origin (though naturally they are stopped at the frontier), until someone realises that their brethren are already there, moving around freely and disguised as another order. They are all around us, but we need to find out where. We know that back in the days of the Roman Republic some used to go to your grandfather's house. It seems unlikely you have not kept in touch with them, and we ask you therefore to sound out their mood and their intentions. There's a general feeling that the order is gaining influence again in France – and whatever happens in France might just as well be happening here in Turin."

He was quite wrong to imagine I was still in touch with the good fathers, but I had been learning much about the Jesuits, and from a reliable source. During those years Eugène Sue had published his last masterpiece, *Les Mystères du Peuple*. He completed it shortly before his death in Annecy, in Savoy, where he was in exile, because he had long been a socialist sympathiser and had fiercely opposed Louis-Napoleon's *coup d'état* and proclamation of the Empire. Since no more *feuilletons* were being published as a result of the Riancey Amendment, Sue's works were being issued in slim volumes, and had fallen foul of the rigours of many censors, including those of Piedmont, and therefore were very difficult to come by. I remember finding it deathly tedious trying to follow this rambling story of two families, one of Gauls and the other Franks, from prehistory up to the time of Napoleon III, where the wicked oppressors are the Franks, while the Gauls seem to have all been socialists since the time of Vercingetorix. But Sue, like all idealists, was now gripped by one obsession alone.

He had obviously written the last pages of his work while in exile, at the same time as Louis-Napoleon had seized power and made himself emperor. To make these designs more odious, Sue had had a clever idea: since the Jesuits were the other great enemy of republican France from the time of the Revolution, all he had to do was show how Louis-Napoleon's seizure of power was inspired and directed by the Jesuits. It is true that the Jesuits had been banished from France since the July 1830 revolution, but in reality they had managed covertly to survive, and more easily after Louis-Napoleon had begun his rise to power, tolerating them so as to remain on good terms with the Pope.

There is a long letter in the book from Father Rodin (who had appeared in *The Wandering Jew*) addressed to the Superior General of the Jesuits, Father Roothaan, in which the plan was set out in great detail. The last events in the novel take place during the final socialist and republican struggle against the *coup d'état*, and the letter seems to be written in such a way that what Louis-Napoleon actually did is made to appear as if it hadn't yet been done, which made his prediction all the more disturbing.

The opening of Dumas' novel *Joseph Balsamo* naturally came to mind: it would have been quite sufficient to substitute Thunder Mountain with some more ecclesiastical setting – perhaps the crypt of an old monastery – and instead of Masons, to gather down there Loyola's sons from around the world, and to replace Balsamo with Rodin, and there you'd have the same old pattern of the universal conspiracy tailored to present times.

Hence the idea that I might sell Bianco not only a few scraps of gossip I had picked up here and there, but an entire document taken from the Jesuits. Obviously, I'd have to change a few details, removing Father Rodin, whom somebody would probably remember as a fictional character, and bringing in Father Bergamaschi, wherever he may be, though someone in Turin might well have heard mention of him. Also, the Superior General of the order was Father Roothaan when Sue was writing, whereas a certain Father Beckx was now said to have taken over.

The document would have to seem like an almost word-for-word transcript of information passed on by a reliable informer, and the informer should not appear as a spy (since it is well known that the Jesuits never betray the Society) but rather as an old friend of my grandfather who had confided these matters in him as proof of the greatness and power of his order.

I'd have liked to have included the Jews in the story, as a tribute to my grandfather, but Sue made no mention of them and I could find no way of fitting them in with the Jesuits – and anyway the Jews in Piedmont were then of little importance to anyone. It is better not to fill the heads of government agents with too much information. All they want is clear, simple ideas – black and white, good and bad, and there must only be one villain.

But I didn't want to leave the Jews completely out of it, so I used them for the setting. All the same, it was a way of arousing some suspicion in Bianco's mind about the Jews.

An event set in Paris or, worse still, in Turin could, I thought, have been checked out. I had to bring my Jesuits together in a place out of the reach of the Piedmont secret service, about which even they had only apocryphal news. The Jesuits, however, were everywhere – the Lord's octopuses, with their tentacles coiling out even into Protestant countries.

Anyone falsifying documents must always be well informed, which is why I used to spend time in libraries. Libraries are fascinating places: sometimes you feel you are under the canopy of a railway station, and when you read books about exotic places there's a feeling of travelling to distant lands. This is how I came across a book with some fine engravings of the Jewish cemetery at Prague. Now abandoned, there were almost twelve thousand gravestones in a very cramped area, but there must have been far more burials as many layers of earth had been added over the course of several centuries. Once the cemetery had been abandoned, someone had lifted a few of the buried stones, with their inscriptions, so as to create an irregular mass of gravestones leaning in all directions (or perhaps the Jews themselves had dug them up, without any consideration, uninterested as they are in beauty and order).

The abandoned site seemed appropriate, not least for its

incongruity. By what cunning had the Jesuits decided to gather in a place that had been sacred to the Jews? And what control did they have over this place that was forgotten by everyone, and perhaps inaccessible? All questions without an answer, which would have given credibility to the story, since I reckoned Bianco would be firmly convinced that when all the facts appear fully explainable and likely, the story is false.

As a faithful reader of Dumas, I felt a certain pleasure describing that night, and that dark and fearful company, with that burial ground, sparsely lit by a deathly pale crescent moon, and the Jesuits massed in a semicircle so that, when seen from above in their flowing black robes, the ground would appear as if it were crawling with cockroaches – or, there again, describing Father Beckx's devilish leer as he proclaimed the sinister designs of those enemies of humanity (and my father's ghost would rejoice from the heavens above – I mean, from the depths of hell where the Almighty most probably casts Mazzinians and republicans), and then to show the vile messengers as they disperse, like evil crows flying away into the pallid dawn, carrying news to all their various houses about the new and diabolic plan to conquer the world, and so bringing to an end that fiendish night.

But I had to be succinct and to the point, as is fitting for a secret report, since it is well known that police agents are not great readers and can handle no more than two or three pages.

My presumed informant therefore described how the Society's representatives from various countries had gathered in Prague that night to hear Father Beckx, and how he had

. . . or, there again, describing Father Beckx's devilish leer as he proclaimed the sinister designs of those enemies of humanity (and my father's ghost would rejoice from the heavens above – I mean, from the depths of hell where the Almighty most probably casts Mazzinians and republicans) . . .

[PAGE 127]

presented Father Bergamaschi, who through a series of providential circumstances had become an advisor to Louis-Napoleon.

Father Bergamaschi told how Louis-Napoleon Bonaparte was demonstrating his submission to the Society's orders.

"We must," he said, "admire the cunning with which Bonaparte has deceived the revolutionaries by pretending to support their doctrines, and his skill in conspiring against Louis Philippe, bringing about the fall of that godless government, and his trust in our counsel, when in 1848 he presented himself as a true republican, so as to be elected President of the Republic. Nor should it be forgotten how he helped to destroy Mazzini's Roman Republic and restore the Holy Father to his throne.

"Napoleon," Bergamaschi continued, "had sought once and for all to destroy the socialists, revolutionaries, philosophers, atheists and all those vile rationalists who espouse national sovereignty, free inquiry, religious, political and social freedom. He had sought to dissolve the legislative assembly, to arrest the representatives of the people on allegations of conspiracy, to decree a state of siege in Paris, to shoot without trial those bearing arms at the barricades, to ship the most dangerous figures to Cayenne, to crush freedom of association and of the press, to send the army into its fortresses and then to bombard the capital, reducing it to ashes, until no stone was left standing, and thereby bringing victory to the Holy Catholic and Apostolic Church on the ruins of modern Babylon. Then he had called upon the people by universal suffrage to extend his presidential power for ten years, and afterwards transformed the Republic back into an empire, universal suffrage being the only remedy against democracy because it includes the rural populations still loyal to the voice of their priests."

Most interesting of all was what Bergamaschi had to say in conclusion about their policy towards Piedmont. Here I got him to set out the Society's future intentions, though by the time I was compiling the report these had already been fully realised.

"That faint-hearted king, Vittorio Emanuele, dreams about the Kingdom of Italy, his minister Cavour encourages his ambitions, and both of them seek not only to drive Austria from the peninsula but also to destroy the temporal power of the Holy Father. They will look to France for support, and so it will be easy to drag them first into a war against Russia by promising to help them against Austria, but asking at the same time for Savoy and Nice in exchange. Then the emperor will pretend to help Piedmont but – after some insignificant local victory – will sue for peace with the Austrians without consulting them, and will promote the formation of an Italian confederation presided over by the Pope, which Austria will join, while keeping the rest of its possessions in Italy. In this way Piedmont, the only liberal government in the peninsula, will remain subject both to France and to Rome and will be controlled by French troops occupying Rome or garrisoned in Savoy."

This was the document. I didn't know how much the Piedmont government would appreciate the accusation that Napoleon III was an enemy of the Kingdom of Piedmont, but I had already sensed what experience would confirm

– that men in the secret service find it useful to have some document they can use (even if they don't produce it immediately) to blackmail government officials, create confusion, or upset the course of events.

Bianco read the report with great care, looked up from what he had been reading, fixed me in the eye and said it was material of the greatest importance. Once again, he had confirmed my view that when a spy sells something entirely new, all he need do is recount something you could find on any second-hand bookstall.

But even though Bianco didn't know much about literature, he knew plenty about me, and he added with a sly expression, "All this stuff you've invented, of course."

"I beg your pardon!" I said, scandalised, but he raised his hand to stop me. "Not to worry, Avvocato Simonini. Even if this document is all your own handiwork, it suits me and my superiors to present it to the government as genuine. You will be aware – since it is widely known – that our minister Cavour was convinced he had Napoleon III in his power, all because he'd sent Contessa Castiglione to be his, shall we say, companion. She is without question a beautiful woman and the Frenchman enjoyed her favours without needing to be asked twice. But it's clear now that Napoleon is not prepared to do all that Cavour wants and the Contessa has wasted much charm on him for nothing – perhaps she enjoyed it, but we cannot allow the affairs of state to depend upon the whims of a lady of easy virtue. It is most important that His Majesty, our sovereign, should distrust Bonaparte. Before long – indeed very soon – Garibaldi or Mazzini (or both together) will organise an expedition to the Kingdom of Naples. If by chance this venture is successful, Piedmont will have to step in so as not to leave those regions in the hands of mad republicans and, to do so, it will have to march down the peninsula through the Papal States. To achieve this end we must therefore instil in our sovereign feelings of suspicion and grievance towards the Pope so that he pays little heed to the advice of Napoleon III. As you will have realised, Avvocato Simonini, policies are often decided by us humble servants of the State rather than by those who in the eyes of the people govern. . . ."

That report was my first truly serious job, where I wasn't merely scribbling out a will for the benefit of nobody special, but had to construct a document of political complexity, through which I may have contributed to the policies of the Kingdom of Piedmont. I remember feeling very proud of it.

In the meantime the momentous year of 1860 had arrived – momentous for the country, though not yet for me. I followed events from a distance, listening to idle café gossip. Sensing that I ought to become more closely involved in political matters, I realised the most attractive news to fabricate would be what these idle minds were expecting, rather than what the newspapers reported as solid fact.

Thus I came to hear that the inhabitants of the Grand Duchy of Tuscany, the Duchy of Modena and the Duchy of Parma had deposed their rulers, that the so-called papal legations of Emilia and Romagna had broken away from papal control, and that they all wanted to be annexed to the

Kingdom of Piedmont. In April 1860, insurrectional rebellions broke out in Palermo, Mazzini wrote to the heads of the revolt that Garibaldi would be coming to their aid, it was rumoured that Garibaldi was looking for men, money and arms for his expedition and that the Bourbon navy was already crossing the waters of Sicily to prevent an enemy expedition.

"Did you know Cavour is using one of his most trusted men, La Farina, to keep Garibaldi under control?"

"What do you mean? The minister has approved a subscription for the purchase of twelve thousand rifles for Garibaldi's men."

"In any case, the distribution was stopped, and by whom? By the Royal Carabineers!"

"But please, oh please! Cavour, far from stopping it, helped with the distribution."

"Quite so! Except that they're not the fine Enfield rifles Garibaldi was expecting, but bits of old scrap metal. Our hero will be lucky if they're any use even for shooting skylarks!"

"I've been told by someone at the royal palace, mentioning no names, that La Farina has given Garibaldi eight thousand lire and a thousand rifles."

"Yes, but there should have been three thousand, and two thousand have been kept back by the Governor of Genoa."

"Why Genoa?"

"Because you don't expect Garibaldi to go to Sicily on the back of a mule. He's signed a contract for the purchase of two ships which should be sailing from Genoa or

... "But what lodge are you
talking about? Freemasonry is an
invention of the Jesuits!"
"You'd best keep quiet – you're a
Mason and everyone knows it!" ...

[PAGE 135]

thereabouts. And you know who's guaranteed the debt? The Masons, or to be more precise a lodge in Genoa."

"But what lodge are you talking about? Freemasonry is an invention of the Jesuits!"

"You'd best keep quiet – you're a Mason and everyone knows it!"

"We'll pass over that one . . . Anyway, I happen to know from a reliable source that those present at the signing of the contract," and here his voice fell to a whisper, "were Avvocato Riccardi and General Negri di Saint Front. . . ."

"And who the hell are they?"

"You don't know?" his voice dropping lower still. "They are the heads of the Department of Secret Affairs, or rather the State Department for Political Surveillance, which is the information service for the head of the government. They are powerful – more important than the Prime Minister himself. That's who they are, far from being Masons!"

"Really? Of course, it's quite possible to be a member of the secret service as well as a Freemason – indeed it helps."

On the 5th of May it became public knowledge that Garibaldi and a thousand volunteers had left by sea on their way to Sicily. No more than ten of them were from Piedmont, and they included foreigners and a large number of lawyers, doctors, pharmacists, engineers and landowners. Few of them were ordinary folk.

On the 11th of May, Garibaldi's ships landed at Marsala. And on whose side was the Bourbon navy? It was apparently intimidated by two British ships moored in the port, officially there to protect the interests of their fellow countrymen who had a flourishing trade in fine Marsala wine. Or were the English helping Garibaldi?

In short, within a few days Garibaldi's Thousand (as they were now known) had routed the Bourbons at Calatafimi and grown in number, thanks to the arrival of local volunteers. Garibaldi proclaimed himself dictator of Sicily in the name of Vittorio Emanuele II, and by the end of the month Palermo had been captured.

And France? What did France have to say? France seemed to be watching cautiously, but one Frenchman, the great novelist Alexandre Dumas, at that time more famous than Garibaldi, rushed to join the liberators in his private yacht, the *Emma*, carrying with him money and arms.

In Naples, Francesco II, the unfortunate King of the Two Sicilies, already fearful that Garibaldi's men had won in various places because his generals had betrayed him, hastened to grant an amnesty to political prisoners and to reintroduce the constitution of 1848 that had been repealed, but it was too late and there were public riots even in his capital.

It was during the first days of June that I received a note from Cavalier Bianco, telling me to wait that same day at midnight for a carriage which would pick me up at the door of my office. An unusual appointment, but I sensed an interesting opportunity, and at midnight, sweating in the stifling heat that was tormenting the city at the time, I waited in front of my office. There a closed carriage arrived, with curtains drawn and inside it a man I did not know. He drove me somewhere not far, it seemed, from the centre – indeed

I had the impression the carriage may have passed two or three times along the same streets.

It stopped in the dilapidated courtyard of an old tenement block which was all a jumble of loose balustrades. Here I was shown through a small doorway and down a long corridor, at the end of which another small door led to the entrance hall of a building of very different character. We had reached the foot of a wide staircase but did not climb here and instead took a small flight of steps at the far end of the hallway. It brought us to a room with walls lined in damask, a large portrait of the king on the far wall, and a table covered with a green baize around which four people sat, one of whom was Cavalier Bianco, who introduced me to the others. No one shook hands, limiting themselves to a nod.

"Please be seated, Avvocato Simonini. The gentleman to your right is General Negri di Saint Front, to your left here is Avvocato Riccardi, and before you Professor Boggio, parliamentary deputy for Valenza Po."

From the rumours I'd heard in the bars, I realised the first two characters were in charge of the State Department for Political Surveillance who (vox populi) had helped Garibaldi's men to buy their two famous ships. As for the third, I recognised his name: he was a journalist, professor of law already by the age of thirty, a parliamentary deputy and one of Cavour's closest advisors. He had a ruddy face with a fine pair of whiskers, a monocle as large as the base of a glass, and the air of the most inoffensive man in the world. But the deference shown towards him by the other three was clear evidence of his power in the government.

Negri di Saint Front was the first to speak: "My dear

Avvocato Simonini, being well aware of your ability to gather information, as well as your prudence and discretion in handling it, we would like to send you on a mission of great delicacy to the territories recently conquered by General Garibaldi. You needn't worry – we don't propose asking you to march the Redshirts into battle. It's a question of obtaining information. But so that you're aware exactly what information the government is interested in obtaining, we are obliged to entrust you with what I have no hesitation in describing as State secrets. You will therefore understand the need for great caution from this evening onwards, until the end of your mission, and beyond. This is also – how shall I say – to ensure your own personal safety, about which, naturally, we are most concerned."

He could hardly have been more diplomatic. Saint Front was most concerned about my health and for this reason was warning me that if I started telling others what I was about to hear, I'd be putting my health in serious jeopardy. But this introduction enabled me to imagine what I stood to gain, considering the importance of the mission. With a respectful nod of assent, I invited Saint Front to continue.

"No one can explain it better than Professor Boggio, whose position allows him access to information and instructions from the highest source, to which he is very close. Please continue, Professor."

"You see, Avvocato Simonini," Boggio began, "no one in Piedmont admires that generous, upright man, General Garibaldi, more than I do. What he has achieved in Sicily, with a handful of courageous men, against one of the best armies in Europe, is miraculous."

This introduction was enough to make me think that Boggio was Garibaldi's worst enemy, but I preferred to keep my silence.

"Yet," Boggio continued, "though it is true that Garibaldi has assumed dictatorship over the territories he has conquered in the name of our king, Vittorio Emanuele II, the person behind him does not support this decision at all. Mazzini is hanging over him, breathing down his neck, anxious to ensure that the great insurrection in the south leads to the creation of a republic. And we know the great persuasive power of this fellow Mazzini who, comfortably ensconced abroad, has already convinced many foolish men to go to their deaths. Among the general's most intimate collaborators are Crispi and Nicotera – Mazzinians through and through. They are a bad influence on a man like the general, a man incapable of seeing malice in others. Let us be clear: Garibaldi will soon reach the Strait of Messina and continue across into Calabria. The man is a shrewd strategist, his volunteers are enthusiastic, and many islanders have joined them, out of either patriotism or opportunism. And many Bourbon generals have already proven to be such poor commanders that it is suspected their military prowess has been compromised by secret payments. It is not for us to say whom we suspect to be the author of such payments. Certainly not our government. Sicily is now in the hands of Garibaldi, and if Calabria and Naples were also to fall, then the general, with the support of Mazzini's republicans, would have the resources of a kingdom of nine million inhabitants at their disposal and, being surrounded by an irresistible popular prestige, he would be stronger than our own sovereign. In order to avoid such a disaster our sovereign has only one possibility: to head southwards with our army, passing not without some difficulty through the Papal States, and arriving in Naples before Garibaldi. Is that clear?"

"Yes. But I don't see how I . . ."

"Wait just a moment. Garibaldi's expedition has been inspired by feelings of patriotism, but to intervene in order to control it, or shall I say neutralise it, we must be able to show, through well-grounded rumours and newspaper articles, that the whole venture has been compromised by people who are unreliable and corrupt, thereby creating the need for Piedmont to step in."

"In short," said Avvocato Riccardi, who had not yet spoken, "our task is not to undermine confidence in Garibaldi's expedition but to weaken support for the revolutionary administration which has followed it. Count Cavour is sending La Farina to Sicily. That great Sicilian patriot has spent many years in exile and should therefore enjoy Garibaldi's trust. But, at the same time, he has also been our government's faithful collaborator as well as founder of the Italian National Society which supports the annexation of the Kingdom of the Two Sicilies into a united Italy. La Farina has been appointed to investigate some most disturbing rumours. It would seem that Garibaldi, out of good faith and ineptitude, is establishing a government which is the negation of all government. Clearly the general cannot control everything. His honesty is beyond doubt. But in whose hands is he leaving public affairs? Cavour is waiting for a full report from La Farina about possible misappropriation of public funds, but Mazzini's men will do all they can

SERVING THE SECRET SERVICE

to keep him away from the people, by which I mean, from those segments of the population where it is easiest to gather up-to-date news about any scandals."

"In any event our department trusts La Farina only to a certain extent," added Boggio. "Not that I wish to be critical, far from it, but he's also Sicilian – fine people no doubt, but different from us, don't you think? You will have a letter of introduction to La Farina, and can obtain his assistance, but you'll have greater freedom to move around. And you'll not be required simply to gather documented facts, but (as you have done on previous occasions) to fabricate them when they are lacking."

"And in what manner and under what capacity shall I travel there?"

"As usual, we have thought of everything," said Bianco with a smile. "Monsieur Dumas, whom you will know by name as a celebrated novelist, is about to reach Garibaldi in Palermo, sailing in his own yacht, the *Emma*. We are not entirely sure what he intends to do down there. Perhaps he simply wants to write a few fictional stories about Garibaldi's expedition, or perhaps he is a vain man seeking to flaunt his friendship with the hero. Whatever it is, we know that in two days' time he will be stopping off in Sardinia, in the bay at Arzachena, and therefore on our own doorstep. You will set off tomorrow morning for Genoa and board our vessel for Sardinia, where you will join Dumas, carrying a letter of introduction signed by someone to whom Dumas is greatly indebted and whom he trusts. You will appear as a correspondent for the newspaper edited by Professor Boggio, sent to Sicily to celebrate Dumas' enterprise as well as that of Garibaldi. In this way, you will be part of the novelist's entourage and will land with him in Palermo. Arriving in Palermo with Dumas will give you prestige and will place you beyond suspicion, which would not be the case if you arrived alone. Then you can mingle with the volunteers and at the same time with the local people. Another letter from a well-known and respected person will provide you with an introduction to one of Garibaldi's young officers, Captain Nievo, whom Garibaldi has apparently appointed Deputy Quartermaster General. It is believed that on the departure of the *Lombardo* and the *Piemonte*, the two ships that took Garibaldi to Marsala, he was entrusted with fourteen thousand of the ninety thousand lire that made up the expedition's funds. We are not sure why they appointed Nievo to carry out these administrative duties. We are told he is a man of letters and it seems he has a reputation for being a most upright man. He will be delighted to talk with someone who writes for the newspapers and presents himself as a friend of the famous Dumas."

The rest of the evening was spent agreeing on the technical aspects of the undertaking, and the question of payment. The following day I closed the office indefinitely, gathered together a few essential odds and ends and, by some stroke of inspiration, took with me the cassock that Father Bergamaschi had left at my grandfather's house and which I had salvaged before everything had been handed over to the creditors.

7

WITH THE THOUSAND

29th March 1897

I don't know whether I could have recalled all those events, and especially what I felt, during my travels in Sicily between June 1860 and March 1861, had it not been for a bundle of dog-eared papers I found yesterday evening while rummaging through some old documents in the bottom of a bureau downstairs in the shop. There I had noted down what had happened, and I had probably written them as a rough draft towards a more detailed report for my paymasters in Turin. The notes are incomplete and I obviously recorded only what I thought was relevant, or *wanted* to seem relevant. What I might have left out I do not know.

By the 6th of June I am on board the *Emma*. Dumas welcomed me with much cordiality. He was wearing a pale brown lightweight coat and looked unmistakably like the half-caste he was – olive skin, protruding fleshy sensual lips and a head of frizzy hair like an African savage. Otherwise he had a lively, wry expression, a cordial smile and the rotundity of a bon vivant. . . . I remembered one of the many stories about him: some impudent young Parisian had made a malicious reference in his presence to the latest theories suggesting a link between primitive man and lower species. And he replied, "Yes, sir, I do indeed come from the monkey. But you, sir, are returning to one!"

He introduced me to Captain Beaugrand, the second-in-command Brémond, the pilot Podimatas (a man as hirsute as a wild boar, his face so completely covered by hair and beard that he seems to shave only the whites of his eyes) and, in particular, the cook Jean Boyer – Dumas seemed to regard the cook as the most important member of the crew. He travelled with a retinue, like some grand lord from the past.

As he showed me to my cabin, Podimatas told me Boyer's speciality was *asperges en petits pois*, a curious recipe since peas were not among its ingredients.

We rounded the island of Caprera, where Garibaldi hides out when he's not fighting.

"You'll soon be meeting the general," said Dumas, and his face lit up with admiration at the mere mention of the man. "With his fair beard and blue eyes he seems like Jesus in Leonardo's *Last Supper*. His movements are full of elegance, his voice has an infinite gentleness. He seems an even-tempered man, but when the words 'Italy' and 'independence' are uttered you will see him stir like a volcano, with eruptions of fire and torrents of lava. He is never armed for combat; at the moment of action he draws the first sabre he comes across, throwing aside the scabbard, and launches himself upon the enemy. He has only one weakness: he thinks he's a champion bowls player."

Shortly afterwards, there was great commotion aboard. The sailors were about to haul up a large turtle of the kind to be found south of Corsica. Dumas was delighted.

. . . *"You'll soon be meeting the general,"* said Dumas, *and his face lit up with admiration at the mere mention of the man. "With his fair beard and blue eyes he seems like Jesus in Leonardo's* Last Supper." . . .

[PAGE 144]

145

"There'll be work to do. First you have to turn it on its back. The turtle innocently stretches out its neck and you take advantage of its imprudence to cut off its head – thwack! – before hanging it by the tail to let it bleed for twelve hours. Then you turn it on its back again, insert a strong blade between the carapace and the breastplate, being very careful not to perforate the gall bladder, otherwise it becomes inedible. The innards are removed and only the liver is retained – the transparent pulp inside serves no purpose but there are two lobes which, because of their whiteness and their flavour, seem like two veal noisettes. Finally, you remove the membranes, the neck and the flippers. They are cut into pieces the size of walnuts, left to soak, then added to a good broth, with pepper, cloves, carrot, thyme and bay leaf, and cooked together for three or four hours on a low heat. In the meantime, prepare strips of chicken seasoned with parsley, chives and anchovy, cook them in boiling broth, then add them to the turtle soup, into which you've poured three or four glasses of dry Madeira. If there's no Madeira, then you can use Marsala with a small glass of brandy or rum, though it would be a second best, *un pis aller*. We'll taste our soup tomorrow evening."

I felt a certain liking for a man who so enjoyed good food, despite his dubious breeding.

(13th June) The *Emma* arrived in Palermo the day before yesterday. With Redshirts coming and going everywhere, the city looks like a poppy field. But many of Garibaldi's volunteers are dressed and armed any old way, some with no more than a feather in their hat and wearing ordinary civilian dress. Red cloth is now hard to find, and a shirt of that colour costs a fortune – perhaps it is more readily available to the many sons of local aristocrats, who didn't enlist with Garibaldi's men until after the first bloody battles, than to the volunteers who came here from Genoa. Bianco had given me enough money to survive in Sicily and, so as not to look like a dandy, I immediately found myself a well-worn uniform with a shirt that was beginning to turn pink after many washes, and some threadbare trousers; the shirt alone had cost me fifteen francs and I could have bought four for the same price in Turin.

Here everything is expensive – an egg costs four soldi, a pound of bread six soldi, a pound of meat thirty. I don't know if it's because the island is poor and the occupiers are using up the few remaining resources, or if the people of Palermo have decided that the Garibaldini are manna from heaven and are fleecing them for all they can.

The meeting between the two great men at the Palazzo del Senato ("like the Hôtel de Ville in Paris in 1830!" cried Dumas ecstatically) was very theatrical. Of the two, I don't know who was more histrionic.

"My dear Dumas, how I've missed you!" the general shouted. When Dumas offered him his congratulations, he replied, "Not me, not me, congratulate these men. They have been giants!" And then to his men, "Give Monsieur Dumas the finest apartment in the building, right now. Nothing is too good for a man who has brought me letters announcing the arrival of two and a half thousand men, ten thousand rifles and two steamships!"

I viewed the hero with the suspicion I had felt for all heroes since my father's death. Dumas had described him as an Apollo, but to me he seemed of modest stature, not fair but mousy, with short bandy legs and, judging from his gait, suffering from rheumatism. I saw him mount his horse with some difficulty, helped by two of his men.

Towards the end of the afternoon, a crowd had gathered below the royal palace shouting, "Long live Dumas, long live Italy!" The writer was clearly delighted but I had the impression the whole thing had been staged by Garibaldi, who understood his friend's vanity and badly needed the promised rifles. I mingled with the crowd and found it hard to understand what they were saying in their incomprehensible dialect, like the language of Africans, but I did catch one brief exchange. Someone asked who this fellow Dumas was that they were cheering, and the other replied he was a Circassian prince who was rolling in money and had come to place his wealth at Garibaldi's service.

Dumas introduced me to some of the general's men, and I was struck by the hawk-like gaze of Garibaldi's lieutenant, the terrible Nino Bixio, and felt so intimidated that I left. I needed to look for an inn where I could come and go without being seen.

The locals now think I'm one of Garibaldi's men, while the expedition corps think I'm a reporter.

I saw Nino Bixio again as he was passing through the city on horseback. He is said to be the real military leader behind the expedition. Garibaldi gets distracted, always thinking about tomorrow. He is fine during attacks, urging his men onwards, but Bixio looks after the here and now and keeps the troops in line. As he was passing, I heard one of Garibaldi's men saying to his comrade, "Look at that gaze, flashing everywhere. His figure cuts like a sabre. Bixio! Even his name sounds like a bolt of lightning."

It's obvious that Garibaldi and his lieutenants have hypnotised these volunteers. That's bad – leaders with too much charisma should be removed immediately, for the peace and security of the kingdom. My masters in Turin are right. This Garibaldi myth mustn't be allowed to spread north, otherwise all the king's subjects up there will be wearing a red shirt and it'll become a republic.

(15th June) Difficult to talk to the local people. The only thing certain is that they're trying to exploit anyone who, according to them, looks Piedmontese, even though very few volunteers come from Piedmont. I've found a tavern where I can dine cheaply and try various dishes with unpronounceable names. I managed to choke on some bread rolls stuffed with spleen, but with a good local wine was able to get through two or three of them. Over dinner I befriended two volunteers, one called Abba, just over twenty years old, from Liguria, and the other Bandi, a journalist about my own age from Livorno. Their accounts enabled me to build up a picture of the arrival of Garibaldi's men, and their first battles.

"Ah, my dear Simonini," said Abba, "if you only knew. The landing at Marsala was a complete circus! There in front of us are the Bourbon ships, the *Stromboli* and the *Capri*. Our ship, the *Lombardo*, gets caught on a reef and Nino Bixio says it's better they capture it with a hole in its belly than safe and sound, and indeed we ought to sink the *Piemonte* as well. 'Fine waste,' say I, but Bixio was right, we shouldn't give away two ships to the Bourbons. And anyway, that's what great leaders do – they burn their boats after landing so there's no retreat. The *Piemonte* starts the landing, the *Stromboli* begins its cannonade but fires wide. The commander of an English ship in port goes aboard the *Stromboli* and tells the captain there are English subjects ashore and he'll hold him responsible for any international incident – the English, you know, have large financial interests in Marsala because of the wine. The Bourbon captain says he couldn't care less about international incidents and once again gives the order to fire but the cannon shoot wide again. When the Bourbon ships finally manage to score a few hits, the only damage they cause is to chop a dog in half."

"So the English were helping you?"

"Shall we say they were quite happy to get in the way to embarrass the Bourbons."

"But what contact does the general have with the English?"

Abba made a gesture to indicate that foot soldiers like him obey orders without asking too many questions. "But listen to this one. Arriving in the city, the general had given orders to take over the telegraph and cut the wires. They send a lieutenant with a few men, and the fellow in the telegraph office runs off when he sees them coming. The lieutenant goes into the office and finds a copy of the dispatch just sent to the military commander at Trapani: 'Two steamships flying a Piedmont flag have just arrived in port and are landing men.' At that very moment the reply arrives. One of the volunteers who had worked at the telegraph office in Genoa translates: 'How many men and why are they landing?' The officer gets him to transmit: 'Sorry, I've made a mistake, they're two merchant ships from Girgenti with a cargo of sulphur.' Answer from Trapani: 'You are an idiot.' The officer reads it, very pleased with himself, cuts the wires, and leaves."

"Let's be honest," commented Bandi, "the landing wasn't a complete circus as Abba suggests. When we came alongside the Bourbon ships, the first grenades and gunfire finally got going. We were having fun, of course. In the midst of the explosions, a plump old friar, hat in hand, turned up to welcome us. Someone shouted, 'Come to make yourself a pain in the arse, Friar?' but Garibaldi raised his hand and said, 'Good Friar, what are you looking for? Can't you hear the bullets whistling?' And the friar answered, 'I'm not afraid of bullets. I'm a servant of poor St Francis and a son of Italy.' 'You're with the people, then?' asked the general. 'With the people, yes, with the people,' replied the friar. And that was when we realised that Marsala was ours. The general sent Crispi to the tax collector in the name of Vittorio Emanuele, King of Italy, to requisition all revenues. These were handed over to Acerbi, the quartermaster general, who issued a receipt. A Kingdom of Italy did not yet exist, but that receipt given by Crispi to the tax collector is the first document in which Vittorio Emanuele is described as King of Italy."

I took the opportunity to ask, "But isn't Nievo the quartermaster?"

"Nievo is Acerbi's deputy," explained Abba. "So young, and already a great writer. A true poet. His brilliance shines out. He's always alone, gazing into the distance, as if trying to reach to the horizon. I understand that Garibaldi's about to appoint him colonel."

Bandi's praises went further: "At Calatafimi he was getting a little behind, distributing bread. Bozzetti called him into battle and he leapt into the fray, swooping down towards the enemy like a great black bird, the wings of his cloak wide open, so that a bullet immediately tore a hole through it. . . ."

This was quite enough for me to feel an antipathy towards this Nievo. He and I must have been about the same age and he already thought himself famous. The warrior poet. Of course your cloak will get shot through if you flap it open like that – a fine way of showing off a hole which could have been in your breast. . . .

At that point Abba and Bandi described the battle of Calatafimi – a miraculous victory, a thousand volunteers on one side and twenty-five thousand well-armed Bourbons on the other.

"Garibaldi's leading us," said Abba, "on a bay gelding fit for a Grand Vizier, with a magnificent saddle and fretted stirrups, wearing a red shirt and Hungarian-style cap. At Salemi we're joined by local volunteers. They arrive from all directions, on horseback, on foot, an evil-looking mob, mountain folk armed to the teeth, with bandit faces and eyes like the barrels of pistols. But led by gentry, local landowners. Salemi is filthy, its streets like open sewers, but the monks had fine monasteries and we're billeted there. We get conflicting information about the enemy – four thousand, no, ten thousand, twenty thousand, with horses and cannon, north, no south, advancing, retreating . . . And all of a sudden the enemy appears. There'd be about five thousand men, but someone said, 'Nonsense, there's ten thousand of them.' Between us and them a barren plain. The Neapolitan riflemen make their way down from the hills. How calm, how confident – you can see they're well trained, not like our rabble. And their bugles, what a mournful sound! The first shots don't ring out until half past one in the afternoon. They're fired by the Neapolitan riflemen who have come down through the prickly pear cactuses. 'Don't reply, don't fire back!' our captains shout. But the rifle bullets whistle past us with such a din that we can hardly keep still. We hear a bang, then another, then the general's bugler sounds the call to arms and the charge. The bullets rain down like hailstones. On the hill there's a cloud of smoke from the cannon firing on us. We cross the plain and break through the enemy's front line. I turn back and see Garibaldi standing on the hill, his sword still sheathed over his right shoulder, advancing slowly and keeping an eye on the action. Bixio gallops to shelter him with his horse and shouts, 'What are you trying to do, General? You'll get killed.' And he answers, 'What better way to die than for my country?' And he continues on, heedless of the hail of bullets. I feared, in that instant, the general had decided it was impossible to win and was trying to get killed. But straight away one of our cannon blasts out from the road. We seem to have the support of a thousand men. 'Onwards, onwards, onwards!' All you can hear is the bugle which has never stopped sounding the charge. With bayonets fixed we pass through the first, the second, the third line, up the hill. The Bourbon battalions retreat higher, regroup and seem to grow in strength. They still seem invincible – they're up there on the summit and we're beneath the ridge, tired and exhausted. There's a moment's rest with them above and us flat on the ground. Gunfire here and there. The Bourbons start rolling boulders, throwing stones. Someone says the general's been hit. I see a fine-looking youth among the prickly pear cactuses, fatally injured, supported by two companions. He's pleading with his companions to take pity on the Neapolitans because they too are Italians. The whole slope is strewn with dead and wounded, but not a groan is to be heard. Now and then, from the summit, the Neapolitans cry, 'Long live the king.' Meanwhile reinforcements arrive. Bandi, I remember that was when you appeared, covered in wounds, but worst of all with a bullet stuck in your left breast, and I thought you'd be dead in half an hour. And yet there you were on the final assault, ahead of everyone – what spirit you had!"

"Nonsense," said Bandi, "they were only scratches."

"And what about the Franciscans who were fighting with us? One friar, all filth and bones, was loading a blunderbuss with handfuls of shot and pebbles, then clambering up to within sight of the enemy and firing it. I saw one who'd been hit in the thigh pull the bullet out of his flesh and carry on firing."

Abba then began to describe the battle at Ponte dell'Ammiraglio: "By God, Simonini, a day out of Homer! Pure poetry. We are at the gates of Palermo and a troop of local insurgents come to help us. Someone – perhaps he's the first sentry we take by surprise – cries out, 'Oh, God!', staggers backwards, takes three or four steps sideways like a drunkard, and falls into a ditch beneath two poplar trees, near to a dead Neapolitan rifleman. And I can still hear one of our Genoese comrades, just as lead shot was hailing down on us, shouting, 'Hell, which way?' And a bullet hits him in the forehead, splitting open his skull. At Ponte dell'Ammiraglio, along the road, over the arches, under the bridge and in the fields, they're massacred by bayonets. Near dawn we hold the bridge, but we're cut off by fierce gunfire from an infantry line behind a wall, and charged by cavalry from the left, but we drive them back into the fields. Once over the bridge, we regroup at the crossroads by Porta Termini, but we're bombarded by cannon from a ship in the port and are under fire from a barricade in front of us. We carry on regardless. A bell rings out the tocsin. We continue on through the narrow streets and at a certain point . . . dear God, what a vision! Three ravishing young girls, dressed in white, clinging to a railing with hands as white as lilies, are watching us in silence. They look like angels you see in church frescoes. 'Who are you?' they ask, and we tell them we're Italians and ask who they are and they tell us they're nuns. 'Oh, poor young things,' we say – we wouldn't mind releasing them from that prison and offering them some sweet amusement – and they cry, 'Long live St Rosalia!' We reply, 'Long live Italy!' And they also shout, 'Long live Italy!' with gentle holy voices, and wish us victory. We fought for another five days in Palermo before the armistice . . . but with no young nuns to comfort us, just whores!"

*   *   *

. . . *"At Ponte dell' Ammiraglio,*
along the road, over the arches,
under the bridge and in the fields,
they're massacred by bayonets." . . .

[PAGE 155]

How far can I rely on these two fanatics? They are young and this is their first experience of war. They had worshipped their General from the very start and in their own way are storytellers like Dumas, embellishing their recollections so that all their geese are swans. They certainly fought well during those skirmishes, but it sounds very strange that Garibaldi could wander around in the midst of the battle (and his enemies would have been able to see him clearly from far away) without ever being hit. Or was the enemy shooting wide on orders from higher up?

I had already begun to form these opinions based on various rumours I'd heard from my innkeeper – he must have travelled around other parts of the peninsula, and speaks a language almost comprehensible. And it was he who suggested I should have a chat with Don Fortunato Musumeci, a lawyer who apparently knows everything about everyone, and has shown his distrust of the new arrivals on several occasions.

I certainly couldn't approach him wearing my red shirt and I thought about Father Bergamaschi's cassock which I'd brought with me. A comb through my hair, a sufficiently unctuous tone, eyes lowered, and there I am slipping out of the inn, unrecognisable to everyone. It was, in fact, most unwise as there was a rumour abroad that the Jesuits were to be expelled from the island. But all in all, it went well. And then again, as the victim of an imminent injustice, I could also inspire confidence among those opposing Garibaldi.

I made contact with Don Fortunato by surprising him, one morning after mass, as he was quietly sipping his coffee. The café was central, almost elegant, and Don Fortunato was relaxed, his face angled towards the sun, eyes closed, a few days' growth of beard, a black jacket and cravat even in those days of searing heat, and a barely lit cigar between his nicotine-stained fingers. I noticed they add lemon peel to the coffee down here – I hope they don't also put it into *caffelatte*.

Sitting at a nearby table, all I had to do was complain about the heat and our conversation had begun. I told him I'd been sent by the Roman Curia to find out what was going on in these parts, and this allowed Musumeci to speak freely.

"Most reverend Father, do you think that a thousand men, gathered together from all over the place, armed any old way, are able to land at Marsala without losing a single man? Why was it that the Bourbon navy – the finest fleet in Europe after the English – fired here and there without hitting a single person? And later at Calatafimi, how did the same band of a thousand bunglers – plus several hundred young scoundrels sent out there with a kick up their backsides by a few landowners who wanted to curry favour with the occupying forces – when put in front of one of the best trained armies in the world (and I don't know whether you're aware exactly what a Bourbon military academy is like) . . . how did that thousand or so bunglers manage to drive back twenty-five thousand men, even if only a few thousand of them had actually been sent into battle and the others had been held back in their barracks? It took money, my dear sir, large quantities of money to pay off the naval officials at Marsala. And General Landi, after a day at Calatafimi when everything was still in the balance, had enough fresh troops to see off those volunteers. But instead he retreated to Palermo! It is said, you know, that they've tipped him fourteen thousand ducats. And his superiors? General Ramorino was shot by firing squad in Piedmont some twelve years ago for far less than that – not that I'm particularly fond of the Piedmontese, but they certainly understand a thing or two about military matters. Yet Landi was simply replaced by Lanza who, I reckon, had already been paid off. In fact, look at this famous conquest of Palermo . . . Garibaldi had reinforced his band with three thousand five hundred scoundrels rounded up from among Sicily's convicts, and Lanza had around sixteen thousand men – yes, sixteen thousand. And rather than using them en masse, Lanza sent them off against the rebels in small groups, and they were overwhelmed – inevitably – not least because various local turncoats were paid to shoot at them from the rooftops. Here at the port, Piedmontese ships unload rifles for the volunteers under the eyes of the Bourbon ships, and on land Garibaldi is allowed to reach Vicaria prison and the forced labour camp where he liberates another thousand common criminals, recruiting them into his band. And I can hardly tell you what is now happening in Naples. Our poor sovereign is surrounded by wretches who have already received their money and are sapping the ground from under his feet. . . ."

"But where does all this money come from?"

"Most reverend Father! I am astonished that you in Rome know so little! It is English Freemasonry! Can't you see the connection? Garibaldi a Mason, Mazzini a Mason, Mazzini exiled in London in contact with the English Masons, Cavour a Mason who receives orders from the English lodges, all Garibaldi's men are Masons. The plan is not so much to destroy the Kingdom of the Two Sicilies but to inflict a fatal blow on His Holiness, because it is clear that, after the Two Sicilies, Vittorio Emanuele also wants Rome. You believe the yarn about these volunteers setting off with ninety thousand lire in their pockets, which would hardly be enough to feed that band of gluttons and drunkards during the voyage? Just look at the way they're devouring Palermo's last supplies of food and pillaging the surrounding countryside. The fact is the English Freemasons have given three million French francs to Garibaldi in gold Turkish piastres which can be spent anywhere in the Mediterranean!"

"And who is looking after the gold?"

"The general's trusted Freemason, Captain Nievo, a young whippersnapper, not yet thirty years old, who is no less than the official paymaster. But these devils are paying off generals, admirals and anyone you like, while poor people starve. The peasants were expecting Garibaldi to divide up their masters' estates, and instead the general has obviously sided with those who own land and money. Mark my words, those young ruffians who went off to risk their lives at Calatafimi, as soon as they realise nothing has changed, will start shooting at the volunteers and with the very same rifles they've stolen from the dead."

Abandoning the cassock, I wandered about the city in my red shirt and happened upon a monk, Father Carmelo, on the steps of a church. He said he was twenty-seven but

looked forty. He wanted to join us, he confided, but something was holding him back. I asked him what it was – after
all, there had been friars at Calatafimi.

"I would come with you," he said, "if I was sure you were
doing something truly great. All you can say is that you want
to unite Italy so as to create one country. If the people are
suffering, they will suffer whether united or divided, and I
don't know if you'll be able to stop that suffering."

"But the people will have freedom and schools," I told
him.

"Freedom is not bread, nor are schools. Perhaps such
things are enough for you up there in Piedmont but not for
us Sicilians."

"What do you want, then?"

"Not a war against the Bourbons, but a war by the poor
against those who are starving them, who aren't just at court,
but all over the place."

"And that includes you monks, whose monasteries and
lands are everywhere?"

"Yes, it includes us – indeed us first, before everyone
else! But with the Gospel and with the Cross. Then I'd come.
Your way is not enough."

From what I learned at university about the famous
Communist Manifesto, this monk must be one of them. I
understand so little about this island of Sicily.

Perhaps it's because I have been obsessed by the idea since
my grandfather's time, but I immediately began to wonder

whether the Jews were also involved in this conspiracy to support Garibaldi. They are nearly always involved somehow. So I went back to see Musumeci.

"But of course," he said. "First of all, while not all Masons are Jews, all Jews are Masons. And what about Garibaldi's men? I was amused to look at the list of volunteers at Marsala, published 'in honour of those gallant men'. And there I found names such as Eugenio Ravà, Giuseppe Uziel, Isacco D'Ancona, Samuele Marchesi, Abramo Isacco Alpron, Moisé Maldacea and Colombo Donato, formerly known as Abramo. Do you suppose they're good Christians with names like that?

(16th June) I went to visit Captain Nievo, carrying the letter of introduction. He's a young blade with a pair of well-groomed whiskers and a tuft beneath his lip, who cultivates the attitude of a dreamer. A mere pose – while we were speaking, a volunteer came in to ask about blankets of some kind to be collected and, like an officious bookkeeper, he reminded him that his company had already been given ten the previous week. "Are you eating blankets?" he asked. "If you want to eat any more I'll send you off to a cell to digest them." The volunteer saluted and disappeared.

"You see what work I have to do? They'll have told you I'm a man of letters. And yet I have to supply soldiers with money and clothing, and order twenty thousand new uniforms because every day new volunteers arrive from Genoa, La Spezia and Livorno. Then there are pleas for money – counts and duchesses who want an allowance of two hundred ducats a month and think that Garibaldi is the archangel of the Lord. Everyone here expects matters to be sorted out from above. It's not like the north – if we want something, we get going and do it. They've entrusted the coffers to me, perhaps because I graduated at Padua in civil and canon law, or because I'm not a thief, which is a great virtue on this island where prince and shyster are one and the same."

He clearly enjoyed playing the absent-minded poet. When I asked him whether he'd already been made colonel he said he didn't know: "The situation here is rather confused," he said. "Bixio is trying to impose the sort of discipline you find in Piedmont, as if it were a military academy, but we're just a band of irregular troops. Leave out such trifles, however, if you're writing articles for Turin. Try to convey the true excitement, the enthusiasm everybody feels. There are people here who are laying down their lives for something they believe in. The rest are treating it as an adventure in colonial lands. Palermo's an amusing place to live: people gossip here as they do in Venice. We are admired as heroes, and two spans of red smock and seventy centimetres of scimitar make us desirable in the eyes of many beautiful women, whose virtue is but skin deep. There's hardly an evening when we don't have a box at the theatre, and the sherbets are excellent."

"You tell me you have to deal with so many expenses, but how do you manage on the little you had when you left Genoa? Are you using the money you impounded at Marsala?"

"That was small change. No, no, as soon as we arrived in Palermo, the general sent Crispi to draw money from the Bank of the Two Sicilies."

"Yes, I heard. There was talk of five million ducats. . . ."

At that point the poet became the general's trusted deputy once again. He gazed up towards the sky: "They say all sorts of things, you know. But you must remember the donations from patriots throughout Italy and, I should say, throughout Europe – and write that in your newspaper in Turin, for those who haven't been keeping up with events. But the most difficult business is keeping the books in order, because when this officially becomes the Kingdom of Italy I'll have to hand everything over to His Majesty's government, accounting for every cent."

And what will you do with those millions from the English Masons? I thought to myself. Or perhaps you, Garibaldi and Cavour are all agreed – the money's there but not to be talked about. Then again, perhaps the money's there and you know nothing about it – you're the front man, the virtuous little fellow whom they (whoever *they* are) are using as a cover, and you imagine all these battles have been won by the grace of God alone. I still wasn't clear about the man. The only note of sincerity I found in his words was his bitter regret that while, over those weeks, the volunteers had been heading, victory after victory, towards the eastern coast and preparing to cross the strait into Calabria and on to Naples, he had been ordered to remain behind the lines, keeping the accounts in Palermo, and he was champing at the bit. Some people are like that. Instead of being thankful that fate had offered him fine sherbets and pretty women, he wanted his cloak to be peppered with more bullets.

I have heard it said that over a billion people inhabit this earth. I don't know how anyone could count them but from one look around Palermo it's quite clear that there are too many of us and that we're already stepping on each other's toes. And most people smell. There isn't sufficient food. Just imagine if there were any more of us. We therefore have to cull the population. True, there are plagues and suicides, capital punishment, those who challenge each other to duels or who get pleasure from riding at breakneck speed through woods and meadows. I've even heard of English gentlemen who go swimming in the sea and, of course, drown. But it is not enough. Wars are the most effective and natural way imaginable for stemming the increase in human numbers. Once upon a time, when people went off to war, didn't they say it was God's will? But to do so you need people who want to fight. If no one wants to fight, no one will die. Then wars would be pointless. And so it's vital to have men like Nievo, Abba or Bandi who want to throw themselves in the line of fire. Others like me can then live without being harassed by so many people breathing down our necks.

In other words, although I don't like them, we do need noble-spirited souls.

I introduced myself to La Farina, carrying my letter of presentation.

"If you're expecting me to give you some good news to send to Turin," he said, "you can forget it. There's no government here. Garibaldi and Bixio think they're in charge of Genoese people like them, not Sicilians like me. In a country that has no conscription, they actually thought they could call up thirty thousand men. In many towns there were serious revolts. They've decreed that all former royal officials are disqualified from local councils, but they are the only ones who can read and write. The other day some rabid anti-clericalists suggested burning down the public library because it had been founded by Jesuits. The Governor of Palermo is a youngster called Marcilepre of whom no one's ever heard. In inland areas, crimes of every kind are being committed and those who should be keeping order are often murderers themselves – control is now in the hands of out-and-out brigands. Garibaldi is an honest man, but unable to see what is happening under his nose. From one single consignment of horses requisitioned in the province of Palermo, two hundred have disappeared! Permission to assemble a battalion is given to anyone who asks and so we have some battalions, complete with brass band and officers, and only forty or fifty soldiers at most! The same job is given to three or four people! The whole of Sicily has been left without civil, criminal or commercial courts because all of the judges have been sacked and military commissions have been set up to judge everything and everyone, as in the time of the Huns! Crispi and his band say that Garibaldi doesn't want civilian courts because judges and lawyers can't be trusted, that he doesn't want a parliament because its members use the pen rather than the sword, that he doesn't want a police force because citizens must arm and defend themselves. I've no idea whether this is true – I'm no longer even able to confer with the general."

On the 7th of July I heard that La Farina had been arrested and sent back to Turin on Garibaldi's orders, evidently urged on by Crispi. Cavour no longer has an informer. All will depend, then, on my report.

It's pointless now dressing up as a priest to collect information: there's plenty of gossip in the taverns and it's sometimes the volunteers themselves who complain how badly things are going. I hear that some fifty of the Sicilians who enlisted with Garibaldi's men when they arrived in Palermo have deserted, some taking their weapons with them. "They're peasants who flare up like straw and quickly tire," explains Abba. The council of war passes death sentences on them but then lets them wander off where they choose, provided it's far away. I try to understand the true feelings of these people. The excitement that prevails throughout Sicily is entirely dependent on the fact that this land was godforsaken, sunburned and waterless (apart from the sea), with a few prickly fruits. Then, in this country where nothing had happened for centuries, Garibaldi and his followers arrive. It's not that the people support him, or that they still support the king whom Garibaldi is overthrowing. They are simply intoxicated by the fact that something different is going on – and everyone interprets "different" as they please. Perhaps this great wind of change is just a south wind that will lull everyone back to sleep.

(30th July) Nievo, with whom I have now become quite friendly, confides in me that Garibaldi has received a formal letter from Vittorio Emanuele ordering him not to cross the strait. But the order is accompanied by a secret message from the king saying more or less, "I wrote the first message to you as king, but now I'm advising you to reply that you'd like to follow my advice but your duty to Italy prevents you from making any effort not to help the people of Naples when they appeal to you to liberate them." The king is double-bluffing, but against whom? Against Cavour? Or against Garibaldi himself, whom first he orders not to cross to the mainland, then encourages to cross . . . and after he has done so, will punish him for his disobedience by marching his troops from Piedmont down to Naples?

"The general is too naive; he'll fall into a trap," says Nievo. "I'd like to be with him, but it's my duty to stay here."

This man is highly intelligent, but I've realised he too is fired by adoration for Garibaldi. In a moment of weakness he let me see a slim volume of his poetry that had just arrived, entitled *Amori garibaldini*, printed up north without him being able to check the proofs.

"I hope my readers will allow me in my role as hero to be a bit of a brute. Here they've done all they can to demonstrate this by leaving a series of shameful printing errors."

I glanced through one of his compositions, dedicated to Garibaldi, and have come to the conclusion that Nievo must indeed be a bit of a brute:

_... In his eyes such strange
appeal / It fills each mind with
splendour / That people feel the
urge to kneel / And incline
their heads in prayer. ..._

[PAGE 170]

169

In his eyes such strange appeal
It fills each mind with splendour
That people feel the urge to kneel
And incline their heads in prayer.
Around the crowded city squares,
Courteous, human as he passes
Tending his hand left and right
To the assembled lasses.

Everyone here is going mad over this bow-legged little man.

(12th August) I visit Nievo to ask whether it is true what they say about Garibaldi and his men having landed on the coast of Calabria. But I find him in low spirits, almost in tears. News has reached him from Turin that there are unpleasant rumours about the way he's handling matters.

"But I keep everything noted down here," and he slams his fist on the account books, each bound in red cloth. "Every receipt and every expense. And if anything has been stolen, my accounts will show it. When I hand this over to the appropriate authorities, several heads will roll. Not mine."

(26th August) I am no strategist, but from the news I receive I think I can see what is going on. Certain ministers in Naples, spurred on by Masonic gold or by their conversion to the Savoy cause, are plotting against King Francesco. A revolt is about to take place in Naples, the rebels will ask the Piedmont government for help, and Vittorio Emanuele will come south. Garibaldi seems not to be aware of anything, or perhaps he's aware of everything and is hastening his manoeuvres so he can reach Naples before Vittorio Emanuele.

I find Nievo in a rage, waving a letter: "Your friend Dumas," he says, "plays at being Croesus, then imagines that I am Croesus! Look what he's written – and he has the gall to say he's doing it in the general's name! Swiss and Bavarian mercenaries around Naples, hired by the Bourbons, smell defeat and are offering to desert for four ducats a head. And there are five thousand of them, which means twenty thousand ducats or ninety thousand francs. Dumas, who had seemed to be his own Count of Monte Cristo, doesn't have that much, and grandly offers the paltry sum of one thousand francs. He says they'll collect three thousand from patriots in Naples and asks if, by any chance, I could put up the rest. But where does he think I could get such a sum?"

He offers me a drink. "You see, Simonini, everyone is now getting excited about the landings on the mainland, and no one seems to know anything about a tragedy which will weigh shamefully on the history of our expedition. It took place at Bronte, near Catania, a town of ten thousand inhabitants, mostly sharecroppers and shepherds, still slaves to a system akin to medieval feudalism. The whole area had been presented as a gift to Lord Nelson, along with the title

171

of Duke of Bronte, and in any event the land had always been in the hands of a few wealthy people, or *galantuomini* as they are called down there. The people were exploited and treated like animals – they couldn't even go into the landowners' woods to gather wild plants for food and had to pay a toll when they went into the fields. When Garibaldi arrives, these people imagine that the time has come for justice and that the land will be returned to them. They form committees of so-called liberals, and the leading figure is a lawyer named Lombardo. But Bronte is owned by Nelson's English heirs and the English had helped Garibaldi at Marsala. So whom should he support? At this point the people stop listening even to Avvocato Lombardo and other liberals and lose all control, triggering off a popular riot, a mass slaughter, and they massacre the landowning gentry. They've done wrong, that's perfectly obvious, and among the rebels were also ex-convicts – with the havoc reigning on the island, many rogues had been set free who ought to have been kept inside. . . . But it all happened because of our arrival. Under pressure from the English, Garibaldi sends Bixio to Bronte, and he's not a man to beat around the bush. He orders a siege, begins harsh reprisals against the population, hears the allegations made by the gentry, and identifies Avvocato Lombardo as the ringleader of the riot, which isn't true, but that doesn't matter. An example had to be made and Lombardo is executed by a firing squad, along with four others, including a wretched lunatic who long before the massacres had been walking the streets shouting insults against the gentry without upsetting anyone. Apart from my sadness over this cruelty, the whole business affects me personally. You understand, Simonini? On the one hand, news of such actions is reaching Turin, from which we appear to be colluding with the old landowners; on the other hand, there are those rumours I told you about concerning money. You don't need much to put the two together – landowners pay us to shoot the poor wretches, and we enjoy ourselves here on their money. And see how people are dying around us, all the time. It augurs ill."

(8th September) Garibaldi has entered Naples without meeting any resistance. He's obviously getting rather cocky because Nievo says he has asked Vittorio Emanuele to dismiss Cavour. Turin will now be needing my report, and I realise it must be as unfavourable as possible to Garibaldi. I will have to exaggerate the Masonic gold, portray Garibaldi as irresponsible, play up the Bronte massacre, refer to other crimes, embezzlement, extortion, corruption and general extravagance. I will use Musumeci's account to describe the behaviour of the volunteers, carousing in the convents, deflowering maidens (perhaps even nuns – there's no harm in laying on the colour).

I'll then produce a few orders requisitioning private property. A letter from an anonymous informer telling me about continual dealings between Garibaldi and Mazzini via Crispi and about their plans for establishing a republic, even in Piedmont. In other words, a good strong report to put Garibaldi into a tight corner. Not least because Musumeci gave me another good point to include:

. . . Garibaldi has entered
Naples without meeting
any resistance. . . .

[PAGE 173]

Garibaldi's men are for the most part a band of foreign mercenaries. These thousand men include adventurers from France, America, England, Hungary and Africa too, the dregs of every nation, and many were buccaneers with Garibaldi himself in the Americas. It's enough to hear the names of his lieutenants: Turr, Eber, Tukory, Teloky, Magyarody, Czudafy, Frigyesy (Musumeci spat out these names as best he could and, apart from Turr and Eber, I've never heard any mention of the others). Then there were Poles, Turks, Bavarians, and a German called Wolff, commander of the German and Swiss deserters who had previously served the Bourbons. And the English government provided Garibaldi with Algerian and Indian battalions. Hardly Italian patriots! Out of a thousand, only half were Italians. Musumeci is no doubt exaggerating, because all around I hear Venetian, Lombard, Emilian or Tuscan accents, and I haven't seen a single Indian. But I don't think it will do any harm to play up this hotchpotch of races.

And of course I've added a few references to the Jews working hand in glove with the Masons.

I think the report should reach Turin as soon as possible, and it mustn't fall into the wrong hands. I've found a Piedmontese naval vessel about to return to the Kingdom of Piedmont, and it won't take much to forge an official document ordering the captain to land me at Genoa. My stay in Sicily ends here, and I'm rather sorry I won't see what is going on in Naples and beyond, but I wasn't here to enjoy myself, nor to write an epic. At the end of these travels I remember with pleasure only the *pisci d'ovu,* the *babbaluci a picchipacchi* (a way of cooking snails), and the *cannoli* . . . ah, the *cannoli*! Nievo also promised to let me taste a certain swordfish *a' sammurigghu* but there wasn't enough time, and so all I can savour is the aroma of its name.

8

THE ERCOLE

From the diary for 30th and 31st March and 1st April 1897

The Narrator is beginning to find this amoebaean dialogue between Simonini and his intrusive abbé rather tiresome, but it would appear that on the 30th of March Simonini completed a partial reconstruction of the final events in Sicily, and his writing is complicated by many lines cancelled out, and others crossed through with an X but still legible – and disturbing to read. On the 31st of March Abbé Dalla Piccola intervenes in the diary, as if to prise open tightly closed doors in Simonini's memory, revealing to him what he is desperately refusing to remember. And on the 1st of April, after a restless night in which he recalls having attacks of nausea, Simonini makes a further entry, annoyed, apparently seeking to correct what he considers to be the abbé's exaggerations and moralistic indignation. But the Narrator being unsure, in short, who in the end is right, has allowed himself to describe these events as he feels they might best be reconstructed, and naturally accepts responsibility for his reconstruction.

Simonini sent his report to Cavalier Bianco upon his return to Turin. A message came the following day calling him to a meeting that evening at the same place where he'd been taken by carriage the first time, where Bianco, Riccardi and Negri di Saint Front awaited him.

"Avvocato Simonini," Bianco began, "I don't know whether the nature of our relationship now permits me to express my full feelings, but I have to say you're a fool."

"Cavalier, how dare you!"

"He's quite right," intervened Riccardi, "and he speaks for us all. And I might add, a dangerous fool. So much so that we have to consider whether it's wise to leave you wandering around Turin with such ideas in your head."

"Excuse me, I may have got something wrong, but . . ."

"You have, you have. You've got it all wrong. Don't you realise that in just a few days (even the fishwives know about it by now) General Cialdini and our troops will be entering the Papal States? And our army will probably be at the gates of Naples within a month. At that point we'll have prepared the ground for a popular plebiscite in which the Kingdom of the Two Sicilies and its lands will be officially annexed to the Kingdom of Italy. If Garibaldi is the gentleman and realist we think he is, he will resist the demands of that hothead Mazzini. He'll accept the situation, *bon gré mal gré*, he'll hand over the conquered lands to the king and he'll have done a splendid job as a patriot. Then we'll have to dismantle Garibaldi's army, which now numbers almost sixty thousand men – they're better not left roaming about as they please, so the volunteers will be accepted into the Savoy army and the others sent home with money in their pockets. All fine fellows, all heroes. And you want us, by releasing that damned report of yours to the newspapers and the general public, to say that these Garibaldini, who are about to become our own soldiers and officers, were a bunch of scoundrels, for the most part foreign, who pillaged their way through Sicily? You want us to say that Garibaldi is not the selfless hero to whom the whole of Italy should be grateful, but an adventurer who defeated a bogus enemy by buying them off? And that he plotted with Mazzini to the very end to make Italy a republic? And you want us to say that Nino Bixio went around Sicily executing liberals and massacring shepherds and peasants? You're mad!"

"But gentlemen, you employed me . . ."

"We did not employ you to slander Garibaldi and those fine Italians who fought with him, but to find documents which might show how the hero's republican entourage were misgoverning the occupied lands, so as to justify an intervention from Piedmont."

"But gentlemen, you are well aware that La Farina . . ."

"La Farina wrote private letters to Count Cavour, which he certainly hasn't been waving around. And then La Farina is La Farina – someone who bears a particular grudge against Crispi. And last of all, what's this nonsense about gold from the English Masons?"

"Everyone's talking about it."

"Everyone? We're not. And what are these Masons anyway? Are you a Mason?"

"No I'm not, but . . ."

"So don't involve yourself in matters that are of no concern to you. Let the Masons stew in their own juice."

Simonini evidently hadn't realised that the whole Savoy government were Freemasons – and with all the

Jesuits he'd had around him as a child, perhaps he should have done so. But Riccardi had already moved on to the question of the Jews, asking by what twisted notion he had included them in his report.

Simonini stammered, "The Jews are everywhere, and don't you think . . ."

"It doesn't matter what we think or don't think," interrupted Saint Front. "The fact is that in a united Italy we also need the support of the Jewish community. What is more, it's pointless telling good Italian Catholics that Garibaldi's selfless heroes also included Jews. In short, with all these blunders of yours, we'd have every reason to send you off for a good long time to enjoy the air at one of our comfortable Alpine fortresses. But regrettably we still need you. It would seem that this Captain Nievo (or Colonel or whatever) is still down there, with all his account books. We have no idea, *in primis*, whether or not he's been keeping them correctly and, *in secundis*, whether it is politically wise for these accounts to be disclosed. You tell us Nievo intends to hand them over to us, and that would be good, but if he shows them to others before they reach us, then it would not. And so you will return to Sicily, once again as correspondent for Professor Boggio reporting on the new and momentous events. You will attach yourself like a leech to Nievo and make sure the accounts disappear, vanish into thin air, go up in smoke, so there's no further talk of them. It is for you to decide how to do this, and you are authorised to use any means, provided of course they are lawful, nor should you expect further orders from us. Cavalier Bianco will give you a contact at the Bank of Sicily to assure the necessary funds."

At this point Dalla Piccola's account is also fairly sketchy and incomplete, as if he too was having difficulty recalling what his counterpart was constrained to forget.

It seems, however, that having returned to Sicily at the end of September, Simonini remained there until March of the following year, trying unsuccessfully to get his hands on Nievo's accounts and receiving a fortnightly dispatch from Cavalier Bianco asking with a certain impatience what point he had reached.

Nievo was now dedicating body and soul to those confounded accounts, increasingly worried about malicious rumours, expending more and more energy investigating, examining, scrutinising thousands of receipts so as to be sure of what he was recording. He had now been given considerable authority since Garibaldi was also anxious not to create scandal and gossip, and had arranged for him to have an office with four assistants and two guards at the entrance and on the stairways so that no one could, so to speak, wander in at night in search of the accounts.

Indeed, Nievo had let it be known that he suspected someone might not be very happy about what they contained. He feared the accounts might be stolen or tampered with and had therefore done his best to ensure they were impossible to find. And all that Simonini could do was consolidate his friendship with the poet, with whom he was now on more informal terms, so as to understand what he planned to do with those wretched books.

They spent many evenings together, in an autumnal Palermo that still languished in heat untempered by the sea breezes, sipping an occasional water and anisette, allowing the liqueur to diffuse gradually in the water like a cloud of smoke. Little by little, Nievo abandoned his military reserve and came to trust Simonini, perhaps because he liked him, perhaps because he now felt himself to be a prisoner in the city and needed the company of someone else with whom he could daydream. He talked about a love he had left behind in Milan, an impossible love, because her husband was not only his cousin but also his best friend. Nothing could be done about it. Other loves had already driven him to hypochondria.

"That's how I am, and how I'm condemned to remain. I will always be a moody, dark, sombre, irritable individual. I'm now thirty and have always fought wars to distract me from a world I do not love. And so I've left a great novel at home, still in manuscript. I'd like to get it printed but can't because I still have these bloody accounts to look after. If I were ambitious, if I thirsted for pleasure . . . if I were at least bad . . . at least like Bixio. Never mind. I'm still a child, I live a day at a time, I love the excitement of rebellion, the air I breathe. I'll die for the sake of dying. . . . And then it will all be over."

Simonini did not try to console him. He considered him incurable.

*   *   *

In early October there was the battle of Volturno, where Garibaldi fought off the Bourbon army's last offensive. During that same period, General Cialdini had defeated the papal army at Castelfidardo and invaded Abruzzo and Molise, formerly part of the Bourbon kingdom. At Palermo, Nievo was champing at the bit. He had heard that among his accusers in Piedmont were followers of La Farina, who was now apparently speaking ill of anyone connected with the Redshirts.

"It makes you want to give up," said Nievo, dejected, "but it's exactly at moments like this that we mustn't abandon the helm."

On the 26th of October the great event took place – Garibaldi met Vittorio Emanuele at Teano. He practically handed over southern Italy. For this, said Nievo, he should at least have been appointed a senator. And yet, at the beginning of November, Garibaldi lined up fourteen thousand men and three hundred horses at Caserta and waited for the king to come and review them, and the king never appeared.

On the 7th of November, the king made his triumphal entry into Naples but Garibaldi, a modern-day Cincinnatus, withdrew to the island of Caprera. "What a man," said Nievo. And he cried, as poets do (which greatly irritated Simonini).

A few days later, Garibaldi's army was disbanded. Twenty thousand volunteers were accepted into the Savoy army, but so too were three thousand Bourbon officers.

"That's fair, they're Italians too," said Nievo. "But it's

a sad ending to our epic campaign. I'm not signing up. I'll take six months' pay, then goodbye. Six months to complete my job – I hope I'll manage it."

It must have been a dreadful job. By the end of November he had barely completed the accounts to the end of July. At a rough guess, another three months were needed, perhaps more.

When Vittorio Emanuele reached Palermo in December, Nievo told Simonini, "I'm the last Redshirt down here and I'm looked upon as a savage. What's more I have to answer the slanders of La Farina's lot. Good Lord, if I knew it would end like this, instead of leaving Genoa for this prison I'd have drowned myself, and been better off."

Simonini had still not found a way of laying his hands on those wretched accounts. Then all of a sudden, in mid-December, Nievo announced he was returning to Milan for a short period. Leaving the accounts in Palermo? Taking them with him? It was impossible to know.

Nievo was away for almost two months and Simonini tried to make use of that bleak period by visiting the area around Palermo (I'm no romantic, he thought, but what is Christmas in a snowless desert strewn with prickly pears?). He bought a mule, put on Father Bergamaschi's cassock, and went from town to town listening to the gossip of curates and farmers, but also uncovering the secrets of Sicilian cooking.

In secluded countryside inns he came across excellent rustic delicacies which cost little, including *acqua cotta*: all you had to do was put slices of bread in a tureen, dress

*. . . Everyone called him
Bronte, and in fact it seems he
had escaped from the Bronte
massacres. . . .*

[PAGE 186]

them with plenty of olive oil and freshly ground pepper; then some chopped onions, peeled sliced tomatoes and wild mint were boiled in three quarters of a litre of water; after twenty minutes this was poured over the bread in the tureen and allowed to rest for a few minutes before it was served hot.

On the outskirts of Bagheria he found an inn with a few tables in a dark hall. But in that pleasant shade, welcoming even during the winter months, a landlord of grubby appearance prepared wonderful offal dishes such as stuffed heart, pork brawn, sweetbreads and every type of tripe.

There he met two characters, each quite different from the other, whom only later, by a stroke of genius, was he able to bring together as part of a single plan. But let us not rush ahead.

The first seemed half mad. The landlord said he gave him food and lodging out of pity, though he was actually able to perform many useful chores. Everyone called him Bronte, and in fact it seems he had escaped from the Bronte massacres. He was continually haunted by memories of the rebellion and after a few glasses of wine would bang his fist on the table, shouting in thick dialect which might roughly be translated as, "You masters, beware, the hour of judgement is at hand! Fear not, citizens, be ready!" This was what his friend Nunzio Ciraldo Fraiunco, one of the four later executed by Bixio, had shouted before the insurrection.

He wasn't particularly intelligent, but at least he had one fixed idea. He wanted to kill Nino Bixio.

Bronte was, for Simonini, just a simpleton with whom he could pass a few winter evenings. Of more immediate interest was another figure, a hirsute individual who, at first, kept himself to himself, but when he heard Simonini asking the landlord about the recipes for various dishes, joined the conversation and turned out to be a fellow gastronome. Simonini told him how to make *agnolotti alla piemontese*, while he revealed the secrets of *caponata;* Simonini described *tartare all'albese* until his mouth watered, and he expounded on the alchemy of marzipan.

Master Ninuzzo spoke something approaching Italian, and hinted that he'd also travelled abroad. And then, after describing his great devotion to the various effigies in the local sanctuaries and respect for Simonini's ecclesiastical dignity, he confessed his curious situation. He had been an explosives expert with the Bourbon army – not an ordinary soldier but the keeper of a nearby powder magazine. Garibaldi's men had driven back the Bourbon army and seized the munitions and powder but, instead of dismantling the bunker, they'd kept Ninuzzo in their service to guard the place, in the pay of the military authorities. And there he was, getting bored, awaiting orders, resentful of the northern occupiers, faithful to his King, dreaming of rebellion and insurrection.

"I could blow up half Palermo if I wanted to," he whispered, as soon as he understood that neither was Simonini on the side of the Piedmontese. And he described how, to his amazement, the usurpers had failed to realise that beneath the magazine was a vault containing more kegs of gunpowder, grenades and other weaponry. These were to be kept for the imminent counterattack, seeing that resistance groups were organising themselves in the hills to make life difficult for the Piedmontese invaders.

His face gradually lit up as he talked about explosives, and his pug-nosed features and gloomy eyes became almost handsome. Then one day he took Simonini to his bunker and, reappearing from an exploration of the vault, he showed him some blackish granules in the palm of his hand.

"Ah, most reverend Father," he said, "there's nothing more beautiful than fine-quality powder. Look at that slate-grey colour. The granules don't crumble when pressed between the fingers. If you had a piece of paper and put the powder on it and ignited it, it would burn without touching the paper. They used to make it with seventy-five parts of saltpetre, twelve of charcoal and twelve of sulphur. Then they moved on to what they called the English blend, which was fifteen parts charcoal and ten of sulphur, and that's how you lose wars because your grenades don't explode. Today we experts (though unfortunately, or thank God, there are few of us) use Chilean nitrate instead of saltpetre, and that's quite another thing."

"Better?"

"It's the best. You see, Father, they're inventing new explosives every day, and each is worse than the other. One of the king's officials (by which I mean the real King) appeared to know everything and told me I should use a brand-new invention, pyroglycerine. He didn't understand that it only works on impact. It's difficult to detonate because you have to be there banging it with a hammer, and you'd be the first to blow up. Let me tell you . . . if you ever want to blow someone up, old-fashioned gunpowder's the only thing. And it makes a fine show."

Master Ninuzzo seemed overjoyed, as if there were nothing more beautiful in the world. Simonini didn't attach much importance there and then to his ramblings. But later on, in January, he thought about it again.

Mulling over ways of getting his hands on the expedition's account books, he reasoned as follows: either the accounts are here in Palermo or they will be back in Palermo when Nievo returns from the north. Nievo will then have to take them back to Turin by sea. It's pointless therefore following him night and day as that won't get me near the secret safe, and even if I do get near the secret safe, I won't be able to open it. If I did get there and opened it, there'd be a scandal, Nievo would report the disappearance of the accounts, and my masters in Turin might be blamed. Nor could I keep the matter quiet even by surprising Nievo with the accounts and knifing him in the back. The dead body of someone like Nievo would always be a cause for embarrassment. They told me in Turin that the accounts had to go up in smoke. But Nievo ought to go up in smoke with them, so that when he disappears (in a way that seems accidental and natural) the disappearance of the accounts fades into the background. Therefore why not burn down or blow up the revenue offices? Too obvious. The only other solution is for Nievo to disappear, along with his accounts, while he's sailing from Palermo to Turin. Nobody would think when fifty or sixty people lose their lives in a disaster at sea that it was done to destroy a few scruffy account books.

It was certainly a bold and imaginative idea. Simonini was apparently growing older and wiser and this was no longer the time for silly games with a few university friends. He had seen war, he was used to seeing death (fortunately that of others) and was most anxious to avoid ending up in the dungeons of those fortresses described by Negri di Saint Front.

Simonini had, of course, thought long and hard about this project, not least because he had nothing else to do. Meanwhile, he spent time with Master Ninuzzo, offering him excellent lunches.

"Master Ninuzzo, you ask why I've come here, and I can tell you that I am here on the orders of the Holy Father, to re-establish the kingdom of our Sovereign of the Two Sicilies."

"Then I'm at your service, Father. Tell me what to do."

"On a certain date – I don't yet know when – a steamship will sail from Palermo to the mainland. It will carry a safe containing orders and plans designed to destroy for ever the authority of the Holy Father and humiliate our King. This steamer must go down before it reaches Turin, with every soul on board."

"Nothing could be simpler, Father. You could use a very recent discovery apparently developed by the Americans. It's called a 'coal torpedo', a bomb that looks like a lump of coal. You hide this lump under the heaps of coal used to fuel the ship, and once it's in the furnace the torpedo heats up and explodes."

"Not bad. But the piece of coal has to be thrown into the furnace at the right moment. The ship mustn't explode too early or too late – in other words as it's leaving or just about to dock – otherwise it would be too obvious. It has to explode halfway through the journey, far from prying eyes."

"That's more difficult. You can't bribe a stoker, since he'd be the first victim, so you'd have to calculate the exact time when a certain quantity of coal is to be put into the furnace. Not even the Witch of Benevento could predict something like that. . . ."

"And so?"

"And so, dear Father, the only solution that never fails is once again a keg of gunpowder with a good fuse."

"But who's going to stay on board to light a fuse knowing the whole thing's going to explode?"

"No one, unless he's an expert. There are – thank God or unfortunately – still a few of us left. The expert can work out the length of the fuse. Fuses were once just pieces of straw filled with black gunpowder, or a sulphur-coated touchpaper, or string soaked in saltpetre and tarred. You never knew how long they'd take to reach the point. But for thirty years or so, thank God, the slow-burning fuse has been available, of which, as it happens, I have a few metres in the crypt."

"And with that?"

"With that you can work out how long it will take from the moment the fuse is lit to when the flame reaches the powder, and you can calculate the time according to the length of the fuse. So that if the artificer, having lit the fuse, knows he can reach a point in the ship where someone is waiting for him with a boat lowered into the water, and the ship blows up when they are a good distance away, then I reckon all would be perfect, a work of art!"

"Master Ninuzzo, there's just one problem. . . . Let's imagine there's a storm that evening, and no one can lower a boat. Would an artificer like you run such a risk?"

"To be honest, Father, no."

No one could ask Master Ninuzzo to go to his almost certain death. But perhaps there was someone less perspicacious than him.

At the end of January, Nievo returned from Milan to Naples, where he had been for a fortnight, perhaps gathering documents there too. He was then ordered to return to Palermo, collect all his account books (thus indicating that he'd left them there) and take them to Turin.

His meeting with Simonini was affectionate and brotherly. Nievo indulged in a few sentimental reflections upon his journey in the north, about that impossible love which had been disastrously, or marvellously, rekindled during this brief visit. . . . Simonini's eyes seemed tearful as he listened to his friend's elegiac stories but in truth all he could think of was how the account books were to leave for Turin.

Finally, Nievo told him. In early March he would be leaving Palermo for Naples aboard the *Ercole*, and from Naples would continue on to Genoa. The *Ercole* was a respectable twin-paddlewheel steamship of English construction with a crew of fifteen and accommodation for several dozen passengers. It had been sailing for many years but its days were not over, it was still a decent vessel. From then on, Simonini was eager to gather as much information as he could. He discovered where her captain, Michele Mancino, was lodging, and with the help of the sailors he was able to get an idea about the internal arrangement of the ship.

Then, having donned his cassock and resumed his priestly air, he returned to Bagheria and took Bronte to one side.

"Bronte," he told him, "a ship is about to leave Palermo for Naples with Nino Bixio on board. Now is the moment for us, the last defenders of the throne, to avenge ourselves for what he did to your town. You have the honour of taking part in his execution."

"Tell me what I have to do."

"Here is a fuse. Its duration has been calculated by someone who knows more about it than you or I. Wrap it around your waist. One of our men, Captain Simonini, an officer of Garibaldi's but secretly loyal to our King, will have loaded on board a chest containing secret military documents, and with instructions that the hold is to be kept under constant guard by one of his trusted men, which is you. The chest is, of course, full of gunpowder. Simonini will be boarding with you. When you arrive at a certain point, within sight of the island of Stromboli, you will be ordered to take out the fuse, lay it and light it. In the meantime he will lower a boat into the sea. The length and thickness of the fuse will allow you to climb out of the hold and reach the stern. Simonini will be waiting for you there, and you will have plenty of time to get away from the ship before she blows up, and that accursed Bixio along with her. But you're not to look for this Simonini, nor must you talk to him if you see him. Ninuzzo will take you to the boat by cart. When you reach the gangplank, you'll find a sailor called Almalò. He'll take you into the hold and you'll remain there quietly until Almalò comes to tell you to do what I've just told you."

Bronte's eyes lit up, but he wasn't entirely stupid. "And if the sea's rough?" he asked.

"If you feel the ship rocking while you're in the hold, don't worry. The ship's dinghy is large and well built, it has a mast and sail, and land will not be far away. And then, if Captain Simonini decides the waves are too high, he won't want to risk his life. You won't receive the order, and he'll kill Bixio another time. But if you receive the order it's because someone, who knows more about the sea than you do, has decided you'll arrive safe and sound at Stromboli."

Enthusiasm and full agreement from Bronte. Long deliberations with Master Ninuzzo to set up the infernal machine. At the appropriate moment, dressed in almost funereal fashion, as people imagine spies and secret agents look, Simonini went to see Captain Mancino with a document of safe conduct covered with stamps and seals, from which it appeared that by order of His Majesty Vittorio Emanuele II he was required to transport a large chest containing top-secret material to Naples. It had to be deposited in the hold so as to merge in with the other cargo and remain inconspicuous, but one of Simonini's trusted men must remain beside it day and night. He was to be received by the sailor Almalò who had on previous occasions carried out important missions for the army, and the captain must otherwise take no interest in the matter. At Naples an infantry officer would arrive to take care of the chest.

The plan was simple, and the operation would not have been noticeable to anyone, especially Nievo who was more interested in looking after his own chest of account books.

The *Ercole* was expected to weigh anchor around one in the afternoon, and the voyage to Naples would last fifteen or sixteen hours. It would be best to blow up the ship when it had reached the island of Stromboli, whose volcano in continual eruption shoots out flames of fire at night, so that even at the first glimmer of dawn the explosion would pass unobserved.

Naturally, Simonini had met Almalò some time earlier. He seemed the most venal of the crew, was purchased for a handsome sum and given the essential instructions. He was to wait for Bronte on the quay and stow him in the hold, along with the chest. "Then," Simonini told him, "towards evening, whatever the state of the sea, look out for the fires of Stromboli on the horizon, climb down into the hold, and tell that man, 'The captain says now's the hour.' Don't worry what he says or does. It's no business of yours. All you need to know is that in the chest he has to find a bottle with a message and throw it from the porthole. Someone will be close by with a boat to recover the bottle and take it to Stromboli. All you have to do is return to your cabin and forget all about it. So, repeat what you have to tell him."

"The captain says now's the hour."

"Well done."

At the moment of departure, Simonini was on the quay to say goodbye to Nievo. It was a touching farewell. "My dearest friend," said Nievo, "you've been my companion for so long, I've bared my soul to you. We may not see each other again. Once I've handed over my accounts in Turin, I'll return to Milan, and there . . . we shall see. I'll think about my novel. Goodbye, let me embrace you. Long live Italy."

"Goodbye my dear Ippolito. I'll always remember you," said Simonini, managing even to shed a tear or two, as his role required.

Nievo had a heavy box unloaded from his carriage, and followed his assistants as they lugged it aboard, careful not to lose sight of it. Shortly after he'd climbed the ship's gangplank, two friends of his, whom Simonini didn't recognise, arrived and urged him not to leave with the *Ercole* which, they said, was unseaworthy. A better ship, the *Elettrico*, was due to set sail the following morning. Simonini had a moment's anxiety, but Nievo shrugged his shoulders, saying that the sooner his documents reached their destination, the better. Shortly afterwards, the *Ercole* left the waters of the harbour.

To suggest that Simonini passed the next hours in cheerful spirit would be to give him too much credit for his cool-headedness. Indeed, he passed the whole day and evening anxiously awaiting the event which he could not have witnessed even from the summit of Punta Raisi outside Palermo. Calculating the time, he reckoned it would all perhaps be over by nine in the evening. He wasn't sure whether Bronte would be able to carry out the orders precisely. He imagined his sailor sighting Stromboli and going down to give the order, the poor fellow bent down inserting the fuse into the chest, setting light to it and running fast up to the stern to find no one there. Perhaps he would realise he'd been tricked and rush down to the hold like a madman (for what else was he?) to snuff out the fuse. But it would be too late and the explosion would have caught him as he returned.

Simonini felt such relief that his mission had been accomplished that he dressed once again in his ecclesiastical garb and returned to the tavern at Bagheria to indulge in a substantial dinner of *pasta con le sarde* and *piscistocco alla ghiotta* (dried cod soaked in cold water for two days and cut into fillets, an onion, a stick of celery, a carrot, a glass of olive oil, chopped tomatoes, pitted black olives, pine nuts, sultanas, pear, desalted capers, salt and pepper).

Then he thought about Master Ninuzzo. . . . It wasn't a good idea to let such a dangerous witness wander free. He climbed back on his mule and returned to the powder magazine. Master Ninuzzo was by the entrance, smoking an old pipe, and welcomed him with a broad smile. "You think it's done, Father?"

"I think so. You should feel very proud, Master

*. . . Calculating the time, he
reckoned it would all perhaps be
over by nine in the evening. . . .*

[PAGE 197]

Ninuzzo," said Simonini, and embraced him saying, "Long live the king," as was the custom in those parts. And as he did so, he thrust twenty inches of dagger into his belly.

Who was to know when the body would be found, seeing that no one passed that way. In the highly unlikely event of the police or anyone else tracing Ninuzzo's movements back to the tavern at Bagheria, they would find he had spent many evenings over the previous months with a priest who enjoyed his food. But the priest would be nowhere to be found, since Simonini was about to leave for the mainland. As for Bronte, no one would be much concerned about his disappearance.

Simonini returned to Turin around mid-March, anxious to see his paymasters – it was time for them to settle the account. Bianco appeared one afternoon in his office, sat down, and said, "You never do anything right, Simonini."

"What do you mean?" Simonini protested. "You wanted the accounts to go up in smoke and I challenge you to find them!"

"That's right, but Colonel Nievo also went up in smoke, and that's more than we intended. There's far too much talk about the disappearance of this ship and I don't know whether we'll be able to keep things quiet. It will be hard to keep the secret service out of this whole business. We'll no doubt work it out in the end, but the only weak link in the chain is you. Sooner or later someone's going to remember you were Nievo's friend at Palermo and – surprise, surprise – that you were working down there for Boggio. Boggio, Cavour, government . . . Good

Lord, I'd hate to think what unsavoury gossip would follow. So you must disappear."

"To the fortress?" Simonini asked.

"Even keeping someone in a fortress could encourage rumours. We don't want to repeat the farce of the man in the iron mask. We're proposing a less theatrical solution. You close up shop here in Turin and disappear abroad. Go to Paris. Regarding initial expenses, half of our agreed remuneration should be sufficient. After all, you went too far, and that's as bad as only doing half the job. And since we cannot suppose you'll survive for long in Paris before getting into trouble, we'll refer you directly to our colleagues there. They may have something for you to do. You'll pass, shall we say, onto the payroll of another administration."

9

PARIS

Since I began this diary I have not been out to a restaurant. This evening to keep my spirits up I decided to go to a place where anyone who met me would have been so drunk that, even if I didn't recognise them, they wouldn't recognise me. It is the cabaret at *Père Lunette*, near here in rue des Anglais, which takes its name from an enormous pair of pince-nez over the entrance – no one knows when or why they were put there.

Rather than providing food, the owners give you bits of cheese to gnaw, almost for free, to make you feel thirsty. Otherwise you drink and sing – or rather the "artistes" Fifi l'Absinthe, Armand le Guelard and Gaston Trois-Pattes sing. The first room is a corridor, half taken up by a long zinc counter, with the landlord, landlady, and a child who sleeps amidst the swearing and laughter of the customers. In front of the counter, along the wall, there is a rough bench where patrons can sit once they have taken a glass. On a shelf behind the counter is the finest collection of gut-rotting concoctions to be found in all Paris. But the real customers go to the room at the end, with two tables around which drunkards sleep on each other's shoulders. The walls have been decorated by customers, and for the most part with obscene drawings.

This evening I sat next to a woman intently drinking her umpteenth absinthe. I thought I recognised her. She had worked as an artist for illustrated magazines but was gradually letting herself go, perhaps because she was consumptive and knew she hadn't long to live. She now offered to do customers' portraits in return for a glass, but her hand trembled. If she's lucky she'll end up falling into the Bièvre one night, before the consumption takes her.

We exchanged a few words (I've been so holed up the past ten days that I found comfort even in conversation with a woman) and each time I offered her a glass of absinthe I could hardly avoid having one myself.

And that is why, as I write, my vision is blurred and my head befuddled – ideal conditions for remembering little and badly.

All I know is that I was naturally apprehensive when I arrived in Paris (after all, I was going into exile), but the city won me over, and I decided I would spend the rest of my life here.

I didn't know how long my money would have to last and so I rented a room in a hotel in the Bièvre district. Fortunately I could afford one to myself – a room in those places often had as many as fifteen straw mattresses and sometimes no window. It was furnished with second-hand odds and ends, the bedding was verminous, there was a zinc bath for washing, a bucket for urine, not even a chair . . . and soap and towels were out of the question. A notice on the wall required the key to be left in the keyhole on the outside, apparently so the police would not have to waste time on their frequent raids, when they would grab sleepers by the hair, peering closely at them by the light of a lantern,

flinging back those they didn't recognise and dragging downstairs those they'd come looking for, after giving a good
thrashing to anyone who tried to put up any kind of
resistance.

As for eating, I found a tavern in rue du Petit Pont where
you could have a meal for a song. All the meat was bad,
having been thrown away by the butchers at Les Halles – the
fat had turned green and the lean meat black . . . it was
salvaged from the bins at dawn, cleaned up, covered with
salt and pepper and steeped in vinegar, then hung for forty-
eight hours in the open air at the far end of the courtyard,
by which time it was ready for the customer. Dysentery
guaranteed, price affordable.

After the life I'd been leading in Turin and the plentiful
meals in Palermo, I would have been dead in a few weeks
if it weren't for the fact that I soon collected my first wages
(as I shall shortly recount) from the people to whom Cavalier
Bianco had sent me. I could now afford to eat at *Noblot*, in
rue de la Huchette. You entered a large room overlooking
an old courtyard, bringing your own bread with you. Close
to the entrance was a cash desk managed by the landlady
and her three daughters, where they kept a tab for the more
expensive dishes – roast beef, cheese, jams, or stewed pear
with two walnuts. Those, such as artisans, penniless artists
or copy clerks, who ordered at least half a litre of wine were
allowed behind the cash desk.

Beyond was a kitchen, where on an enormous stove
simmered mutton ragout, rabbit or beef, puréed peas or
lentils. There was no service: you had to find a plate and
cutlery and queue up in front of the cook. Diners then

pushed and shoved their way, plate in hand, to find a place at the enormous table d'hôte. Two sous for broth, four sous for beef, ten centimes for the bread you'd brought with you – the whole meal would cost forty centimes. It all seemed excellent, and indeed I noticed even respectable people went there for the pleasure of slumming.

Even before I could afford to go to *Noblot*, I didn't mind those first few weeks of hell: I made useful acquaintances and was able to get to know a world in which I would later have to learn to swim like a fish in water. And listening to the talk in the alleyways I found out about other streets in other parts of Paris, such as rue de Lappe, entirely dedicated to ironmongery for artisans and their families, or of a less reputable kind such as instruments for picklocks or skeleton keys, or retractable daggers to be concealed up the sleeve of a jacket.

I stayed in my room as little as possible and only allowed myself the pleasures available to penniless Parisians. So I walked the boulevards. I hadn't realised just how much larger Paris was than Turin. I was enthralled by the sight of so many people of all classes walking beside me. Few of them had any particular errand to perform and most were there just to look at each other. Respectable Parisian women dressed with great taste and if they didn't draw my attention, their hairstyles did. Unfortunately there were also, shall we say, those less respectable women who were most ingenious in inventing ways of dressing up to gain the attention of our sex.

These were the prostitutes, though not of the vulgar sort I was later to encounter in the *brasseries à femmes*. They were

*. . . I was enthralled by the sight
of so many people of all classes
walking beside me. . . .*

[PAGE 204]

strictly for wealthy gentlemen, as was apparent from the devilish techniques they used to seduce their victims. An informant of mine explained that at one time only *grisettes* were seen on the boulevards. These were young women of no particular intelligence, of easy virtue but undemanding, who asked their lovers neither for clothes nor jewellery, knowing the lovers were even poorer than they were. Then, as a breed, they vanished, just like the pug. Later *lorettes*, or *biches* or *cocottes* appeared. These were no more amusing or cultured than *grisettes* but were eager for cashmere and frills. By the time I arrived in Paris, the *lorette* had been replaced by the courtesan: rich lovers, diamonds, carriages. It was rare by then for a courtesan to walk the boulevards. These *dames aux camélias* had decided as a matter of principle to reveal neither heart, nor tenderness, nor gratitude, and to exploit the impotent souls who paid just to display them in their box at the Opéra. What a repulsive sex.

Meanwhile I went to meet Clément Fabre de Lagrange. My former contacts in Turin had directed me to a certain office in an apparently derelict building, in a street which professional discretion prevents me from naming, even on a sheet of paper which no one is ever going to read. I believe that Lagrange was involved with the Political Division of the *Direction Générale de Sûreté Publique*, but I never knew whether he was at the top or bottom of the pyramid. He didn't seem answerable to anyone else and I would be unable, even under torture, to say anything about that political intelligence machine. I wasn't even sure, in fact, whether Lagrange had an office in the building. I wrote to that address informing him that I had a letter of introduction from Cavalier Bianco, and two days later received a card arranging a meeting in place Notre Dame. I would recognise him by a red carnation in his buttonhole. Lagrange thereafter always met me in the most unlikely places – a cabaret, a church, a public garden, and never in the same place twice.

Lagrange needed a particular document at the time and I produced it perfectly for him. He was immediately impressed and from that day I worked for him as an *indicateur*, as it is commonly described around here, receiving three hundred francs each month plus a hundred and thirty for expenses (with a few occasional bonuses and money on top for producing documents). The Empire spends a great deal on its informers, certainly more than the Kingdom of Piedmont, and I've heard it said that out of a police budget of seven million francs a year, two million are set aside for political intelligence. But others say the total budget is fourteen million, which includes the cost of crowds to applaud as the emperor passes, and of groups sent out to keep watch on Mazzini's supporters, as well as agitators and actual spies.

I used to make at least five thousand francs a year with Lagrange, but through him I was introduced to private clients, so that I was soon able to set up my present office (under the cover of dealing in *brocantage*). With forged wills and the sale of consecrated hosts my business brought me another five thousand francs, and with ten thousand francs a year I was what could be described in Paris as a comfortably off bourgeois. These earnings were obviously never secure, and my dream was to make ten thousand francs, not as earned but as unearned income, and with three per cent on State bonds (the safest) I would have to accumulate a capital of three hundred thousand francs. Such a sum might have been possible at that time for a courtesan but not for a completely unknown notary.

While awaiting some stroke of fortune, I could nevertheless transform myself from spectator to active participant in the pleasures of Paris. I have never been interested in the theatre, in those horrible tragedies declaimed in alexandrines, and museum rooms depress me. But Paris offered me something much better – restaurants.

The first place where I wanted to indulge myself was *Le Grand Véfour*, in the arcades of the Palais-Royal. Though extremely expensive, I had heard it praised even in Turin, and Victor Hugo apparently used to go there to eat breast of mutton with haricot beans. The other place which had immediately seduced me was the *Café Anglais*, on the corner of rue de Gramont and the boulevard des Italiens. It had once been a restaurant for coachmen and servants and now served *le tout Paris* at its tables. There I discovered *pommes Anna, écrevisses bordelaises, mousses de volaille, mauviettes en cerises, petites timbales à la Pompadour, cimier de chevreuil, fonds d'artichauts à la jardinière* and champagne sorbets. The mere mention of these names makes me feel that life is worth living.

Apart from the restaurants, I was fascinated by the *passages*. I adored passage Jouffroy, perhaps because it held three of Paris's best restaurants – the *Dîner de Paris*, the *Dîner du Rocher* and the *Dîner Jouffroy*. It seems, even today, that the whole of Paris gathers there, especially on Saturdays, in the glass-covered arcade where you are continually jostled by world-weary gentlemen and ladies who are too heavily scented for my taste.

Perhaps I was more intrigued by passage des Panoramas. The crowd you saw there was more working class, bourgeois and provincial, people who looked longingly at antiques they could never afford, but there were also young girls who had just come out of the factories. If you really must go to ogle petticoats, then the women in passage Jouffroy are better dressed (if that's what you like) but here, wandering up and down watching the factory girls, are the *suiveurs*, middle-aged men who conceal their gaze behind green-tinted glasses. It is doubtful whether all the girls really are factory workers – that they are plainly dressed with a tulle bonnet and pinafore means nothing. Look carefully at their finger-tips. Girls without cuts, scratches or small burns lead a more leisurely life, thanks to the *suiveurs* that they manage to enchant.

It is not the factory girls I gaze at in the arcade, but the *suiveurs* (who said that the philosopher is someone who watches the audience and not the stage at the *café chantant*?). They may one day become my clients, or useful in some way. I even follow some of them home, perhaps to see them being greeted by a fat wife and half a dozen brats. I make a note of their addresses. You never know. I could easily ruin them with an anonymous letter. One day, perhaps, if the need arises.

I remember almost nothing about the various assignments Lagrange gave me in the early years. All I can remember is a name – Abbé Boullan – but that must have been much

*. . . It is not the factory girls
I gaze at in the arcade, but
the* suiveurs *. . .*

[PAGE 209]

later, perhaps even just before or after the war (it had something to do with a war, I believe, with Paris in chaos).

The absinthe is doing its job and if I were to blow on a candle a great flame would spurt from the wick.

10

DALLA PICCOLA PERPLEXED

3rd April 1897

Dear Captain Simonini,

This morning I woke with a heavy head and a strange taste in my mouth. God forgive me . . . it was the taste of absinthe! I assure you, I hadn't yet read your account of last night. How could I know what you had been drinking unless I'd drunk it myself? And how could a priest recognise the taste of something forbidden and therefore unfamiliar? Or perhaps my head is confused. Perhaps I'm writing about the taste I felt in my mouth when I woke up, but am writing after reading your diary, and what you wrote has influenced me. I have, in fact, never tasted absinthe, so how could I know that the taste in my mouth is absinthe? It is the taste of something else, which your diary has induced me to think is absinthe.

Oh, good Lord, the fact remains that I woke in my own bed, and everything seemed normal, as if I had done nothing else all last month. Except that I knew I had to go to your apartment. Having reached there, or rather here, I read those pages of your diary, which I hadn't yet seen. I saw your mention of Boullan and some vague, confused picture came to mind.

I repeated that name aloud, several times, and it produced a sudden flash in my mind, as if your Drs Bourru and Burot had touched a piece of magnetised metal to some part of my body, or a Dr Charcot had waved – I don't know what – a finger, a key, a hand before my eyes and had sent me into a state of lucid somnambulism.

I saw the image of a priest spitting into the mouth of a woman possessed.

11

JOLY

From the diary for 3rd April 1897, late at night

That page in Dalla Piccola's diary ended abruptly. Perhaps he had heard a noise, maybe a door opening downstairs, and must have vanished. Please understand that the Narrator is himself puzzled. Abbé Dalla Piccola seems to reawaken only when Simonini needs a voice of conscience to accuse him of becoming distracted and to bring him back to reality, otherwise he appears somewhat forgetful. To be frank, if it were not for the fact that these pages refer to events which actually took place, such alternations between amnesic euphoria and dysphoric recall might seem like a device of the Narrator.

In the spring of 1865, Lagrange summoned Simonini to meet him one morning on a park bench in the Jardin du Luxembourg and showed him a tattered book with yellowish cover which appeared to have been published in October 1864 in Brussels, with the title *Dialogue aux enfers entre Machiavel et Montesquieu ou la politique de Machiavel au XIXe siècle, par un contemporain.*

"Here," he said. "It's by a certain Maurice Joly. We know who he is and found him smuggling copies of the book into France. He'd had them printed abroad and was distributing them secretly. We had some difficulty catching him, or perhaps I should say it took time but wasn't difficult, since many smugglers of political material are agents of ours. You should know that the only way of controlling a subversive sect is by taking over its command, or at least having its ringleaders in our pay. You don't find out about the plans of enemies of the State by divine inspiration. Someone said, perhaps exaggerating, that out of every ten followers of a secret society, three of them are working for us as *mouchards* – please excuse the expression but that is what they're commonly called – while six are fools who completely believe in what they're doing, and one man is dangerous. But let us not digress. Joly is now in prison, at Sainte-Pélagie, and we'll keep him there as long we can. But we're interested in finding out where he got his information."

"What's the book about?"

"I must admit I haven't read it. It's over five hundred pages long, which is a mistake – any defamatory work ought to be readable in half an hour. One of our agents who specialises in these matters, a certain Lacroix, has prepared us a summary. But I'll give you the only other surviving copy. In these pages you'll find an imaginary dialogue in hell between Machiavelli and Montesquieu, where Machiavelli proposes a cynical vision of power, and supports the legitimacy of a course of actions aimed at curbing the freedom of the press and freedom of expression, and all those other things espoused by republicans. He does so in such detail, with such relevance to our own times, that even the simplest reader can see that the object of the tract is to defame our emperor, alleging that he seeks to thwart the powers of the National

Assembly, to ask the people to extend the power of the President by ten years, to transform the Republic into an empire. . . ."

"Please excuse me, Monsieur Lagrange – we are speaking in confidence and you are well aware of my devotion to the government – but I cannot help noting from what you say that this Joly alludes to matters which the emperor has actually done, and I don't see why we need ask where Joly got his information from. . . ."

"But the insinuations in Joly's book are not just about what the government has done but what it may be proposing to do, as if Joly is able to see certain things not from the outside but from within. You see, in every ministry, in every government office, there's always a mole, a *sous-marin*, who reveals information. He is usually allowed to remain there so he can leak false information that the ministry wishes to circulate, but sometimes he may become dangerous. We must find out who is informing Joly or, worse still, who has trained him."

Despotic governments, Simonini reflected, all follow the same logic – it was enough to read Machiavelli in order to understand what Napoleon would do. But this reflection led him to another thought which had crossed his mind during Lagrange's description of the book. Joly had made his Machiavelli-Napoleon use almost the same words that he, Simonini, had put into the mouths of the Jesuits in the document he'd created for the secret service in Piedmont. Evidently Joly had been influenced by the same source, in other words Father Rodin's letter to Father Roothaan in Sue's *Les Mystères du Peuple*.

"And so," continued Lagrange, "we are proposing to have you taken to Sainte-Pélagie as one of Mazzini's political exiles suspected of having links with French republican groups. There's a prisoner, a certain Gaviali, who was involved in Orsini's bomb attack. It's natural that you, being a follower of Garibaldi, a Carbonaro or whatever else, would try to make contact with him. Through Gaviali you'll get to know Joly. There's a fellow feeling among political prisoners. They're alone among villains of every kind. Get him to talk – the prison inmates bore him."

"And how long am I to stay there?" Simonini asked, concerned about what he would have to eat.

"That depends on you. The sooner you get the information, the sooner you leave. The word will be that the examining magistrate has acquitted you on all charges thanks to the skill of your lawyer."

Prison was something Simonini hadn't yet experienced. With the stink of sweat and urine, and soup that made you retch, it was not very pleasant. Simonini, thank God, like other prisoners in respectable financial circumstances, was able to receive a daily food basket.

As one entered from the courtyard, there was a large hall dominated by a central stove, with benches around the walls. Those receiving food from outside generally took their meals here. Some ate hunched over their baskets, using their hands to protect their dinner from the sight of their compatriots, while others showed more generosity towards their friends and any casual neighbours. Simonini realised that the kinder ones were either the hardened criminals, who had developed a solidarity with their fellow inmates, or they were political prisoners.

Through his years in Turin, his experience in Sicily and his first years in the most disreputable backstreets of Paris, he had gained sufficient experience to recognise the born criminal. He did not share the views which had begun to circulate at the time that all criminals were supposed to be runtish, or hunchbacked, or harelipped or scrofulous or, as the celebrated Vidocq had suggested (and Vidocq knew a thing or two about criminals, not least because he was one himself), were all bow-legged. But they certainly presented many characteristics typical of the coloured races, such as lack of body hair, small cranial capacity, receding forehead, well-developed chest, highly pronounced protruding jaw and cheekbones, squint-eyes, swarthy complexion, thick curly hair, large ears, uneven teeth, as well as emotional indifference, exaggerated passion for carnal pleasures and for wine, lack of sensitivity to pain, laziness, impulsiveness, improvidence, great vanity, passion for gambling and superstition.

Not to mention characters such as the one who sat next to him each day, as if to beg some morsel from his basket, his face etched all over by deep, livid scars, his lips swollen by the corrosive action of vitriol; the bridge of his nose slashed, his nostrils replaced by two formless holes, his arms long, hands stubby and broad, with hairs down to the fingers. . . . Except that Simononi was obliged to change his ideas about the marks of delinquency upon meeting a fellow by the name of Oreste who showed himself to be a man of such mildness and became, after

. . . That was how Simonini
identified Gaviali, and came
to meet him. . . .

[PAGE 220]

Simonini had eventually offered him some of his food, so affectionate as to demonstrate an almost canine devotion towards him.

His story was quite straightforward: he had simply strangled a girl who had not appreciated his advances, and was now awaiting sentence. "I don't know why she was so nasty," he said. "I'd asked to marry her, after all. And she had laughed. As if I was a monster. I'm really sorry she's gone but what else could a self-respecting man do in the circumstances? If I can avoid the guillotine, I suppose hard labour won't be so bad. They say you get plenty to eat."

One day he pointed someone out to me. "That one there," he said, "he's really bad. He tried to kill the emperor."

That was how Simonini identified Gaviali, and came to meet him.

"You conquered Sicily thanks to our sacrifice," said Gaviali. And then he corrected himself. "Or rather, not mine. They couldn't prove anything against me, except that I'd had contact with Orsini. Orsini and Pieri were guillotined, Di Rudio was sent to Cayenne. But if all goes well, I'll soon be out."

Everyone knew about Orsini, an Italian patriot who had gone to England and come back with six bombs packed with fulminate of mercury. On the 14th of January 1858, as Napoleon III was on his way to the theatre, Orsini and two companions threw three bombs at the emperor's carriage, but they failed to hit their target – a hundred and fifty-seven people were injured, eight of whom died, but the emperor and empress escaped unhurt.

Before going to the scaffold Orsini wrote a moving letter to the emperor urging him to defend the unity of Italy, and many said that this letter had had some influence on Napoleon III's later policies.

"I was originally the one who was supposed to make the bombs," said Gaviali, "along with a group of friends who, I may say, were geniuses when it came to explosives. But Orsini wasn't sure. Foreigners, you know, are always better than us, and he took a fancy to a certain Englishman, who took a fancy to fulminate of mercury. You could buy the ingredients in any chemist's shop in London, where they were used for making daguerreotypes, and here in France they put it into the paper used for making 'Chinese bonbons' so that when you unwrapped them, bang, there was a big explosion – what fun. The trouble is that a bomb with a detonating explosive is not very effective unless it explodes on contact with the target. A gunpowder bomb would have produced large shards of metal shrapnel which would have covered a radius of ten metres, whereas a fulminate bomb disintegrates immediately and it kills you only if you're there where it falls. And at that point it's better to use a bullet, which goes as far as it goes."

"You could always try again," suggested Simonini, and then added, "I know someone who'd be interested in the services of a group of good explosives experts."

The Narrator is not sure why Simonini dangled this bait. Did he already have something in mind or did he dangle bait out of instinct, habit, or prudence, since you never know what might happen? In any event Gaviali was enthusiastic. "Let's talk about it," he said. "I'm told you'll soon be out of here, and so should I. Come and see me at *Père Laurette* in rue de la Huchette. I go there most evenings with my friends. It's a place where the gendarmes have stopped bothering us – they'd end up having to put all the regulars in prison, and that would be too much work and, besides, it's a place where a gendarme can go in but can't be sure of getting out."

"What a place," Simonini laughed. "I'll be there. But tell me, I've heard there's a certain Joly here who's written malicious things about the emperor."

"He's an idealist," said Gaviali. "Words don't kill. But he's probably a good enough fellow. I'll introduce you."

Joly was dressed in clothes that were still clean and he had obviously found some way of shaving. When the privileged inmates arrived with their food baskets, he generally left the hall with the stove, keeping his own solitary company so as not to suffer the sight of other people's good fortune. He seemed about the same age as Simonini, had the piercing gaze of a visionary, though cloaked with sadness, and appeared to be a man of many contradictions.

"Sit with me," Simonini told him. "Take something from my basket. It's too much for me. I could see straight away that you're not one of this bunch."

Joly thanked him silently with a smile, was pleased to accept a piece of meat and a slice of bread, but kept to generalities. "Thank goodness my sister hasn't forgotten me," said Simonini. "She's not rich but she looks after me well."

"Lucky you," replied Joly. "I have no one."

The ice had been broken. They spoke about Garibaldi's epic deeds which the French had been following with great excitement. Simonini referred to his difficulties first with the Piedmont government and then with the French, and here he was now awaiting trial for conspiracy against the State. Joly said he was in prison not even for conspiracy but through a simple enjoyment of gossip.

"To imagine that we are a necessary part in the order of the universe is, for well-read people like us, the same as superstition is for uncultured people. You cannot change the world through ideas. People with few ideas are less likely to make mistakes; they follow what everyone else does and are no trouble to anyone; they're successful, make money, find good jobs, enter politics, receive honours; they become famous writers, academics, journalists. Can anyone who is so good at looking after their own interests really be stupid? I'm the stupid one, the one who wanted to go tilting at windmills."

By their third meal Joly was still reluctant to get to the point and so Simonini tried to prompt him a little further by asking what sort of dangerous book he could have written. Joly began to describe his *Dialogue in Hell* and, as he did so, became more and more indignant about the iniquities he had exposed, naming them one by one and analysing them in greater detail than he had done in his tract.

"Tyranny, you understand, has been achieved thanks to universal suffrage! The scoundrel has carried out an authoritarian *coup d'état* by appealing to the ignorant mob! This is a warning to us about the democracy of tomorrow."

"Quite right," thought Simonini. "This Napoleon is a man for our times. He understands how to keep a grip on people who only seventy years ago were getting excited about the idea of cutting off a king's head. Lagrange might well think that Joly had had his informers, but what is clear is that he used simple facts that were plain for all to see, so as to anticipate the dictator's next moves. More importantly, I'd like to know what he actually used as a model."

So Simonini made a veiled reference to Sue and to Father Rodin's letter. Joly immediately smiled, almost blushing, and admitted that the idea for portraying Napoleon's sinful plans was inspired by Sue's description of them, except that he thought it more useful to date the Jesuitical influence back to classical Machiavellianism.

"When I read Sue's book I realised I had found the key to writing something that would shake this country. What folly. Books are seized, they're destroyed, and you . . . it's as if you've done nothing. And I'd forgotten that Sue was forced into exile for saying even less."

Simonini felt he'd been deprived of something that was his. It is true that he too had copied his Jesuit discourse from Sue, though no one knew that, and he wanted to use this model of conspiracy again for other ends. And here was Joly taking it from him, bringing it into the public domain, so to speak.

Then he calmed down. Joly's book had been confiscated and he held one of the few copies still in circulation. Joly would still be in prison for a few more years, by which time Simonini would have copied the whole book, using its contents perhaps to support a conspiracy by Cavour, or by the Prussian chancellery. Nobody would realise it, not even Lagrange, who at most would recognise that the document was credible. The secret service in each country believes only what it has already heard elsewhere and would discount as unreliable any information that is entirely new. He could relax. He was in the fortunate position of knowing what Joly had told him, without anyone else knowing anything about it . . . except for Lacroix, to whom Lagrange had given the task of reading the *Dialogue in Hell* – the only one brave enough to read all of it. All he had to do, then, was eliminate Lacroix and that would be that.

Meanwhile, the time had come for his release from Sainte-Pélagie. He went to find Joly, bidding him farewell with brotherly warmth. Joly was greatly moved and said, "Perhaps you could do me a service. I have a friend, a man called Guédon. He may not know I'm here. Perhaps he might send me a basket of something decent to eat every now and then. That disgusting soup is giving me stomach ache and dysentery."

He told him he would find Guédon in a bookshop in rue de Beaune owned by Mademoiselle Beuque, where a group of Fourierists met. Fourierists, so far as Simonini knew, were socialists who sought to reform the human race, but without a revolution, and were therefore held in scorn by communists and conservatives alike. But Mademoiselle Beuque's bookshop, it seemed, had become a safe haven for all republicans who stood against the Empire, and they could meet there undisturbed because the police thought the Fourierists would not hurt a fly.

On leaving prison, Simonini hastened to present his report to Lagrange. He had no interest in making Joly's position any worse. After all, he felt almost sorry for that Don Quixote.

"Monsieur de Lagrange," he said, "our man is just a naive fellow hoping for a moment of fame, and everything has gone wrong for him. I had the impression that if he hadn't been encouraged by a certain colleague of yours, he wouldn't even have thought of writing his tract. And his source of information, it pains me to say, is Lacroix himself. You say he read the book in order to prepare a summary of it, but he'd probably read it, so to speak, even before it was written. Perhaps it was he who'd arranged for it to be printed in Brussels. Though why he did it I have no idea."

"No doubt on the instructions of some foreign service, perhaps the Prussians, to create unrest in France. I'm not surprised."

"A Prussian agent in a department such as yours? I find that hard to believe."

"Stieber, the head of Prussian espionage, has received nine million thalers to cover the whole of France with spies. He is said to have sent five thousand Prussian peasants and nine thousand domestic servants to France in order to have agents in cafés, restaurants, in the families that count, everywhere. It's not true, mind you. Very few of their spies are Prussian, or even Alsatian – they'd be recognised straight away by their accent. Most of them are good Frenchmen who do it for money."

"And can't you identify and arrest these traitors?"

"It's not worth it. They'd only arrest ours. You don't deal with spies by killing them, but by passing them false information. And to do this we need people who act as double agents. Having said this, your information about Lacroix is quite new to me. Heavens above, what a world we live in. No one's to be trusted – we must be rid of him straight away."

"But if you put him on trial, neither he nor Joly will admit a thing."

"No one working for us must ever appear in a court of law and – excuse me if I state a general rule – this applies just as well to you. Lacroix will be the victim of an accident. His widow will have a proper pension."

Simonini didn't mention Guédon and the bookshop in rue de Beaune. He preferred to wait and see what he might find out from his visit there. He had also been exhausted by his few days in Sainte-Pélagie.

So he went at the earliest opportunity to *Laperouse*, in quai des Grands-Augustins, and not downstairs, where they served oysters and entrecôtes as they used to, but upstairs, in one of the *cabinets particuliers* where you could order *barbue sauce hollandaise, casserole de riz à la Toulouse, aspics de filets de laperaux en chaud-froid, truffes au champagne, pudding d'abricots à la Vénitienne, corbeille de fruits frais,* and *compotes de pêches et d'ananas.*

And to the devil with those convicts – idealists, murderers or whoever they were – and their soup. Prisons are there to ensure that a gentleman can go to a restaurant without coming to any harm.

Simonini's recollections here, as in similar instances, become confused, and some passages in his diary are disjointed. All the Narrator can do is rely upon comments added by Abbé Dalla Piccola. The two are now working at full pace and in perfect coordination. . . .

In short, Simonini realised that to be viewed favourably by the imperial service he had to give Lagrange something more. What makes a police informer truly believable? Discovering a conspiracy. He therefore had to organise a conspiracy so that he could then uncover it.

It was Gaviali who had given him the idea. Simonini went to Sainte-Pélagie and learned when he was to be released. He remembered where he would find him – at *Cabaret Père Laurette* in rue de la Huchette.

Towards the end of the road, you entered a house through a narrow opening, though hardly narrower than rue du Chat qui Pêche which led off from the same rue de la Huchette, and indeed so narrow that it was hard to understand why they had made it so, seeing that you had to enter sideways. At the top of the staircase, you walked along corridors whose stone paving exuded grease, with doorways so low that it was hard to imagine how anyone could enter the rooms. On the second floor,

. . . sitting at a table with
companions who seemed to share
his regicidal ideas, almost all of
them Italian exiles, and almost all
experts in explosives . . .

[PAGE 230]

through a rather more practicable doorway, you reached a large room, created perhaps by knocking together three or more former apartments. This was the salon or hall or cabaret of Père Laurette, whom no one knew because he was thought to have died some years earlier.

There were tables all around, crowded with pipe smokers, lansquenet players and girls prematurely wrinkled, with pallid complexions, as if they were dolls for poor children, who were interested only in finding customers who hadn't quite finished their glass so that they could beg them for the last drop.

There was a commotion on the evening when Simonini arrived – someone in the area had stabbed someone else and the smell of blood seemed to have created a general tension. At a certain point a madman with a cobbler's knife stabbed one of the girls, hurled the landlady to the ground when she tried to intervene, lashed out at whoever tried to stop him, and was brought down only when a waiter smashed a carafe over the back of his head. After which everyone returned to what they had been doing earlier, as if nothing had happened.

Simonini found Gaviali sitting at a table with companions who seemed to share his regicidal ideas, almost all of them Italian exiles, and almost all experts in explosives, or enthusiasts. Once those around the table had had a reasonable amount to drink, they held forth on the failings of great terrorists of the past. The infernal machine, with which Cadoudal had tried to assassinate Napoleon when he was still First Consul, was a mixture of saltpetre and grapeshot which might have worked in the narrow backstreets of the old capital but would be totally useless today (as indeed it had been even then). Fieschi, in order to assassinate Louis Philippe, had built a machine with eighteen barrels that all fired at the same time, and had killed eighteen people, but not the king.

"The problem," said Gaviali, "is the composition of the explosive. Look at potassium chlorate. They decided to mix it with sulphur and charcoal to make gunpowder, but all they managed to do, once they'd built a factory to produce it, was to blow the whole place up. Then they decided it could be used at least for making matches, but to light them you had to dip the chlorate and sulphur match head in sulphuric acid. Not exactly easy. Until the Germans invented phosphorous matches more than thirty years ago, which burst into flame on friction."

"And what about picric acid," said another. "They realised that it blew up when heated with potassium chlorate and this led to a series of powders, each more explosive than the other. Several experimenters were killed and the idea had to be abandoned. It would have been better with cellulose nitrate. . . ."

"Of course."

"Look at what the old alchemists had to say. They discovered that a mixture of nitric acid and oil of turpentine, after a while, burst into flame spontaneously. It's been a hundred years since they discovered that when sulphuric acid, which absorbs water, is added to nitric acid, it almost always ignites."

"I'd be more minded towards xyloïdine. Combine nitric acid with starch or wood fibres . . ."

"It sounds as if you've just read that novel by Verne where he uses xyloïdine to shoot a manned projectile to the moon. But today there's more interest in nitrobenzene and nitro-naphthalene. Or if you treat paper and cardboard with nitric acid you obtain nitramidine, which is similar to xyloïdine."

"All these products are unstable. Perhaps there's more interest today in guncotton – weight for weight, its explosive power is six times greater than that of gunpowder."

"But it's unreliable."

And so they continued for hours, always returning to the virtues of good honest gunpowder and, for Simonini, it seemed as if he was back in Sicily, in conversation with Ninuzzo.

After offering them a few jugs of wine, it was easy to rouse that bunch into hatred for Napoleon III, who was likely to oppose the now imminent Savoy invasion of Rome. The cause of a unified Italy required the death of the dictator. Simonini had the feeling that those drunkards didn't care much about the unification of Italy and were more interested in exploding a few good bombs. But they were also the type of maniacs he was looking for.

"Orsini's attack had failed," explained Simonini, "not because he couldn't carry it out but because the bombs were badly made. We now have someone who's prepared to risk the guillotine to throw a few bombs at the right moment, but we don't yet have a clear idea about the type of explosive to use, and my conversations with our friend Gaviali have convinced me that your group could be very useful."

"Who do you mean when you say 'we'?" asked one of the patriots.

Simonini gave the impression of hesitating, then came out with the story he had concocted to gain the trust of his student friends in Turin – that he represented the *Alta Vendita* and was one of the lieutenants of the elusive Nubius, but they could ask him no more since the Carbonari were organised in such a way that each of them knew only their immediate superior. The problem was that you couldn't produce new bombs of assured effectiveness just like that – it required experiment after experiment, the work almost of an alchemist, mixing the right substances and testing them in open countryside. He was able to offer them a place, right there in rue de la Huchette, where they wouldn't be disturbed, and all necessary money for expenses. As soon as the bombs were ready, the group need not be involved in the attack but the premises would also be used to store handbills announcing the death of the emperor and explaining the attackers' purposes. Once Napoleon was dead, the group would have to distribute the handbills in various parts of the city and leave some of them outside the offices of the main newspapers.

"You'll have no trouble. There's someone in high office who will look favourably upon the attack. One of our men working for the prefect of police is called Lacroix. I'm not sure he's completely reliable, so don't try to contact him. If he finds out who you are then he'd be quite capable of reporting you, just to get promotion. You know what these double agents are like. . . ."

The deal was accepted with enthusiasm, and Gaviali's eyes sparkled with delight. Simonini gave them the keys to the premises and a large sum of money for the initial purchases. A few days later he went to visit the conspirators. It seemed the experiments were proceeding well. He took with him several hundred handbills produced by an obliging printer, gave them another sum of money for their expenses, cried, "Long live united Italy – Rome or death," and left.

That evening, as he was walking along rue Saint-Séverin, deserted at that hour, he thought he heard footsteps behind him. And when he stopped, the sound behind him also stopped. He quickened his pace, but the sound came nearer and nearer until it was clear that somebody was not just tailing him, but closing in. All of a sudden he heard a gasp of breath at his shoulder, was struck violently and flung into impasse della Salembrière, a passageway even narrower than rue du Chat qui Pêche, which led off from rue Saint-Séverin at that very point. His pursuer, it seemed, knew the area well and had chosen exactly the right moment and place. Flattened against the wall, all Simonini could see was the glint of a knife blade against his face. His assailant's features were hidden in the darkness but he had no difficulty in recognising the voice, with its Sicilian accent, hissing, "Six years it's taken me to hunt you down, my good Father, but I've done it!"

It was the voice of Master Ninuzzo, whom Simonini was quite sure he had left with twenty inches of dagger in his stomach, at the powder magazine in Bagheria.

"I'm alive, you see, thanks to a merciful soul who was passing in those parts just after you, and came to my rescue. I spent three months between life and death. There's a scar on my stomach that goes from one hip to the other. . . . But as soon as I got up from my bed I began my search, looking for anyone who'd seen a priest of such and such an appearance. . . . It turned out that someone had seen him at a café in Palermo talking to Notaio Musumeci and thought he looked very much like one of Garibaldi's men from Piedmont who was a friend of Colonel Nievo. Then I get to hear that Nievo had been lost at sea, as if his ship had disappeared into thin air, and I knew all too well how and why it had disappeared, and who'd done it. From there it was easy to trace him to the army of Piedmont, and then to Turin, and I spent a bitterly cold year in that city questioning everyone. Finally I found out that this Garibaldino's name was Simonini, who ran a notary's office. But he'd sold it, letting slip to the purchaser that he was leaving for Paris. I still had no money, and somehow – don't ask me how I did it – I got to Paris, except that I had no idea the city was so big. I was wandering about for a long time before I tracked you down. And I made my living on streets like these, holding a knife to the throat of any well-dressed gentleman who'd taken a wrong turn – one a day was enough to keep me alive. And I always wandered these parts, imagining that someone like you would go to the *tapis francs,* as they call them here, rather than to decent places. . . . You should have grown a fine black beard if you didn't want to be recognised so easily. . . ."

It was from that time onwards that Simonini adopted his bearded bourgeois appearance, but at that juncture he had to admit he had done far too little to cover his tracks.

"But I'm not here to tell you my whole history," Ninuzzo concluded. "All I want is to slash your stomach in just the same way as you did to me . . . but I'll do it properly this time. No one passes here at night . . . just like that powder magazine at Bagheria."

The moon had just risen and Simonini could now see Ninuzzo's bulldog nose and evil glistening eyes.

"Ninuzzo," he had the presence of mind to say, "what you don't know is that I did what I did in obedience to orders – orders from very high up, and from an authority so sacred that I had to carry them out without any care for my own personal feelings. And it is still in obedience to those orders that I am here, to prepare other actions in support of throne and altar."

Simonini was panting breathlessly as he spoke, but saw that the point of the knife was very gradually moving away from his face. "You have dedicated your life to your king," he continued, "and you must understand that there are missions – sacred missions, let me say – when it is justifiable to carry out an act that could never otherwise be pardoned. You understand?"

Master Ninuzzo still didn't understand, but indicated that vengeance was no longer his only purpose: "My stomach's been empty for too long, and seeing you dead isn't enough. I'm fed up living in the dark. Since I caught up with you I've seen you even going into gentlemen's restaurants. Shall we say I'll let you live in exchange for a sum of money each month, enough for me to eat and sleep like you, and better than you."

"Master Ninuzzo, I promise you more than a small sum each month. I'm preparing an attack on the French emperor – and remember, your king lost his throne due to Napoleon's secret help to Garibaldi. You know a great deal about gunpowder – you should meet the group of valiant men who are working together in rue de la Huchette to prepare what can truly be called an infernal machine. If you join up with them, you'll take part not only in an act that will go down in history, while also proving your extraordinary ability as an explosives expert, but – remembering that this attack is being supported by people at the highest level – you'll have your share of a reward that will make you rich for the rest of your days."

The mention of gunpowder was enough to calm the rage which had festered within Ninuzzo since that night at Bagheria, and Simonini realised he had him in the palm of his hand when he asked, "So what do I have to do?"

"It's simple. In two days' time, around six o'clock, go to this address, knock, enter the warehouse and say that Lacroix has sent you. Our friends will be expecting you. But you must wear a carnation in the buttonhole of your jacket so they'll recognise you. I will arrive around seven – with money."

"I'll be there," said Ninuzzo, "but remember – if it's a trick, I know where you live."

Next morning Simonini returned to Gaviali and warned him that time was pressing. They should all be there at six the following afternoon. First of all, a Sicilian explosives expert would arrive, sent by Simonini to examine the state of progress. He would appear shortly afterwards, then Monsieur Lacroix himself, to give all necessary guarantees.

Then he went to Lagrange and told him he had information about a conspiracy to kill the emperor. He knew that the plotters would be meeting at six o'clock the following day in rue de la Huchette to hand over the explosives to the people they were working for.

"But beware," he said. "You once told me that out of every ten members of a secret society, three of them are spies working for us, six are fools and one is dangerous. Well, you'll find only one spy there, which is me, eight of them are fools, but the one who's really dangerous will be wearing a carnation in his buttonhole. And since he's also a danger to me, I'd like a small disturbance to break out, and this fellow not to be arrested but killed on the spot. Believe me, it is a way of making sure this business causes as little fuss as possible. Heaven help us if he starts talking, even to one of your people."

"I accept what you say, Simonini," said Lagrange. "The man will be eliminated."

Ninuzzo arrived in rue de la Huchette at six o'clock, wearing a fine carnation, Gaviali and the others proudly showed him their bombs, and Simonini arrived half an hour later announcing the arrival of Lacroix. At six forty-five the police burst in. Simonini shouted out that they'd been betrayed and pointed a pistol at the police, but he fired in the air. The police replied and hit Ninuzzo in the chest. And since everything had to be done properly they also killed another conspirator. Ninuzzo was still rolling about on the ground, uttering colourful Sicilian blasphemies, when Simonini, pretending once more to shoot at the police, delivered the *coup de grâce*.

Lagrange and his men had caught Gaviali and the others red-handed, with the prototypes of half-constructed bombs and a pile of handbills explaining why they were making them. During some pressing interrogation, Gaviali and his companions gave the name of the mysterious Lacroix who had betrayed them (or so they thought). One more reason why Lagrange decided to get rid of him. The police report suggested he'd been involved in arresting the conspirators and had been killed from a shot fired by one of the villains. An honourable commendation.

As for the conspirators, it seemed pointless attracting publicity with a trial. There were continual rumours of attacks on the emperor at that time, as Lagrange explained to Simonini, and it was thought that many of these stories were not genuine but had been cunningly circulated by republican agents to encourage fanatics to follow suit. It was useless creating the idea that attacks on the life of Napoleon III had become a popular sport. The conspirators were therefore shipped off to Cayenne where they would die of malarial fever.

Saving the life of the emperor had been most profitable. While the Joly assignment was worth ten thousand francs, discovering the conspiracy brought Simonini another thirty thousand. Rental of the warehouse and purchase of the bomb-making materials had cost him five thousand francs, leaving him a clear thirty-five thousand francs – more than a tenth of that three hundred thousand capital he was hoping for.

Though pleased with what had happened to Ninuzzo, he felt rather sorry for Gaviali. He was, after all, a good sort who had placed his trust in him. But anyone involved in conspiracies has to accept the risks, and trust no one.

And it was a shame about Lacroix who, after all, had done no wrong. But his widow would get a good pension out of it.

12

A NIGHT IN PRAGUE

4th April 1897

All that remained was for me to approach Guédon, the man
Joly had spoken about. The bookshop in rue de Beaune was
run by a wizened old maid, always dressed in an immense
black woollen skirt and a bonnet, like something from Little
Red Riding Hood, which half covered her face . . . and a
good thing too.

I immediately came across Guédon, a sceptic who looked
mockingly upon the world around him. I like unbelievers.
Guédon immediately responded favourably to Joly's plea,
saying he would send him food and a little money. Then
he joked about the friend he was about to help. Why write
a book and run the risk of prison when those who read
books were already republicans by nature, and those who
supported the dictator were illiterate peasants who'd been
granted universal suffrage by the grace of God?

The Fourierists? They're good people, but how can you
believe in a prophet who declares that in a new world oranges
would be grown in Warsaw, seas would become lemonade,
men would grow tails, and incest and homosexuality would
be recognised as the most natural human impulses?

"So why then do you mix with them?" I asked.

"Because they're still the only honest people standing
up against Bonaparte's infamous dictatorship," he replied.

"You see that fine lady across there. She is Juliette

Lamessine, one of the most influential women in Countess d'Agoult's salon, and with her husband's money she's trying to establish her own salon in rue de Rivoli. She's charming, intelligent, and a writer of considerable talent; an invitation to her house would be something indeed."

Guédon pointed out another tall, handsome, imposing figure: "That's Toussenel, the celebrated author of *L'Esprit des bêtes*. He's a socialist, a staunch republican and madly in love with Juliette, who won't even look at him. But he has the most brilliant mind here."

Toussenel spoke to me about capitalism, which was poisoning modern society.

"And who are the capitalists? The Jews, the rulers of our time. The Revolution last century cut off the head of Louis Capet. This century's revolution ought to cut off the head of Moses. I shall write a book about it. Who are the Jews? They're all those who suck the blood out of the defenceless, the people. They're Protestants, Freemasons. And, of course, the people of Judah."

"But Protestants are not Jews," I ventured.

"Jew and Protestant are the same. The English Methodists, the German Pietists, the Swiss and the Dutch all learn to read the will of God from the same book as the Jews – the Bible, a story of incest and massacres and barbarous wars, where the only way to win is through treachery and deception, where kings have men murdered so they can take their wives, where women who call themselves saints enter the beds of enemy generals and cut off their heads. Cromwell had the head of his king cut off while quoting the Bible. Malthus, who denied the children of the poor the right to life, was steeped in the Bible. It's a race which spends its time recalling its slavery, and which is always ready to yield to the cult of the golden calf ignoring every sign of divine wrath. The battle against the Jews ought to be the main purpose of every socialist worthy of the name. I am not talking about communists – their founder is a Jew. But the problem is exposing the conspiracy of money. Why does an apple in a Paris restaurant cost a hundred times more than in Normandy? There are unscrupulous races who live on the flesh of others, merchant races like the ancient Phoenicians and Carthaginians. And today it's the English and the Jews."

"So for you, the Englishman and the Jew are the same?"

"Almost. You ought to read what a leading English politician has written in his novel *Coningsby* – a certain Disraeli, a Sephardic Jew who converted to Christianity. He had the temerity to write that the Jews were going to take over the world."

The following day he brought me a book by Disraeli, in which he had underlined whole passages: "You never observe a great intellectual movement in Europe in which the Jews do not greatly participate. The first Jesuits were Jews. That mysterious Russian diplomacy which so alarms Western Europe, who is running it? The Jews! Who is taking over almost all of the professorial chairs of Germany?

"Note that Disraeli is not a *mouchard* who is denouncing his own people. On the contrary, he is praising their virtues. He writes quite shamelessly that the Russian minister of finance, Count Cancrin, is the son of a Lithuanian Jew, in the same way that the Spanish minister Mendizábal is the son of a convert from Aragon. Soult, an imperial marshal in Paris, is the son of a French Jew, and Massena was also a Jew, whose original name was Manesseh. . . . And there again, that mighty revolution being plotted at this very moment in Germany, who is behind it? The Jews. Look at Karl Marx and his communists."

I wasn't sure if Toussenel was right, but his philippics indicated how the more revolutionary circles were thinking and it gave me several ideas. . . . I was doubtful that documents against the Jesuits would be saleable. Perhaps to the Freemasons, but I still had no point of contact with their world. Writings against the Freemasons might have been of interest to the Jesuits, but I didn't yet feel able to produce any. Against Napoleon? Certainly not to sell them to the government. And the republicans were a good potential market but, after Sue and Joly, there was little more to be said. Against the republicans? Here again, it seemed as if the government had all it needed. And if I offered Lagrange information on the Fourierists he would have laughed – who knows how many of his informers already visited that bookshop in rue de Beaune.

Who was left? The Jews, for heaven's sake! Deep down I thought it was only my grandfather who had been so obsessed, but after listening to Toussenel I realised there was an anti-Jewish market not just among all the descendants of Abbé Barruel (and there were quite a few of them) but also among revolutionaries, republicans and socialists. The Jews were the enemy of the altar, but also of the ordinary people, whose blood they sucked. And they were also the enemy of the throne, depending on who governed. I had to work on the Jews.

I realised that the task would not be easy. Some church circles might perhaps be impressed by a recycling of Barruel's material, with the Jews in league with the Freemasons and the Templars to bring about the French Revolution, but it would be of no interest to a socialist like Toussenel. I needed to say something more specific about the relationship between Jews, accumulation of capital, and conspiracy with the British.

I began to feel a certain regret that I had never wanted to meet a Jew in my life. I realised there was so much I didn't know about the object of my repugnance, which was becoming more and more suffused with resentment.

I was grappling with these thoughts when Lagrange presented me with an opportunity. Lagrange, as I have already noted, was always arranging meetings in the most improbable places, and this time it was to be at Père-Lachaise. This was a good idea. Here, after all, we could be mistaken for relatives searching for the grave of a dear departed, or as romantics revisiting the past. On this occasion we were standing reverently beside the tomb of Abelard and Héloïse, a place of pilgrimage for artists, philosophers and lovers, appearing like ghosts among ghosts.

"Simonini, I want to arrange for you to meet Colonel Dimitri – that's the only name he's known by in our circles. He works in the Third Department of the Imperial Russian Chancellery. If, of course, you were to go to St Petersburg and ask for the Third Department everyone would look at you blankly, as officially it doesn't exist. They are agents appointed to keep an eye on revolutionary groups – the problem there is much worse than it is here. They have to watch for those taking the place of the Decembrists, for the anarchists, and now for the discontented so-called emancipated peasants. Tsar Alexander abolished serfdom several years ago, but there are now around twenty million free peasants who are supposed to pay rent to their old masters for plots of land too small to give them a living, and large numbers of them are invading the cities in search of work. . . ."

"And what does this Colonel Dimitri want of me?"

"He's collecting documents on the Jewish problem which are, shall we say, compromising. There are many more Jews in Russia than here, and in the villages they pose a threat to the Russian peasants since they can read, write, and above all count. That's not to mention the cities, where many of them are thought to belong to subversive sects. My Russian colleagues have two tasks: first, to see whether and where the Jews pose a real danger, and then to direct the peasants' discontent against them. But Dimitri will explain everything. It's no concern of ours. Our government is on good terms with the Jewish financiers in France and has no interest in stirring up resentment against them. All we want is to be of service to the Russians. In our job, Simonini, it's a question of you scratch my back and I'll scratch yours, and we're only too pleased to offer you to Colonel Dimitri – though officially, of course, you're nothing to do with us. I forgot to mention . . . before Dimitri arrives, you might wish to know about the *Alliance Israélite Universelle*, established about six years ago in Paris. They are doctors, journalists, lawyers, businessmen, the cream of Parisian Jewish society – all, shall we say, of liberal persuasion, and certainly more republican than Bonapartist. Their aim is apparently to help victims of persecution from every religion and country in the name of the rights of man. Until proved otherwise, they are citizens of the utmost integrity, but it is hard for our informers to infiltrate them because Jews know and recognise each other, sniffing each other's bottoms like dogs. But I'll put you in contact with someone who has managed to gain the trust of some *Alliance* members. He's a certain Jakob Brafmann, a Jew who converted to the Orthodox faith and became professor of Hebrew at the Theological Seminary in Minsk. He's in Paris for a short stay, working for Colonel Dimitri and his Third Department. And being thought a member of the same religion, it was easy for him to make contact with the *Alliance Israélite*. He'll be able to tell you something about them."

"Excuse me, Monsieur de Lagrange. But if this Brafmann is Colonel Dimitri's informer, then he will already have told Dimitri all he knows, and there's no point my going to tell him all over again."

"Don't be naive, Simonini. Of course there's a point. If you give Dimitri the same information that he's already heard from Brafmann, then he'll regard you as someone whose news is reliable, since it confirms what he already knows."

Brafmann. From my grandfather's stories I expected to meet someone with the profile of a vulture, with fleshy lips, the lower lip heavily protruding like a negro, eyes deep set and generally watery, eyelids less open than other races, wavy or curly hair, ears sticking out. . . . Instead, the man I met had a monkish appearance, a fine grey beard and thick bushy eyebrows with those Mephistophelian tufts at each corner that I had seen among the Russians or Poles. Religious conversion evidently transforms not just the soul but also facial appearances.

He had a particular liking for good food, though he displayed the voraciousness of a provincial who wants to try everything but has no idea how to create a proper menu. We had lunch at *Au Rocher de Cancale* in rue Montorgueil, which used to serve the finest oysters in Paris. It had closed twenty years earlier and then been reopened under new ownership – it wasn't what it used to be, but they still had oysters, and for a Russian Jew it was good enough. Brafmann began with just a few dozen *belons*, then ordered a *bisque d'écrevisses*.

"For such a thriving race to survive over forty centuries, it had to establish a single government in every country where it was living – a state within a state – which it has maintained ever since, even when its people have been scattered for thousands of years. And I have found documents which prove the existence of this state, this law, the Kahal."

"And what is it?"

"The institution dates back to the times of Moses. After the diaspora, it no longer operated openly but was confined to the synagogues. I have found documents for the Kahal in Minsk from 1794 to 1830. It's all written down, every detail is recorded."

He unrolled various scrolls covered with symbols I couldn't understand.

"Every Jewish community is governed by a Kahal and

. . . the man I met had a monkish
appearance, a fine grey beard and
thick bushy eyebrows with those
Mephistophelian tufts at each
corner that I had seen among
the Russians or Poles. . . .

[PAGE 248]

249

subject to an autonomous tribunal, the Bet-Din. These documents are from one Kahal, but they're obviously just the same as those for every Kahal. They tell us how members of a community must obey only their own court and not that of their host state, how festivities are to be carried out, how animals must be specially killed and prepared (the impure and corrupt parts sold to the Christians), how every Jew can obtain a Christian from the Kahal whom he can exploit through usury until he has taken all his property, and no other Jew has rights over that same Christian. . . . The lack of mercy towards lower classes, the exploitation of the poor man by the rich man, are not crimes according to the Kahal but virtues when practised by a son of Israel. Some say that Jews are poor, especially in Russia. This is true. Large numbers of Jews are the victims of a secret government run by rich Jews. I'm not against the Jews – I was, after all, born a Jew – but against the *Jewish ideal* that wants to replace Christianity. I love the Jews . . . may Jesus whom they assassinated be my witness. . . ."

Brafmann had found his second wind and ordered *aspic de filets mignons de perdreaux*. But he returned almost immediately to his scrolls, which he handled lovingly: "And as you see, they're all genuine. That is proved by the age of the paper, by the uniformity of the scribe's handwriting when he drew up the various documents, and by the identical signatures from different dates."

Brafmann had already translated the documents into French and German. He had been told by Lagrange that I could produce authentic documents, and asked me to make him a French version that would appear to date from the same period as the originals. He also needed these documents in other languages to show the Russian services how the model of the Kahal was being followed in various European countries, and particularly by the Parisian *Alliance Israélite*.

I asked how it was possible, from documents produced by a remote Eastern European community, to demonstrate the existence of a global Kahal. Brafmann replied that I need not worry about that. These documents would be useful as supporting evidence, proving that what he had to say was no mere invention, and in any event his book would be sufficiently persuasive in its condemnation of the true Kahal, that great octopus whose tentacles extended across the whole civilised world.

His expression hardened and he assumed almost that eagle-like appearance that would have given him away as a Jew which, after all, he still was.

"The fundamental feelings animating the Talmudic spirit are an overweening ambition to dominate the world, an insatiable lust to possess all the riches of those who are not Jewish, and a grudge against Christians and against Jesus Christ. Until such time as Israel is converted to Jesus, those countries that offer a home to such people will always be regarded by them, to quote the Talmud, as an open lake where every Jew can fish freely."

Exhausted by this tirade of accusations, Brafmann ordered a dish of *escalopes de poularde au velouté,* but it was not to his taste and so he changed it for some *filets de poularde piqués aux truffes.* Then he took a silver pocket watch from his waistcoat. "Oh dear, it's late," he said. "French cuisine is exquisite but the service is slow. I have an urgent meeting and must go. Let me know, Captain Simonini, whether you can find the right kind of paper and inks."

Brafmann had just concluded the meal with a vanilla soufflé. I was expecting that a Jew, although converted, would leave me to pay the bill. On the contrary, with a lordly gesture, Brafmann insisted that he should pay for our snack, as he casually described it. No doubt the Russian secret service allowed him princely expenses.

I returned feeling puzzled. A document produced fifty years ago in Minsk with detailed instructions about whom to invite or not invite to a religious festivity hardly demonstrates that such rules also apply to the actions of great bankers in Paris or Berlin. And what is more, never, never, never work with genuine or half-genuine documents! If they already exist, someone can always search them out to prove that they are incorrect. . . . If a document is to be convincing, it must be created *ex novo*. And where possible, the original must not be seen but only talked about, without any reference to any precise source, as happened with the Three Kings, whom only Matthew mentions in a couple of verses, not saying what they were called, or even how many they were, or that they were kings, and all the rest is tradition. And yet people think of them as being just as real as Joseph and Mary, and I know their bodies are venerated somewhere or other. Revelations have to be out of the ordinary, shocking and fantastical. Only then do they become credible and arouse indignation. Is a peasant in a vineyard in Champagne going to care whether Jews make their fellow Jews do this or that at their daughter's marriage

festivities? Does this prove that the Jews are trying to pick
the Champagne peasants' pockets?

And then I realised I already had the document I needed,
or at least a convincing framework – much better than
Gounod's *Faust*, which the Parisians had been raving over
for the last few years. All I had to do was find the right
contents. I was, of course, thinking of the Masonic gathering
on Thunder Mountain, of Joseph Balsamo's plan and the
Jesuits' night in the Prague cemetery.

Where should the Jewish plan for the conquest of the
world start? Obviously from their possession of its gold, as
Toussenel had suggested. Conquest of the world, to frighten
monarchies and governments; possession of its gold, to
satisfy the socialists, anarchists and revolutionaries; destruction of healthy Christian principles, to worry pope, bishops
and clergy. And introduce a bit of that Bonapartist cynicism
which Joly had used so well, and the Jesuitical hypocrisy
that both Joly and I had taken from Eugène Sue.

I went back to the library, but this time I was in Paris,
where I could find much more than in Turin, and here I
found more pictures of the Prague cemetery. It has been
there since the Middle Ages. The burial ground could not
be extended beyond the permitted area and so more graves
were added over the centuries, one on top of the other, until
there were perhaps a hundred thousand bodies, and the
number of gravestones grew, until one was almost touching
the next, covered by fronds of elder and without any portraits
to decorate them, since the Jews have a terror of images. In
their fascination with the site, engravers had perhaps exaggerated their depiction of the stones which mushroomed

from the ground like moorland shrubs bent back by the winds – the space seemed like the gaping mouth of a gap-toothed old witch. But thanks to some of the more imaginative engravers who had portrayed it in moonlight, I immediately saw how I could make use of that unearthly atmosphere, placing – among the stones that looked like paving slabs upended by some subterranean tumult – the bent, cloaked and hooded figures of rabbis, with their greying and goatish beards, intently conspiring, inclined like the gravestones against which they were leaning, so that they formed a forest of wizened ghosts in the night. And at the centre stood the tomb of Rabbi Löw who, in the seventeenth century, had created the Golem, a monstrous creature who was supposed to avenge all Jews.

Better than Dumas, and better than the Jesuits.

My document, of course, had to appear in the form of an oral testimony by a witness to that terrible night – a witness forced on pain of death to remain anonymous. He must have been able to enter the cemetery at night, dressed as a rabbi, before the ceremony had begun, hiding behind the heap of stones that formed Rabbi Löw's tomb. On the stroke of midnight – as if the distant bell of a Christian church had blasphemously summoned the Jewish gathering – twelve figures wrapped in dark cloaks would arrive and a voice, rising up almost from the depths of a tomb, would welcome them as the twelve Rosche-Bathe-Abboth, leaders of the twelve tribes of Israel, and each of them would answer, "Greetings to you, O son of the damned."

This is the scene. And just as on Thunder Mountain, the voice that summoned them asks, "One hundred years have passed since our last assembly. From whence do you come and whom do you represent?" And the voices answer in turn, Rabbi Juda from Amsterdam, Rabbi Benjamin from Toledo, Rabbi Levi from Worms, Rabbi Manasse from Pest, Rabbi Gad from Krakow, Rabbi Simeon from Rome, Rabbi Sebulon from Lisbon, Rabbi Ruben from Paris, Rabbi Dan from Constantinople, Rabbi Asser from London, Rabbi Isascher from Berlin, Rabbi Naphtali from Prague. Then the voice of the thirteenth member of the gathering calls each of them to declare the wealth of their communities, and calculates the wealth of the Rothschilds and the other great Jewish bankers around the world. In this way he arrives at the figure of six hundred francs for each of the three million five hundred thousand Jews living in Europe – in other words two billion francs. "It is still not enough to destroy two hundred and sixty-five million Christians," says the thirteenth voice, "but enough to start off."

I still had to decide what they would say, but I had mapped out the conclusion. The thirteenth voice invoked the spirit of Rabbi Löw, a bluish light shone from his tomb, becoming harsher and more dazzling, each of the assembled twelve threw a stone upon the grave and the light gradually faded. The twelve began to melt away in different directions, swallowed up (as they say) by the darkness, and the cemetery returned to its spectral, lifeless melancholy.

So Dumas, Sue, Joly and Toussenel. The only thing missing, apart from the mastery of Father Barruel, my spiritual guide in the whole plan, was the point of view of a fervent Catholic. Lagrange, at that very time, while urging me to hasten my contact with the *Alliance Israélite*, had spoken of Gougenot des Mousseaux. I knew something about him. He was a Catholic monarchist journalist, who had been interested in magic, satanic practices, secret societies and Freemasonry.

"So far as we know," said Lagrange, "he's about to finish a book on the Jews and the Judaisation of Christian nations, if you follow my meaning. You may find it helpful to meet him to gather any information you need for our Russian friends. And it would be useful for us to know more about what he's up to – we wouldn't wish any harm to come to the fine relationship between our government, the Church and the Jewish financial world. You could describe yourself as an expert on Jewish affairs who admires his work. There is someone who could introduce you – a certain Abbé Dalla Piccola who has performed quite a few services for us."

"But I don't know a word of Hebrew," I said.

"And who says Gougenot does? To hate someone, you don't have to speak his language."

And now (suddenly!) I remember my first meeting with Abbé Dalla Piccola. I see him as if he were standing here in front of me. And in seeing him, I realise that he is not my double, or even anything like me, because he looks at least sixty and is almost hunchbacked, squint-eyed and has protruding teeth (Abbé Quasimodo, I thought, seeing him now). What is more he had a German accent. I remember Dalla Piccola whispering to me that it would be a good idea to keep an eye on not just the Jews but also the Freemasons as, after all, they are all part of the same conspiracy. I felt it would be better not to open up two fronts at the same time, but from the abbé's various comments I realised the Jesuits were interested in information on the Masonic sects as the Church was preparing a very violent attack on the Masonic plague.

"In any event," Dalla Piccola had said, "when the time comes to make contact with such groups, let me know. I'm a brother in a Paris lodge and well connected in such circles."

"You, a priest?" I had said, and Dalla Piccola had smiled. "If you only knew how many priests are Masons. . . ."

I had, in the meantime, arranged an interview with Chevalier Gougenot des Mousseaux. He was about seventy, already weak in spirit, sure of the few ideas he had, and interested only in proving the existence of the Devil and in magicians, sorcerers, spiritualists, hypnotists, Jews, idolatrous priests, and even "electricians" who believed in some kind of vital force.

He spoke in torrents, and began at the very beginning. I listened patiently to the old man's ideas about Moses, the Pharisees, the Great Sanhedrin and the Talmud. As he spoke, Gougenot offered me an excellent cognac, inadvertently leaving the bottle on a small table in front of him, and I listened patiently.

He told me the proportion of women of ill-repute was higher among Jews than among Christians (and don't we know it, I thought, from the Gospels, where Jesus meets fallen women wherever he goes?) and went on to demonstrate how in Talmudic teaching there is no mention of neighbours, nor any suggestion of duties towards them, which explains and justifies in its own way the ruthlessness of Jews in ruining families, seducing young girls, and putting widows and old people on the streets after bleeding them of all their money. The number of criminals, as well as prostitutes, was also higher among Jews than Christians. "Did you know," said Gougenot, "that eleven out of twelve cases of theft brought before the courts in Leipzig were committed by Jews?" adding with a malicious smile, "And in fact on Calvary there were two criminals for a single just man. And generally speaking, the crimes committed by Jews are the more heinous, such as deception, forgery, usury, fraudulent bankruptcy, smuggling, producing counterfeit money, extortion, commercial fraud. . . . I need hardly continue."

After almost an hour of details about usury, he then reached the more lurid part, on infanticide and cannibalism, before ending, almost by way of contrast to such dark practices, with the description of a matter that was clear and visible in the light of day – the harmful effects of Jewish finance on the public economy and the weakness of French governments in combating and punishing it.

Most interesting of all, though hardly of any use to me, was when des Mousseaux recalled the intellectual superiority of the Jews over Christians, almost as if he too were Jewish, quoting those assertions by Disraeli which I had heard from Toussenel. And here it was clear that socialists, Fourierists and Catholic monarchists shared the same view of Judaism and seemed to reject the popular view of the runtish, sickly Jew. It is true that Jews had weak, fragile constitutions, never having trained their bodies or practised military arts (unlike, say, the Greeks who valued physical competition) but they lived long, were remarkably fertile (an effect of their insatiable sexual appetite) and were immune from many illnesses which afflicted the rest of humanity, thus making them more dangerous as invaders of the world.

"Explain to me," said Gougenot, "why the Jews are almost always spared from cholera epidemics, even when they live in the most dank and insalubrious parts of the city. Referring to the plague in 1346, a historian of that period said that for some mysterious reason the Jews had not been stricken in any country; Frascator tells us the Jews alone were saved from the typhoid epidemic of 1505; Daguer shows how the Jews were the only survivors of the dysentery epidemic in Nijmegen in 1736; Wawruch proves that the tapeworm is not found in the Jewish population in Germany. What do you say? How is it possible, if these are the filthiest people in the world, who marry only among members of their own race? It's against all the laws of nature. Is it their diet, whose rules still remain obscure? Or is it circumcision? What secret makes them stronger than us even when they seem weaker? Such a treacherous and powerful enemy, I say, has to be destroyed by whatever means. You realise when they arrived in the Promised Land there were only six hundred thousand men. If you count four people for each adult male, that makes a total population of two and a half million. But by the time of Solomon they had one million three hundred thousand soldiers, and therefore five million people, and that's double. And today? It's hard to calculate how many there are, spread throughout every continent, but the more prudent estimates talk of ten million. And they're growing, growing. . . ."

He seemed so racked by resentment that I felt tempted to offer him a glass of his own cognac. But he recovered, and

. . . He seemed so racked by resentment that I felt tempted to offer him a glass of his own cognac. . . .

[PAGE 259]

by the time he had reached Messianism and the Cabala (and was about to embark on a description of his books on magic and Satanism), I had fallen into a gentle slumber and only managed by some miracle to rouse myself, whereupon I thanked him and took my leave.

Too much of a good thing, I thought. If I put all this into one document for people like Lagrange I'd be in danger of ending up (courtesy of the secret service) in a dungeon, maybe in the castle at If, as would befit a devotee of Dumas. Perhaps I should have taken des Mousseaux's book more seriously because now, as I write, I recall that *Le juif, le judaïsme et la judaïsation des peuples chrétiens* was published in 1869 – almost six hundred pages of small print – and received the blessing of Pope Pius IX and great public acclaim. But it was the feeling that so many books and pamphlets were being published from every corner of the world against the Jews that encouraged me to be selective.

In my Prague cemetery the rabbis had to say something easily understood, which would capture the popular imagination and would, in some way, be new – not like the ritual child-killing that people had been talking about for centuries . . . they believed in that as much as they believed in witches, and it was enough to prevent their children from playing around the ghettos.

And so I went back to writing my report on the dark dealings of that fateful night. The thirteenth voice spoke first: "Our forefathers ordained that the elders of Israel should gather together once each century around the tomb of our blessed Rabbi Simeon-Ben-Jehuda. Eighteen centuries have passed since the power pledged to Abraham was snatched from us by the Cross. The people of Israel, downtrodden, humiliated by their enemies, under constant threat of death and rape, have resisted. If they are spread across the whole earth, that means the whole earth must belong to them. The Golden Calf has been ours since the days of Aaron."

"Yes," said Rabbi Isascher, "when we are the sole possessors of all the earth's gold, true power will pass into our hands."

"This is the tenth occasion," continued the thirteenth voice, "after a thousand years of fierce and endless battling with our foes, that the elders of each generation of the people of Israel have gathered together in this cemetery, around the tomb of our Rabbi Simeon-Ben-Jehuda. But in none of the previous centuries were our forefathers able to concentrate in our hands so much gold, and therefore so much power. In Paris, London, Vienna, Berlin, Amsterdam, Hamburg, Rome, Naples, and through the Rothschilds, the Israelites have control over all financial affairs. Speak, Rabbi Ruben. You know the position in Paris."

"All reigning emperors, kings and princes," said Ruben, "are overwhelmed by debts they have incurred with us to maintain their armies and shore up their tottering thrones. We must therefore encourage more lending and, as security for the capital we supply to countries, we must take control of their railways, their mines, their forests, their foundries and factories, and other property, as well as tax collection."

"Do not forget agriculture," said Simeon from Rome. "It is still the great wealth of every country. The ownership of great estates still seems unattainable but if we manage to persuade governments to break up these vast landholdings, they can then be more easily acquired."

Rabbi Juda from Amsterdam then said, "But many of our brothers in Israel are converting and accepting Christian baptism. . . ."

"That's no matter!" replied the thirteenth voice. "Those who are baptised can serve us just as well. Despite the baptism of their bodies, their spirit and their souls remain faithful to Israel. In a hundred years' time no child of Israel will want to become Christian, but many Christians will seek to join our holy faith. Then Israel will turn them away with contempt."

"But most of all," said Rabbi Levi, "let us regard the Christian Church as our most dangerous enemy. We must spread ideas of free thought, of scepticism, among Christians. We must bring down the ministers of this religion."

"Let us spread the idea of progress which leads to equality for all religions," said Rabbi Manasse. "Let us fight to stop lessons about the Christian religion in school syllabuses. Israelites, through their skill and education, will have no difficulty in finding teaching posts in Christian schools. Religious education will then be relegated to the family, and since most families have little time to concern themselves with this branch of learning, religious feeling will gradually fade."

It was now the turn of Rabbi Dan from Constantinople: "And above all, business and speculation must never slip out of Israelite hands. We must take over trade in alcohol, butter, bread and wine. In this way we will have complete control over agriculture, and over the whole rural economy."

And Naphtali from Prague said, "We must set our sights on the judiciary and the legal profession. And why should Israelites not become government ministers for education, when they have so often held that role for finance?"

And finally, Rabbi Benjamin from Toledo spoke: "We must not be strangers to any important profession: philosophy, medicine, law, music, economics . . . in short, all branches of science, the arts, literature are a vast field in which we must prove ourselves and show our abilities. And above all medicine! A doctor is privy to a family's most intimate secrets, and is responsible for a Christian's life and health. And we must encourage marriages between Israelites and Christians – the introduction of a tiny quantity of impure blood into our race, elected by God, cannot taint it, and our sons and our daughters will acquire relatives in Christian families who hold positions of power."

"Let us conclude our assembly," said the thirteenth voice. "If gold is the first power in this world, the second is the press. We must take over the running of all daily newspapers in every country. Once we are in absolute control of the press, we can change public ideas about honour, virtue, integrity, and carry out our first attack on the family as an institution. Let us appear to be concerned about social questions of current interest. We have to maintain control over the proletariat, plant our agitators in social movements so that we can stir up trouble when we want to, driving workers to the barricades, to revolution. And each of these catastrophes brings us closer to our purpose – that of ruling the earth, as was promised to our forefather Abraham. Our power will now increase like a gigantic tree, whose branches will bear the fruits of wealth, pleasure, happiness and power, as compensation for that vile condition which was the sole destiny of the people of Israel over long centuries."

If I remember rightly, that was how the report from the Prague cemetery ended.

At the end of my reconstruction I feel exhausted – perhaps because I've taken some libation to accompany these hours of feverish writing, to give me physical strength and raise my spirits. But since yesterday I've had no appetite and eating sickens me. I wake up and vomit. Perhaps I'm working too hard. Or perhaps I'm being throttled by a hatred which is consuming me. At this distance in time, looking back over the pages I wrote about the Prague cemetery, I understand how that experience, the powerful, convincing reconstruction of the Jewish conspiracy, the repugnance which through my childhood and early youth had been no more than (how can I say?) imaginary, all in my head, like voices of a catechism instilled by my grandfather, had now become flesh and blood. And only when I had succeeded in reliving that terrible night was my resentment, my aversion towards Jewish perfidy, transformed from an abstract idea into a deep irrepressible passion. By God, it must indeed have been that night at the Prague cemetery – or at least reading my account of the event – that had made me understand how that accursed race could no longer be allowed to corrupt our lives!

Only after I had read and reread the document did I fully understand that this was my mission. I had to sell my report to someone, but only if they paid its weight in gold would they believe it, and help in making it credible. . . .

But it's better for me to stop writing for the evening. This hatred (or just the memory of it) is twisting my mind. My hands are trembling. I must go and sleep, sleep, sleep.

13

DALLA PICCOLA SAYS HE IS NOT DALLA PICCOLA

5th April 1897

This morning I awoke in my own bed and dressed myself, adding that touch of make-up which my character requires. Then I came to read your diary, where you say you met Abbé Dalla Piccola, and you describe him as being older certainly than me and, what is more, hunchbacked. I went to look at myself in the mirror in your room – in mine there is no mirror, as is appropriate for a priest – and, without wishing to indulge in vanity, I can only say that my features are regular, that I am certainly not squint-eyed and my teeth do not protrude. And I have a fine French accent with, if anything, a certain Italian inflexion.

So who then is the abbé you met with my name? And at this point, who am I?

14

BIARRITZ

5th April 1897, late morning

I awoke late and found your brief note on my diary. You're
an early riser. Good God, Monsieur Abbé – assuming, that
is, you'll read these lines in the next few days (or nights).
Who then are you? Because I now recall, at this very moment,
having killed you, back before the war! How can I be talking
to a ghost?

Did I kill you? Why am I so sure of it now? Let us try
to remember. But first of all I have to eat. Strange, yesterday
the very thought of food disgusted me. Now I'll devour
anything I can find. If I were free to go out, then I should
see a doctor.

Having finished my report on the gathering in the Prague
cemetery, I was ready to meet Colonel Dimitri. I remembered
how much Brafmann enjoyed French food and invited
Dimitri to the same place, *Au Rocher de Cancale*, but he didn't
seem interested in food and picked at what I had ordered.
He had slightly slanted eyes, with small piercing pupils that
made me think of the eyes of a weasel, though I admit I
have never seen one (I hate weasels as much as I hate Jews).
Dimitri, it seemed, had the peculiar virtue of making the
person he was talking to feel uncomfortable.

He had read my report with care. "Very interesting," he
said. "How much?"

It was a pleasure to deal with people like him, and I named a figure that was perhaps excessive – fifty thousand francs – explaining how costly my informants had been.

"Too expensive," said Dimitri, "or should I say, too expensive for me. Let us try to divide the cost. We are on good terms with the Prussian secret service. They also have a problem with Jews. I'll pay you twenty-five thousand francs in gold and authorise you to pass a copy of the document to the Prussians, who will give you the other half. I will inform them. They'll want the original, of course – the same as you have given me – but from what Lagrange tells me you are perfectly capable of duplicating originals. The name of the person who will contact you is Stieber."

That was all he said. He courteously refused a cognac, bowed formally, in the German rather than the Russian way, with his body straight and head bent at almost a right angle, and went. I was left to pay the bill.

I asked for a meeting with Lagrange, who had already spoken to me about Stieber, the chief of Prussian intelligence. He specialised in gathering material beyond the frontier, but was also able to infiltrate sects and movements who compromised the peace of the State. Ten years earlier he had played a valuable part in obtaining information on that man Marx, who had been causing concern both to the Germans and the English. It seems that Lagrange or his agent Krause, who worked under the assumed name of Fleury, had managed to get into Marx's house in London disguised as a doctor, and made off with a list of names of all the supporters of the Communist League. It was quite a coup, Lagrange told me,

*. . . I asked for a meeting
with Lagrange . . .*

[PAGE 269]

and led to the arrest of many dangerous individuals. A useless precaution, I suggested: those communists must have been pretty stupid to be duped like that and wouldn't have got very far. But Lagrange said you never know. Prevention is best – it's better to punish first, before any crimes are committed.

"A good secret agent is lost when he has to deal with something that has already happened. Our job is to make it happen first. We're spending a substantial amount of money organising riots on the boulevards. It doesn't take much: just a few dozen ex-convicts, with several plain-clothed policemen. They'll destroy a few restaurants and a couple of brothels singing 'La Marseillaise', they'll burn down a few kiosks, and then our uniformed police arrive and arrest everyone after a semblance of a fight."

"And for what purpose?"

"To ensure that decent citizens are kept in a state of fear, and to convince everyone that tough measures are needed. If we had to put down real riots, organised by heaven knows who, we would not manage to deal with them quite so easily. But let's return to Stieber. When he became head of Prussia's secret police he travelled around the villages of Eastern Europe dressed as a wandering acrobat, noting down everything and creating a network of informers along the road on which the Prussian army would one day pass from Berlin to Prague. And he's begun to do the same thing in France, in preparation for a war that will one day be inevitable."

"Wouldn't it be better, then, to steer clear of him?"

"No. We have to keep an eye on him. It's better that those who work for him also work for us. In any event, you have to talk to him about a certain matter involving the Jews, which is of no interest to us. So by collaborating with him you won't be doing any harm to our government."

A week later I received a note from Stieber. He asked whether it would be very inconvenient for me to go to Munich to meet his contact, a certain Goedsche, to whom I had to deliver the report. It certainly was inconvenient, but I was far too interested in the other half of the payment.

I asked Lagrange whether he knew Goedsche. He was, he told me, a former postal clerk who had worked as an agitator for the Prussian secret police. After the uprisings of 1848, he forged letters to incriminate the leader of the democrats, from which it appeared that he intended to assassinate the king. There were evidently still some judges left in Berlin, and someone was able to show the letters were false. Goedsche was implicated in the scandal and had to leave his job at the post office. But it had also damaged his credibility with the secret service, who forgive you for counterfeiting documents but not if you're caught while doing it. He reinvented himself, under the name of Sir John Retcliffe, writing second-rate historical novels, and continued to work for *Kreuzzeitung*, an anti-Semitic newspaper. And the secret service still used him to disseminate news, whether true or false, about the Jews.

And this was the man who'd been put on my case, I thought. Lagrange was explaining that perhaps, if they were using him for this, it was because the Prussians weren't particularly interested in my report and had appointed someone low down to have a look at it in order to clear their conscience, and then get rid of me.

"No, that's not true," I said. "My report is important to the Germans. I've already been promised a considerable sum."

"Who has promised it?" asked Lagrange. And he smiled when I replied that it was Dimitri. "They're Russians, Simonini. Need I say more? What does a Russian have to lose if he promises you something on behalf of the Germans? But go to Munich all the same – we too are interested in finding out what they're doing. And don't forget that Goedsche is a devious rogue. Otherwise he wouldn't be in this job."

Lagrange was not exactly a gentleman, but perhaps there was a better kind of scoundrel, of which he was one. And so long as they pay me well I don't complain.

I believe I have already described in this diary my impression of that enormous tavern in Munich, crowded with Bavarians seated elbow to elbow at long communal tables, gorging themselves on greasy sausages and drinking from beer jugs the size of vats, men and women together, the women more boisterous, rowdy and vulgar than the men . . . most definitely an inferior race. And after the journey, tiring in itself, I found having to spend even two days on Teutonic soil a great effort.

It was in just such a tavern that Goedsche had arranged our meeting, and I was obliged to conclude that my German spy seemed born to scratch about in such places: clothes of brazen elegance were insufficient to hide the fox-like cunning of someone who lived on his wits.

In bad French he immediately asked questions about my sources. I evaded them, talking about other matters and mentioning my exploits with Garibaldi's men. He was pleasantly surprised as, he said, he was writing a novel about events in Italy in 1860. It was almost complete, its title would be *Biarritz*, and it would be in several volumes. Not all the events were set in Italy – it moved about between Siberia, Warsaw, Biarritz (of course) and so on. He spoke of it with enthusiasm and a certain smugness, claiming that he was about to complete the Sistine Chapel of historical fiction. I didn't understand the link between the various events he was describing, but the story seemed to revolve around the continual threat from three evil powers that were surreptitiously taking over the world – the Freemasons, the Catholics (in particular the Jesuits) and the Jews, who were also infiltrating the first two in order to undermine the purity of the Protestant Teutonic race.

The story described the Italian conspiracies of Mazzini's Freemasons, then moved to Warsaw, where the Freemasons were conspiring against Russia, along with nihilists – a breed as damned as the Slavs had ever managed to produce, although both (nihilists and Slavs) were mostly Jewish . . . and it is important to note that their system of recruitment resembled that of the Bavarian Illuminati and the *Alta Vendita* of the Carbonari, where every member recruited another nine, none of whom must know each other. Then the story returned to Italy, following the advance from Piedmont southwards to the Kingdom of the Two Sicilies, in a mayhem of wounding, treachery, rape of noblewomen, dramatic exploits, gallant swashbuckling Irish monarchists, secret messages hidden under the tails of horses, a vile Carbonaro prince Caracciolo who molests a young (Irish monarchist) girl, the discovery of magic rings in green-oxidised gold with intertwined snakes and red coral at the centre, a kidnap attempt on the son of Napoleon III, the drama of Castelfidardo where the battlefield is strewn with the blood of German troops loyal to the Pope, and condemnation of the *welsche Feigheit* – Goedsche said it in German, perhaps not to offend me, but I had studied a little German and understood he was referring to that cowardly behaviour typical of the Latin races. At that point events became more and more confused, and we still hadn't reached the end of the first volume.

As he spoke, Goedsche's vaguely porcine eyes gradually lit up, he spluttered and laughed with self-satisfaction at certain witticisms he judged to be excellent. He seemed to be hoping for some first-hand gossip about Cialdini, Lamarmora and other Piedmont generals and, of course, Garibaldi and his men. But since people like him were used to paying for their information, I didn't think it appropriate to give him any Italian titbits for free. And anyway, it was better to keep quiet about what I knew.

This man, I thought, was on the wrong track. You can never create danger which has a thousand different faces – danger has to have one face alone, otherwise people become distracted. If you want to expose the Jews, then talk about the Jews, not the Irish, the Neapolitan monarchy, Piedmontese generals, Polish patriots and Russian nihilists. Too many irons in the fire. How can anyone be so chaotic? And all the more surprising when, apart from his novel, Goedsche seemed so completely fixated on the Jews – and so much the better for me, since I had come for the very purpose of offering him a special document about the Jews.

He was, he said, not writing his novel for money or in hopes of earthly glory but to liberate the German race from the Jewish snare.

"We must return to the words of Luther, when he said that the Jews are evil, poisonous and devilish to the core and had been our plague and pestilence for centuries, and still were in his time. They were, to use his words, perfidious, venomous, bitter serpents, assassins and children of the Devil, who sting and harm in secret, as they cannot do it openly." To deal with them the only possible remedy was a *scharfe Barmherzigkeit*, which he was unable to translate but, as I understood it, meant a *sharp mercy*, by which Luther meant no mercy at all. "Their synagogues had to be burned down and all that would not burn had to be buried with earth so that not a single stone remained in sight; they had to be driven from their homes into cattle sheds like gypsies; all their Talmudic texts which taught only lies, curses and blasphemies had to be removed; they were to be prevented from practising usury and all their gold, money and jewellery was to be taken from them, and their young men given axes and spades and their women flax and spindles. That is because," said Goedsche, sneering contemptuously, "*Arbeit macht frei* . . . work sets you free. The final solution, for Luther, would have been to drive them out of Germany, like rabid dogs."

"No one listened to Luther," continued Goedsche, "at least, not until now. And despite the fact that, since ancient times, non-European people have been considered as base – look at the negro who, still today, is rightly considered an animal – no sure criteria have yet been defined for recognising superior races. Today we know that the more developed level of humanity has white skin, and that the most evolved model of the white race is German. But the presence of Jews poses a continual threat of racial cross-breeding. Look at a Greek statue: such pure lines, such elegant build, and it is no surprise that beauty was identified with virtue, and to be beautiful was to be brave, as we see with our great heroes of Teutonic mythology. Now imagine Apollo with Semitic features, with brown skin, dark eyes, hooked nose, bent body. This is how Homer described Thersites, the very personification of baseness. The Christian legend, still strongly influenced by the Jews (it was, after all, begun by Paul, an Asiatic Jew whom today we'd call a Turk), has convinced us that all races are descended from Adam. No – in separating from the original beast, men have followed different paths. We have to return to that point where our paths separated, and therefore to the true national origins of our people, rather than the ravings of those French *lumières*, with their cosmopolitanism and their *égalité* and universal brotherhood! This is the spirit of our modern times. What in Europe is now called nationalism, is a cry for the purity of the original race. Except that this term – and aim – is only valid for the German race. It is absurd to imagine that in Italy the return to bygone beauty could be represented by your bow-legged Garibaldi, your short-legged king and that dwarf Cavour. The Romans, after all, were a Semitic race."

"The Romans?"

"You haven't read Virgil? They came from a Trojan, and therefore from an Asiatic, and this Semitic migration destroyed the spirit of the ancient Italic people. Look what happened to the Celts: after being Romanised, they became French, and therefore they too are Latin. Only the Germans have managed to remain pure and uncontaminated and to break the power of Rome. But the superiority of the Aryan race and the inferiority of the Jew (and inevitably also of the Latin) is seen in the excellence of the various arts. Neither Italy nor France have given birth to a Bach, a Mozart, a Beethoven or a Wagner."

Goedsche didn't exactly look like the type of Aryan hero he was praising. Indeed, to tell the truth (though why do we always have to worry about the truth?), he had the appearance of a gluttonous, lecherous Jew. In the end, however, I had to accept what he said, seeing that he was working for the service who had to pay me the remaining twenty-five thousand francs.

But I couldn't resist a small gibe. I asked if he thought he was a good example of the superior, Apollonian race. He glowered at me and said that belonging to a race is not just a physical matter but above all a spiritual one. A Jew is still a Jew even if, by accident of nature, he is born with blond hair and blue eyes, in the same way as there are children born with six fingers and women capable of doing multiplication. And an Aryan is an Aryan if he lives the spirit of his people, even if he has black hair.

But my question had tempered his enthusiasm. He calmed down, mopped the sweat from his brow with a large red-chequered handkerchief and asked to see the document for which our meeting had been arranged. I handed it to him and, after all he'd been saying, I thought it would have sent him into raptures. If his government wanted to be rid of the Jews in accordance with Luther's charge, my story about the Prague cemetery seemed an ideal way of alerting the whole of Prussia to the nature of the Jewish conspiracy. Instead I watched him, between one mouthful of beer and another, frowning several times and screwing up his eyes until he looked almost like a Mongol. Finally he said, "I'm really not sure this information is of any interest. It says what we have always known about Jewish conspiracies. It's certainly well said, and if it has been invented, then it's well invented."

"Please, Herr Goedsche! I'm not here to sell you material that's been invented."

"I have no reason to think it is, but I too have certain obligations towards those who pay me. The authenticity of the document still has to be proved. I have to show these documents to Herr Stieber at his offices. Leave them with me, if you wish, and return to Paris. You'll have a reply in a few weeks."

"But Colonel Dimitri told me it was already agreed. . . ."

"Not at all. Not yet, at least. As I say, leave the document with me."

"I'll be frank with you, Herr Goedsche. What you are holding is an original document . . . original, do you understand? It is valuable for the information it contains but, more than that, for the fact that this information appears in an original report, written in Prague after the meeting described. I cannot allow the document out of my hands, or at least not until I have received the amount I have been promised."

"You are far too suspicious. Very well then. Order yourself another beer or two, and give me an hour to make a copy of it. You yourself said that the information it contains is worth what it's worth and, if I wished to deceive you, then all I would have to do is retain it in my memory since, I assure you, I can remember what I have read more or less word for word. But I wish to show the document to Herr Stieber. Therefore allow me to copy it. The original has been brought here by you, and it shall leave with you."

There was no way I could object. I humiliated my palate with several of those disgusting Teutonic sausages and drank a large amount of beer, though I have to say that German beer can sometimes be as good as French beer. I waited while Goedsche carefully copied it all out.

Our parting was cool. Goedsche suggested we should split the bill and, indeed, worked out that I had drunk rather more beer than he did. He promised me news within a few weeks and departed, leaving me seething with rage at the long pointless journey I had made at my own expense without seeing a single thaler of the payment already agreed with Dimitri.

How stupid, I thought. Dimitri knew Stieber wasn't going to pay and had simply secured my document at half the price. Lagrange was right – I shouldn't have trusted a Russian. Or perhaps I had asked too much and should have been satisfied with the half I had received.

I was now convinced I would hear no more from the Germans and, in fact, several months passed without any news. Lagrange, to whom I had confided my worries, smiled indulgently: "These are the risks of our trade. We're not dealing with saints."

I was most irritated by the whole business. My story about the Prague cemetery was too well constructed to be allowed to go to waste on Siberian soil. I could have sold it to the Jesuits. After all, the first real accusations against the Jews, and the first suggestions about their international conspiracy, had come from Barruel, a Jesuit, and my grandfather's letter must have attracted the attention of other leading figures in the order.

The only possible point of contact with the order was Dalla Piccola. It was Lagrange who had put me in contact with him, and Lagrange to whom I now turned. Lagrange told me he'd let him know I was looking for him. And some time later Dalla Piccola came to my shop. I showed him my wares, as they say in the commercial world, and he seemed interested.

"Of course," he said, "I'll have to examine your document and refer it to someone in the Society. These people aren't going to buy sight unseen. I hope you'll trust me with it for a few days. It won't leave my hands."

I felt I could safely trust a priest.

Dalla Piccola returned to the shop a week later. I invited him up to my office and tried to offer him something to drink, but his manner was far from friendly.

"Simonini," he said, "you clearly took me for a fool, making the fathers of the Society of Jesus think I was a counterfeiter and ruining a network of good relationships I'd been developing over the years."

. . . "Simonini," he said, "you clearly took me for a fool" . . .

[PAGE 281]

"Monsieur l'Abbé, I have no idea what you're talking about. . . ."

"Stop playing games with me. You gave me this document, which is supposed to be secret," and he threw my report about the Prague cemetery on the table. "I was about to ask a considerable sum of money for it when the Jesuits, staring at me as if I were a shyster, quietly informed me that my highly confidential document had already appeared as fictional material in a novel called *Biarritz*, by a certain John Retcliffe. Exactly the same, word for word." And he threw the book down on the table as well. "You obviously understand German, and must have read the book as soon as it came out. You found the story of that nocturnal meeting in the Prague cemetery, you liked it, and couldn't resist the temptation of selling fiction for reality. And you had the impudence to presume, as plagiarists do, that no one reads German on this side of the Rhine. . . ."

"Please listen, I think I understand. . . ."

"There's little to understand. I could have thrown this paper into the bin and told you to go to the Devil, but I'm stubborn and vindictive. I warn you, I'll make sure your friends in the secret service know who you are and how much they can trust your information. And why have I come to tell you in advance? Not out of loyalty – someone like you has no right to such a thing – but if the service decides you are worth a dagger in your back, then you'll know who suggested it. There's no point killing someone out of revenge unless he knows you're the person who's having him killed, don't you think?"

It was all quite clear. That villain Goedsche (and Lagrange

had told me he published *feuilletons* under the name of Retcliffe) had never taken my document to Stieber. He realised the story fitted perfectly into the novel he was about to finish, and it appealed to his anti-Jewish frenzy, and so he took a true story (or at least he must have thought it was) and made it into a piece of fiction – his own fiction. Lagrange had even warned me that the rogue was already a well-known forger of documents and the fact that I had so naively fallen victim to a forger enraged me.

But my rage was matched with fear. When Dalla Piccola spoke of being stabbed in the back, he may have been talking metaphorically, but Lagrange had been quite clear. In the service, when someone gets in the way, he's dispensed with. Just imagine an informer who is publicly exposed as untrustworthy because he sells fictitious rubbish as secret intelligence and, what is more, has made the secret service look foolish in the eyes of the Society of Jesus. Who wants to have him around? A quick knifing, and he'll end up floating in the Seine.

This is what Abbé Dalla Piccola was promising me, and it was pointless trying to tell him the truth – there was no reason why he should believe me. He didn't know that I had shown my document to Goedsche before the scoundrel had finished writing his book – all he knew was that I had given it to him (Dalla Piccola) *after* Goedsche's book had appeared.

There seemed no way out.

Apart from stopping Dalla Piccola from talking.

I acted almost out of instinct. I have a heavy wrought-iron candlestick on my desk. I grabbed hold of it and pushed

Dalla Piccola against the wall. He looked at me, eyes wide open, and murmured, "You don't want to kill me. . . ."

"I'm sorry, yes," I replied.

And I really was sorry, but it was a question of making a virtue of necessity. I struck the blow. The abbé fell straight away, blood streaming through his protruding teeth. I looked at the body and felt not the slightest guilt. He had brought it upon himself.

Now all I had to do was get rid of that troublesome corpse.

When I bought the shop and upstairs apartment, the proprietor had shown me a trapdoor in the cellar floor.

"You'll find there are a few steps," he said, "and at first you won't have the courage to go down them because the stink will make you want to faint. But sometimes you'll have to. You're a foreigner and you may not know the whole story. People used to throw all their filth into the streets at one time, and they even made a law that you had to shout, 'Look out, water!' before you threw your business out of the window. But that was too much trouble – you emptied your chamber pot, and it was just too bad for anyone below. Then they made open gutters along the street and eventually these were covered over, and the sewers were created. Baron Haussmann has now, at last, built good sewers for Paris but they serve mostly for draining away the rainwater, and (when the pipes under your lavatory are not blocked up) the excrement flows away by itself, into a pit which is emptied at night and taken off to large dumps. But there is now discussion about whether, at last, to adopt a system of *tout-à-l'égout*, in other words whether the major sewers ought to include not only drain-water but every other kind of rubbish. For this reason a decree, made ten years ago, requires owners to connect their houses to the sewer by a tunnel at least one metre thirty wide. That's what you'll find down there, except that (I need hardly say) it's narrower and lower than the law requires. These laws are laid down for the main boulevards, but not for a dead-end passageway that is of no importance to anyone. And no one will ever come round checking whether you're actually taking your rubbish down there as you ought to be. When you can't face the idea of squelching through all that filth, just throw your rubbish down the steps, and you can be sure that when it rains some of the water will arrive as far as here and carry it away. There again, this route into the sewers could have its advantages. As it turns out every decade or so there's a revolution or a riot in Paris, and an underground escape route isn't such a bad thing. Like every Parisian, you'll have read that novel *Les Misérables* which came out recently, where our hero escapes through the sewers with an injured friend over his shoulder, so you'll understand what I mean."

As an avid reader of *feuilletons*, I was familiar with Hugo's story. I certainly had no wish to repeat the experience, not least because how his character managed to get so far down there I really don't know. Perhaps the underground drains in other parts of Paris are higher and broader, but the one under impasse Maubert must have been a few centuries old. It was already hard enough bringing Dalla Piccola's body downstairs to the shop and then to the cellar – fortunately the little dwarf was quite bent and thin so was fairly easy to handle. But to get him down the steps from the trapdoor I had to roll him. Then I went down and, with my head lowered, dragged him for a few metres to make sure he wouldn't putrefy right beneath my house. With one hand I pulled him along by the ankles and with the other I held a lamp – unfortunately I didn't have a third hand to hold my nose.

This was the first time I'd had to dispose of the body of someone I'd killed. With Nievo and Ninuzzo the matter was sorted out without my having to worry (though with Ninuzzo I should have been more careful, at least that first time in Sicily). I realised that the most irritating aspect of a murder is hiding the body, and it must be for this reason that priests tell us not to kill, except of course in battle, where the bodies are left for the vultures.

I dragged my deceased abbé for ten metres or so, and it is not a pleasant experience having to drag a priest through excrement (not just my own but of goodness-knows-who before me), and even worse having to describe all this to the victim himself – my God, what am I writing? But finally, after squelching through a great deal of effluent, I could see a distant blade of light, indicating a manhole cover in the street at the entrance to the alleyway.

I had originally planned to drag the corpse as far as the main drain and leave it to the mercy of its more plentiful waters. But afterwards, I thought, these waters might have carried the body who knows where, perhaps into the Seine, and someone might have managed to identify it. Quite right, because now, as I write, I discover that in the great rubbish tips below Clichy there have recently been found, over a period of six months, four thousand dogs, five calves, twenty sheep, seven goats, seven pigs, eighty hens, sixty-nine cats, nine hundred and fifty rabbits, a monkey and a boa constrictor. The figures do not mention priests but I could have contributed towards making them even more grotesque. By leaving my deceased in that place, there was a good chance he wouldn't move. Between the wall and the actual channel – which was certainly much older than Baron Haussmann's – there was a narrow walkway, and that was where I left the corpse. I calculated that it would have decomposed fairly quickly in that miasma and humidity, leaving no more than an unidentifiable heap of bones. And then, bearing in mind the nature of the alleyway, it seemed unlikely that this place would merit any maintenance, or that anyone would venture that far. And even if human remains were found there, it would still have to be proved where they'd come from: anyone climbing down through the manhole cover from the street could have brought them there.

I went back to my office and opened Goedsche's novel at the place where Dalla Piccola had left a bookmark. My German was rather rusty but I managed to follow the story, though not in detail. It was certainly my rabbis' gathering in the Prague cemetery, except that Goedsche (evidently someone with a theatrical imagination) had expanded my description of the cemetery at night and introduced a banker, Rosenberg, who was the first to arrive in the cemetery, accompanied by a Polish rabbi wearing a skullcap and with ringlets around his temples, and in order to enter he had to whisper to the custodian a cabalistic seven-syllable word.

The next to arrive was the person who had been my informant in the original, introduced by a certain Lasali, who promised to let him watch a gathering that occurred every hundred years. They had disguised themselves with false beards and broad-brimmed hats, and the story continued more or less as I had told it, including my ending, with the bluish light that rose from the tomb and the outlines of the rabbis walking away, swallowed up into the night.

The blackguard had used my succinct report to conjure up scenes of great melodrama. He was prepared to do anything to scrape together a few thalers. What is the world coming to?

Exactly what the Jews want it to come to.

It's time for bed. I have deviated from my habits of gastronomic moderation and have been drinking not wine but intemperate quantities of Calvados (and intemperance is making my head spin – I fear I am becoming repetitious). It seems I wake up as Abbé Dalla Piccola only when I plunge into a deep dreamless sleep. But now I'd like to see how I can possibly wake up again in the shoes of a dead man whose death I most certainly caused and witnessed.

15

DALLA PICCOLA REDIVIVUS

6th April 1897, at dawn

Captain Simonini, I don't know whether it was during your (immoderate or intemperate) slumber that I woke up and was able to read your diary. At the first light of dawn.

After reading it I thought perhaps, for some mysterious reason, you were lying (nor is it difficult to conclude from your life, as you have so frankly related it, that you do sometimes lie). If there is anyone who should know for sure that you didn't kill me, it would be I myself. I wanted to investigate. I removed my clerical garb and, almost naked, went down to the cellar and opened the trapdoor. But at the entrance to that foul-smelling passageway that you so well describe, I was taken aback by the stench. I asked myself what it was I wanted to find out: whether there were still a few bones from the body you say you left down there over twenty-five years ago? And did I have to go down into that filth to discover those bones weren't mine? If you'll allow me, I already know. Therefore I accept what you say – you did kill an Abbé Dalla Piccola.

So who am I? Not the Dalla Piccola you killed (who in any event didn't look like me), but how then can there be two Abbé Dalla Piccolas?

The truth is perhaps I'm mad. I dare not leave the house. Yet I have to go out to buy food, since my cassock prevents me from visiting taverns. I do not have a fine kitchen like you – even though, to be honest, I am no less of a glutton.

I am gripped by an irresistible urge to kill myself, but I know it's the Devil tempting me.

And then, why kill myself if you have already done it for me? It would be a waste of time.

7th April

Dear Abbé, enough of this.

I have no recollection of what I did yesterday and found your note this morning. Stop tormenting me. You don't remember either? So do as I do – contemplate your navel and then start writing. Allow your hand to think for you. Why is it I who has to recall everything, and you who remember only the few things I wanted to forget?

At this moment I am beset by other memories. I had just killed Dalla Piccola when I received a note from Lagrange. This time he wanted to meet me at place Fürstenberg, at midnight, when the place is fairly ghostly. I had, as God-fearing people would say, a guilty conscience, as I had killed a man, and feared (irrationally) that Lagrange already knew. But he obviously had something else to talk about.

"Captain Simonini," he said, "we need you to keep an eye on a curious character, a priest . . . how can I put it . . . a satanist."

"Where do I find him, in hell?"

"I'm not joking. He's a certain Abbé Boullan, who years ago came to know a certain Adèle Chevalier, a lay sister in the convent of Saint-Thomas-de-Villeneuve at Soissons. Strange rumours began to circulate about her. It was said she had been cured of blindness and had made certain prophecies. The convent began to fill up with followers, her superiors became worried, the bishop moved her away from Soissons and, all of a sudden, our Adèle chooses Boullan as her spiritual guide, and no doubt they're well matched. And so they decide to establish a society for the reparation of souls, in other words dedicating themselves to Our Lord not only through prayer but through various forms of physical atonement, to make good for the wrongs done by sinners against him."

"No harm in that, I'd have thought."

"Except that they start preaching that you have to commit sin in order to free yourself from it, that humanity was debased by the double adultery of Adam with Lilith and Eve with Samael (don't ask me who these people are – in my church I was only taught about Adam and Eve) and that you have to do certain things which are not yet entirely clear, but the abbé, the young lady and many of their followers were apparently involving themselves in gatherings that were, shall we say, indecorous, where each was abusing the other. And it was also rumoured the good abbé had discreetly disposed of the fruit of his illegitimate liaisons with Adèle. All things, you might say, that are of interest to the prefect of police rather than us, except that some time ago a number of respectable women started to join the throng, the wives of high officials, even of a government minister, and Boullan manages to wheedle large sums of money out of these pious ladies. At this point the whole business became a State matter, and we had to take it over ourselves. The two of them were arrested and sentenced to three years' imprisonment for fraud and indecent behaviour, and were released at the end of 'sixty-four. Then we lost track of the abbé and thought he might have turned over a new leaf. But he recently reappeared in Paris, having finally been absolved by the Holy Inquisition after numerous acts of penitence, and is back proclaiming his beliefs that people can redress the sins of others through the cultivation of their own, and if everybody starts thinking like that, then the whole business would no longer be religious, but political. You understand? The Church itself has started to worry once more and the archbishop of Paris has recently banned Boullan from ecclesiastical duties – and about time, I'd say. Boullan's only response has been to make contact with another holy man of heretical leanings, a certain Vintras. Here in this small dossier you'll find all there is to know about him, or at least all that we know. Keep an eye on him and find out what he's up to."

"As I'm not a pious lady in search of a confessor to take advantage of her, how do I approach him?"

"No idea. Dress up as a priest perhaps. I gather you've managed even to pass yourself off as one of Garibaldi's generals, or something like that."

That's what has just come back to mind. But, my dear Abbé, it has nothing to do with you.

16

BOULLAN

Captain Simonini, during the night, after reading your indignant note, I decided to follow your example and have settled down to write almost automatically (though without staring at my navel), allowing my hand to record what my mind had forgotten. That Dr Froïde of yours wasn't such a fool.

Boullan . . . I can see myself walking with him in front of a church, on the edge of Paris. Or was it at Sèvres? I remember him saying to me, "Reparation for the sins committed against Our Lord means taking responsibility for them. Sin can be a mystical burden, and the heavier the better, so that we can relieve that load of iniquities that the Devil exacts from humanity, and we can unburden our weaker brothers who are incapable of exorcising the evil forces to which they are enslaved. Have you ever seen the *papier tue-mouches* which they have recently invented in Germany? Confectioners use it. They cover a piece of tape with treacle and hang it in the window above their cakes. Flies are attracted to the treacle, are caught in the sticky substance on the tape, and die of asphyxiation, or are drowned when the tape, now crawling with insects, is thrown into the gutter. Well, the faithful reparator must be like this fly paper: he must attract every ignominy upon himself and then become the purifying crucible."

I see him in a church where, before the altar, he has to "purify" a devotee, a woman possessed, who squirms on the ground

294

... *"You may know it is the
practice in certain lodges to stab
the host to seal an oath."* ...

[PAGE 296]

uttering disgusting blasphemies and naming demons: Abigor, Abracas, Adramelech, Haborym, Melchom, Stolas, Zaebos . . .

Boullan is wearing purple vestments with a red surplice; he bends over her and pronounces what seems to be the formula for an exorcism, but (if I heard correctly) saying the opposite, "*Crux sacra non sit mihi lux, sed draco sit mihi dux, veni Satanas, veni!*" He bends down over the penitent and spits into her mouth three times, then lifts his vestments, urinates in a chalice, and offers it to the poor woman. Then he takes a substance of evident faecal origin from a bowl (with his hands!) and, having exposed the possessed woman's chest, he smears it over her breasts.

The woman thrashes about on the ground, gasping and letting out groans which gradually subside, until she falls into an almost hypnotic sleep.

Boullan goes into the sacristy where he cursorily washes his hands. Then he goes out with me to the forecourt, sighing as if he has performed a difficult duty. "*Consummatum est,*" he says.

I remember telling him that I had come on behalf of someone who wished to remain anonymous and who wanted to practise a ritual where consecrated hosts were required.

Boullan smiled contemptuously: "A black mass? But if a priest is taking part then he consecrates the hosts there and then, and the whole thing would be valid even if he's been defrocked."

I explained, "I don't think the person I'm referring to is looking for a priest to officiate over a black mass. You may know it is the practice in certain lodges to stab the host to seal an oath."

"I see. I've heard there's a bric-a-brac dealer somewhere near place Maubert who also sells hosts. You could try him."

Was it on that occasion the two of us first met?

17

THE DAYS OF THE COMMUNE

9th April 1897

I killed Dalla Piccola in September 1869. In October I received a note from Lagrange calling me, this time, to a *quai* on the Seine.

What tricks the mind can play. Perhaps I am forgetting facts of vital importance but I remember the excitement I felt that evening when, on the Pont Royal, I was amazed to see a sudden bright light. I was in front of the site for the new offices of the *Journal Officiel de l'Empire Français* which was lit by electricity at night to speed up the work. In the midst of a forest of beams and scaffolding, powerful rays shone down on a group of builders. Words cannot describe the magical effect of that great glow flaring out into the surrounding shadows.

Electric light . . . During those years, some were stupid enough to feel excited about the future. A canal had been opened in Egypt to join the Mediterranean with the Red Sea, so you no longer had to go round Africa to reach Asia (thus harming many honest shipping companies); a great exhibition was opened and, judging from its architecture, it was apparent that what Haussmann had done to ruin Paris was only the beginning; the Americans were completing a railway line that would cross their continent from east to west, and since black slaves had just been given their freedom, they could now invade the whole nation, swamping it with half-bloods, worse than the Jews. Submarine boats had appeared in the American war between North and South, where sailors no longer died from drowning but from suffocation; our parents' fine cigars were being replaced by measly cartridges that burned down in a minute, destroying every pleasure for the smoker; and our soldiers were now eating rotten meat conserved in metal cans. The Americans were said to have invented a hermetically sealed cabin which lifted people to the upper floors of a building using some kind of water piston – and there was already news that some pistons had broken one Saturday evening and people were stuck inside the box for two nights without air, not to mention water or food, so that they were found dead on the Monday.

Everyone was pleased that life was becoming easier. With one machine people could talk to each other over a distance; with another they could write mechanically without a pen. Would there be any original documents left to counterfeit?

People gazed in wonder at the windows of perfume sellers who celebrated the miraculous invigorating qualities of wild lettuce sap for the skin, a hair restorer containing quinine, Crème Pompadour with banana water, cocoa milk, rice powder with Parma violets, all devised to make lascivious women attractive, but now available even to seamstresses ready to become kept women, since many dressmaking firms were introducing a sewing machine to take over their jobs.

The only interesting invention in recent times has been a porcelain contraption that enables you to defecate while seated.

Not even I, though, had realised that this apparent

excitement would mark the end of the Empire. At the *Exposition Universelle*, Alfred Krupp had shown a fifty-ton cannon, a size never before seen, with an explosive charge of one hundred pounds per shell. The emperor was so fascinated by it that he awarded Krupp the *Légion d'honneur*, but when Krupp sent him a catalogue of weapons he was prepared to sell to any European state, the French high command, who had their own preferred arms dealers, persuaded the emperor to decline the offer. The king of Prussia, on the other hand, was evidently buying.

But Napoleon was not able to reason as clearly as he used to: his kidney stones prevented him from eating and sleeping, not to mention riding a horse; he accepted the advice of the conservatives and his wife, who were convinced that the French army was the best in the world, whereas (as it later turned out) it had no more than a hundred thousand men against four hundred thousand Prussians; and Stieber had already sent reports to Berlin about the *chassepots*, which the French believed to be the very last word in rifles, but had already become museum pieces. Moreover, Stieber was pleased to note, the French had failed to assemble an intelligence service equal to theirs.

But let us get to the point. I met Lagrange at the agreed place.

"Captain Simonini," he said, ignoring all formalities, "what do you know about Abbé Dalla Piccola?"

"Nothing. Why?"

"He's disappeared, and precisely while he was doing a small job for us. I believe you were the last person to see him: you asked me if you could speak to him and I sent him. And then?"

"And then I gave him the report I'd given to the Russians, so that he could show it to certain ecclesiastical authorities."

"Simonini, a month ago I received a note from the abbé saying more or less, 'I have to see you as soon as possible, I've something interesting to tell you about your Simonini.' From the tone of his message, whatever he had to say about you couldn't have been very flattering. So what's been going on between you and the abbé?"

"I don't know what he wanted to tell you. Perhaps he thought it improper for me to offer him a document which (he believed) I had produced for you. He obviously wasn't aware of our arrangement. He said nothing to me. I've seen no more of him, and in fact I was wondering what had happened to my proposal. . . ."

Lagrange fixed me in the eye for a moment, then he said, "We shall talk further about this," and left.

There was little more to talk about. Lagrange would be following my every move, and if he really had a clear suspicion, the famous stab in the back would be coming my way, even though I'd closed the abbé's mouth.

I adopted certain precautions. I went to an armourer in rue de Lappe and asked for a swordstick. He had one, but it was badly made. I then remembered having seen the window of a cane seller in my favourite passage Jouffroy, and there I found a splendid example with an ivory handle in the form of a snake and an ebony shaft – remarkably elegant, as well as sturdy. The handle is not particularly suitable for leaning on if you happen to have a bad leg since, though slightly curved, it is more vertical than horizontal; but it works perfectly if the cane is used as a sword.

The swordstick is a fine weapon even when you are confronted by someone with a pistol: you pretend to be frightened, move back and point the cane, preferably with your hand shaking. He starts laughing and takes hold of it to pull it away, but by doing so he helps you draw the sword, which is pointing towards him and deadly sharp, and while he is still bewildered, wondering what he's holding in his hand, in a flash you wield the blade, slashing him almost effortlessly from one temple, crosswise down to the chin, ideally cutting through a nostril, and even if you don't gouge an eye, the blood pouring from his forehead would block his vision. It's the surprise that counts, and at that point your opponent is finished.

If he is an adversary of little importance, then retrieve the shaft and make your departure, leaving him disfigured for the rest of his life. But if he's more dangerous, then after the first slash, following the movement of your arm, slice back with a horizontal thrust, and make a clean cut through his throat – in this way he won't have to worry any more about his scar.

Not to mention the dignified and respectable appearance you make when you're walking with a cane of this kind – it's expensive but worth it, and in certain cases expense should not be spared.

Returning home one evening, I met Lagrange in front of the shop.

I lightly waved my stick but then realised the secret

service would hardly have given someone like him the task of getting rid of someone like me, and so I prepared for what he had to say.

"A fine object," he said.

"What?"

"The swordstick. With a pommel of that kind, it couldn't be anything else. You're worried about someone?"

"You tell me, Monsieur Lagrange."

"You are worried about us, I know. You realise you've become a suspect. However, allow me to be brief. Before long there's going to be a war between France and Prussia, and our friend Stieber has filled Paris with his agents."

"You know them?"

"Not all of them, and that is how you come in. Having offered Stieber your report on the Jews, he regards you as someone, shall we say, who can be bought. . . . Well then, one of his men has arrived in Paris – that fellow Goedsche who I think you've already met. We believe he's looking for you. You'll become the Prussian spy in Paris."

"Against my own country?"

"Don't be a hypocrite. It's not even your country. And if it worries you, you can do it for France. You'll be transmitting false intelligence provided by us to the Prussians."

"That doesn't seem too hard. . . ."

"On the contrary, it's highly dangerous. If you're discovered in Paris then we'll have to pretend we don't know you. You'll therefore be shot. And if the Prussians find out you're a double agent then they'll kill you, though by less lawful means. In this whole business you have, let's say, a fifty per cent chance of saving your skin."

"And if I don't accept?"

"You'd have a one per cent chance."

"Why not zero?"

"Because of your swordstick . . . but don't count too much on it."

"I knew I had loyal friends in the service. Thank you for your consideration. Very well. I accept, and do so freely and patriotically."

"You are a hero, Captain Simonini. Please await further orders."

A week later Goedsche appeared in my shop, looking more sweaty than usual. It was hard to resist the temptation to strangle him.

"You know I regard you as a plagiarist and a counter-feiter," I said.

"No more than you," said the German, with an unctuous smile. "Did you imagine I wouldn't find out eventually how your story about the Prague cemetery is based on that book by Joly, who ended up in prison? I'd have found it for myself, without your help. You just made the task easier."

"Do you realise, Herr Goedsche, being a foreigner on French soil, that all I have to do is mention your name to certain acquaintances and your life would not be worth one centime?"

"Do you realize that yours would be worth no more if, once arrested, I were to mention your name? Peace, therefore. I am trying to sell that chapter of my book as fact, to safe buyers. We shall go halves, seeing that we have to work together from now on."

A few days after the beginning of the war, Goedsche took me to the roof of a house beside Notre Dame, where an old man kept a number of dovecotes.

"This is a good spot for releasing pigeons, since there are hundreds of them around the cathedral and no one notices. Each time you have useful information, write a message and the old man will send one of them off. Similarly, you must pass here each morning to find out whether there are any instructions for you. Simple, no?"

"But what sort of information do you want?"

"We don't yet know what is of interest to us in Paris. For the moment we are keeping an eye on the areas at the front. But sooner or later, if we win, we'll be interested in Paris. And then we'll want news about troop movements, about the presence or absence of the imperial family, about morale among citizens, in other words about everything and nothing. It's up to you to show initiative. We might need maps, and no doubt you'll want to know how we manage to stick geographical charts around the neck of a pigeon. Come downstairs with me."

On the lower floor there was another man in a photographic darkroom, and a room with a wall painted white and one of those machines which at fairs are called magic lanterns, and which project pictures on walls or on large cotton sheets.

"This fellow will take your message, however long it is, and however many pages, he'll photograph it and reduce it on a sheet of collodion, which is sent off by pigeon. When the message arrives, the image is enlarged by projecting it on a wall. And the same will happen if you receive long

. . . "When the message arrives, the
image is enlarged by projecting it
on a wall." . . .

[PAGE 305]

messages. But it's no longer safe here for a Prussian – I'm leaving Paris tonight. We can keep in touch sending messages on the wings of a dove, like two lovers."

The idea disgusted me, but I was stuck with him, damn it, and just because I'd killed a priest. Anyway, what about all those generals who kill thousands of men?

Thus we found ourselves at war. Lagrange passed me the odd piece of news every now and then to send on to the enemy but, as Goedsche had said, the Prussians weren't particularly interested in Paris and were more concerned about finding out how many men the French had in Alsace, at Saint-Privat, at Beaumont, at Sedan.

In the days before the siege, Parisians were still living gaily. In September it was decided to close all entertainment halls, out of solidarity with the plight of the soldiers in action as well as to allow firemen to be sent to the front, but barely a month later the Comédie-Française was given permission to put on performances for the families of dead soldiers, though on a reduced scale, without heating and with candles instead of gas lighting. After that, various productions were resumed at the Ambigu, the Porte Saint-Martin, the Châtelet and the Athénée.

But September marked the beginning of difficult times with the tragedy at Sedan. As soon as Napoleon had been taken prisoner by the enemy, the Empire collapsed and the whole of France fell almost (almost, at that stage) into a state of revolution. The Republic was proclaimed, but in the same republican ranks, so far as I could understand, there were two conflicting forces: one wanted to use the

*. . . By mid-September the
Prussians had reached the gates of
Paris, had occupied the forts that
should have protected it, and were
shelling the city. . . .*

[PAGE 309]

defeat as an opportunity for an out-and-out revolution, while the other was ready to sign for peace with the Prussians so as not to succumb to those reforms which – it was said – would have led to out-and-out communism.

By mid-September the Prussians had reached the gates of Paris, had occupied the forts that should have protected it, and were shelling the city. Five months of terrible siege during which starvation was to become the chief enemy.

I understood little and cared less about the political intrigues and the marches in various parts of the city, and felt at such times it was better not to be seen around too much. But the question of food certainly did concern me, and each day I kept up to date through the local shopkeepers about what we might expect. As I walked through public gardens like the Jardin du Luxembourg, it seemed at first as if the city had been overrun with livestock, as sheep and cows had been herded within the city walls. But by October it was said that no more than twenty-five thousand oxen and a hundred thousand rams were left, which was nothing to feed a metropolis.

Slowly households were reduced to frying goldfish, hippophagy was killing off every horse not under the protection of the army, a bushel of potatoes cost thirty francs, and Boissier the grocer was selling a box of lentils for twenty-five. Rabbits were nowhere to be seen and butchers had no hesitation, first, in displaying fine, plump cats and then dogs. All the exotic animals in the Jardin des Plantes were killed for meat, and on Christmas night, for those with money to spend, a sumptuous menu was on offer at *Voisin* with elephant consommé, roast camel *à l'anglaise*, jugged kangaroo, bear chops *au sauce poivrade*, antelope terrine with truffles, and cat garnished with baby mice, since not only were sparrows no longer seen on the rooftops but even mice and rats were disappearing from the sewers.

The camel was acceptable, and not too bad, but rats no. Even in times of siege there were smugglers and black market-eers, and I well remember one (extremely expensive) meal, not in one of the great restaurants but in a *gargotte* almost on the edge of the city, where along with a few privileged guests (not all belonging to the best of Parisian society, but at such times class differences are forgotten) I was able to taste pheasant and the freshest *pâté de foie d'oie*.

In January, an armistice was signed with the Germans. It allowed them to symbolically occupy the capital in March, and I have to say it was quite humiliating even for me to watch them parading along the Champs-Élysées in their spiked helmets. They established themselves to the north-east of the city, leaving the French government to control the south-western side, in other words the fortresses of Ivry, Montrouge, Vanves, Issy and others, including the heavily fortified stronghold of Mont-Valérien from which the western part of the capital could be easily bombarded (as the Prussians had shown).

The Prussians then left Paris, and the French government under Thiers was formed. But the National Guard, now getting hard to control, had already seized cannon purchased by public subscription and hidden them at Montmartre, and Thiers sent General Lecomte to recapture them. At first Lecomte ordered his men to shoot at the National Guard and upon the crowd, but in the end his soldiers joined the rebels, and he was taken prisoner by his own men. Meanwhile someone, somewhere or other, had recognised another general, General Thomas, who was not well remembered from the repressions of 1848. What was more, he was in civilian dress, perhaps because he was going about his own business, but everyone began to claim he was spying on the rebels. He was led to where Lecomte was waiting, and both of them were shot.

Thiers and the rest of the government withdrew to Versailles and at the end of March the Paris Commune was proclaimed. Now it was the French government (at Versailles) who besieged and bombarded Paris from the Mont-Valérien fortress, while the Prussians let everyone get on with it, indeed they were fairly indulgent in allowing people across their lines, so that Paris had more food during its second siege than it did in the first: though starved by their fellow countrymen, they were being indirectly supplied by their enemies. And someone, comparing the Germans with the Thiers government, suggested that the kraut-eaters were good Christians after all.

While news was arriving of the French government's withdrawal to Versailles, I received a note from Goedsche telling me that the Prussians were no longer interested in what was going on in Paris and so the pigeon loft and photographic darkroom would be dismantled. But on the same day I received a visit from Lagrange, who appeared to have guessed what Goedsche had written.

"My dear Simonini," he said, "you must do for us what

you were doing for the Prussians, and keep us informed. I've just had those two wretches you were working with arrested. The pigeons have returned where they were trained to go, but we can make use of the darkroom materials. We had our own fast line of communication for military information between Issy fort and an attic room in the Notre Dame area. You'll send us your information there."

"You'll send 'us' – us who? You were, how do you say, a member of the imperial police. You ought to have gone with your emperor. But it now seems you're speaking as an emissary of the Thiers government. . . ."

"Captain Simonini, I am one of those who remain even when governments go. I'm now following my government to Versailles – if I stay here I'll end up just like Lecomte and Thomas. These lunatics are quick to shoot. But we'll give them as good as we get. When we need to know something specific you'll receive more detailed orders."

Something specific . . . Easier said than done, given that different things were going on in different parts of the city – platoons of the National Guard were parading with the red flag and with flowers in the barrels of their rifles in the same districts where respectable families had locked themselves inside their houses waiting for the return of the lawful government. Among those elected to the Commune, it was impossible to understand, either from the newspapers or from the gossip in the marketplace, who was on which side, since they included labourers, doctors, journalists, moderate republicans, angry socialists, and diehard Jacobins who dreamt of returning not to the Commune of 'eighty-nine but to the terror of 'ninety-three. But the general atmosphere in the streets was of great gaiety. Had it not been for the men in uniform, you might have imagined a large popular celebration. The soldiers were playing what, in Turin, we used to call *sussi* and here is called *au bouchon*, while officers strutted about in front of the girls.

This morning I remembered I had among my old belongings a large boxful of cuttings from that period, which now come in useful for reconstructing what my memory alone cannot do. They were from newspapers of all leanings: *Le Rappel*, *Le Réveil du Peuple*, *La Marseillaise*, *Le Bonnet Rouge*, *Paris Libre*, *Le Moniteur du Peuple* and others. I don't know who read them – perhaps only those who wrote them. I bought them to see whether they had any facts or opinions that might have been of interest to Lagrange.

I could see how confused the situation was when I met Maurice Joly one day among a confused crowd in an equally confused demonstration. He barely recognised me because of my beard and then, remembering I was a Carbonaro or something similar, assumed I was a supporter of the Commune. For him I had been a kind and generous companion in a time of difficulty. He took me by the arm, led me to his house (a very modest apartment on quai Voltaire) and confided in me over a glass of green chartreuse.

"Simonini," he said, "after Sedan I took part in the first republican revolts; I marched to support the continuation of war, but I realised these fanatics wanted too much. During the Revolution, the Commune saved France from invasion but such miracles of history don't happen twice. Revolution isn't proclaimed by decree – it is born from the womb of the people. There's been a moral canker in this country for twenty years: it cannot be cured in two days. France is capable only of emasculating its finest offspring. I suffered two years' imprisonment for opposing Bonaparte and when I left prison I was unable to find a publisher who would print my new books. You'll say there was still the Empire. But when the Empire fell this republican government indicted me for taking part in a peaceful invasion of the Hôtel de Ville at the end of October. All right, I was acquitted as they couldn't prove I used any violence, but this is the reward to those who have fought against the Empire and against that vile armistice. Now it seems the whole of Paris is basking in this Communard utopia, but you have no idea how many are trying to leave the city to avoid military service. It is said they are about to introduce conscription for all men between eighteen and forty, but look how many young men there are wandering brazenly around the streets and in the districts where the National Guard don't even dare to enter. There are not many who want to get killed for the Revolution. How sad."

Joly seemed an incurable idealist who would never be content with things as they were, though I have to say things always seemed to go wrong for him. But I was concerned about his mention of conscription and decided it was time to whiten my beard and my hair. Now I looked like a dignified sixty-year-old.

In the squares and marketplaces I found many who, unlike Joly, supported the new laws, laws such as the cancellation of rent increases imposed by landlords during the siege, the return of all work tools that workers had pledged to pawnshops during the same period, the granting of pensions to the wives and children of National Guardsmen killed in action, and the postponement of obligations on commercial debts. All these fine things bled the coffers of the Commune and benefited the rabble.

But that same mob (as was clear from discussions around place Maubert and in the local brasseries), while applauding the abolition of the guillotine, condemned (of course) the law that prohibited prostitution, turning onto the streets so many women in the district. So all the Paris whores emigrated to Versailles, and I have no idea where those brave National Guardsmen went to slake their lust.

Then, to alienate the bourgeoisie, there were the anti-clerical laws, such as the separation of Church and State and the confiscation of Church property, and many rumours circulated about the arrest of priests and monks.

In mid-April an army advance guard from Versailles penetrated the north-western districts near Neuilly, shooting every *fédéré* they captured. The Arc de Triomphe was shelled from Mont-Valérien. A few days later I witnessed the most incredible moment of the siege: the procession of Freemasons. I didn't think of the Masons as Communards, but there they were with their standards and their aprons asking the government in Versailles to agree to a truce so the wounded could be evacuated from the districts that had been shelled. They arrived as far as the Arc de Triomphe where, on that occasion, there was no cannon fire as it was clear that most of their brethren were outside the city with the monarchists. But, in short, though there may be honour among thieves, and though the Freemasons at Versailles had worked to obtain a one-day truce, the agreement stopped there and the Freemasons in Paris were siding with the Commune.

If I remember little else about what happened on the surface during the days of the Commune, it is because I was moving around Paris under the ground. A message from Lagrange informed me of what the military high command wanted to know. It is well known that Paris is perforated underground by its system of drains, so often described by novelists, but beneath the city's network of sewers, stretching as far as its boundaries and beyond, is a maze of limestone and chalk caves and ancient catacombs. Much is known about some of these, but little about others. The army knew about the tunnels connecting the ring of fortresses outside central Paris, and when the Prussians arrived they hurriedly blocked up many entrances so as to prevent the enemy from organising an unwelcome surprise. The Prussians, however, hadn't considered entering that maze of tunnels, even when the opportunity arose, for fear of being unable to get out and losing their way in a minefield.

Very few, in fact, knew anything about the tunnels and catacombs, and most of these were criminals who used the labyrinths for smuggling goods past the city customs posts, and to escape from police round-ups. My job was to question as many blackguards as possible, so as to learn my way around these passageways.

I remember, when acknowledging receipt of my orders, that I couldn't resist asking, "But doesn't the army already have detailed maps?" To which Lagrange answered, "Don't ask stupid questions. At the beginning of the war our military leaders were so sure of winning that they distributed only maps of Germany and none of France."

* * *

In times when good food and wine were scarce, it was easy to renew acquaintance with people I'd met at some *tapis francs* and take them to a more reputable tavern where I could offer them chicken and the finest wine. And they'd not only talk, but would take me on some fascinating subterranean excursions. It was just a question of having good lamps and of noting a series of features of every kind along the way so as to remember when to turn left or right, such as the outline of a guillotine, an old sign, a charcoal sketch or a name, perhaps drawn by someone who was never to leave that place again. The ossuaries shouldn't deter you either, since by following the right sequence of skulls, you'll arrive at some stairway leading up into the cellars of an obliging establishment from where you can emerge to see the stars again.

Some of these places were soon to be opened to visitors, but others were known at that time only to my informants.

In short, between late March and the end of May, I gained a certain expertise and sent sketches to Lagrange indicating several possible routes. Then I realised my messages were of very little use since the government forces were now entering Paris without using the underground passageways. Versailles had five army corps by then, with soldiers who were well trained and briefed and had only one purpose, as was quickly apparent: not to take prisoners – every *fédéré* they captured had to be killed. Orders were even given, as I was to see with my own eyes, that when a group of prisoners exceeded ten, the firing squad would be replaced by a machine gun. And the regular soldiers were reinforced with *brassardiers*

– convicts or worse – wearing a tricolour armband, who were even more ruthless than the regular troops.

On Sunday the 21st of May at two o'clock in the afternoon, eight thousand people gathered in festive spirit for the concert in the Jardins des Tuileries in aid of the widows and orphans of the National Guard, no one yet realising that the number of unfortunates to benefit was soon to increase alarmingly. At four-thirty, as the concert was still in progress (though this was only discovered later) the government forces entered Paris by the city gate at Saint-Cloud, occupied Auteuil and Passy and shot all the captured National Guardsmen. It is said that by seven o'clock that evening at least twenty thousand *Versaillais* were in the city, but heaven knows what the leaders of the Commune were doing. It all goes to show that organising a revolution requires men with good military training. But such people don't get involved, and stay on the side with the power. Which is why I can see no reason (by which I mean no good reason) for staging a revolution.

On Monday morning the men from Versailles set up their cannon at the Arc de Triomphe and someone seemed to have ordered the Communards to abandon a coordinated defence of the city and for each to barricade themselves in their own district. If this is true, then the stupidity of the *fédéré* commanders was able to shine through once again.

Barricades were erected everywhere, with the help of an apparently enthusiastic population, even in the most hostile districts of the Commune, such as those of the Opéra or Faubourg Saint-Germain, where the National

Guardsmen drove the most elegant women out of their homes, spurring them to pile their finest furniture in the street. A rope was drawn across the street to mark the line of the next barricade and everyone began depositing uprooted paving slabs or sandbags; chairs, chests of drawers, benches and mattresses were thrown down from the windows, sometimes with the consent of the occupants, sometimes with their owners in tears, cowering in the back room of a now empty apartment.

An officer pointed to his men at work and said to me, "You too can lend a hand, citizen. We're here to die for your liberty as well!"

I pretended to join in, and made as if to pick up a stool at the far end of the street, then continued on round the corner.

The fact that Parisians have enjoyed building barricades for at least a century, and then taking them down at the first cannon shot, seems quite irrelevant: barricades are built out of a feeling of heroism, though I'd like to see how many of those who build them stay there up to the right moment. They'll follow my example, and only the most stupid ones will be left to defend them, and will be shot where they stand.

The only way of understanding how events were proceeding in Paris would have been from a dirigible balloon. Rumours suggested that the École Militaire, where the cannon of the National Guard were kept, had been occupied, others that there was fighting at place Clichy, while others claimed that the Germans were allowing the government forces to enter

319

from the north. Montmartre was seized on the Tuesday, and forty men, three women and four children were taken to the place where the Communards had shot Lecomte and Thomas, made to kneel, and were shot one by one.

On the Wednesday I saw many public buildings in flames, including the Tuileries – some said they had been set ablaze by the Communards to stop the advance of the government troops, and indeed that there were mad Jacobins, *les petroleuses*, who went around with a bucket of petroleum to start up fires; others swore they had been caused by government howitzers while yet others blamed old Bonapartists who were taking advantage of the situation to destroy compromising archives – and at first I thought that was what I would have done if I had been in Lagrange's position, but then it occurred to me that a good secret service agent hides information but never destroys it, since it may come in useful one day against someone.

Out of an excess of scruples, but with much fear of finding myself in the midst of fighting, I went for the last time to the pigeon loft, where I found a message from Lagrange. He told me I need no longer communicate by pigeon, and gave me an address at the Louvre, which had been occupied by now, and a password to get me through the government roadblocks.

At that same moment I heard that government forces had reached Montparnasse. I remembered how at Montparnasse I had been taken to visit a vintner's cellar. From there, you entered an underground passageway that followed rue d'Assas as far as rue du Cherche Midi and then emerged in an abandoned storeroom in a building at carrefour de la Croix-Rouge, a crossroads still heavily occupied by Communards. Seeing that my underground investigations had so far been of no benefit, and that I had to obtain some results in order to earn my pay, I went to see Lagrange.

It wasn't difficult to reach the Louvre from the Île de la Cité, but behind Saint-Germain-l'Auxerrois I saw a scene that, I confess, made quite an impression upon me. A man and woman with a child were passing by, and they certainly didn't seem to be running away from a stormed barricade; but there was a squad of drunken *brassardiers* who were obviously celebrating the capture of the Louvre, and they tried to pull the man from the arms of his wife, who was holding onto him crying, and the *brassardiers* pushed all three against the wall and riddled them with bullets.

I tried to make sure I passed only through the lines of regular soldiers to whom I could give my password, and was then led to a room where several people were marking a large map of the city with coloured pins. I couldn't see Lagrange, and asked for him. A middle-aged man with an excessively normal face (by which I mean that if I had to describe him I could point out no salient feature) turned and greeted me courteously, not extending his hand.

"Captain Simonini, I presume. My name is Hébuterne. From now on whatever you had to do with Monsieur Lagrange you will do with me. You are aware that change is necessary, even in State services, especially at the end of a war. Monsieur Lagrange deserved an honourable retirement, and perhaps he is right now fishing *à la ligne* somewhere or other, away from this disagreeable confusion."

. . . A middle-aged man with
an excessively normal face . . .
turned . . .
"Captain Simonini, I presume.
My name is Hébuterne." . . .

[PAGE 321]

This wasn't the moment to ask questions. I told him about the underground passage from rue d'Assas to the Croix-Rouge, and Hébuterne commented that an operation at the Croix-Rouge would be extremely useful as he had received news that the Communards were amassing large numbers of troops there awaiting the arrival of government forces from the south. He therefore ordered me to go to the vintner's shop, whose address I had given, and to wait there for a squad of *brassardiers*.

I was thinking of taking it gently from the Seine to Montparnasse to allow enough time for Hébuterne's messenger to arrive before me, when I saw, there on the pavement on the right bank, twenty corpses laid out in a line. They must have just been shot, and seemed to be of various ages and social origins. There was a young man who looked like a labourer, his mouth gaping slightly open; next to him an older, more respectable man with curly hair and a well-groomed moustache, with hands crossed over a slightly crumpled frock coat; and beside him someone with the face of an artist; and another whose features were almost unrecognisable, with a black hole where his left eye should have been, and a towel tied around his head, as if some pious soul, or some ruthless renegade, had sought to bind up his head which had been blown apart by who knows how many bullets. There was also a woman who had perhaps once been pretty.

They were lying there in the late May sun, the first flies of the season buzzing around them, attracted by the feast. They looked as if they had been taken almost at random and shot just to set someone an example, and had been lined up on the pavement to clear the street for a platoon of government soldiers who were passing at that very moment, pulling a cannon behind them. What struck me about those faces was . . . I find it difficult to write down . . . was their *casualness*: in their sleep they seemed to show an acceptance of their common destiny.

Having reached the end of the row I was shocked to see the corpse of the last executed man, slightly apart from the others, as if it had been added to the group later. Part of the face was caked with blood, but I had no difficulty in recognising Lagrange. Changes certainly were under way in the secret service.

I have no womanish sensitivity, and had been perfectly capable of dragging a priest's corpse down into the sewers, but this sight disturbed me. Not out of pity, but because I realised it could have happened to me. All that was needed was to meet someone on the way to Montparnasse who recognised me as one of Lagrange's men – and it could just as well have been a *Versaillais* or a Communard: both sides had reason to distrust me . . . and distrust, in those days, meant death.

I decided to cross the Seine and follow the whole of rue du Bac above ground as far as the Croix-Rouge, assuming that in those areas where buildings were still on fire I'd be unlikely to find any Communards and that the government forces would not yet be on patrol. From there I could go straight into the abandoned storeroom and take the rest of the route below ground.

I feared that the defences at the Croix-Rouge would have prevented me from reaching the building but they didn't.

Armed groups stood at the entrances of various houses, awaiting orders. Conflicting information was circulating – it wasn't clear from which direction the government forces would arrive and someone was laboriously building and dismantling barricades, changing the entrance of the road according to various rumours. A larger contingent of National Guardsmen was arriving, and many of the people living in that respectable district tried to persuade the soldiers not to attempt useless acts of heroism. After all, they said, the men from Versailles were compatriots and, what is more, also republicans, and Thiers had promised an amnesty for all Communards who surrendered. . . .

I found the door of my building ajar, went inside and closed it firmly behind me, climbed down into the storeroom, then down into the underground passageway, and found my way to Montparnasse without difficulty. There I met thirty or so *brassardiers* who followed me back along the same route. From the storeroom, the men went up into various top-floor apartments, ready to overpower the occupants, but were welcomed with relief by well-dressed people who pointed out the windows commanding the best positions over the crossroads. At that moment, an officer arrived on horseback from rue du Dragon, carrying an order of alert. The order was obviously for them to prepare for an attack from rue de Sèvres or rue du Cherche-Midi, and at the corner of the two streets the Communards were pulling up paving slabs to build a new barricade.

While the *brassardiers* were readying themselves at the various windows of the occupied apartments, I did not think it fit to remain in a place where Communard bullets would, sooner or later, be arriving and so returned downstairs while there was still plenty of commotion below. Knowing the direction of fire from the windows of the building, I positioned myself at the corner of rue du Vieux Colombier so that I could slip away in the event of danger.

Most of the Communards had stacked their weapons in a pile while they worked away, so that when the shooting began from the windows they were caught unprepared. Then, even when they had retrieved them, they failed to understand where the shots were coming from and began shooting straight down towards the junctions of rue de Grenelle and rue du Four, so that I had to move back, fearing that the shots would also reach rue du Vieux Colombier. Finally, someone realised their enemy was shooting from above, and there was an exchange of fire between the crossroads and the windows of the houses, except that while the government soldiers could clearly see who they were shooting at, and fired into the mob, the Communards were still unsure which windows to aim for. In short, it was an easy massacre. Meanwhile, someone at the crossroads was shouting that they'd been betrayed. It's always the same. When you fail in something, you always try to blame someone else for your incompetence. But what betrayal, I thought – you simply have no idea how to fight. And you call this a revolution. . . .

Someone eventually managed to work out which building was occupied by the government troops and the survivors began to try breaking down the door. I imagine that by then the *brassardiers* had already returned into the underground tunnel and the Communards had found the house empty, but I decided not to wait around to find out. As I later discovered, the government forces were indeed arriving from rue du Cherche-Midi, and in large numbers, so that the last defenders of the Croix-Rouge must have been easily wiped out.

I returned to my own alleyway by the backstreets, avoiding those directions from which I could hear the rattle of gunshot. Along the walls I saw notices, freshly pasted up, from the Committee for Public Safety, urging citizens to make a last stand (*"Aux barricades! L'ennemi est dans nos murs. Pas d'hesitations!"*).

In a brasserie in place Maubert I received the latest news: seven hundred Communards had been shot in rue Saint-Jacques, the powder keg went up at the Luxembourg, and in revenge the Communards had taken various hostages from the prison of La Roquette, including the archbishop of Paris, and lined them up against the wall. The execution of the archbishop marked the point of no return. There had to be a complete bloodbath for things to return to normal.

But just as these events were being described to me, several women arrived to shouts of jubilation from the other customers. They were *les femmes* returning to their brasserie! The prostitutes banned by the Commune had been brought back from Versailles by the government forces, who allowed them once again to circulate in the city, as if to show that all was returning to normal.

I couldn't stay there in the midst of that mob. They were undoing the one good thing the Commune had achieved.

In the next few days the Commune came to an end with the last hand-to-hand combat in Père-Lachaise cemetery. It was said that a hundred and forty-seven survivors were captured and executed on the spot.

That way they learned not to stick their noses into other people's affairs.

18

THE PROTOCOLS

From the diary for 10th and 11th April 1897

The war over, Simonini resumed his normal work. Fortunately, with all the deaths, problems of inheritance were an everyday occurrence. Large numbers of those killed on or in front of the barricades were young and hadn't yet thought about making a will, and Simonini was inundated with work – and handsome profits. How wonderful it was to have peace, even if there had first been a sacrificial purification.

His diary makes little mention of the legal routine of the following years and refers only to his hope, which during that period he had never abandoned, of finding new contacts for the sale of his document on the Prague cemetery. He had no idea what Goedsche had been up to in the meantime, but had to keep ahead of him, not least because the Jews seemed to have curiously disappeared during almost the whole period of the Commune. Were they inveterate conspirators, secretly pulling strings in the Commune? Or were they, on the contrary, accumulators of capital hiding at Versailles waiting for the war to finish? But they were behind the Freemasons, and the Paris Freemasons had sided with the Commune, and the Communards had shot an archbishop. The Jews had to be involved in some way. They killed children, so killing archbishops was hardly a problem.

One day in 1876, while Simonini was pondering this question, he heard the bell downstairs. At the door was an elderly man in a cassock. He thought at first it was the usual satanist priest come to sell consecrated hosts, but then, studying him more closely, under that mass of grey but still curly hair, he recognised Father Bergamaschi. It had been almost thirty years since he'd last seen him.

For the Jesuit it was rather more difficult to be sure that the person in front of him was indeed the Simonini he had known as an adolescent, mainly because of the beard (which, after the return of peace, had become black again, with a touch of grey, as befitted a forty-year-old). Then his eyes brightened and he said, with a smile, "But of course. Simonino, it's you my boy, isn't it? Why keep me at the door?"

He was smiling: hardly, we would suggest, the smile of a tiger – more that of a cat. Simonini invited him upstairs and asked, "How did you manage to find me?"

"Ah, my boy," said Bergamaschi, "didn't you know we Jesuits are always one step ahead of the Devil? Even though the Piedmontese had driven us out of Turin, I still managed to maintain a good circle of contacts. I discovered, first of all, that you were working at a notary's office and forging wills and then, alas, that you had sent a report to the Piedmont secret service in which I appeared as advisor to Napoleon III, and was supposed to be plotting against France and the Kingdom of Piedmont at the Prague cemetery. A fine invention, there's no denying it, but then I realised you'd copied the whole thing from that heathen Sue. I tried to find you but was told you were in Sicily with Garibaldi and then that you'd left Italy. General Negri di Saint Front is still on friendly terms with the Society and directed me to Paris, where my brethren had good connections with the imperial secret service. That was how I discovered you were in touch with the Russians and that your report about us at the Prague cemetery had become a report on the Jews. But at the same time I learned you'd been spying on a certain Joly. I was able secretly to obtain a copy of his book, left in the office of someone called Lacroix who had died heroically in an armed encounter with Carbonaro bombers, and I could see that, even though Joly had taken his ideas from Sue, you had copied from Joly. Finally my German brethren informed me that a certain Goedsche had written about a ceremony, once again at the Prague cemetery, where the Jews said more or less the same things you had written in your report to the Russians. Except that I knew the first version, involving us Jesuits, was yours, and predated Goedsche's potboiler by many years."

"At last someone who gives me my due!"

"Let me finish. After that, what with war, siege and the days of the Commune, Paris was better avoided by a man of the cloth like me. I decided to come and search you out because that same story about the Jews at the Prague cemetery appeared in a booklet published in St Petersburg. But it was presented as a passage from a novel based on true facts, and therefore originated from Goedsche. And now, this year, more or less the same text has appeared in a pamphlet in Moscow. In short, up there (or down there . . . however you wish to put it) the whole question of the Jews is turning into a State matter. They're becoming a threat, but they're also a threat to us. Hidden behind this *Alliance Israélite* are the Masons, and His Holiness has now decided to start a thorough campaign against all enemies of the Church. And here we come back to you, Simonino, who must seek forgiveness for the trick you played on me with the Piedmontese. After slandering our Society, you owe something in return."

Hell, these Jesuits were even cleverer than Hébuterne, Lagrange and Saint Front. They knew everything about everyone. They needed no help from the secret services because they were a secret service themselves; they had brethren in every part of the world and followed what had been said in every language since the fall of the tower at Babel.

After the collapse of the Commune, everyone in France, even those against the Church, had become deeply religious. There was even talk of erecting a sanctuary at Montmartre, in public atonement for that tragedy caused by such godless people. If there was a climate of restoration, it was therefore just as important to work as a good restorer. "All right Father," he said, "tell me what you want."

"Let us continue along the same line. First of all, seeing that Goedsche is selling the rabbis' speeches in his own name, we have to produce a version that is more detailed and shocking; then we have to put Goedsche

. . . Bergamaschi added that, in order to make the rabbis' speeches more credible, it would be worth looking again at what Abbé Barruel had written, and above all the letter Simonini's grandfather had sent to him. . . .

[PAGE 334]

into such a condition that he can no longer continue to circulate his version."

"And how can I stop that cheat?"

"I'll tell my German brethren to keep an eye on him and, if necessary, to take steps to deal with him. From what we know of him, he can be blackmailed in all sorts of ways. But now you have to turn the rabbis' speeches into another document, more detailed, with more references to current political events. Look at Joly's satire. You have to bring out – how shall I put it – the Machiavellian character of the Jews, and the plans they have for corrupting governments."

Bergamaschi added that, in order to make the rabbis' speeches more credible, it would be worth looking again at what Abbé Barruel had written, and above all the letter Simonini's grandfather had sent to him. Perhaps he had kept a copy of it, which could very well pass as the original sent to Barruel?

Simonini found the copy of the letter in the bottom of a cupboard, in its original small casket, and agreed a sum with Father Bergamaschi as payment for such a valuable document. The Jesuits were avaricious, but they were obliged to collaborate. And that was how an issue of *Contemporain* was published in July 1878 containing the recollections of Father Grivel, a one-time confidant of Barruel, with much information that Simonini recognised from another source, and his grandfather's letter. "The Prague cemetery will follow later," said Father Bergamaschi. "If you break a sensational story all at once, after the first impact people forget it. Instead, you have to parcel it out, and each new piece of news brings the whole story back to mind."

As he wrote, Simonini found great satisfaction in this *repêchage* of his grandfather's letter and, with a tremor of righteousness, convinced himself that what he was doing was in furtherance of a clear obligation.

He set to work with renewed energy to expand the rabbis' speeches. Rereading Joly, he noticed that his attacks obviously depended less upon Eugène Sue than he had imagined on first reading it, and that he had attributed other iniquities to his Machiavelli–Napoleon which seemed ideally suited to the Jews.

In gathering together this material, Simonini realised that it was too rich and too vast. In order to impress Catholics, the rabbis' speeches had to contain lots of references to plans to corrupt public morals, and should perhaps borrow from Gougenot des Mousseaux the idea of the physical superiority of the Jews, or from Brafmann the rules for exploiting Christians through usury. Republicans, on the other hand, would be disturbed about references to greater control of the press, while for businesses and small investors, who were increasingly distrustful of the banks (which public opinion already considered the exclusive domain of the Jews), references to the economic plans of international Judaism would touch a raw nerve.

Thus he gradually developed in his mind an idea which, unbeknown to him, was very Jewish and cabalistic. Rather than a single scene at the Prague cemetery and a single gathering of rabbis, he had to prepare different speeches, one for the priest, one for the socialist, one for the Russians, another for the French. And he didn't have to prefabricate all the speeches: he had to produce separate sheets which, when shuffled into a different order, would provide the basis for one or other speech – in this way he could sell the appropriate speech to different buyers according to the requirements of each one. In other words, it was as if, like a good notary, he were drawing up different depositions, witness statements or confessions which would then be supplied to the lawyers for them to defend different cases. He therefore began to draft out his notes as protocols, and was careful not to show everything to Father Bergamaschi, allowing him only to look at those texts of a more specifically religious nature.

Simonini ends this brief description of his work during those years with a curious note: towards the end of 1878 he learned, to his great relief, that both Goedsche and Joly had died, the former probably asphyxiated by the beer which had been bloating him more and more each day, while poor Joly – desperate as ever – had shot himself in the head. May he rest in peace: he wasn't a bad fellow.

Perhaps, in recalling the dear late departed, the diarist had drunk too much. As he wrote, his words become muddled and the page eventually comes to a halt, suggesting that he had fallen asleep.

* * *

But the next day, waking when it was almost evening, Simonini found on his diary a note from Abbé Dalla Piccola who had somehow entered his office that morning, had read what his alter ego had written and, in moralistic tones, had hastened to set the record straight.

Saying what? That the deaths of both Goedsche and Joly ought not to have come as a surprise to our captain who, unless he was intentionally trying to forget, was evidently incapable of any clear recollection.

After his grandfather's letter had appeared in *Contemporain*, Simonini had received a letter from Goedsche, written in a French that was grammatically imperfect but quite explicit. "Dear Captain," the letter said, "I imagine the material appearing in *Contemporain* is just a taste of other you propose to publish, and we well know that part of that document belongs to me, considering that I can show (*Biarritz* in hand) that I am author of the whole work and you have nothing to show, not even to have assisted in the tiniest detail. Consequently, I require you first of all to desist and agree with me a meeting, preferably in the presence of a lawyer (but not of your kind) to decide the ownership of the report on the Prague cemetery. If you fail to do so then I will publish news of your deception. Immediately afterwards I will inform a certain Monsieur Joly, who is currently unaware of the matter, that you have robbed him of his literary creation. Unless you have forgotten that Joly is a lawyer by profession, you will understand that this will also cause you serious inconvenience."

Alarmed, Simonini immediately contacted Father

Bergamaschi. "You look after Joly," he said, "and we'll deal with Goedsche."

While he was still hesitating over what to do about Joly, Simonini received a note from Father Bergamaschi informing him that poor Herr Goedsche had passed away peacefully in his bed, and urging him to pray for his eternal rest, even though he was a damned Protestant.

Simonini now understood the meaning of looking after Joly. He didn't like having to do certain things, and he was after all indebted to Joly, but he could hardly compromise the successful outcome of his plans with Bergamaschi out of mere moral scruple, and we have just seen how Simonini now wanted to rely heavily upon Joly's book, without having to worry about any threat of legal proceedings from its author.

So he went once again to rue de Lappe, and bought a pistol that was small enough to be kept at home, not very powerful but with the advantage of making little noise. He remembered Joly's address and had noted that the apartment, though small, had fine carpets and wall hangings which would muffle loud noises. In any event it was better to act in the morning, when there was a clatter of carriages and omnibuses in the street below coming from the Pont Royal and rue du Bac, or passing up and down the Seine embankment.

He rang at the lawyer's door, taking him by surprise, but Joly immediately offered him some coffee and began to recount his latest misfortunes. In the eyes of most of those who read the newspapers – mendacious as always (both their readers and their editors) – despite having rejected violence and revolutionary notions, he was still regarded as a Communard. He thought it right to oppose the political ambitions of Grévy who had stood as candidate for the presidency of the Republic; and had made accusations against him in a manifesto printed and posted up at his own expense. He himself was then accused of being a Bonapartist who was plotting against the Republic; Gambetta spoke scornfully of "venal writers with a criminal record behind them", and Raymond About had portrayed him as a forger. In short, half of the French press attacked him, and only *Le Figaro* had published his manifesto, while all of the others refused to print his letters in defence.

He had, in fact, won his battle since Grévy had decided to stand down as candidate, but Joly was one of those people who was never satisfied and would go to great lengths to ensure justice was done. After challenging two of his accusers to a duel, he began legal proceedings against ten newspapers for refusal to publish, defamation and public insult.

"I presented my case in person and can assure you, Simonini, that I denounced all the scandals which the press had kept silent, as well as those already talked about. And do you know what I said to all those scoundrels (including the judges)? 'Gentlemen, I did not fear the Empire, which silenced you when it was in power, and now I care not a fig about you, who imitate it in its worst aspects!' And when they tried to prevent me speaking, I said, 'Gentlemen, the Empire put me on trial for incitement to hatred, contempt of the government, and insulting

... "A time comes when something
breaks inside, and there is no more
energy or will. They say you must live,
but living becomes a burden which
ultimately leads to suicide." ...

[PAGE 341]

the emperor, but Caesar's judges allowed me to speak. And now I demand that the judges of the Republic grant me the same freedom that I enjoyed under the Empire!'"

"And what happened?"

"I won. All but two newspapers were convicted."

"So what's still troubling you?"

"Everything. The opposing lawyer, though praising my work, said I'd ruined my future through my passionate intemperance. He told me that relentless failure followed my every step as punishment for my pride; that by attacking this and that I had become neither parliamentary deputy nor minister; that perhaps I'd been more successful as a writer than as a politician. But that's not true either, because what I have written has been forgotten, and after winning these cases I've been banished from any salons of importance. I have won so many battles and yet I am a failure. A time comes when something breaks inside, and there is no more energy or will. They say you must live, but living becomes a burden which ultimately leads to suicide."

Simonini believed what he was about to do was entirely justified. It would be saving that unfortunate soul from an extreme and humiliating gesture, the ultimate act of failure. He was about to commit an act of charity . . . and would be rid of a dangerous witness.

He asked Joly if he would take a quick look at some papers on which he wanted his opinion. He handed him a large file: they were old newspapers, but it would take a little time to understand what they were about, and Joly was sitting in an armchair, carefully collecting up pieces of paper that were slipping out of the bundle.

He began to read, unaware of what was going on, while Simonini moved quietly behind him, put the muzzle of the pistol to his head and fired the trigger.

Joly slumped forward, with a trickle of blood flowing from a hole in his temple, and his arms dangling. It wasn't hard to put the pistol in his hand. Fortunately this occurred six or seven years before the discovery of a miraculous powder that allowed the prints of fingers that had touched a weapon to be clearly detected. At the time Simonini had settled his score with Joly, the methods of a certain Bertillon were still followed, based on the measurements of the skeleton and particular bones of the suspect. No one could have suspected that Joly's death was other than suicide.

Simonini retrieved the bundle of newspapers, washed the two cups they had used for drinking their coffee and left the apartment in good order. Two days afterwards, as he later discovered, the doorkeeper, noticing the tenant's absence, went to call at the police commissariat for the Saint-Thomas-d'Aquin district. The door was broken down and the body found. According to a short newspaper report the pistol was apparently on the ground. Simonini had obviously failed to fix it properly in his hand, but it made no difference. By extraordinary good fortune there were letters on the table addressed to Joly's mother, sister and brother. None of them spoke specifically about suicide but they were all tinged with deep and noble pessimism and seemed to have been written for that very purpose. And who knows whether the poor fellow hadn't actually meant to kill himself, in which case Simonini had gone to a great deal of trouble for nothing.

This was not the first time Dalla Piccola had revealed matters to his fellow occupant which he might perhaps have learned only in confession, and which Simonini himself did not wish to recall. Simonini was somewhat offended and had written several angry comments beneath Dalla Piccola's account.

Certainly, the papers your Narrator is browsing are full of surprises, and might perhaps be worth using one day as the basis for a novel.

19

OSMAN BEY

11th April 1897, evening

Dear Abbé, I'm striving as hard as I can to reconstruct my past and you continually interrupt like a pedantic tutor correcting me every time I make a spelling mistake. . . . You are distracting me. And you're upsetting me. Very well, perhaps I did kill Joly, but I was intent on achieving an end that justified the small means I was forced to use. You should follow the example of Father Bergamaschi, with his political acumen and sangfroid, and control your own morbid petulance. . . .

Now that I was no longer beholden to Joly or Goedsche, I could work on my Prague Protocols (as I called them). I had to devise something new since the old setting of the Prague cemetery had become a commonplace almost worthy of a novel. A few years after my grandfather's letter, *Contemporain* had published "the Rabbi's Speech", purporting to be a factual report by an English diplomat, a certain Sir John Readcliff. Since the pseudonym used by Goedsche as the author of his novel was Sir John Retcliffe, it was clear where the text had come from. I lost count of the number of times the scene in the cemetery was reused by other authors – as I write, I seem to recall that a certain Bournand recently published *Les juifs nos contemporains*, where "the Rabbi's Speech" appears once again, except that John Readclif had become the name of the rabbi himself. My God, how is life possible in a world of counterfeiters?

I was therefore looking for new material to add to my protocols, and I was not averse to taking it from published works, well aware that – save for the unfortunate case of Abbé Dalla Piccola – my potential clients didn't seem the sort of people who spent their time in libraries.

Father Bergamaschi said to me one day, "Someone called Lutostansky has published a book in Russian on the Talmud and the Jews. I'll try to get a copy and have it translated by my brethren. But more importantly, there's another person who may be useful. Have you ever heard of Osman Bey?"

"A Turk?"

"He might be Serbian, but he writes in German. His book on the Jewish conquest of the world has been translated into several languages, but I think he may be in need of more information since his campaigns against the Jews are what he lives by. It is said that the Russian political police have given him four hundred roubles to come to Paris and investigate the *Alliance Israélite Universelle*. If I remember correctly, you had information about them from your friend Brafmann."

"Very little, to be honest."

"Then make it up. Offer something to this Bey and he'll give you something in return."

"How do I find him?"

"He'll find you."

I worked very little now for Hébuterne, but made contact with him every so often. We met up at the central doorway of Notre Dame and I asked for information about Osman Bey. It seems he was known to the police halfway round the world.

"He may be Jewish by origin, like Brafmann and other fanatical enemies of their race. He has a long history: he used to call himself Millinger or Millingen, then Kibridli-Zade and some time ago claimed to be Albanian. He's been deported from many countries for shady dealings, generally fraud; in others he has spent several months in prison. He's interested in the Jews because he has sensed it would be profitable. In Milan, on some occasion or other, he publicly retracted everything he'd written on the Jews, then had new anti-Jewish pamphlets printed in Switzerland and went selling them from door to door in Egypt. But his real success was in Russia, where he began writing stories about the murder of Christian children. Now he's interested in the *Alliance Israélite*. That's why we want to keep him out of France – as I've mentioned before, we don't want to start any dispute with these people. It's not in our interests, at least not for the moment."

"But he's on his way to Paris, or may already be here."

"I see you're better informed than I am. Well, if you'd like to keep an eye on him, we'd be much obliged, as always."

And so I had two good reasons for meeting Osman Bey – first, to sell him whatever I could on the Jews and, second, to keep Hébuterne informed of his movements. And a week later Osman Bey got in touch with me, leaving a note under my shop door with the address of a boarding house in the Marais.

I had imagined he might enjoy his food, and wanted to invite him to *Le Grand Véfour* to let him taste *fricassée de poulet Marengo* and *les mayonnaises de volaille*. But there was an exchange of messages in which he refused any form of invitation and told me to meet him that evening at the corner of place Maubert and rue Maître-Albert. I would see a fiacre draw up and I should approach it and make myself known.

When the vehicle stopped at the corner of the square, the face that appeared was of someone I wouldn't wish to meet on a dark night in the streets of my area: long, dishevelled hair, hooked nose, hawk-eyed, pasty complexion, as spindly as a contortionist, and a nervous tic in his left eye.

"Good evening, Captain Simonini," he said immediately. "In Paris even the walls have ears, as they say. The only way for a quiet chat is by taking a drive around the city. Here the coachman can't hear us, and even if he could he's as deaf as a post."

And so our first conversation took place as evening fell on the city and a light drizzle condensed from the thick mist which slowly advanced until it almost obscured the cobbles in the streets. It seemed as if the coachman had received instructions to wind his way through the most deserted districts and along the darkest lanes. We could have spoken undisturbed even in boulevard des Capucines, but Osman Bey was evidently enjoying the *mise en scène*.

"Paris seems deserted. Look at the passersby," said Osman Bey, with a smile that lit his face as a candle might light a skull (despite his ravaged face he had magnificent teeth). "They move like ghosts. Perhaps at the first light of day they hurry back to their graves."

I was losing my patience: "I admire your turn of phrase, it reminds me of Ponson du Terrail at his best, but perhaps we can talk about more concrete matters. For example, what can you tell me about a certain Hippolyte Lutostansky?"

"He's a swindler and a spy. He was a Catholic priest, defrocked for doing, shall we say, things he shouldn't have done with young boys – and this in itself is a very poor recommendation since, heavens above, man is weak, as we know, but if you're a priest you have a duty to maintain a certain dignity. Instead, he became an orthodox monk . . . and I know enough about Holy Russia to say that in those monasteries, remote as they are from the world, older monks and novices are bound together in mutual . . . how shall I put it? . . . brotherly affection. But I'm not a gossipmonger and have no interest in other people's affairs. All I know is that your Lutostansky has taken huge amounts of money from the Russian government for writing tales about human sacrifices by Jews, the usual story about the ritual killing of Christian children. As if he treated children any better himself. There are also rumours that he approached several groups of Jews saying that for a sum of money he would retract everything he'd published. You can hardly imagine the Jews forking out a single sou. No, he is not to be trusted."

Then he added, "And I forgot . . . he's syphilitic."

I have been told that the great storytellers always portray themselves in their characters.

Osman Bey listened patiently to what I had to tell him, smiling knowingly at my vivid description of the Prague cemetery, and then interrupted: "Captain Simonini, this certainly sounds like literature, just as much as what you were suggesting about me. All I'm looking for is clear evidence about relations between the *Alliance Israélite* and Freemasonry and – if it's possible not to dig around in the past but to forecast the future – about relations between French Jews and the Prussians. The *Alliance* is a power which is casting a net of gold around the world so that it will own everything and everyone, and this is what has to be proved and exposed. Powers like the *Alliance* have existed for centuries, even before the Roman empire. That's what makes them work; they've existed for three thousand years. Just think how they've taken over France through a Jew like Thiers."

"Was Thiers a Jew?"

"And who isn't? They're all around us, watching over us, controlling our investments, directing our armies, influencing the Church and governments. I bribed someone working for the *Alliance* (the French are all corrupt) and have copies of the letters sent to various Jewish committees in countries bordering Russia. These committees extend along the whole frontier and, while the police watch the major roads, their messengers travel over fields, marshlands and waterways. It's a single web. I have informed the Tsar of this conspiracy and have saved Holy Russia. I alone. I love peace. I would like a world ruled by moderation, where the word *violence* no longer has any meaning. If the world were rid of Jews, who use their money to finance arms dealers, we'd have a hundred years of happiness."

"And so?"

"And so one day we'll have to try out the only reasonable solution, the final solution – the extermination of all Jews. Even children? Yes, even children. I know the idea might seem Herodian, but when the seed is bad it's not enough for the plant to be cut down – it has to be eradicated.

If you don't want mosquitoes, you kill the larvae. Concentrating on the *Alliance Israélite* can only be a first step. The *Alliance* can only be destroyed through the complete elimination of the race."

At the end of that journey through the deserted streets of Paris, Osman Bey made a proposal.

"What you have offered me, Captain, is very little. You cannot expect me to give you important information on the *Alliance*, about which I will soon know everything. But I propose a pact: I am able to investigate the Jews of the *Alliance*, but not the Freemasons. Coming from mystical, orthodox Russia, and without any particular acquaintances in this city's financial and intellectual circles, I cannot join the Freemasons. They take people like you, with watches in their waistcoat pockets. It shouldn't be difficult to find your way in among them. I'm told you claim to have been part of one of Garibaldi's campaigns – a Mason if ever there was one. So then, you tell me about the Masons and I'll tell you about the *Alliance*."

"A verbal agreement and no more?"

"Between gentlemen there's no need to put things in writing."

20

RUSSIANS?

12th April 1897, nine in the morning

Dear Abbé, we are definitely two different people. I have proof of it.

This morning – around eight o'clock – I awoke (in my own bed), went into my office, still in my nightshirt, and caught sight of a black figure slipping away downstairs. I immediately noticed that someone had interfered with my papers. I grabbed my swordstick, which was fortunately within easy reach, and went down into the shop. I saw a dark shadow like some bird of ill omen passing into the street. I pursued it and – either by pure misfortune or because the intruder had carefully planned his escape – I tripped over a stool which shouldn't have been there.

I rushed out limping into the passageway, with my swordstick unsheathed, but, alas, I could see no one. My visitor had gone. But it was you, I swear it. And, as a matter of fact, I returned to your apartment and your bed was empty.

12th April, midday

Captain Simonini,

I am replying to your message having only just woken up (in my bed). I swear I could not have been in your apartment this morning as I was asleep. But just as I was awakening, around eleven o'clock, I was terrified by the sight of a man – certainly you – disappearing along the corridor where the costumes hang. Still in my nightshirt I followed you as far as your apartment, saw you descend like a phantom into your junk shop and slip out through the door. I too tripped over a stool and by the time I had reached impasse Maubert there was no trace of the figure. But I could swear it was you. Tell me whether I'm right, I beg of you . . .

12th April, early afternoon

Dear Abbé,

What is happening to me? I'm clearly ill. There are moments when I seem to go faint and then regain consciousness to find you have been writing in my diary. Are we the same person? Think a moment, in the name of good sense rather than logical reasoning. If our two encounters had both happened at the same time, it would be possible to imagine that one person was me and the other was you. But what each of us experienced happened at different times. Certainly, if I arrive home and see someone running off, then I can be sure that person is not me; but the idea that he must be you is based upon the belief, with very little basis to it, that this morning there were only the two of us in this house.

If there were only the two of us, then something is not right. You would have been rummaging through my things at eight o'clock in the morning and I would have pursued you. Then I'd have gone rummaging through your things at eleven and you'd have followed me. But why does each of us remember the time and moment in which he found the intruder in his house and not the time and moment in which *he* entered the other's house?

We could, of course, have forgotten, or have wanted to forget, or we could have kept quiet about it for some reason. But I, for example, am quite sure, in absolute honesty, that I have not kept quiet about anything. And there again, let's be honest, the idea that two different people would both have the same desire at the same time to conceal a certain fact from the other seems rather fanciful, and not even Montépin would have dreamt up such a story.

It is more likely that three people were involved. A mysterious Monsieur Mystère, who I thought was you, enters my apartment in the early morning. At eleven o'clock the same Monsieur Mystère, who you think is me, enters your place. Does it seem so incredible, with all the spies around?

But this does not confirm that we are two different people. The same person can, as Simonini, remember Mystère visiting at eight, then lose his memory and, as Dalla Piccola, remember Mystère visiting at eleven.

The whole story, therefore, doesn't really answer the problem of our identity. It has simply complicated the lives of both of us (or of that person who we both are) by involving a third person who is able to enter our apartments as and when he pleases.

And what if, rather than three of us, there are four? Mystère 1 enters my place at eight and Mystère 2 enters your place at eleven. What relationship is there between Mystère 1 and Mystère 2?

There again, can we be entirely sure that the person who

pursued your Mystère was you and not me? That's a fine question, you must admit.

In any event, let me warn you. I have my swordstick. As soon as I see another figure in my house, I'll strike and won't check first who it is. It's unlikely to be me, and that I'd be killing myself. I might kill Monsieur Mystère (either 1 or 2). Or I might kill you. So beware.

12th April, evening

Your words, which I read on awakening from a long slumber, troubled me. And, as if in a dream, a picture came to mind of Dr Bataille (but who was he?) at Auteuil, who, while rather drunk, gave me a small pistol, saying, "I'm frightened, we've gone too far, the Masons want us dead, you'd better be armed." I was afraid, more about the pistol than the threat, since I *knew* (how?) I could take care of the Masons. The following day I left the gun in a drawer here in the apartment in rue Maître-Albert.

This afternoon you frightened me, and so I went back to the drawer. I had a strange feeling, as if I were repeating something I had already done, but then I pulled myself together. Enough about dreams. Around six o'clock this evening I ventured cautiously towards your apartment, along the corridor where the costumes hang. I saw a dark figure coming towards me, a man who was bent forwards, holding just a small candle. It might have been you, my God, but I lost my head. I shot him and he fell at my feet, motionless.

... *He was dead, with a single*
shot to his heart. ...

[PAGE 356]

He was dead, with a single shot to his heart. I had fired a gun for the first time in my life, and I hope the last. How appalling.

I rummaged through his pockets. All he had were letters written in Russian. And then, looking at his face, it was obvious he had the high cheekbones and slightly slanting eyes of a Kalmuk, not to mention his blond, almost white hair. He was certainly a Slav. What did he want from me?

I couldn't let the corpse remain in the house. I carried it down into your cellar, opened the trapdoor leading to the sewer and this time found the courage to climb down the steps, dragging the body with great difficulty and, at the risk of being suffocated by the miasma, took it as far as the point where I thought I should find the bones of the other Dalla Piccola. Instead, I had two surprises. First, that those vapours and that underground mould, by some miracle of chemistry, the supreme science of our time, had helped to preserve for decades what ought to have been my mortal remains, which had been reduced to a skeleton, but with some vestige of a substance similar to leather, so as to retain a form that was still human, though mummified. The second surprise was that beside the presumed Dalla Piccola I found two other bodies, one of a man in a cassock, the other of a half-naked woman, both in a state of decomposition, but one of whom seemed very familiar. Who were these corpses that put me in such turmoil and filled my mind with such unspeakable images? I do not know, nor do I wish to find out. But our two stories are much more complicated than they seem.

Don't tell me now that something similar has happened to you. I cannot bear this game of double coincidence.

12th April, night

Dear Abbé, I don't go round killing people – at least, not without cause. But I went down to have a look at the sewer, where I haven't been for years. Good Lord, there are indeed four corpses. One of them I left there a long time ago, another one you yourself took down this evening, but the other two?

Who is visiting my sewer and dumping bodies? The Russians? What do the Russians want from me – from you – from us?

Oh, quelle histoire!

21

TAXIL

From the diary for 13th April 1897

Simonini was anxious to understand who had entered his house – and Dalla Piccola's. He thought back to the early years of the 1880s when he used to visit the salon of Juliette Adam (whom he had met as Madame Lamessine at the bookshop in rue de Beaune). There he had come to know Juliana Dimitrievna Glinka, and through her made contact with Rachkovsky. If someone had broken into his (or Dalla Piccola's) apartment, he had certainly been sent by one of those two who, he seemed to remember, were rivals hunting for the same treasure. But fifteen years or so had passed since then, during which so much had happened. How long had the Russians been following him?

Or was it the Freemasons? He must have done something to upset them. Perhaps they were looking for compromising papers. Back at that time he had tried to make contact with the Freemasons to satisfy Osman Bey, as well as Father Bergamaschi, who was breathing down his neck because Rome was about to launch a full-scale attack on the Freemasons (and on the Jews who were supporting them) and needed fresh material – they had so little that *Civiltà cattolica*, the Jesuit journal, had been forced to republish his grandfather Simonini's letter to Barruel, even though it had already been printed three years earlier in *Contemporain*.

He thought back: at the time he had been unsure whether it was a good idea for him to join a lodge. He would be subject to certain rules of obedience, would have to attend meetings and could not refuse favours to brethren. All of this would have reduced his freedom of movement. And what was more, he could not exclude the possibility of the lodge, before accepting him, carrying out investigations into his current situation and his past, something he could not allow. Perhaps it would be better to blackmail some Mason and use him as an informer. A notary who had drawn up so many false wills (and for inheritances of a considerable value) must surely have come across some Masonic dignitary or other.

There again, perhaps he didn't have to make outright threats of blackmail. Simonini had felt for some time that his move from *mouchard* to international spy had certainly been profitable, but had not proved sufficient to satisfy his ambitions. Being a spy obliged him to live an almost hidden existence, but as he grew older he felt an increasing need for a more rewarding and respectable social life. This was how he saw his true vocation: not to be a spy, but for everyone to think he was a spy, and one who played at different tables, so that no one was ever sure for whom he was collecting information, and how much information he might have.

Being thought of as a spy was very profitable as everyone was trying to get what they believed to be price-less secrets from him, and they were prepared to spend a great deal for them. But because they did not want to be open about it, they used his business of lawyer as a pretext, paying his exorbitant bills without batting an eyelid and, indeed, not only paying excessively for trivial legal services but doing so without receiving any information. They thought quite simply they had paid their bribe and were waiting patiently for some news.

The Narrator feels that Simonini was ahead of his time: in reality, with the spread of a free press and new ways of communication, with telegraph and radio now imminent, confidential information was becoming increasingly rare, and this could have led to difficulties for the secret agent. Better not to have any secrets, but to make people believe you have. It was like living on a private income or enjoying earnings from patent rights – you enjoy a life of leisure while others boast about having received amazing revelations from you, your fame increases, and the money rolls in without you lifting a finger.

Whom could he contact? Who might fear being blackmailed without any actual blackmail taking place? The first name that leapt to mind was Taxil. He recalled he had met him when he had forged some letters (from whom? to whom?) and that he had spoken with a certain self-importance about his membership of a lodge called *Le Temple des amis de l'honneur français*. Was Taxil the right man? He didn't want to make a false move and sought advice from Hébuterne. His new contact, unlike Lagrange, never changed meeting place: it was always a point to the rear of the central nave in Notre Dame.

Simonini asked him what the secret service knew about Taxil. Hébuterne began to laugh: "It's usually we who ask you for information, not the other way round. But this time I'll see what help I can give. The name rings a bell, but it's nothing to do with the secret service, it's a police matter. I'll let you know in a few days."

The report arrived by the end of the week and was most interesting. It stated that Marie Joseph Gabriel Antoine Jogand-Pagès, alias Léo Taxil, was born in Marseilles in 1854, had been taught by the Jesuits and by the age of eighteen, as an obvious consequence, had begun working for anti-clerical newspapers. In Marseilles he mixed with women of ill repute, including a prostitute later sentenced to twelve years' hard labour for killing her landlady, and another subsequently arrested for attempting to murder her lover. The police may have been unkind in alleging other casual relationships, and this was strange since it appeared that Taxil had also worked for them in providing information about his dealings with republican circles. But perhaps the police also found him an embarrassment as he was once prosecuted for advertising what were described as *Bonbons du Serrail,* which were in effect aphrodisiac pills. In 1873, again in Marseilles, he sent letters to local newspapers, all with the false signatures of fishermen, warning that the coastal waters were infested with sharks, and creating considerable alarm. Later, when convicted for writing articles offending religion, he escaped to Geneva. There he circulated stories about the existence of a ruined Roman city submerged beneath Lake Geneva, attracting hordes of tourists. He was expelled from Switzerland for spreading false and misleading information and moved first to Montpellier and then Paris, where he established a *Librairie Anticléricale* in rue des Écoles. He had recently joined a Masonic lodge but was expelled soon after for unworthy conduct. It appeared that his anti-clerical activity was no longer as profitable as it had been and he was heavily in debt.

Simonini now remembered all about Taxil. He had produced a series of books which, as well as being anti-clerical, were also distinctly anti-religious, such as a *Life of Jesus* told through highly irreverent illustrations (for example, depicting relations between Mary and the dove of the Holy Spirit). He had written a scurrilous novel, *The Jesuit Son*, which proved that the author was a charlatan. It carried a dedication on the front page to Giuseppe Garibaldi ("whom I love like a father"). So far so good. But the title page promised an "Introduction" by Giuseppe Garibaldi. The title of the introduction was "Anti-clerical thoughts" and it took the form of a furious tirade ("When I see a priest before me, and especially a Jesuit, the quintessential priest, I am struck by the whole baseness of his nature to the point that it makes me shudder and feel sick") but there was absolutely no mention of the work it apparently introduced – and it was clear that Taxil had taken this text by Garibaldi from somewhere else and had presented it as if it had been written for his book.

Simonini did not wish to take any risks with someone of this kind. He decided to present himself as a notary by the name of Fournier, and dressed himself in a fine well-groomed wig of indeterminate colour, tending

. . . *a* Life of Jesus *told through
highly irreverent illustrations
(for example, depicting relations
between Mary and the dove
of the Holy Spirit). . . .*

[PAGE 362]

towards auburn, with a parting to one side. He added side whiskers of the same colour to lengthen his face, which he lightened with a suitable cream. In the mirror, he tried to fix a slightly vacant smile which would reveal two gold incisors, thanks to a minor masterpiece of dentistry which enabled him to cover his natural teeth. This small denture also distorted his speech and thus altered his voice.

He sent a *petit bleu* by pneumatic post to his man in rue des Écoles, inviting him to the *Café Riche* the following day. This was a fine way of introducing himself, since many illustrious people had passed through that restaurant and a parvenu inclined to bragging could hardly have resisted the delights of sole or woodcock *à la Riche*.

Léo Taxil had a chubby, oily face ornamented with a fine moustache. He had a broad forehead and balding pate from which he was continually wiping sweat, a rather overly accentuated elegance, and spoke loudly with an insufferable Marseillais accent.

He didn't know the exact reasons why this notary wished to talk to him, but gradually began to flatter himself that Maître Fournier was an acute observer of human nature, like many of those whom novelists of the time described as "philosophers", and was interested in his anti-clerical arguments and in his singular experiences. And he therefore entertained his host with stories about his juvenile pranks, talking while he ate: "When I spread the story about the sharks around Marseilles, all the resorts from Plage des Catalans as far as Prado were empty for weeks. The mayor said the sharks had definitely come from Corsica following a ship that had been throwing the rotten remains of smoked meat in the sea, the municipal commission asked for a company of *chassepots* to be sent out on a tug-boat expedition and a hundred of them actually arrived at General Espivent's headquarters! And the story about Lake Geneva? Journalists arrived from every part of Europe! Word got around that the underwater city had been built during the time of Caesar's *De bello gallico*, when the lake was so narrow that the River Rhone could cross it without their waters merging. The local boatmen did good business carrying tourists to the middle of the lake, and used to pour oil on the water so they could see better. . . . A famous Polish archaeologist sent an article back home in which he described having seen a crossroads with an equestrian statue on the bed of the lake! Man's principal trait is a readiness to believe anything. Otherwise, how could the Church have survived for almost two thousand years in the absence of universal gullibility?

Simonini asked for information about *Le Temple des amis de l'honneur français*.

"Is it difficult to join a lodge?" he asked.

"All you need is to be well off and ready to pay the annual dues, which are steep. And to show you're willing to comply with the rules on mutual care between brothers. And as for morality, they talk a great deal about it, but even last year the speaker of the Grand College of Rites was the owner of a brothel in the Chaussée-d'Antin, and one of the thirty-three most influential brethren in Paris is a spy, or rather the head of the secret service, which is the same thing – a certain Hébuterne."

"But what do you have to do to be admitted?"

"There are certain rites – if only you knew! I have no idea whether they really believe in the Great Architect of the Universe they're always talking about, but they certainly take their ceremonies seriously. You'd never guess what I had to do to become an apprentice!"

And here Taxil began to tell some hair-raising stories.

Simonini wondered whether Taxil, a compulsive liar, might not have been inventing it all. Wasn't he revealing things that an adept should have jealously guarded? Hadn't he perhaps described the whole ritual in a rather ludicrous fashion? Taxil replied casually, "Ah, you know, I'm no longer bound by any duty. Those imbeciles have expelled me."

He seemed to have a hand in a new newspaper in Montpellier, *Le Midi Républicain,* which in its first issue had published letters of encouragement and solidarity from various important people, including Victor Hugo and Louis Blanc. Then, suddenly, all those supposed signatories had sent letters to other newspapers with Masonic leanings denying ever having given such support and complaining bitterly about the way their names had been used. This was followed by several Masonic trials, during which Taxil's defence consisted, firstly, in presenting the originals of those letters and, secondly, in attributing Hugo's behaviour to the illustrious old man's senile decay – thus harming his first argument with an intolerable insult to a figure revered both by nation and Freemasonry.

Simonini now remembered the moment when, as Simonini, he had forged the two letters from Hugo and Blanc. Taxil had obviously forgotten the episode. He was so accustomed to lying, even to himself, that he was able to describe the letters with an apparent glint of honesty in his eyes, as if they had been genuine. And though he might have vaguely recalled a notary called Simonini, he wouldn't have connected him with Maître Fournier.

What mattered was that Taxil professed a deep hatred towards those who had once been fellow members of his lodge

Simonini immediately realised that, by encouraging Taxil's storytelling skills, he would be able to gather some toothsome material for Osman Bey. But another idea was forming in his fertile imagination, first of all as a mere impression, the seed of an intuition, and then as a plan which was complete in almost every detail.

After the first meeting, when Taxil had tucked into his food with such great enthusiasm, the fake Maître Fournier invited him to *Père Lathuile*, a popular little restaurant at the Barrière de Clichy, where you could eat a renowned *poulet sauté* and an even better-known *tripes à la mode de Caen* – to say nothing of its cellar – and between one smack of the lips and another, he asked whether, for a respectable payment, he might be prepared to write his memoirs as an ex-Mason for some publisher or other. At the mention of payment, Taxil indicated he was most interested in the idea. Simonini arranged a further appointment and went straight off to see Father Bergamaschi.

"Bear in mind, Father," he said, "we are dealing here with a diehard enemy of the Church, whose anti-clerical books are no longer bringing him the income they once did. He's also well acquainted with the Masonic world against which he holds a deep grudge. All that's needed is for Taxil to convert to Catholicism, to recant all his anti-religious works and expose all the secrets of Freemasonry, and you Jesuits would have a tireless propagandist at your service."

"But a person doesn't convert just because you tell him to."

"With Taxil, I think it's only a question of money. And all you have to do is tickle his fancy for spreading false information, and let him imagine himself on the front page, and he'll change his allegiances straight away – what was the name of that Greek who burned down the Temple of Diana at Ephesus just so everyone would talk about him?"

"Herostratus. Yes, of course," said Bergamaschi, pondering. "And there again, the ways of the Lord are infinite. . . ."

"How much can we give him for a clear conversion?"

"Having said that a sincere conversion ought to be made freely, *ad majorem Dei gloriam*, we shouldn't be too fussy. But don't offer him more than fifty thousand francs. He'll say it's too little, but point out to him that first of all he's saving his soul, which is priceless, and secondly, if he writes against the Masons he will enjoy the benefit of our distribution system, which means hundreds of thousands of copies."

Simonini wasn't sure he'd be able to secure the deal, so took the precaution of going to Hébuterne and telling him there was a Jesuit plot to persuade Taxil to turn against the Masons.

"If only it were true," said Hébuterne. "Just for once my opinions coincide with those of the Jesuits. You see, Simonini, I speak to you as a dignitary of no little importance in the Grand Orient, the only true Masonic order, which is lay, republican and, although anti-clerical, not anti-religious, since it recognises a Great Architect of the Universe – so each person is free to recognise him as the Christian God or as an impersonal cosmic force. The presence of that rascal Taxil is still causing us embarrassment, even though he's been expelled. What is more, we wouldn't be upset if an apostate began saying things about Freemasonry that were so terrible that no one could believe them any longer. We are expecting an attack from the Vatican, and we don't expect the Pope to be particularly gentlemanly. The Masonic world is tainted by various confessions and the writer Ragon, many years ago now, listed seventy-five kinds of Freemasonry, fifty-two rites, thirty-four orders (including twenty-six androgynous orders) and fourteen hundred grades of ritual. And I could tell you about the Knights Templar and Scottish Freemasonry, about the Rite of Heredom, the Rite of Swedenborg, the Rite of Memphis and Misraim (established by that scoundrel and charlatan Cagliostro), and then Weishaupt's 'Unknown Superiors', the Satanists,

Luciferians or Palladians as they are otherwise known . . . it's all Greek to me. The various satanic rites bring us the worst publicity of all, and even some of our more respectable brethren have taken part in them, perhaps for purely aesthetic reasons, without realising the harm they're doing us. Proudhon may have been a Freemason for only a short time, but forty years ago he wrote a prayer to Lucifer: 'Come, Satan, come, thou the calumniated of priests and kings! Let me embrace thee and press thee to my bosom!' That Italian Rapisardi wrote *Lucifero*, which was just the usual myth about Prometheus, and Rapisardi wasn't even a Freemason, but Garibaldi praised him to the skies, and so it's now taken as gospel that the Freemasons worship Lucifer. Pope Pius IX never failed to find the Devil behind everything that Freemasonry did. Then some time ago the Italian poet Carducci, part republican and part monarchist, a great windbag and unfortunately a great Freemason, wrote a hymn to Satan, even crediting him with the invention of the railways. Carducci then claimed that Satan was a metaphor, but by that time everyone seemed to think the cult of Satan was the Masons' principal amusement. In short, our brethren wouldn't be displeased if a person who had already been long disgraced, notoriously expelled from Freemasonry, and a blatant turncoat, were to start a series of violently libellous pamphlets against us. It would be a way of getting back at the Vatican, driving it onto the side of a pornographer. If you accuse a man of murder you might be believed, but if you accuse him of eating children for lunch and dinner like Gilles de Rais, then no one will take you seriously. If you reduce anti-Masonry to the level of the *feuilleton* then you have reduced it to colportage. So, yes, we could do with people who bury us in mud."

From this, it was clear that Hébuterne was shrewder and more intelligent than his predecessor Lagrange. He was unable to say there and then how much the Grand Orient might be able to invest in such a venture, but his reply came a few days later: "One hundred thousand francs. But on condition that it is complete and utter rubbish."

Simonini therefore had one hundred and fifty thousand francs for buying rubbish. If he offered Taxil only seventy-five thousand francs, with the promise of a large circulation, he would say yes immediately, considering the difficulty he was in. And seventy-five thousand would be left for Simonini. A fifty per cent commission wasn't bad.

On whose behalf could he make the offer to Taxil? On behalf of the Vatican? Maître Fournier, the notary, didn't have the appearance of a papal plenipotentiary. Perhaps he could arrange a visit from someone like Father Bergamaschi. After all, that's the whole point of priests, so that people can convert and confess their murky past to them.

But, when it came to murky pasts, should Simonini trust Father Bergamaschi? Taxil mustn't be left in the hands of the Jesuits. There had been atheist writers who had sold a hundred copies of a book and then fallen to their knees before the altar and recounted the story of their experience as converts, boosting their sales to two or three thousand. After all, when it came to it, the anticlericalists counted for something among the republicans in the city, but the reactionaries who dreamt of the good old days, of king and curate, lived in the countryside and, even excluding those who couldn't read (though the priest would read to them), were legion, like demons. By keeping Father Bergamaschi out of it, Taxil could be offered a deal on his new publications, and invited to sign a contract where whoever was collaborating with him would be entitled to ten or twenty per cent on his future works.

In 1884 Taxil had dealt the ultimate blow to the feelings of good Catholics by publishing *The Secret Loves of Pius IX*, defaming a pope now dead. In the same year the reigning pope, Leo XIII, published his encyclical *Humanum Genus*, which was a "condemnation of the philosophical and moral relativism of Freemasonry". And, in the same way as he had railed against the monstrous errors of socialists and communists in his encyclical *Quod Apostolici muneris*, this time he directed his attack towards the doctrines of Freemasonry, exposing the secrets that made their followers captives and prone to every kind of crime, since "this continual pretence and desire to remain hidden, this binding of men, like vile slaves, to the arbitrary will of others, and to abuse them as blind instruments for any enterprise, however evil it be, and to arm their right hands for bloodshed after securing impunity for the crime, are excesses from which nature recoils". Not to mention, obviously, the naturalism and relativism of their doctrines, which made human reason the sole judge of everything. And it was perfectly clear what the results would be: the Pope stripped of his temporal power, the intention to annihilate the Church, marriage made into a simple civil contract, the education of children no longer carried out by priests but by lay teachers, and the teaching that "all men have the same rights, and are in every respect of equal and like condition; that every man is, by nature, independent; that no one has the right to command another; that it is tyranny to require men to obey any authority other than that which emanates from themselves". So that for the Freemasons "the origin of all civil rights and duties is in the people, or in the State" and the State could only be godless.

It was obvious that "once the fear of God and reverence for divine laws is taken away, the authority of rulers trampled upon, sedition permitted and approved, and the popular passions urged on to lawlessness, with no restraint save that of punishment, revolution and universal subversion will necessarily follow . . . which is the deliberate plan and open purpose of many associations of communists and socialists: to such intentions the Masonic sect cannot properly describe itself as hostile".

News of Taxil's conversion had to break as soon as possible.

At this point Simonini's diary becomes confused. It seemed he could no longer remember how Taxil was converted, or by whom. It was as if his memory were leaping ahead, allowing him to remember only that Taxil, in just a few

. . . *he published* Les frères trois-points
*(the three points being those of the thirty-third
Masonic degree),* Les Mystères de la Franc-
Maçonnerie *(with dramatic illustrations of
satanic invocations and hideous rites)* . . .

[PAGE 375]

years, had become a Catholic voice against Freemasonry. After proclaiming *urbi et orbi* his return to the bosom of the Church, he published *Les frères trois-points* (the three points being those of the thirty-third Masonic degree), *Les Mystères de la Franc-Maçonnerie* (with dramatic illustrations of satanic invocations and hideous rites) and immediately afterwards *Les soeurs maçonnes*, which described the (hitherto unknown) female lodges – and a year later *La Franc-Maçonnerie dévoilée*, followed by *La France Maçonnique*.

From these first books the description of an initiation was enough to make readers shudder. Taxil had been summoned to attend the Masonic lodge at eight o'clock one evening, and was met at the door by a brother. At eight-thirty he was closed in the Chamber of Reflection, a small closet decorated with black walls, death's heads and crossbones, and inscriptions such as, "If vain curiosity brings you here, depart now!" All of a sudden the gaslight flame dimmed, a false panel slid back along grooves hidden in the wall, and Taxil looked down into an underground chamber lit with grave lamps. A freshly cut human head lay on a block from which trickled blood and, as he recoiled in horror, a voice which seemed to come out of the wall cried, "Tremble, O Profane one! You see before you the head of a false brother who revealed our secrets! . . ."

It was of course a trick, observed Taxil, and the head must have been that of a stooge whose body was hidden in the empty cavity of the block. The wicks of the lamps had been soaked in camphorated alcohol mixed with coarse cooking salt, known by fairground conjurers as the "infernal blend", which emits a greenish light and gives a cadaverous appearance to the face of the person pretending to be beheaded. But he had heard of other initiations where walls were made with frosted mirror onto which, as soon as the flame of the gas jet was lowered, a magic lantern made moving ghostlike figures appear, and masked men who surrounded a figure in chains raining dagger blows upon him. This all goes to show what shameful means were used by the lodge to exert control over impressionable aspirants.

After this, a so-called Brother Terrible prepared the profane, removing his hat, coat and right shoe, rolling up his right trouser leg above his knee, exposing his arm and chest on the side of his heart, blindfolding him, turning him around several times and, having made him climb up and down various steps, took him to the Hall of the Lost Steps. A door opened, while a Brother Expert, using an instrument consisting of large clashing springs, simulated the sound of enormous chains. The postulant was taken into a room where the Expert held the point of a sword to his bare chest and the Master asked, "Profane, what do you feel at your chest? What do you have on your eyes?" The aspiring Mason had to reply, "A thick blindfold covers my eyes, and I feel the point of a weapon at my chest." And the Master, "This metal, sir, always raised to punish disobedience, is the symbol of remorse that would strike your heart if, to your disgrace, you should become a traitor to the society you wish to enter; and the blindfold over your eyes is the symbol of the blindness of the man who was ruled by his passions and immersed in ignorance and superstition."

Then someone took hold of the aspiring Mason, turned him round several times until he began to feel dizzy, then pushed him in front of a large screen made of several layers of thick paper, similar to the hoops through which circus horses jump. At the command for him to enter the cavern, the poor fellow was pushed with great force against the screen, the paper broke and he fell onto a mattress positioned on the other side.

Then there was the *everlasting staircase*, which was actually a tread-wheel, so that the blindfolded aspirant found there was always another step to climb, and each step lowered as he climbed it, so that he remained at exactly the same height, and thus he continued to climb for half an hour without knowing what height he had reached, though obviously he was still at exactly the same level as when he started.

They even pretended to subject the apprentice to bloodletting and baptism by fire. For the blood, a Brother Surgeon bound his arm, pricked it fairly forcefully with the point of a toothpick, and another brother dripped a tiny amount of warm water over the postulant's arm so that he thought it was his blood that was flowing. For the trial of the red-hot iron, one of the Experts rubbed a part of his body with a dry cloth and then placed a piece of ice on it, or the hot part of a candle which had just been blown out, or the base of a liqueur glass heated with burning paper. Finally the Master told the aspirant

. . . At the command for him to enter the cavern, the poor fellow was pushed with great force against the screen, the paper broke and he fell onto a mattress positioned on the other side. . . .

[PAGE 377]

about the secret signs and special mottoes used by the brothers to recognise each other.

Simonini now recalled these works of Taxil, not as an instigator but as a reader. Nonetheless he remembered that before each new work of Taxil's appeared, he would go (having therefore read it in advance) and describe its contents to Osman Bey as if they were extraordinary revelations. It was true that on the following occasion Osman Bey would point out that everything he had told him on the previous occasion had then appeared in a book by Taxil. But it was easy for Simonini to reply that, yes, Taxil was his informer, and it was hardly his fault that, having revealed Masonic secrets to him, Taxil had sought financial gain by publishing them in a book. Otherwise he would have had to pay to stop him publishing his experiences – and in saying this, Simonini fixed Osman Bey with an eloquent stare. But Osman replied that money spent on persuading a chatterbox to keep quiet was money wasted. Why should Taxil be made to hold his tongue about the very secrets he had just revealed? And, understandably suspicious, Osman offered Simonini no revelation in exchange concerning what he had learned about the *Alliance Israélite*.

At which point Simonini stopped passing information to him. But Simonini reflected, as he wrote, that the problem is, "Why do I remember giving Osman Bey information I'd received from Taxil, but nothing about my dealings with Taxil?"

Good question. If he remembered everything then

he wouldn't be here writing down what he was gradually piecing together. *Quelle histoire!*

With that sage comment, Simonini went to bed, reawakening on what he thought to be the following day, bathed in sweat as if after a night of bad dreams and indigestion. But returning to his desk he discovered he had awoken, not the next day, but two days later. During not one but two nights of restless sleep, Abbé Dalla Piccola, not content at dumping corpses in Simonini's own personal sewer, had made his inevitable appearance, describing events about which the captain clearly knew nothing.

22

THE DEVIL IN THE NINETEENTH CENTURY

14th April 1897

Dear Captain Simonini,

Once again: where your ideas are confused, my memories are much clearer.

So I remember meeting first Monsieur Hébuterne and then Father Bergamaschi as if it were today. I go on your behalf to receive the money I had to give (or should have given) to Léo Taxil. Then I visit Taxil, this time on behalf of Maître Fournier the notary.

"Monsieur Taxil," I say, "I have no wish to use my clerical attire as a ploy to persuade you to recognise our Lord Jesus Christ whom you deride. Whether or not you go to hell is a matter of supreme indifference to me. I am not here to offer you any promise of eternal life, but rather to inform you that a series of publications condemning the crimes of Freemasonry would find a readership of right-thinking people which I have no hesitation in describing as vast. Perhaps you have no idea what it is worth for a book to have the support of every monastery, every parish church, every diocese, not just in France but far away throughout the world. As proof that I am not here to convert you but to help you make money, I will tell you straightaway what my modest proposals are. All you must do is sign papers assuring me (or rather the religious congregation I represent) twenty per cent of your future rights, and I'll introduce you to someone who knows even more than you about the mysteries of Freemasonry."

I imagine, Captain Simonini, that we agreed the famous twenty per cent of Taxil's rights would be split between the two of us. I then made him the further offer: "There are also seventy-five thousand francs for you – don't ask where they come from, though my priestly dress might offer you some clue. Seventy-five thousand francs are yours, on trust, even before you begin, but on one condition: that tomorrow you publicly announce your conversion. On these seventy-five thousand francs – seventy-five thousand, I say – you have no percentage to pay. That's because when you deal with people like me and those who have sent me, you're dealing with people for whom money is the Devil's excrement. Count it: there are seventy-five thousand here."

I can still picture the scene, as if I were looking at a daguerreotype.

I immediately had the feeling that Taxil was not so much interested in the seventy-five thousand francs and the promise of future rights (even though the money on the table brought a twinkle to his eye), as in the idea of doing a complete about-turn and, from hardened anti-clerical, becoming a fervent Catholic. He relished the idea of shocking others and reading the news about himself in the newspapers. Much better than inventing a Roman city at the bottom of Lake Geneva.

He laughed heartily, and was already planning his forth-coming books, even with ideas for the illustrations.

"Yes," he said, "I can already see a whole book, more fantastic than a novel, on the mysteries of Freemasonry. A winged Baphomet on the cover, and a severed head to suggest the satanic rites of the Templars. . . . By God (excuse the expression, Monsieur Abbé), it will be the news of the day. And despite what those evil books of mine have said, to be a Catholic, and a believer, and on good terms with the clergy, would bring me such respectability, even among my family and neighbours, who often look at me as if it was I who had crucified Our Lord Jesus. But who do you say could help me?"

"I'll introduce you to an oracle, a creature who, when hypnotised, has incredible stories to tell about Palladian rituals."

The oracle must have been Diana Vaughan. It seemed I knew all about her. I remember going one morning to Vincennes, as if I already knew Dr Du Maurier's address. His clinic is a house of modest dimensions, with a small but attractive garden. Various patients are seated in apparent tranquillity, enjoying the sun, and blankly ignoring each other.

I introduced myself to Du Maurier, reminding him that you had spoken about me. I vaguely mentioned a society of charitable ladies who cared for mentally disturbed young women and he seemed much relieved.

"I must warn you," he said, "that today Diana is in what I term her normal state. Captain Simonini will have told you the story. In this state we have the depraved Diana, so to speak, who believes she is a disciple of a mysterious Masonic sect. So as not to alarm her, I'll introduce you as a brother Mason . . . wishing no disrespect to a member of the clergy. . . ."

He took me to a room that was simply furnished with a wardrobe and bed and where, on an armchair covered in white cloth, sat a woman with regular delicate features, soft auburn hair gathered on top of her head, a haughty gaze and a small, shapely mouth. Her lips immediately curled with scorn: "Does

Dr Du Maurier wish to thrust me into the maternal arms of the Church?" she asked.

"No, Diana," Du Maurier said. "Despite the cassock, he's one of our brethren."

"Which obedience?" Diana immediately asked.

I evaded her question with a certain skill: "I am not permitted to say," I murmured cautiously, "perhaps you know why. . . ."

Her reaction seemed fitting: "I understand," said Diana. "The Grand Master of Charleston sends you. I am glad you can give him my version of events. The meeting took place in rue Croix Nivert, at *Les Coeurs Unis Indivisibles* lodge, which I am sure you know. I was due to be initiated as a Mistress Templar, and I presented myself in all possible humility to worship the only worthy god, Lucifer, and to abominate the evil god, Adonai, God the Father of the Catholics. I approached the altar of Baphomet, believe me, full of ardour, where Sophia Sapho was waiting for me. She began to question me about the Palladian dogmas, and I replied, once again with humility, 'What is the duty of a Mistress Templar?' 'To execrate Jesus, curse Adonai, venerate Lucifer.' Is this not how the Grand Master wanted it?" and in asking this, Diana took hold of my hands.

"Certainly, it is," I replied cautiously.

"And I pronounced the ritual oration . . . 'Come, come, O great Lucifer, O great one, vilified by priests and kings!' And I trembled with emotion when the whole assembly, each person raising a dagger, shouted, '*Nekam Adonai, Nekam!*' But just as I was stepping up to the altar, Sophia Sapho gave me a paten of the kind I had seen only in the windows of shops selling religious objects, and while I was wondering what that horrible paraphernalia from the Roman cult was doing there the Grand Mistress explained to me that, since Jesus had betrayed the true God, had signed on the Tabor an evil pact with Adonai, and had subverted the order of things by transforming the bread into his own body, it was our duty to stab that blasphemous host with which priests repeat each day the betrayal of Jesus. Tell me, sir, does the Grand Master wish this act to form part of an initiation?"

"It is not for me to say. Perhaps it is better you tell me what you did."

"I refused, of course. To stab the host means believing that it really is the body of Christ, whereas a Palladian must refuse to believe this lie. Stabbing the host is a Catholic ritual for Catholic believers!"

"I believe you are right," I said. "I will pass on your justification to the Grand Master."

"Thank you, brother," said Diana, and she kissed my hands. Then, almost unthinkingly, she unbuttoned the upper part of her blouse, revealing a marble-white shoulder, and looked at me with an inviting gaze. But suddenly she fell back into the chair, as if struck by a convulsive attack. Dr Du Maurier called a nurse, and together they carried the girl to the bed. "When she has a crisis of this kind," the doctor said, "she generally passes from one state to the other. She hasn't yet lost consciousness – there's just a contracture of the jaw and tongue. All that's required is light ovarian compression. . . ."

After a short while her lower jaw dropped, flexing to the left, the mouth distorted, remaining open so that her tongue could be seen at the back, curled into a semicircle, with the tip invisible, as if the patient were about to swallow it. Then the

. . . her body curved into an arc
as though she were an acrobat,
supporting herself on just the back
of her head and her feet. . . .

[PAGE 387]

tongue relaxed, suddenly stretched out so that part of it emerged from her mouth, and moved rapidly in and out several times, as if from the mouth of a snake. Finally the tongue and jaw returned to their natural state, and the patient spoke a few words: "My tongue . . . my mouth's sore . . . there's a spider in my ear. . . ."

After a brief pause, there was a further contracture of the patient's jaw and tongue. She was once again calmed with ovarian compression, but shortly afterwards her breathing became laboured, she uttered a few disjointed phrases, her stare became fixed, the pupils directed upwards, and her whole body grew rigid. Her arms contracted and made a rotating movement, her wrists came together behind her back, her lower limbs stretched outwards. . . .

"Equinovarus feet," commented Du Maurier. "The epileptoid stage. It's quite normal. You'll see it followed by a clown-like phase. . . ."

Her face gradually tightened, her mouth opened and closed, and large white bubbles frothed out. The patient was now moaning and howling, "Ah! Ah!", her facial muscles gripped by spasms, her eyelids flickering up and down, and her body curved into an arc as though she were an acrobat, supporting herself on just the back of her head and her feet.

This terrible circus scene of a disjointed puppet who seemed weightless continued for several seconds, then the patient collapsed on the bed and assumed an attitude which Du Maurier described as "passionate", at first almost threatening, as if she were trying to fight off an aggressor, then almost childish, as if she were winking at someone. Immediately afterwards she adopted the lewd expression of a seductress luring her prey with the obscene movements of her tongue, then assumed a pose of amorous entreaty, eyes moist, arms held out, hands together, lips protruding as if to invite a kiss. Finally, peering up so high that only the whites of her eyes could be seen, she fell into an erotic swoon: "O my good Lord," she said hoarsely, "O beloved serpent, sacred asp . . . I am your Cleopatra . . . here on my breasts . . . I will feed you . . . O my love enter, the whole of you, within me. . . ."

"Diana sees a sacred serpent which penetrates her. Others see the Sacred Heart which merges with them. For an hysteric," said Du Maurier, "seeing a phallic form or a dominating masculine image is sometimes almost equivalent to seeing the man who raped her as a child. Perhaps you have seen engravings of Bernini's St Teresa: you'd see no difference between her and this unfortunate girl. A mystic is an hysteric who has met her confessor before her doctor."

Diana was meanwhile stretched out in the form of a crucifix and had entered a new state, in which she began to utter strange threats to somebody and was announcing terrifying revelations, while rolling violently on the bed.

"Let us leave her to rest," said Du Maurier. "When she reawakens, she'll have entered her second state, and will be upset about the horrible things she'll remember having said to you. You must tell your charitable ladies not to be frightened if crises such as this occur. All they have to do is hold her firm and place a handkerchief in her mouth so she doesn't bite her tongue, but it wouldn't be a bad idea to feed her a few drops of the tincture that I will give you."

Then he added, "The fact is, this creature has to be kept segregated. And I cannot keep her here. This is not a prison, it is a nursing home. People walk about, and it is useful, indeed essential, for their treatment, that they talk to each other and get the idea of living a normal, happy life. My patients are not mad. They are simply people whose nerves are shattered. Diana's attacks mustn't be allowed to affect other patients, and the intimate stories she tells during her 'bad' state, whether true or false, unsettle everyone. I hope your charitable ladies are able to keep her isolated."

The impression I gained from the meeting was that the doctor was anxious to rid himself of Diana, but that he was asking for her to be kept practically imprisoned, and was concerned about her having contact with others. Moreover, he seemed worried that someone might take what she said seriously, and therefore was safeguarding himself by immediately suggesting it was the delirium of a madwoman.

I had rented the house at Auteuil a few days before. It was nothing special, but reasonably comfortable. You entered the typical drawing room of a bourgeois family, with a mahogany divan upholstered in old Utrecht velvet, red damask curtains, a mantel clock on the fireplace between two vases of flowers under glass domes, a console table beneath a mirror and a well-polished tiled floor. Off it was a bedroom which I had prepared for Diana. The walls were hung with a pearl-grey moiré fabric and the floor had a thick carpet with large red rosettes; the curtains around the bed and the windows were of the same cloth, woven with broad stripes of violet to break up the monotony. Over the bed hung a chromolithograph depicting two pastoral lovers and on a console table a pendulum clock inlaid with small artificial stones, on either side of which two cherubs held a bunch of lilies arranged to form a candelabrum.

Upstairs were another two bedrooms. One was set aside for an old woman who was half-deaf and partial to the bottle, who had the merit of not coming from the local area and was willing to do anything to earn some money. I don't remember who recommended her, but she seemed the ideal person to look after Diana when no one else was there, and to calm her down when she had one of her attacks.

It occurs to me, as I write, that the old lady must have received no news of me for a month. Perhaps I left her enough money to get by, but for how long? I should go to Auteuil immediately, but I realise I cannot remember the address: where in Auteuil? I can hardly wander the whole area knocking at every door to ask whether there's a Palladian hysteric with a split personality living there.

Taxil publicly announced his conversion in April and his first book, *Les frères trois-points,* was already out by November, with sensational revelations about Freemasonry. I took him to see Diana at about that time. I didn't conceal her double state, and had to explain to him that she was useful to us not in her state as a God-fearing maiden, but as an unrepentant Palladian.

I had carefully studied the girl over the previous months, and had kept her changes of condition under control, sedating her with Dr Du Maurier's tincture. But I realised it was stressful waiting for her unpredictable crises. A way had to be found of changing Diana's condition upon command: this, after all, is what Dr Charcot seems to do with his hysterics.

I didn't have Charcot's magnetic power and so I went to the library to search out some more traditional treatises, such as *De la cause du sommeil lucide* by the old (and authentic) Abbé Faria. Following the indications in that book, and several others, I decided to clamp the girl's knees between my own, take her thumbs between my two fingers and stare into her eyes, then, after at least five minutes, withdraw my hands, place them on her shoulders, move them down her arms to her fingertips five or six times, then rest them on her head, bringing them down over her face, five or six centimetres apart, as far as the hollow of her stomach, with my other fingers under her ribs, and finally to let them continue down her body as far as her knees or even to the tips of her toes.

From the point of view of decency, this was too forward for the "good" Diana, and at first it seemed she was about to scream, as if (God forgive me) I was assaulting her virginity, but it was so effective that she calmed down almost immediately, became drowsy for a few minutes, and reawakened in the first state. It was easier to make her return to the second state because the "bad" Diana showed considerable pleasure in being touched, and tried to prolong my manipulation, accompanying it with unseemly movements of her body and stifled groans. Fortunately, before long, she was no longer able to avoid its hypnotic effect and, once again, she became drowsy, otherwise I would have had difficulty, both in prolonging contact, which disturbed me, and in controlling her repulsive lust.

I believe that any one of the male sex would consider Diana as a creature of singular charm, at least so far as I can judge, being one who, by disposition and vocation, has remained well away from the miseries of sex; and Taxil was clearly a man of vivacious appetites.

Dr Du Maurier, when handing his patient over to me, had also given me a trunk full of fairly elegant clothes which Diana had brought with her when she arrived for treatment – an indication that she came from a relatively prosperous family. And with evident coquettishness, on the day I told her she would be receiving a visit from Taxil, she carefully dressed up. Although she appeared vacant in both states, she was most attentive to these small feminine details.

Taxil was immediately fascinated ("Fine woman," he muttered to me, smacking his lips) and later, when he tried to imitate my hypnotic procedures, he tended to prolong his groping even when the patient had clearly already fallen asleep, so that I had to intervene with a mild "I think that's enough for now."

I suspected that if I had left him alone with Diana while she was in her primary state, he would have indulged in other liberties, and she would have allowed him. I therefore made sure that our conversations with the girl always took place when the three of us were present. Indeed, sometimes there were four. Because to stimulate the memories and energies of Diana the satanist and luciferian (and her luciferine humours) I though it appropriate that she should meet Abbé Boullan.

Abbé Boullan. After being interdicted by the archbishop of Paris, he moved to Lyon to join the Church of Carmel, founded by Vintras, a visionary who officiated wearing a large white robe embroidered with a red upturned cross, and a diadem with an Indian phallic symbol. Vintras levitated when he prayed, sending his followers into ecstasy. During his liturgies the host oozed blood but there were various rumours of homosexual practices, of the ordination of priestesses of love, of redemption through free expression of the senses – in other words, all those things to which Boullan was much inclined. So when Vintras died, he was named his successor.

He came to Paris at least once a month. Having the chance to study a creature like Diana from the demonological point of view seemed too good to be true (so as to exorcise her more effectively, he claimed, though I already knew how he went about his exorcising). He was over sixty, but still a vigorous man, with a gaze I can only describe as magnetic.

Boullan listened to what Diana had to say – which Taxil religiously noted down – but he seemed intent on other purposes and sometimes, out of our hearing, whispered words of incitement or advice to the girl. Nonetheless he was useful to us. The Masonic mysteries to be exposed certainly included the stabbing of the sacred hosts and various forms of black mass, on which Boullan was an authority. Taxil took notes about various demonic rites and, as his books gradually appeared, he concentrated more and more on these liturgies which his Masons practised whenever they had the chance.

. . . Vintras levitated when he prayed, sending his followers into ecstasy. . . .

[PAGE 393]

After publishing several books, one after the other, Taxil had almost exhausted what little he knew about Freemasonry. Fresh ideas came to him only from the "bad" Diana who appeared under hypnosis; with eyes wide open, she described scenes she might have witnessed, or might have heard spoken about in America, or might simply have imagined. They were stories that left us spellbound, and I have to say that though I am (I think) a man of experience, I was scandalised. For example, one day she began talking about the initiation of her enemy, Sophie Walder, otherwise known as Sophia Sapho. I wasn't sure whether she was aware of the incestuous character of the whole scene. She certainly didn't describe it with any tone of disapproval but rather with the excitement of someone who had been privileged to witness it.

"It was her father," Diana said slowly, "who had put her to sleep, and passed a red-hot iron over her lips. . . . He had to be sure her body was isolated from any snare that might come from outside. She had a pendant around her neck, a coiled snake. . . . Here, her father removes it, opens a basket and takes out a live snake, placing it on her stomach. . . . It is beautiful, it seems to dance as it slithers upwards towards Sophie's neck and wraps itself around her in place of the pendant. . . . Now it slides up to her face, thrusting out its tongue, which flickers towards her lips and, hissing, it kisses her. How . . . splendidly . . . slimy it is. . . . Sophie now wakes up, her mouth frothing; she gets up and remains standing, rigid as a statue. Her father unlaces her corset, revealing her naked breasts! And now with a rod he traces out a question upon her breast, and the letters appear in red on her skin, and the snake, who appeared to be asleep, wakes up hissing and moves its tail to trace out the answer, once again on Sophia's naked flesh."

"How do you know these things, Diana?" I asked her.

"I know them from when I was in America. . . . My father initiated me into Palladism. Then I came to Paris. Maybe they wanted to send me away. . . . In Paris I met Sophia Sapho. She has always been my enemy. When I refused to do what she wanted, she sent me to Dr Du Maurier. Telling him I was mad."

I go to Dr Du Maurier to find out more about Diana: "You have to understand, Doctor, my confraternity cannot help this girl unless we know where she comes from, who her parents are."

Du Maurier looks at me blankly: "I don't know anything, I've told you. She was entrusted to me by a relative who is dead."

"And the address of this relative?"

"It may seem strange, but I no longer have it. There was a fire in my office a year ago and many papers were lost. I know nothing of her past."

"But did she come from America?"

"Maybe, but she speaks French without any accent. Tell your charitable ladies not to concern themselves too much since it's quite impossible for the girl to escape her current condition and live a normal life. And they must treat her gently, allowing her to end her days peacefully – I tell you, she won't survive very long in such an advanced stage of hysteria. Before long she'll have a violent inflammation of the uterus and medical science will be powerless to do any more."

I am convinced he is lying. Perhaps he too is a Palladian (so much for the Grand Orient!) and had agreed to deal with an enemy of the sect, walling her up alive. But these are mere conjectures. It is a waste of time talking any longer to Du Maurier.

I question Diana, both in her first as well as her second state. She seems to recall nothing. Around her neck she has a gold chain with a medallion: it has the picture of a woman whom she greatly resembles. I have realised that the medallion can be opened and I have repeatedly asked her to show me what is inside. But she emphatically refuses, with an expression of fear and wild determination: "My mother gave it to me," is all she says each time.

It must now be four years since Taxil began his campaign against the Freemasons. The reaction from the Catholic world has gone far beyond our expectations: in 1887 Taxil is called by Cardinal Rampolla to a private audience with Pope Leo XIII. Official approval of his battle, and the start of a great publishing success. And economic success.

Around that time I received a curt, but eloquent note: "Most reverend Abbé, it seems that matters are going well beyond what we intended: please deal with the situation. Hébuterne."

There is no way of turning back. I'm not talking here about the author's rights which continue to flood in, but the series of tensions and alliances that have been created with the Catholic world. Taxil is now a hero in the fight against satanism, and certainly does not want to relinquish that position.

Meanwhile another short note arrived, from Father Bergamaschi: "All seems to be going well. But the Jews?"

Father Bergamaschi had already been urging that Taxil's scandalous revelations should be not just about Freemasonry but also about the Jews. And yet both Diana and Taxil were silent on that score. I wasn't surprised about Diana. Perhaps there were fewer Jews in the Americas from where she came than there were here, so the problem seemed irrelevant. But Freemasonry was full of Jews, and I pointed this out to Taxil.

"And how should I know?" he answered. "I've never come across Jewish Masons, or at least not knowingly. I've never seen a rabbi in a lodge."

"They don't go there dressed as rabbis. But I've been told by a certain well-informed Jesuit father that Monsignor Meurin, who's not just any priest but an archbishop, will prove in a forthcoming book that all the Masonic rituals have cabalistic origins, and that it's the Jewish Cabala which leads Masons to demonolatry."

"Then let us leave it to Monsignor Meurin to speak. We have enough irons in the fire."

Taxil's reluctance intrigued me (Is he Jewish? I wondered) until I discovered that during the course of his various journalistic and book-selling enterprises he was prosecuted on many occasions for defamation or obscenity and had had to pay some very harsh fines. He was therefore heavily in debt to several Jewish moneylenders, nor had he yet been able to release himself (not least because he freely spent the substantial earnings from his new anti-Masonic activity). He therefore feared that these Jews, who were content for the moment, might send him off to the debtors' prison if they felt they were under attack.

Was it just a question of money, though? Taxil was a scoundrel but yet was capable of some feelings and was, for example, closely attached to his family. And for some reason he felt a certain compassion towards Jews, the victims of many persecutions. He used to say that the popes had protected the Jews in the ghetto, if only as second-class citizens.

Success had gone to his head: believing himself to be the herald of Catholic monarchist and anti-Masonic thought, he decided to turn to politics. I was unable to follow him through all his intrigues, but he stood as candidate for a district council in Paris and found himself in competition, and in dispute, with an important journalist called Drumont, who was involved in a violent campaign against Jews and Freemasons. Drumont had a considerable following among people in the Church, and began to insinuate that Taxil was a schemer – and perhaps the word "insinuate" is too weak.

In 1889, Taxil had written a pamphlet against Drumont and, not knowing what accusations to make (both of them denouncing the Masons), he described his phobia about Jews as a form of mental alienation. And he got carried away with some recrimination about the Russian pogroms.

Drumont was a born polemicist and replied with an attack in which he spoke sarcastically about this self-appointed champion of the Church, a man who received embraces and congratulations from bishops and cardinals yet only a few years earlier had written outrageous filth about the Pope and the clergy, not to mention Jesus and the Virgin Mary. But there was worse.

I had visited Taxil several times at his house, where on the ground floor he had once had his anti-clerical bookshop, and we were often interrupted by his wife who would come and whisper in his ear. As I later discovered, many unrepentant anti-clericals still went to that address in search of anti-Catholic works, copies of which Taxil, though now a devout Catholic, still had in his storehouse in such vast quantities that he couldn't easily destroy them. And so, with great discretion, he continued to exploit this excellent line of business, always sending his wife out and never appearing in person. I was never under any illusions about the sincerity of his conversion: the only philosophical principle he adhered to was money *non olet*.

Except that Drumont had found out about this, and so attacked his Marseillais rival not only for being linked in some way with the Jews, but also for remaining an unrepentant anticlericalist. This was enough to raise grave doubts among our more God-fearing readers.

It was time to strike back.

"Taxil," I said, "I'm not interested in why you don't want to be personally involved against the Jews, but isn't it possible to bring in someone else who can deal with the matter?"

"Provided I'm not directly involved," Taxil replied. And then he added, "In fact my own revelations are no longer enough, nor even the nonsense our Diana tells us. We've created a readership that wants more. Perhaps they no longer read me to learn about conspiracies by the enemies of the Cross, but purely and simply out of love for a good story, as in those tales of intrigue where the reader is drawn to the side of the criminal."

And that is how Dr Bataille was born.

Taxil had discovered, or re-found, an old friend, a naval doctor who had travelled widely in exotic countries, nosing about here and there among the temples of various religious conventicles, but who above all had a boundless knowledge when it came to adventure stories, including the books of Boussenard or the fanciful accounts of Jacolliot, such as *Le spiritisme dans le monde* or *Voyage aux pays mystérieux*. I fully approved of the idea of going off to look for new subjects in the world of fiction (and from your diaries I notice that you yourself have been much influenced by Dumas and Sue). People are voracious readers of travel adventures or crime stories. They read for simple pleasure, then quickly forget what they have learned, and when they're told about something they have read in a novel as if it were true, they have just a vague recollection of already having heard some mention of it, and their ideas are confirmed.

The man Taxil had rediscovered was Dr Charles Hacks, who had been a specialist in Caesarean birth, had published several books on the merchant navy but had never exploited his talents as a storyteller. He seemed to suffer from serious bouts of alcoholism and was clearly penniless. From what he said, it appeared he was about to publish an important attack on religions and Christianity, which he described as "crucifixion hysteria", but when confronted with Taxil's offer he was ready to write a thousand pages against devil-worshippers, to the glory and defence of the Church.

I remember that in 1892 we began a mammoth work, a series in two hundred and forty instalments to be published over about thirty months, entitled *Le diable au XIXe siècle*. It had a great sneering Lucifer on the cover, with the wings of a bat and the tail of a dragon, and was subtitled "the mysteries of modern satanism, occult magnetism, luciferian mediums, fin de siècle cabala, Rosicrucian magic, possessions in the latent state, the precursors of the Antichrist" – all attributed to a mysterious Dr Bataille.

The work contained nothing which hadn't been written elsewhere, as was intended: Taxil or Bataille had plundered all the previous literature and had built up a hotchpotch of subterranean cults, devilish apparitions, spine-chilling rituals, more Templar liturgies featuring the usual Baphomet, and so forth. Even the illustrations had been copied from other books on occult science, which illustrations themselves had been copied. The only unpublished pictures were the portraits of Masonic grand masters, which were rather like those posters in the American prairies showing outlaws who had to be tracked down and handed over to the law, dead or alive.

Work progressed at a frenetic pace: Hacks-Bataille, after liberal doses of absinthe, described his inventions to Taxil, who wrote them up and embellished them, or Bataille busied himself over details concerning medical science, the art of poisoning, and the description of cities and esoteric rites which he had actually seen, while Taxil embroidered upon Diana's latest delusions.

Bataille, for example, began depicting the rock of Gibraltar as a spongy mass crisscrossed with passageways, cavities and subterranean caves where some of the most blasphemous sects celebrated their rituals, or describing the Masonic antics of the

. . . a mammoth work [. . .]
entitled Le diable au XIXe siècle.
It had a great sneering Lucifer on
the cover, with the wings of a bat
and the tail of a dragon . . .

[PAGE 402]

Indian sects, or the apparitions of Asmodeus, while Taxil gave a profile of Sophia Sapho. Having read the *Dictionnaire infernal* by Collin de Plancy, he suggested that Sophia had revealed that there were six thousand six hundred and sixty-six legions, each legion consisting of six thousand six hundred and sixty-six demons. Although he was drunk by this time, Bataille managed to work out that the final number of devils and she-devils totalled forty-four million, four hundred and thirty-five thousand five hundred and fifty-six. We checked his calculation, admitting with surprise that he was right, while he banged his fist on the table and shouted, "You see then, I'm not drunk!" And he was so pleased with himself that he slid under the table.

It was fascinating to imagine the Masonic toxicology laboratory in Naples, where poisons were prepared to be used on the enemies of the lodges. Bataille's masterpiece was to invent what, for no chemical reason whatsoever, he called *manna*: a toad is closed up in a jug filled with vipers and asps; there it is fed on poisonous toadstools, then digitalis and hemlock are added, and the animals are left to starve and their bodies are sprayed with a foam of powdered crystal and euphorbia; everything is placed in a still so that the moisture is slowly distilled, and finally the ash from the bodies is separated from the incombustible powders, thus obtaining not one but two poisons, one which is liquid and the other a powder, each identical in their lethal effects.

"I can already imagine how many bishops these pages will send into ecstasy," Taxil smirked, scratching his groin, as he did in moments of great satisfaction. And he said this with good reason, since with each new instalment of *Le Diable* came a letter from some prelate thanking him for his courageous revelations, which were opening the eyes of so many faithful followers.

Diana came in useful now and then. Only she could invent the *Arcula Mystica* of the Grand Master of Charleston, a small chest of which only seven examples existed in the world. Opening the lid you saw a silver megaphone, like the bell of a hunting horn but smaller; to the left a thin rope made of twisted silver threads fixed at one end to the apparatus and at the other to a contraption you put into your ear so as to hear the voice of people talking from one of the other six chests. To the right a vermilion toad emitted small flames from its open mouth, as an assurance that the communication had been activated, and seven small golden statuettes represented the seven cardinal virtues of the Palladian ladder as well as the seven main Masonic directories. In this way the Grand Master, by pressing a statuette on the pedestal, could contact his correspondent in Berlin or Naples; if the correspondent was not at his *Arcula* at that moment, he would feel a warm breeze on his face, and would whisper, for example, "I'll be ready in an hour," and on the table of the Grand Master the toad would say out loud, "In an hour."

At first we wondered whether the story wasn't rather preposterous, not least because some years earlier a certain Meucci had already patented his telectrophone, or telephone as it is now called. But such contrivances were still only for rich people and our readers were unlikely to know anything about them. In any event, such an extraordinary invention as the *Arcula* was bound to be diabolically inspired.

We met sometimes at Taxil's house, sometimes at Auteuil. We occasionally tried to work in Bataille's rathole, but the general stench that reigned there (of cheap alcohol, unwashed clothes and food left about for weeks) persuaded us to avoid the premises.

One of the problems we had was describing General Pike, the Grand Master of Universal Freemasonry who directed the destiny of the world from Charleston. But nothing is more original than what has already been published.

We had just started publishing our issues of *Le Diable* when *La Franc-Maçonnerie Synagogue de Satan* appeared, the long-awaited book by Monsignor Meurin, Archbishop of Port-Louis (where the devil was that?). Dr Bataille, who had a smattering of English, had also picked up on his travels a book called *The Secret Societies*, published in Chicago in 1873, by General John Phelps, an avowed enemy of the Masonic lodges. All we had to do was reuse what we found in those books to build up a fuller picture of this Grand Old Man, high priest of Universal Palladism, perhaps founder of the Ku Klux Klan and participant in the conspiracy that led to the killing of Lincoln. We decided that the Grand Master of the Supreme Council of Charleston bore the titles of Brother General, Sovereign Commander, Master Adept of the Grand Symbolic Lodge, Secret Master, Perfect Master, Intimate Secretary, Provost and Judge, Master Elect of the Nine, Illustrious Elect of the Fifteen, Sublime Knight Elect, Chief of the Twelve Tribes, Grand Master Architect, Scottish Grand Elect of the Sacred Visage, Perfect and Sublime Mason, Knight of the East or of the Sword, Prince of Jerusalem, Knight of the East and West, Sovereign Prince of the Rose Croix, Grand Pontiff, Venerable Master *ad vitam* of all Symbolic Lodges,

Noachite or Prussian Knight, Grand Master of the Key, Prince of Libanus and of the Tabernacle, Knight of the Brazen Serpent, Knight Commander of the Temple, Knight of the Sun, Prince Adept, Scottish Knight of Saint Andrew, Grand Elect Knight Kadosh, Perfect Initiate, Grand Inspector Inquisitor, Clear and Sublime Prince of the Royal Secret, Thirty-Three, Most Powerful Sovereign Commander General Grand Master Conservator of the Sacred Palladium, Sovereign Pontiff of Universal Freemasonry.

We quoted a letter of his which condemned the excesses of certain brethren in Italy and Spain who, "moved by a legitimate hatred towards the God of priests" glorified his adversary under the name of Satan – a being invented by priestly deception, whose name should never be pronounced in a lodge. Thus it condemned the practices of a Genoese lodge which had paraded a flag in a public procession on which was written "Gloria a Satana!", but then it was discovered that this condemnation was against satanism (a Christian superstition) whereas the Masonic religion had to maintain its purity by following the principles of Luciferian doctrine. It was the priests, with their faith in the Devil, who created Satan, satanists, witches, sorcerers, magicians and black magic, whereas the luciferians were disciples of an enlightened magic, like that of the Templars, their ancient masters. Black magic was performed by the followers of Adonai, the evil god worshipped by Christians, who had transformed hypocrisy into sanctity, vice into virtue, falsehood into truth, faith in the absurd into theological science, and whose every act testifies to his cruelty, perfidy, hatred towards mankind, barbarity and rejection of science. Lucifer, on the other hand, is the good god who opposes Adonai, as light opposes darkness.

Boullan tried to explain the differences between the various cults of what, as far as we were concerned, was simply the Devil: "For some people Lucifer is the fallen angel who has now repented and could become the future Messiah. There are sects, entirely of women, who regard Lucifer as a good female being, opposed to the wicked male God. Others see him as Satan cursed by God, but believe that Christ hasn't done enough for humanity and therefore devote themselves to adoring the enemy of God – and these are the real satanists, those who celebrate the black masses and so forth. There are worshippers of Satan who pursue only their taste for witchcraft, *envoûtement*, fortune-telling; and there are others who practise satanism as an actual religion. Among them are people who seem to be organisers of cultural gatherings, such as Josephin Péladan or, worse still, Stanislas de Guaita, who cultivates the art of poisoning. And then there is Palladism – a rite for few initiates, in which even a Carbonaro like Mazzini took part; and it is said that Garibaldi's conquest of Sicily was the work of the Palladians, enemies of God and of the monarchy.

I asked him why he accused his rivals Guaita and Péladan of satanism and black magic, when rumours I'd heard in Paris suggested that they themselves were accusing him of satanism.

"Ah," he said, "in this universe of occult sciences the boundaries between Good and Bad are extremely subtle, and what is Good for one person is Bad for others. Sometimes, even in ancient times, the difference between an angel and a witch was simply a question of age and physical charm."

"But how does this sorcery work?"

"They say that the Grand Master of Charleston fell out with a certain Gorgas from Baltimore, the head of a breakaway

Scottish Rite. He managed to obtain Gorgas's handkerchief by bribing his laundress. He left it to soak in salt water, and each time he added salt he murmured, 'Sagrapim melanchtebo rostromouk elias phitg.' He left it to dry in front of a fire of magnolia branches, then every Saturday for three weeks he offered an invocation to Moloch, holding out his arms with the handkerchief spread out over his open hands, as if in offering to the demon. On the third Saturday, towards dusk, he burned the handkerchief in flaming alcohol, put the ash on a bronze plate, left it overnight, and the following morning mixed the ash with wax and made it into a doll, a diabolical creation called a *dagyde*. He placed the *dagyde* under a glass dome attached to a pneumatic pump which removed all the air until there was a complete vacuum in the dome. At that moment his rival began to feel a series of terrible pains and couldn't understand what was causing them."

"And did he die?"

"That's not the point. Perhaps he didn't want to go quite that far. The important thing is that magic works over a distance, and that is what Guaita and his friends are doing to me."

He did not want to say any more but Diana, who had been listening, followed him with an adoring gaze.

At the appropriate point Bataille had, at my insistence, devoted a substantial chapter to the Jews in Masonic sects, going back to the eighteenth-century occultists and revealing the existence of five hundred Jewish Freemasons who were secretly confederated alongside the official lodges, so that their own lodges carried no name but only a number.

Our timing was excellent. It was more or less during that period that certain newspapers began to use a fine expression, *anti-Semitism*. We became part of an "official" current; the spontaneous mistrust of Jews became a doctrine, like Christianity or idealism.

Diana was present during these sessions and when we referred to the Jewish lodges she uttered the words "Melchisedec, Melchisedec" several times. What was she recalling? She continued, "During the Patriarchal Council, the emblem of the Jewish Masons . . . a silver chain around their neck holding a gold plaque . . . represents the Tablets of the Law . . . the Law of Moses . . ."

The idea was a good one, and here were our Jews, gathering in the Temple of Melchisedec, exchanging signs of recognition, passwords, greetings and oaths that obviously had to look fairly Hebrew, such as *Grazzin Gaizim, Javan Abbadon, Bamachec Bamearach, Adonai Bego Galchol*. The lodge, of course, was bent on undermining the Holy Roman Church and the ubiquitous Adonai.

In this way, Taxil (under the cover of Bataille) could ensure those he was working for in the Church were kept happy, without upsetting his Jewish creditors. By now, however, he could have paid them off – after all, during the first five years, Taxil had made three hundred thousand francs (net) in royalties . . . and another sixty thousand came to me.

Around 1894, I think it was, the newspapers talked of nothing but the case of an army captain, a certain Dreyfus, who had sold military intelligence to the Prussian embassy. By sheer coincidence, the villain was Jewish. Drumont pounced on the Dreyfus case straight away and I thought that our periodical *Le Diable* should also contribute a few sensational revelations. But Taxil said it was always better not to get mixed up in stories involving military espionage.

Only later did I realise what he had sensed – that it was one thing to talk about the Jewish involvement in Freemasonry, but the introduction of Dreyfus would mean suggesting (or revealing) that Dreyfus, as well as being a Jew, was also a Mason. And that would have been unwise, given that (since Masonry thrived particularly well in the army) many of the senior officers who were prosecuting Dreyfus were probably Masons.

On the other hand, there was no shortage of alternative avenues to explore – and from the point of view of the readership we had built up, our cards were better than Drumont's.

About a year after *Le Diable*'s first appearance, Taxil said to us, "You know, when it comes down to it, everything that appears in *Le Diable* is the work of Dr Bataille. Why should anyone believe what he writes? We need a Palladian convert who reveals the sect's innermost mysteries. What is more, has there ever been a good story without a female character? We presented Sophia Sapho in a negative light. She couldn't stir the sympathies of Catholic readers, even if she were to convert. We need someone who is immediately likeable, though still a satanist, as if her face shone with her imminent conversion, a naive Palladian ensnared by the sect of Freemasons, who gradually breaks free from that yoke and returns to the arms of the religion of her forebears."

"Diana," I said. "Diana is more or less the living image of what a converted sinner might be, given that she is either one or the other almost on command."

And that is how Diana arrived on the scene in issue number 89 of *Le Diable*.

Diana was introduced by Bataille, but to make her appearance more credible he immediately wrote a letter expressing dissatisfaction with the way in which she had been presented, and even criticising the picture that had been published, according to the style of the *Le Diable* periodicals. I have to say that her portrait was rather mannish and immediately we offered a more feminine picture of Diana, claiming that it was done by an artist who had been to visit her at her Paris hotel.

Diana also made her first appearance in the journal *Le Palladium régéneré et libre*, which presented itself as the voice of breakaway Palladians who had the courage to describe the cult of Lucifer down to the smallest detail, and the blasphemous expressions used during the course of their rituals. The horror still felt about Palladism was so apparent that a certain Canon Mustel, in his *Revue Catholique,* spoke about Diana's Palladian dissidence as the beginnings of a conversion. Diana contacted Mustel, sending him two one-hundred-franc notes for the poor. Mustel invited his readers to pray for Diana's conversion.

I swear that Mustel was neither invented by us nor did we bribe him, but he behaved exactly as we had hoped. And alongside his magazine came support from *La Semaine Réligieuse,* inspired by Monsignor Fava, Bishop of Grenoble.

It was, I think, in June 'ninety-five that Diana converted and *Mémoires d'une ex-palladiste* was published over the next six

*. . . we offered a more feminine
picture of Diana . . .*

[PAGE 412]

months, once again in instalments. Those who subscribed to instalments of *Palladium Régéneré* (which of course stopped publication) could transfer their subscription to the *Mémoires* or receive their money back. My impression is that, apart from a few fanatics, the readers accepted the change of position. Diana the convert, after all, was telling stories that were just as bizarre as those of Diana the sinner, and it was what the public wanted. This was Taxil's basic idea — there was really no difference between describing the private love life of Pope Pius IX and the homosexual rituals of Masonic satanists. People want what is forbidden to them, and that's that.

And this is exactly what Diana promised: "I will be writing to reveal all that happened in the Triangles and which I did everything I could to prevent, all that I have always despised and all that I believed to be good. Let the public judge. . . ."

Well done, Diana. We had created a myth. But she herself knew nothing about it. She lived under the effect of the drugs we administered to tranquillise her, and she responded only to our (my God, no, *their*) caresses.

I recall so vividly those times of great excitement. Diana, the angelic convert, received the love and admiration of priests and bishops, pious mothers and repentant sinners. *Le Pèlerin* recounted how a woman called Louise, who had been seriously ill, had been sent on a pilgrimage to Lourdes under the auspices of Diana and was miraculously cured. *La Croix*, the leading Catholic newspaper, wrote, "We have just read the draft of the first chapter of *Mémoires d'une ex-palladiste*,

shortly to be published by Miss Vaughan, and are still overcome by an indescribable emotion. How wonderful is the
grace of God in those souls who give themselves to Him. . . ."
A certain Monsignor Lazzareschi, the Holy See's delegate to
the Central Committee of the Anti-Masonic Union, authorised
a three-day thanksgiving to be celebrated for Diana's conversion at the Church of the Sacred Heart in Rome, and a hymn
to Joan of Arc, supposedly composed by Diana (though it was
in fact an aria from a musical operetta composed by one of
Taxil's friends for a Muslim sultan or caliph) was performed
at the Roman Committee's anti-Masonic feasts and sung in
several basilicas.

And then, as if the whole thing had been invented by us,
a mystic Carmelite nun from Lisieux, already regarded as a
saint despite her youth, interceded on behalf of Diana. This
Sister Teresa of the Child Jesus and of the Holy Face, having
received a copy of the converted Diana's *Mémoires*, was so
moved by this creature that she included her as a character
in her theatrical operetta, *The Triumph of Humility*, written for
her sister nuns, in which even Joan of Arc makes an appearance. And she sent Diana a photograph of herself dressed as
Joan of Arc.

Diana's *Mémoires* were translated into several languages;
the Cardinal Vicar Parocchi congratulated her upon her conversion which he described as a "magnificent triumph of Grace";
Monsignor Vincenzo Sardi, Apostolic Secretary, wrote that
Providence had allowed Diana to become part of that vile sect
so that it could be crushed more effectively; and *Civiltà Cattolica*
stated that Miss Diana Vaughan, "summoned from darkness into
the divine light, is now using her experience in the service of

the Church with publications that are unequalled for their accuracy and utility".

I saw Boullan more regularly at Auteuil. What was his relationship with Diana? Sometimes, returning to Auteuil unexpectedly, I surprised them in each other's arms, Diana staring at the ceiling with an expression of ecstasy. But perhaps she had entered her second state, had just confessed, and was enjoying the moment of absolution. More suspicious, it seemed, was her relationship with Taxil. Returning, once again without warning, I had surprised her on the couch, half-dressed, in intimate contact with a cyanotic-faced Taxil. Fine, I thought. Someone has to satisfy those carnal urges of the "bad" Diana, provided it isn't me. The idea of sexual contact with a woman is bad enough, but with a mad woman . . .

When I find myself once again with the "good" Diana, she rests her virginal head on my shoulder and cries, begging my forgiveness. The warmth of her head against my cheek and the breath of penitence cause me to shudder and I immediately withdraw, inviting her to go and kneel before a holy image and to pray for forgiveness.

Among Palladian circles (do they really exist? many anonymous letters seem to prove it and, in any event, it's quite enough to talk about something to make it exist) dark threats were being made against Diana the traitress. And in the meantime something happened that escapes me. I was about to say, the death of Abbé Boullan. And yet I have a hazy memory of him and Diana together in more recent years.

I've been overtaxing my memory. I must rest.

23

TWELVE YEARS WELL SPENT

From the diary for 15th and 16th April 1897

At this point not only do the pages of Dalla Piccola's diary intersect almost, I would say, frenetically with those of Simonini, both sometimes speaking of the same event, though from differing points of view, but Simonini's own pages become erratic as if it was difficult for him to remember the various events as well as the characters and organisations with which he'd had contact over those years. The period of time that Simonini reconstructs (often confusing dates, placing first what in all probability must have occurred later) runs from Taxil's supposed conversion until 'ninety-six or 'ninety-seven – at least twelve years – in a series of rapid notes, some almost in shorthand as if he feared leaving out things that suddenly came to mind, interspersed with more detailed descriptions of conversations, thoughts, dramatic events.

So the Narrator, finding himself without that well-balanced *vis narrandi* which even our diarist seems to lack, will limit himself to separating the recollections under different headings, as if the events had occurred one after the other, or each separate from the other, though in all probability they were taking place at the same time – so, for example, after a conversation with Rachkovsky, Simonini left to meet Gaviali that same afternoon. But, as they say, that's how it is.

Salon Adam

Simonini remembers how, after urging Taxil on the path to conversion (he does not know why Dalla Piccola had then taken the whole business out of his hands, so to speak) he decided, while not actually joining the Masons, to move among circles with more or less republican sympathies where, he imagined, he would find Masons aplenty. And thanks to the good offices of people he had met at the bookshop in rue de Beaune – in particular Toussenel – he gained admittance to the salon of Juliette Lamessine, now Madame Juliette Adam, wife of a parliamentary deputy from the republican left who was the founder of Crédit Foncier and later a senator for life. Money, high politics and culture graced the house in boulevard Poissonnière (later in boulevard Malesherbes) whose hostess was herself a writer of some note (she had indeed published a life of Garibaldi). It also attracted such statesmen as Gambetta, Thiers and Clemenceau, and writers like Prudhomme, Flaubert, Maupassant and Turgenev, and it was here that Simonini met Victor Hugo, shortly before his death, already transformed into a living monument, fossilised by age, with the title of senator and the after-effects of an apoplectic stroke.

These were not circles Simonini was used to. It must have been around that time that he had met Dr Froïde at Magny (as he recalled in his diary of the 25th of March) and had smiled when the doctor described how he'd had to buy a dress coat and a fine black cravat to go to dinner at Charcot's house. Now Simonini had to buy a dress coat and cravat as well, and not only that, but a fine new beard, from the best (and most discreet) wigmaker in Paris. Yet though his early studies had left him with a modicum of education, and during his years in Paris he had read a fair amount, he felt a certain unease in the midst of the sparkling, informed, often learned conversation in which its participants were always *à la page*. He preferred to remain silent, listened carefully to what was said and confined himself to describing certain distant military exploits during the expedition in Sicily – Garibaldi was still well looked upon in France.

Simonini was most surprised. He had expected to hear conversation that was not just republican – the least to be expected for that period – but strongly revolutionary. And yet Juliette Adam adored being surrounded by Russians of obviously Tsarist leanings and was an Anglophobe like her friend Toussenel. In her *Nouvelle Revue* she also published a figure like Léon Daudet who was rightly regarded as a reactionary to just the same extent that his father Alphonse was considered to be a genuine democrat – though let it be said, to Madame Adam's credit, that both were admitted to her salon.

Nor was it clear what was the origin of the anti-Jewish debate that often animated the conversation. Was it from socialist hatred of Jewish capitalism, of which Toussenel was an illustrious representative, or from the mystical anti-Semitism circulated by Juliana Glinka, a woman very closely linked to Russian occultism – whose practices were reminiscent of the Brazilian *Candomblé* rituals into which she was initiated as a girl when her father was serving down there as a diplomat – and, it was whispered, an intimate friend of Madame Blavatsky, the great pythoness of Paris occultism at that time?

Juliette Adam's distrust of Jewry was no secret, and Simonini was present one evening during the reading of various pieces by the Russian writer Dostoevsky, who had obviously made use of what that man Brafmann, whom Simonini had met, had revealed about the great Kahal.

"Dostoevsky tells us that to have lost their lands and their political independence, their laws and almost even their faith so many times, and always to have survived, almost more united than before, these Jews – people so dynamic, so extraordinarily strong and energetic – could not have resisted without a state over and above the existing states, a *status in statu*, which they have preserved, always and everywhere, even during the most terrible persecutions, isolating themselves, cutting themselves off from the people with whom they lived, without integrating with them, and observing one fundamental principle: 'Even when you are spread over the face of the earth, fear not, have faith that all that has been promised you will come to pass, and meanwhile live, loathe, unite, exploit, and wait, wait . . .'"

"This Dostoevsky is a great master of rhetoric," commented Toussenel. "See how he begins by professing an understanding, a sympathy, dare I say a respect for the Jews: 'Am I too perhaps an enemy of the Jews? Might it be that I am an enemy of that unfortunate race? On the contrary, I say and I write that everything demanded by humanity and justice, everything required by humanity

and Christian law, all of this must be done for the Jews
. . . .' A fine start. But then he shows how this unfortunate
race seeks to destroy the Christian world. Great move.
Not new – perhaps you've not read Marx's *Communist
Manifesto*. It begins with an incredible *coup de théâtre*,
'a spectre is haunting Europe', then offers us a bird's-
eye view of the class struggle from ancient Rome to
today. The pages dedicated to the bourgeoisie as a
revolutionary class are breathtaking. Marx shows us this
new unstoppable power that is affecting the whole planet,
as if it were God's creative breath at the beginning of
Genesis. And at the end of this eulogy (which, I promise,
is truly remarkable) the subterranean powers arrive on
the scene, invoked by the bourgeois triumph: from the
bowels of capitalism, its own gravediggers, the proletariat, emerge. They proclaim, loud and clear, 'Now we
want to destroy you and take away all that belonged to
you.' Marvellous. And that's what Dostoevsky does with
the Jews – he justifies the conspiracy that has determined
their survival throughout history, and denounces them
as the enemy to be wiped out. Dostoevsky is a true
socialist."

"He isn't a socialist," interrupted Juliana Glinka with
a smile. "He's a visionary, and so tells the truth. You see
how he anticipates even the most apparently reasonable
objection, namely that even if there has been a state within
the state over the centuries, it was the persecutions that
led to its creation, and it would disappear if the Jew were
given equal rights to those of the native populations.
Wrong, warns Dostoevsky! Even if the Jews were given

. . . *"They now run the stock
exchanges and control credit.
This is why socialism has to
be anti-Semitic."* . . .

[PAGE 424]

the same rights as other citizens, they would never abandon the obstinate idea that a Messiah will arrive who will subdue all nations with his sword. For this reason, the Jews prefer one activity alone, trading in gold and jewels. On the coming of the Messiah they will then feel no attachment to the land where they have lived, and can easily carry their belongings away with them, when – as Dostoevsky so poetically puts it – the ray of dawn casts forth its glow and the chosen people will carry their cymbal, drum and pipe and their silver and their sacred objects to their ancient Home."

"In France, we have been too indulgent towards them," concluded Toussenel. "They now run the stock exchanges and control credit. This is why socialism has to be anti-Semitic. . . . It is no coincidence that the success of the Jews in France came exactly when the new principles of capitalism triumphed, brought in from across the English Channel."

"You simplify things too much, Monsieur Toussenel," said Madame Glinka. "Among those in Russia who have been tainted by the revolutionary ideas of that Marx whom you praise, there are many Jews. They are everywhere."

And she turned towards the windows of the drawing room, as if *They* were waiting for her with their daggers on the street corner. And Simonini, overcome once again by his childhood nightmares, imagined Mordechai coming up the staircase at night.

Working for the Okhrana

Simonini quickly identified Madame Glinka as a possible client. He would sit next to her, courting her discreetly, though with some effort. Simonini was not a good judge of feminine charms, but he had always noted that she had the face of a weasel and eyes too close to the bridge of her nose. Juliette Adam, on the other hand, though no longer as she had been when he had first known her twenty years earlier, was still a lady of fine bearing and majestic appearance.

He had little to say, and instead listened to Madame Glinka's fantasies, feigning interest as she told how at Wurzburg she had had a vision of a Himalayan guru who initiated her into some kind of mystical revelation. She was someone, therefore, to whom he could offer anti-Jewish material in keeping with her esoteric inclinations, all the more since it was rumoured that Juliana Glinka was the niece of General Orzheyevsky, a figure of great importance in the Russian secret police. It was through him that she had been recruited by the Okhrana, the imperial secret service – and in that role she had links (it wasn't clear whether as employee, collaborator or rival) with Pyotr Rachkovsky, the new head of all foreign investigations. *Le Radical,* a left-wing newspaper, had voiced the suspicion that Glinka was earning her living from regularly exposing Russian terrorists in exile – which meant she attended not only Salon Adam but other circles about which Simonini knew nothing.

The scene in the Prague cemetery had to be adapted to Glinka's tastes, cutting out the long-winded passages on economic plans and emphasising the more messianic aspects of the rabbinical speeches.

Taking a few ideas from Gougenot and other writings of the time, Simonini let the rabbis imagine the return of the Sovereign chosen by God as King of Israel, appointed to wipe away all the iniquities of the Gentiles. And he added at least two pages of messianic phantasmagoria to the story of the cemetery, such as, 'With all the power and terror of Satan, the triumphant reign of the king of Israel is drawing near to our degenerate world; the king born of the blood of Zion, the Antichrist, is drawing near to the throne of universal power.' But, remembering that republican ideas struck fear into Tsarist minds, he added that only a republican system with a popular vote would enable the Jews, once they had acquired a majority, to introduce laws to achieve their purposes. Only those Gentile fools, said the rabbis in the cemetery, believe there is greater freedom under a republic than under an autocracy. Yet the contrary is true: wise men govern in an autocracy, while a liberal regime is run by common people who are easily manipulated by Jewish agents. That the Republic would be able to coexist with a *Rex Mundi* didn't seem to cause any concern: the case of Napoleon III was still there to demonstrate that republics can create emperors.

But Simonini, remembering his grandfather's stories, had the idea of embellishing the rabbis' speeches with a long description of how the secret world government had operated, and should operate. It was curious that Glinka hadn't realised that the arguments were the same as Dostoevsky's – or perhaps she had, and so was delighted that an ancient text should confirm Dostoevsky, thus proving itself to be authentic.

In the Prague cemetery it was therefore revealed that the Jewish cabalists had been the inspiration behind the Crusades to restore Jerusalem's position as the centre of the world, thanks also, it went without saying, to the Templars (and here Simonini knew he was delving into very rich terrain). What a shame, then, that the Arabs had driven the Crusaders into the sea, and the Templars had met such a nasty end: otherwise the plan would have succeeded several centuries earlier.

In this regard, the rabbis at Prague remembered how humanism, the French Revolution and the American War of Independence had helped to undermine the principles of Christianity and respect for kings, preparing the way for the Jewish conquest of the world. To achieve this plan, the Jews obviously had to construct a respectable facade for themselves, namely Freemasonry.

Simonini had ably recycled the old writings of Barruel, about which Glinka and her paymasters in Russia were evidently unaware. General Orzheyevsky, when he received Glinka's report, in fact thought it appropriate to use two extracts – the shorter of them corresponded more or less to the original scene in the Prague cemetery, and was published in various Russian magazines, forgetting (or deciding that the public had forgotten, or indeed was unaware) that a rabbi's speech, taken from Goedsche's book, had already been in circulation more than ten years earlier in St Petersburg, and had subsequently appeared in the *Antisemiten-Katechismus* by Theodor Fritsch; the other extract was published as a pamphlet with the title *Tayna Yevreystva* ('The Secrets of the Jews'), graced with a preface by Orzheyevsky himself, stating that the text, finally rediscovered, revealed for the first time the profound links between Masonry and Judaism, both harbingers of nihilism (an accusation taken extremely seriously in Russia at that time).

Orzheyevsky obviously arranged for Simonini to receive a proper fee and Glinka made the dreadful – and dreaded – gesture of offering her body in gratitude for that magnificent enterprise – a horror from which Simonini escaped by intimating, with hands trembling and plenty of virginal sighs, that his fate was not dissimilar to that of Octave de Malivert, about whom all of Stendhal's readers had been speculating for decades.

From that moment Glinka lost interest in Simonini, and he in her. One day, though, on entering *Café de la Paix* for a simple *déjeuner à la fourchette* (cutlets and grilled kidneys) Simonini noticed her sitting at a table with a portly, vulgar-looking man of bourgeois appearance with whom she was clearly having a heated argument. He stopped to greet her, and Glinka was obliged to introduce Monsieur Rachkovsky, who eyed him with great interest.

Simonini failed at the time to understand the reason for this interest and it was only later when he heard the shop bell ring and saw it was Rachkovsky himself that all became clear. He walked through the shop with a broad smile and authoritative self-assurance, climbed the staircase to the upper floor and entered the office, seating himself comfortably in an armchair beside the desk.

"Let us please talk business," he said.

Blond as a Russian, though greying, as might be expected for a man now over thirty, Rachkovsky had fleshy, sensual lips, a prominent nose, the eyebrows of a Slavic demon, a wild, feral smile and a mellifluous voice. He resembled a cheetah more than a lion, Simonini thought, and wondered what would be less worrying: to be summoned to meet Osman Bey at night on the Seine embankment or Rachkovsky early in the morning at the Russian embassy in rue de Grenelle. He decided in favour of Osman Bey.

"So, Captain Simonini," began Rachkovsky, "you may not know very much about what you in the West improperly call Okhrana, and the Russian emigrants disparagingly call Okhranka."

"I've heard rumours about it."

"No rumours. All as clear as daylight. It is the *Ochrannye otdelenija*, which means Department for Public Security, the secret intelligence service, part of our Ministry of Internal Affairs. It was created after the assassination of Tsar Alexander II in 1881 to protect the imperial family. But little by little it has had to deal with the threat of nihilist terrorism, and has also had to set up various surveillance departments abroad, where exiles and emigrants are flourishing. And this is why I am here, in the interests of my country. As clear as day. It is the terrorists who hide. You understand?"

"I understand. But where do I come in?"

"Let's take it step by step. If by chance you have any information on terrorist groups, you need hide nothing from me. I understand in your time you have reported to the French secret service about dangerous anti-Bona-partists. And the only people who can do that are their friends, or at least those who know them. I am not shy. I too in my time have had contact with Russian terrorists. It's all water under the bridge now, but that's how I climbed the ladder in the anti-terrorist services, where those who are efficient are the ones who've worked their way through the ranks of subversive groups. You have to break the law before you can serve it properly. Here in France you have the example of your Vidocq, who became head of police only after serving time in gaol. Beware of policemen who are too, how do you say, clean. They are prigs. But let's return to us. We have recently become aware that a number of Jewish intellectuals are working among the terrorists. I have been appointed by certain persons at the court of the Tsar to try to show that the Jews are undermining the moral fibre of the Russian people and threatening their very survival. You may hear it said that I am regarded as a protégé of Witte, the minister, a well-known liberal who would not agree with me on such matters. But you should never serve only your present master, remember that. Always be ready for the next one. However, I shall not waste time. I've seen what you have given Madame Glinka. Most of it is rubbish. You have, of course, chosen the occupation of junk dealer as a cover – someone, in other words, who sells used stuff for more than it costs new. But several years ago in

Contemporain you published some most interesting documents you had received from your grandfather, and I would be surprised if you didn't have more. I have heard it said you know a great deal about many things . . ." (and here Simonini was reaping the benefits of being a spy in appearance more than reality). "Therefore I would like some reliable material from you. I know the difference between wheat and chaff. I will pay. But if the material is no good, then I get annoyed. Is that clear?"

"But what exactly do you want?"

"If I knew that, I wouldn't be paying you. There are people in my department who are very good at constructing a document but I have to give them the contents. And I cannot tell the good Russian people that the Jews are waiting for the Messiah, which is of no interest to either the peasant or the landowner. If they're waiting for the Messiah, it must be explained in terms of their pockets."

"But why are you after the Jews in particular?"

"Because in Russia there are Jews. If I were living in Turkey, I would be after the Armenians."

"So you want the Jews to be destroyed, as Osman Bey does. . . . I assume you know him."

"Osman Bey is a fanatic. He's also a Jew. Better to keep away from him. I don't want to destroy the Jews. I might even say the Jews are my best allies. I'm interested in the morale of the Russian people. It is my wish (and the wish of those I hope to please) that these people do not direct their discontent against the Tsar. We therefore need an enemy. There's no point looking for an enemy among, I don't know, the Mongols or the Tatars, as despots have done in the past. For the enemy to be recognised and feared, he has to be in your home, or on your doorstep. Hence the Jews. Divine Providence has given them to us and so, by God, let us use them and pray there's always some Jew to fear and to hate. We need an enemy to give people hope. Someone said that patriotism is the last refuge of cowards: those without moral principles usually wrap a flag around themselves, and the bastards always talk about the purity of the race. National identity is the last bastion of the dispossessed. But the meaning of identity is now based on hatred, on hatred for those who are not the same. Hatred has to be cultivated as a civic passion. The enemy is the friend of the people. You always want someone to hate in order to feel justified in your own misery. Hatred is the true primordial passion. It is love that's abnormal. That is why Christ was killed: he spoke against nature. You don't love someone for your whole life – that impossible hope is the source of adultery, matricide, betrayal of friends . . . But you can hate someone for your whole life – provided he's always there to keep your hatred alive. Hatred warms the heart."

Drumont

Simonini found the meeting unsettling. Rachkovsky appeared to be serious about what he was saying. Unless Simonini gave him some new material he would get "annoyed". It wasn't so much that he was short of material, indeed he'd put together a considerable number of documents for his series of protocols, but he felt that something more was needed – not just the stories about the Antichrist which were fine for characters like Glinka, but something that was more relevant to current events. After all, he didn't want to sell his updated version of the Prague cemetery story for less than it was worth – on the contrary, he wanted to raise the price. And so he waited.

He went to see Father Bergamaschi, who had been pursuing him for material against the Masons.

"Look at this book," said the Jesuit. "*La France juive* by Édouard Drumont. Hundreds of pages. Here's someone who obviously knows more about it than you."

Simonini flicked cursorily through the book: "But these are the same things that old Gougenot wrote more than fifteen years ago!"

"And so? The book is selling like hot cakes. His readers clearly know nothing about Gougenot. And you imagine that your Russian client has read Drumont? You're the master of recycling, aren't you? Go and sniff about, find out what Drumont's companions are saying and doing."

Making contact with Drumont was easy. At Salon Adam, Simonini had become well acquainted with Alphonse Daudet, who had invited him to the soirées which were held, when it was not the turn of Salon Adam, at his house at Champrosay. Kindly received there by Julia Daudet, he met personalities such as the Goncourts, Pierre Loti, Émile Zola, Frédéric Mistral and Drumont himself, whose fame took off after the publication of *La France juive*. And over the next few years he took to meeting with Drumont, first at La Ligue Antisémitique which he had

. . . he took to meeting with Drumont,
first at La Ligue Antisémitique which
he had founded and then at the offices
of his newspaper, La Libre Parole. *. . .*

[PAGE 433]

founded and then at the offices of his newspaper, *La Libre Parole*.

Drumont had a leonine mane of hair and a large black beard, bent nose and fiery eyes, and you could have described him (judging from the illustrations of the time) as a Jewish prophet. In effect, there was something messianic about his anti-Judaism, as if the Almighty had given him the specific task of destroying the chosen people. Simonini was fascinated by the virulence of Drumont's anti-Semitism. He hated the Jews, you might say, with love, with single-mindedness, with devotion – and with a fervour that substituted all sexual desire. Drumont's anti-Semitism wasn't philosophical and political like Toussenel's, nor theological like Gougenot's. He was an erotic anti-Semite.

It was enough to hear him talk during the long, leisurely editorial meetings.

"I was more than willing to do the preface for that book by Abbé Desportes on the Jewish blood mystery. And they're not just medieval practices. Even today, those splendid Jewish baronesses who hold salons put the blood of Christian children into the sweetmeats they offer their guests."

Or: "The Semite is mercenary, covetous, scheming, shrewd, crafty, whereas we Aryans are enthusiastic, heroic, gentlemanly, disinterested, straightforward, trusting to the point of naivety. The Semite is earthly, never sees anything beyond this life – have you ever seen any mention of the hereafter in the Old Testament? The Aryan is always rapt by a passion for transcendence; he is a child of the ideal.

The Christian God is up there in the heavens; that of the Jews is sometimes on a mountain top, sometimes in a burning bush, never in the sky. The Semite is a shopkeeper, the Aryan a farmer, poet, monk, and above all a soldier, because he challenges death. The Semite has no creative ability. Have you ever heard of Jewish musicians, painters or poets? Have you ever known a Jew who has made scientific discoveries? The Aryan is an inventor, the Semite exploits the inventions of others."

He quoted what Wagner had written: "It is impossible to imagine that a character, whether antique or modern, heroic or amorous, be performed by a Jew without feeling instinctively struck by how ridiculous such a performance would be. What we find most repugnant is the peculiar accent that characterises Jewish speech. Our ears are particularly irritated by sharp, hissing, strident sounds of this kind. Very naturally, the innate barrenness of the Jewish manner which is so distasteful to us finds its greatest expression in song, the most lively, the most authentic manifestation of individual feeling. We might recognise in the Jew an artistic aptitude for any other kind of art except that of song, for which he seems entirely deprived by nature herself."

"So how," someone asked, "do we explain their invasion into musical theatre? Rossini, Meyerbeer, Mendelssohn, or Giuditta Pasta . . . all Jewish."

"Perhaps it is not true that music is a higher art," suggested another. "Didn't that German philosopher say that it is lower than painting and literature because it also disturbs those who don't want to listen? If someone near

436

you plays a tune you dislike, you're forced to listen, in the same way as if someone takes out a handkerchief scented with an essence that disgusts you. The Aryan glory is literature, now in crisis. But music, a sensorial art for milksops and convalescents, triumphs. After the crocodile, the Jew is the most musical of all animals. All Jews are musicians. Pianists, violinists, violoncellists – they're all Jews."

"Yes, but they're performers, parasites of great composers," retorted Drumont. "You have mentioned Meyerbeer and Mendelssohn, second-rate musicians, but Delibes and Offenbach are not Jews."

A great argument grew out of this – whether the Jews were alien to music or whether music was the Jewish art par excellence – and views differed.

Anti-Semitic fury had reached its height back at the time when the Eiffel Tower was being planned, not to mention when it had been completed. It was the work of a German Jew, the Jewish response to the Sacré-Coeur, explained de Biez. He was perhaps the most combative anti-Semite in the group, who began his demonstration about Jewish inferiority from the fact that they write in the opposite way to normal people. "The very form of this Babylonian construction," he said, "demonstrates that their brain is not made like ours. . . ."

They moved on to talk about alcoholism, then a major problem in France. It was said that over fourteen million litres were drunk annually in Paris!

"Alcohol," someone said, "is distributed by Jews and Masons, who have perfected their own traditional form of

CROQUIS PARISIENS, — par Daumier (suite).

— Dire qu'il y a des gens qui boivent de l'absinthe dans un pays qui produit de si bon vin que ça !

. . . *"Alcohol," someone said, "is
distributed by Jews and Masons,
who have perfected their own
traditional form of poison,
Aqua Tofana."* . . .

[PAGE 437]

---

poison, Aqua Tofana. They're now producing a toxin which seems like water but contains opium and Spanish fly. It produces apathy or madness, then leads to death. When mixed into alcoholic drinks it induces suicide."

"And pornography? Toussenel (even socialists can sometimes tell the truth) has written that the swine is the emblem of the Jew who is not ashamed to wallow in baseness and ignominy. After all, the Talmud says it is a good omen to dream about excrement. All obscene publications are produced by Jews. Go to rue du Croissant, the market selling pornographic magazines. There's a series of (Jewish) stalls, one after the other: scenes of fornication, monks copulating with young girls, priests whipping naked women who have only their hair to cover them, priapic scenes, drunken, debauched priests. The people pass by and laugh, even families with children! The triumph – excuse the word – of the Anus. Sodomite priests, buttocks of nuns who allow themselves to be whipped by lecherous curates . . ."

Another regular topic was the nomadic nature of the Jews.

"The Jew is a nomad, but to escape from something, not to explore new lands," observed Drumont. "The Aryan travels, he discovers America and unknown places; the Semite waits for the Aryans to discover new lands and then goes and exploits them. And look at folk tales. The Jews don't have enough imagination to think up a fine story, but their Semitic brothers, the Arabs, told the stories of *The Thousand and One Nights* where someone discovers a pot of gold, a cavern with thieves' diamonds, a bottle containing a kind genie – and all are gifts from heaven. But in the Aryan tales, the quest for the Holy Grail for instance, everything has to be achieved through combat and sacrifice."

"Despite all this," said one of Drumont's friends, "the Jews have managed to overcome all adversity. . . ."

"Certainly," said Drumont, foaming with resentment. "It's impossible to destroy them. When any other race of people migrates to another place, it cannot resist the change of climate, different food, and it becomes weak. Yet when they move about they become stronger, like insects."

"They're like the gypsies who never get sick. Even if they feed on dead animals. Perhaps cannibalism helps them, which is why they kidnap children. . . ."

"I'm not sure, though, that cannibalism lengthens life – look at the negroes in Africa: they're cannibals and yet they die like flies in their villages."

"Then how do you explain the immunity of the Jew? He has an average lifespan of fifty-three years while for Christians it's thirty-seven. They appear more resistant to disease than Christians, through a phenomenon that's been noted since the Middle Ages. They seem to have within them a permanent pestilence which protects them from ordinary plague."

Simonini pointed out that these arguments had already been dealt with by Gougenot, but Drumont and his coterie were less concerned about the originality of ideas than about their truth.

"All right," said Drumont, "they are more resistant

than we are to physical illness, but they are more susceptible to mental illness. Constant involvement in commercial dealings, speculation and scheming affects their nervous system. In Italy there is one lunatic for every three hundred and forty-eight Jews and one for every seven hundred and seventy-eight Catholics. Charcot has carried out some interesting studies on Russian Jews – we have information about them because they're poor, whereas French Jews are rich and pay a great deal of money to hide their sick patients in Dr Blanche's clinic. You know that Sarah Bernhardt keeps a white coffin in her bedroom?"

"They're producing children twice as fast as we are – they now number more than four million throughout the world."

"It was written in the Book of Exodus: the children of Israel were fruitful and increased abundantly, and became mighty and filled the earth."

"And now they are here. And here they've been, even when we had no suspicion they were here. Who was Marat? His true name was Mara, a Sephardic family driven out of Spain, who turned Protestant to hide their Jewish origins. Marat: ravaged by leprosy, died in filth, mentally ill, affected by persecution mania, then homicidal mania, a typical Jew who avenges himself on Christians by sending as many as he can to the guillotine. Look at his picture in the Carnavalet Museum and you'll immediately see the crazed neuropath, like Robespierre and other Jacobins, and that asymmetry in the two halves of the face which is indicative of an unbalanced mind."

"The Revolution, as we know, was caused to a large

extent by the Jews. But Napoleon, with his hatred of the Pope and his Masonic alliances, was he a Semite?"

"So it would seem, even Disraeli said he was. The Balearic Islands and Corsica provided shelter for the Jews driven from Spain, who then became Marranos and took the name of the lords they served, such as Orsini and Bonaparte."

In every group of people there's the *gaffeur*, the one who asks the wrong question at the wrong moment. And that was how the insidious question emerged: "And Jesus, then? He was a Jew. Yet he dies young, has no interest in money and thinks only about the Kingdom of Heaven. . . ."

The reply came from Jacques de Biez: "Gentlemen, the idea that Christ was Jewish is a legend created by people who were Jews themselves, like Saint Paul and the four evangelists. Jesus was in fact of Celtic race, like we French who were only much later conquered by the Romans. And before being emasculated by the Romans, the Celts were a population of conquerors. Have you heard of the Galatians, who reached as far as Greece? Galilee is thus called from the Gauls who had colonised it. There again, the legend of a virgin who gave birth to a son is a Celtic and a Druidic myth. Just look at all the portraits we have of Jesus – he was fair-haired and blue-eyed. And he spoke against the customs, superstitions and vices of the Jews. And unlike what the Jews expected from the Messiah, he said that his kingdom was not of this earth. And while the Jews were monotheists, Christ launched the idea of the Trinity, inspired by Celtic polytheism.

That's why they killed him. Caiaphas, who condemned him, was a Jew . . . Judas, who betrayed him, was a Jew . . . Peter, who denied him, was a Jew. . . ."

The same year that Drumont founded *La Libre Parole*, he had the good fortune or intuition to ride the Panama scandal.

"It's quite simple," he explained to Simonini before launching his campaign. "Ferdinand de Lesseps, the very same man who opened the Suez Canal, is appointed to open up the Isthmus of Panama. Six hundred million francs had to be spent and Lesseps creates a joint-stock company. Work begins in 1881, hampered by countless problems. Lesseps needs more money and launches a public subscription. But he uses part of the money received to corrupt journalists and conceal the difficulties that were gradually emerging, such as the fact that by 'eighty-seven barely half the isthmus had been dug and one thousand four hundred million francs had already been spent. Lesseps seeks the help of Eiffel, the Jew who built that ugly tower, then continues to collect funds and uses them to corrupt the press as well as various ministries. The Canal Company went bankrupt four years later and eighty-five thousand decent Frenchmen who had invested in the company lost all their money."

"That's well known."

"Yes, but we can now show that the people who were aiding and abetting Lesseps were Jewish financiers, including Baron Jacques de Reinach (a baron of Prussian title!). Tomorrow's *La Libre Parole* will cause quite a stir."

And quite a stir it certainly caused, creating a scandal involving journalists and government officials, as well as former ministers. Reinach committed suicide, several important figures went to prison, Lesseps managed to avoid imprisonment by reason of age, Eiffel got out by the skin of his teeth, and Drumont triumphed as the scourge of malpractice, but above all had produced solid arguments in his campaign against the Jews.

A few bombs

Before he could approach Drumont, it seems however that Simonini was summoned by Hébuterne to his usual spot in the nave of Notre Dame.

"Captain Simonini," he said, "some years ago I appointed you to incite a certain Taxil into a campaign against the Masons, one that would prove to be such a circus that it would rebound against the more vulgar opponents of Freemasonry. The man who guaranteed on your behalf that the enterprise would be kept under control was Abbé Dalla Piccola, to whom I entrusted a considerable amount of money. But it now seems this Taxil is going too far. And since it was you who sent the abbé to me, you must put pressure on him, and on Taxil."

At this point in his diary, Simonini admits to himself that his mind is a blank: he seems to remember that Abbé Dalla Piccola had to look after Taxil, but cannot recall appointing him to do any particular task. He remembers saying to Hébuterne only that he would deal with the matter. Then he told him that his present interest was in the Jews and he was about to get in touch with Drumont and his friends. He was surprised to notice how favourably disposed Hébuterne was towards that group. Had he not emphasised repeatedly, Simonini asked him, that the government didn't want to be mixed up in anti-Jewish campaigns?

"Things change, Captain," Hébuterne replied. "Until recently, you see, the Jews were either poor folk who lived in a ghetto, as they still do in Russia and in Rome, or they were great bankers, as here in France. The poor Jews were moneylenders or practised medicine, but those who made their fortune financed the court and grew rich on loans to the king, supplying money for his wars. In this way they always sided with power and didn't get mixed up in politics. And being interested in finance, they didn't get involved in industry. Then something happened that even we were slow in noticing. After the Revolution, countries needed sums of money much larger than the Jews could supply, and so they gradually lost their monopoly position over credit. Meanwhile, little by little – and only now do we realise this – the Revolution had brought equality to all citizens, at least here in France. And the Jews, except for those poor folk still in the ghettos, now joined the bourgeoisie – not only the capitalist upper bourgeoisie but also the petit bourgeoisie, that of the professions, the State authorities and the army. Do you know how many Jewish officers there are today? More than you'd ever imagine. And it's not just the army: the Jews are gradually working their way into the anarchist and communist underworld. Once upon a time, all good revolutionaries were anti-Jewish because they were anti-capitalist, and the Jews were always allies of the government in power, but today it's fashionable to be a Jew *d'opposition.* And what was that man Marx, of whom our revolutionaries so often talk? He was a penniless bourgeois who lived off his aristocratic wife. And we cannot forget, for example, that all higher education is in their hands, from secondary school to the École des Hautes Études, and all the Paris theatres are in their hands, and most of the newspapers – look at the *Journal des débats,* the official journal of the *haute banque.*"

Simonini still didn't understand what it was Hébuterne wanted, now that the Jewish bourgeoisie were becoming a nuisance. When he asked, Hébuterne replied with a vague gesture.

"I don't know. We simply have to keep an eye on the situation. The problem is whether we can trust this new class of Jews. Let's be clear, I am not interested in those fantasies about a Jewish plot to take over the world! Bourgeois Jews no longer identify with their original community and are often ashamed of it. But at the same time they are citizens who cannot be trusted – they have been properly French for only a short while and could betray us tomorrow, in league perhaps with bourgeois Prussian Jews. Most of the spies during the Prussian invasion were Alsace Jews."

As they were about to say goodbye, Hébuterne added, "Incidentally, back in Lagrange's time, you had dealings with a certain Gaviali. It was you who had him arrested."

"Yes, he was head of the bombers at rue de la

Huchette. They're all in Cayenne or thereabouts, if I remember correctly."

"Except for Gaviali, who escaped recently. He's been spotted in Paris."

"Is it possible to escape from Devil's Island?"

"It's possible to escape from anywhere if you're tough enough."

"Why don't you arrest him?"

"Because a good bomb-maker might be useful right now. We've managed to track him down. He's working as a rag-and-bone man in Clignancourt. Why not go and find him?"

Rag-and-bone men weren't hard to track down in Paris. They were spread across the whole city but their main enclave had traditionally been between rue Mouffetard and rue Saint-Médard. They (or at least those described by Hébuterne) were now close to the city gate at Clignancourt, living in a colony of shacks with brushwood roofs, and it was a mystery how sunflowers could grow there, in that putrid atmosphere, in the warmer weather.

Nearby, at one time, had been a restaurant *aux pieds humides*, so named because the customers had to wait their turn in the street, then entered and for one sou could plunge an enormous fork into a cauldron where they fished out whatever they could, and would get a piece of meat if they were lucky, otherwise a carrot – and then out.

Rag-and-bone men had their own *hôtels garnis*. The rooms were not much – a bed, a table, two odd chairs.

On the wall, some holy pictures or engravings from old novels salvaged from the refuse. A piece of mirror, essential for the Sunday wash and brush-up. Here the rag-and-bone man would sort out his finds: bones, china, glass, old ribbons, scraps of silk. The day began at six in the morning, and if the city sergeants (or the *flics*, as everyone now called them) found anyone still at work after seven in the evening, they would be fined.

Simonini went looking for Gaviali. And finally, at a *bibine* that sold not only cheap wine but also an absinthe which was said to be poisoned (as if the ordinary stuff wasn't already bad enough), a figure was pointed out to him. Simonini wasn't wearing his beard since he remembered he hadn't been wearing one when he knew Gaviali. Twenty years had passed but he thought he could still be recognised. It was Gaviali who was unrecognisable.

His face was pale and wrinkled and he had a long beard. Around his scrawny neck, a yellowish cravat resembling a piece of rope hung from a greasy collar. On his head was a tattered cap, he wore a greenish frock coat over a crumpled waistcoat, his splattered shoes looked as if they hadn't been cleaned for years and a layer of mud plastered his laces to the leather. But Gaviali's appearance would hardly have been noticeable among these rag-and-bone men, since no one else was dressed any better.

Simonini introduced himself, expecting a cordial response. But Gaviali looked at him with a piercing gaze.

"You have the gall, Captain, to stand there in front of me?" he said. And seeing Simonini's look of bewilderment he continued, "Do you think I'm quite so stupid? That day, when the police arrived and fired on us, I saw perfectly well how you gave the *coup de grâce* to that wretch you'd sent to us as your agent. And then, all of us survivors ended up on the same boat sailing for Cayenne, and you weren't there. It's easy to put two and two together. Fifteen years' lazing about in Cayenne gives you time to think: you planned our conspiracy so you could then expose it. It must be a profitable business."

"And so? You want your revenge? You're reduced to the shadow of a man. If your theory is right, I must be in league with the police, and one word in the right direction would be quite enough to send you on your way back to Cayenne."

"No, Captain, good heavens no. Those years in Cayenne have made me a wiser man. When you're in a conspiracy there's always the risk of getting mixed up with a *mouchard*. It's like playing cops and robbers. And anyway, it's been said that all revolutionaries over the years become defenders of throne and altar. I'm not much interested in throne or altar but, for me, the time of great ideals is over. With this so-called Third Republic you can't be sure which tyrant you ought to be killing. There's still one thing I know how to do and that's make bombs. And the fact that you've come looking for me means you want bombs. That's fine, as long as you pay. You see where I'm living. A change of lodgings and restaurant would be quite enough. Who do I have to kill off? Like all old revolutionaries I've become a mercenary. That's a job you must know well."

"I want bombs from you, Gaviali. I don't know what kind yet, or where. We'll talk about it at the appropriate time. I can promise you money, a clean slate regarding your past, and new papers."

Gaviali said he was ready to work for anyone who paid well and Simonini in the meantime gave him enough to survive on without having to collect rags for at least a month. There's nothing like gaol to encourage obedience to another's commands.

It was some time later that Hébuterne told Simonini what Gaviali had to do. In December 1893 an anarchist, Auguste Vaillant, had thrown a small explosive device, filled with nails, in the Chamber of Deputies, shouting, "Death to the bourgeoisie! Long live anarchy!" It was a symbolic gesture. "If I had wanted to kill I'd have filled the bomb with shot," said Vaillant at his trial. "You don't expect me to lie to give you the pleasure of cutting off my head." They cut his head off all the same, to set an example, but that was not the problem. The secret service was worried that gestures of this kind might seem heroic and would therefore be imitated.

"There are those who set a bad example," Hébuterne explained to Simonini, "who defend and encourage terror and social unrest, while they remain comfortably ensconced in their clubs and restaurants discussing poetry and drinking champagne. Look at Laurent Tailhade, a gutter journalist who enjoys a double influence on public opinion since he's also a parliamentary deputy. This is what he wrote about Vaillant: 'What does it matter about the victims if the gesture was laudable?' The Tailhades of this world are more dangerous than the Vaillants because it's more difficult to cut off their heads. It is time these intellectuals who never pay for what they do were taught a public lesson."

And the lesson had to be arranged by Simonini, and by Gaviali. At *Foyot*, in the very corner where Tailhade was enjoying one of his expensive meals, a bomb exploded a few weeks later, from which he lost an eye (Gaviali was indeed a genius – the bomb had been devised in such a way that the victim, rather than dying, would be injured just enough). The government newspapers made the most of it, writing sarcastic comments such as, "And so, Monsieur Tailhade, was this a laudable gesture?" A fine success for the government, for Gaviali and for Simonini. And, in addition to his eye, Tailhade lost his reputation.

Most satisfied of all was Gaviali, and Simonini was pleased to restore a livelihood and respect to someone who, through life's vicissitudes, had had the misfortune to lose them.

Hébuterne had entrusted Simonini with other assignments over these same years. The Panama scandal was by now losing its impact on public opinion – people get bored after a while when the news is always the same. Drumont was no longer interested in the case, but others were still fanning the flames and the government was worried that it might (how would one put it today?) all backfire. It was time to distract attention from the last dregs of the story which was now stale, and Hébuterne asked Simonini to organise a riot – nice enough to fill the front pages of the newspapers.

Simonini said organising a riot was not easy and Hébuterne suggested that those most inclined to cause a disturbance were students. The best approach was to get the students to start something and then get a specialist in public disorder involved.

Simonini had no point of contact with the student world but those who did, he immediately thought, were revolutionaries and, better still, anarchists. And who knew the anarchist groups better than anyone? Someone whose job it was to infiltrate and expose them, and therefore Rachkovsky. So he made contact with Rachkovsky who, displaying all his lupine teeth in a smile that was meant to be friendly, asked for details.

"All I want is a few students who can cause a disturbance when required."

"That's easy," said the Russian. "Go to *Le Château-Rouge.*"

Le Château-Rouge in rue Galande appeared to be a meeting place in the Latin quarter for down-and-outs. It stood at the end of a courtyard, with a guillotine-red facade. As you entered, you were hit by the asphyxiating stench of rancid grease and mildew, and of soup which had been cooked and re-cooked over the years leaving tangible traces on those greasy walls, though there was no apparent reason for this, seeing that you had to bring your own food with you, and the house offered wine and plates only. The noxious haze of tobacco smoke and gas escaping from the lamps appeared to have cast a drowsiness over the dozens of tramps sitting there, three or four on each side of the tables, each sleeping on the shoulder of the other.

But the two inner rooms admitted no vagrants. Here, instead, were old whores wearing cheap jewellery, fourteen-year-old tarts with a premature air of insolence, sunken eyes and the pallid mark of tuberculosis, and local rogues wearing showy rings with fake stones and redingotes a cut above the rags in the first room. Wandering about in that reeking confusion were well-dressed women, and men in evening wear. A visit to *Le Château-Rouge* had become an experience not to be missed: late in the evening, after the theatre, elegant carriages arrived – *le tout Paris* came to enjoy the thrill of the underworld, most of whom had probably been recruited by the landlord (with free absinthe) to attract the respectable people who would pay twice the proper price for the same absinthe.

At *Le Château-Rouge*, on Rachkovsky's advice, Simonini made contact with a man called Fayolle, a foetus trader by occupation. He was an elderly man who spent his evenings there drinking eighty per cent eau de vie, spending what he had earned that day from his tour of the hospitals, where he collected foetuses and embryos to sell to students at the École de Médecine. He stank of rotten flesh as well as alcohol and was obliged, due to the stench, to sit alone, even in the fetid atmosphere of the *Château*, but he was said to have good connections with the student world, especially with those who had become professional students over the years – those who were more inclined towards other interests than studying

. . . But the two inner rooms admitted no vagrants.
Here, instead, were old whores wearing cheap
jewellery, fourteen-year-old tarts with a premature
air of insolence, sunken eyes and the pallid mark
of tuberculosis, and local rogues wearing showy
rings with fake stones and redingotes a cut
above the rags in the first room. . . .

[PAGE 453]

foetuses, and ready to cause trouble whenever the occasion arose.

At that very moment, as chance would have it, the youngsters in the Latin quarter had become annoyed at an old prig, Senator Bérenger, whom they had immediately nicknamed Père la Pudeur. He had proposed a law to put a stop to offences against morality for which (he said) the prime victims were the students themselves. The pretext was a series of performances at the *Bal des Quat'z Arts* by a certain Sarah Brown who appeared semi-naked, exposing ample quantities of flesh (and was probably clammy with sweat, Simonini imagined with horror).

Woe to anyone depriving students of the honest pleasures of voyeurism. Fayolle and his group were already planning to go one night and cause a disturbance under the senator's windows. All Simonini had to do was find out when they planned to go, and arrange for a few ruffians to be there in the neighbourhood, ready and waiting for a fight. For a modest sum Fayolle was prepared to handle everything. All Simonini had to do was tell Hébuterne the day and time.

The students had barely begun their disturbance when a company of soldiers or police (or whatever they were) arrived. On any view, there is nothing better than the arrival of policemen to kindle feelings of violence among students. A few stones began to fly and there was plenty of shouting. But then some poor wretch who happened to be passing was struck in the face by a missile fired by a soldier. Here was the vital death. And that was it – barricades straight away, and the beginnings of a proper revolt. At this point Fayolle's heavies arrived. The students stopped an omnibus, politely asked the passengers to leave, unharnessed the horses and overturned the vehicle to use as a barricade, but the professionals weighed in immediately, setting the vehicle alight. In short, a noisy protest turned into a riot, and from a riot to a hint of revolution. Plenty to keep the front pages of the newspapers busy for quite some time. *Adieu,* Panama.

The bordereau

The most profitable year for Simonini was 1894. It happened almost by chance, though chance always needs a helping hand.

Around that time Drumont's bitterness about the number of Jews in the army had become deeper.

"No one talks about it," he ranted. "No one wants to compromise our faith in the army by speaking out about these potential traitors of our fatherland at the very heart of our most glorious institution, or to say that the army is being corrupted by so many of these Jews," and he pronounced the words "*ces Juëfs, ces Juëfs*" with his lips protruding, as if his fierce impetuous words would reach out directly to the whole infamous Israelite race. "But someone must speak out. Do you know how the Jew is now trying to make himself respectable? By making a career as an officer, or mixing in the drawing rooms of the aristocracy as an artist and pederast. Adultery with old-fashioned gentlemen, or with respectable clergymen, no longer amuses our duchesses; they never tire of the bizarre, the exotic, the monstrous; they let themselves be wooed by patchouli-scented characters made up like women. Whatever perversions the aristocracy gets up to are of little interest to me – those countesses who used to fornicate with one Louis after another were no better – but perversion within the army is the end of French civilisation. I am convinced that most of the Jewish officers are Prussian spies, but I need evidence, evidence.

"So find it!" he shouted to his newspaper staff.

At the offices of *La Libre Parole* Simonini made the acquaintance of Major Esterhazy: quite a dandy, he continually boasted his noble origins, his Viennese education, mentioned past and future duels and was known to be heavily in debt. The newspaper staff avoided him when he approached on private business since they expected to be asked for a loan, and money lent to Esterhazy was never repaid. Slightly effeminate, he continually held an embroidered handkerchief to his mouth, and some said he was tubercular. His military career had been very odd: first as a cavalry officer in the Italian military campaign of 1866, then in the Papal Zouaves, before joining the Foreign Legion fighting in the war of 1870. It was rumoured he had been involved in military counter-espionage, but this was clearly not the kind of information anyone paraded on their uniform. Drumont held him in high esteem, perhaps to assure himself of a military contact.

One day Esterhazy invited Simonini to dinner at the *Boeuf à la Mode*. After ordering a *mignon d'agneau aux laitues* and discussing the wine list, Esterhazy came to the point: "Captain Simonini, our friend Drumont is looking for evidence he will never find. The problem is not finding out whether there are Prussian spies of Jewish origin in the army. Heavens above, there are spies everywhere in this world and we can hardly be scandalised by another one here or there. The political problem is to *demonstrate* they exist. And to nail a spy or a conspirator, there's no need, you'll agree, to find the evidence. It is easier and cheaper to create it – and if possible to create not just the evidence but the spy himself. We must therefore, in the national interest, choose a Jewish officer who might be open to suspicion through some weakness, and show he has passed important information to the Prussian embassy in Paris."

"Who do you mean by 'we'?"

"I am speaking on behalf of the Statistics Department of the *Service des Renseignements Français*, directed by Lieutenant Colonel Sandherr. You may know that this department, with such an unassuming name, is concerned primarily with the Germans. It was interested at first in German internal affairs – information of every kind from the newspapers, from reports of officers there on business, from the police, from our agents on both sides of the frontier, trying to find out as much as possible about the organisation of their army, how many cavalry divisions they had, how much their troops were paid . . . in other words, everything. But the Department recently decided to look at what the Germans are doing here in France. There are those who complain about the mixing up of espionage and counter-espionage, but the two activities are closely linked. We have to know what's going on in the German embassy, because it is foreign territory, and this is espionage; but there they gather information on us, and to find out about that is counter-espionage. And so we have a Madame Bastian who's a cleaner at the embassy. She works for us, and pretends to be illiterate when in fact she can read and understand German. She has to empty the wastepaper baskets in the embassy offices each day, and then sends us notes and documents which the Prussians believe they've consigned for destruction (you know how dull-witted they are). So we have to produce a document in which our officer gives highly secret news about French armaments. At that point it will be presumed that the author must be someone who has access to secret information, and he'll be exposed. We therefore need a small note, a memorandum – we call it a *bordereau.* That is why we have come to you, who in such matters, we are told, are a master."

Simonini didn't ask how the Department knew of his skills. They may have heard from Hébuterne. He thanked him for the compliment and said, "I imagine I'll have to reproduce the handwriting of a particular person."

"We have already identified the perfect candidate. His name is Captain Dreyfus, from Alsace of course. He is working for the Department as a trainee. He's married to a rich woman and fancies himself as a *tombeur de femmes,* so that his colleagues can hardly bear him and wouldn't find him any better if he were Christian. He'll arouse no feelings of solidarity. He's an excellent sacrificial victim. Once the document has been received, various

Le Judaïsme, voilà l'ennemi ..

Édouard Drumont

. . . *"After that it will be up to
people like Drumont to whip
up public scandal"* . . .

[PAGE 461]

investigations will be made and Dreyfus's handwriting will be recognised. After that it will be up to people like Drumont to whip up public scandal, expose the Jewish peril and at the same time save the honour of the armed forces who have so masterfully uncovered and dealt with it. Clear?"

Perfectly clear. In early October Simonini found himself in the presence of Lieutenant Colonel Sandherr, an ashen-faced man with insignificant features – the perfect physiognomy for the head of an espionage and counter-espionage service.

"Here we have an example of Dreyfus's handwriting, and here is the text to transcribe," said Sandherr, passing him two sheets of paper. "As you see, the note must be addressed to the military attaché at the embassy, von Schwarzkoppen, and must announce the arrival of military papers on the hydraulic brake for the one-hundred-and-twenty-millimetre gun, and other details of that kind. The Germans are desperate for information like this."

"Might it be appropriate to include some technical detail?" asked Simonini. "It would look more compromising."

"I hope you realise," said Sandherr, "once the scandal has erupted, this *bordereau* will become public property. We cannot let the newspapers have technical information. So down to business, Captain Simonini. For your convenience I have prepared a room with all the necessary writing materials. The paper, pen and ink are those used in these offices. I want it well done. You may take as long and try as many times as you wish, until the handwriting is perfect."

And that is what Simonini did. The *bordereau*, written on onionskin paper, was a document of thirty lines, eighteen on one side and twelve on the other. Simonini had taken care to ensure that the lines of the first page were wider apart than those of the second, where the handwriting was more hurried, since this is what happens when a letter is written in a state of agitation – it is more relaxed at the beginning and then accelerates. But he had also taken into account that a document of this kind, if it is thrown away, is first torn up and would therefore reach the statistics department in several pieces before being reassembled, and it was therefore better to space out the letter, to assist the *collage*, without going too far from the sample of writing he had been given.

All in all, he had done a good job.

Sandherr then had the *bordereau* sent to the Minister of War, General Mercier, and at the same time ordered an examination of all documents circulated by all officials in the department. In the end his staff informed him that the handwriting was that of Dreyfus, who was arrested on the 15th of October. The news was carefully kept secret for two weeks, with just a few details allowed to leak out in order to whet the curiosity of journalists. Then a name began to circulate, first in strictest secrecy, and finally it was admitted that the guilty man was Captain Dreyfus.

As soon as Esterhazy had been authorised by Sandherr,

he immediately told Drumont who ran through the rooms of the newspaper offices, waving the major's message and shouting, "The evidence, the evidence, here's the evidence!"

On the 1st of November *La Libre Parole* ran the headline in block capitals: "HIGH TREASON: ARREST OF THE JEWISH OFFICER DREYFUS". The campaign had begun, the whole of France burned with indignation.

But that same morning, while the newspaper office was celebrating the happy event, Simonini's eye fell on the letter with which Esterhazy had given news of Dreyfus's arrest. It was still on Drumont's desk, stained by his wine glass but completely legible. And to Simonini, who had spent more than an hour imitating what was supposed to be Dreyfus's handwriting, it seemed as clear as day that the handwriting, on which he had worked so carefully, was similar in every respect to that of Esterhazy. No one is more aware of such matters than a forger.

What had happened? Had Sandherr given him a piece of paper written by Esterhazy instead of one written by Dreyfus? Was that possible? Bizarre, inexplicable, but irrefutable. Had he done so by mistake? On purpose? But if so, why? Or had Sandherr been misled by one of his staff who had taken the wrong piece of paper? If Sandherr had been acting in good faith, then he should be told of the mistake. But if Sandherr was acting in bad faith, it would be risky for him to reveal that he knew the game he was playing. Inform Esterhazy? But if Sandherr had swapped the handwriting on purpose so as to harm Esterhazy, if he informed the victim then Simonini would have the whole secret service against him. Keep quiet?

And if the secret services were one day to accuse him of carrying out the swap?

Simonini wasn't to blame for the error. He wanted to make sure this was clear, and above all that his forgery was, so to speak, genuine. He decided to take the risk and went to see Sandherr, who seemed reluctant to talk to him at first, perhaps because he feared an attempt at blackmail.

But when Simonini explained the truth (the only truth in what was otherwise a pack of lies) Sandherr, more ashen-faced than usual, appeared not to want to believe it.

"Colonel," Simonini said, "you have certainly kept a photographic copy of the *bordereau*. Take a sample of Dreyfus's writing and one of Esterhazy's, and let us compare the three texts."

Sandherr gave some orders and after a short while there were three sheets of paper on the desk. Simonini made several observations: "Look here, for example. In all the words with a double 's', such as *adresse* or *intéressant*, in Esterhazy's hand the first of the two 's's is smaller and the second larger, and they are never joined up. This is what I noticed this morning, because I was particularly careful about this detail when I wrote the *bordereau*. Now look at Dreyfus's handwriting – this is the first time I've seen it. Astonishing! The larger of the two 's's is the first and the second is small, and they are always joined up. Shall I continue?"

"No, that's enough. I have no idea how this mistake has happened. I'll investigate. But the problem now is that the document is in the hands of General Mercier who can always compare it with a sample of Dreyfus's writing. But he's not a handwriting expert, and there are also many similarities between these two hands. We simply have to make sure it doesn't occur to him to look for a sample of Esterhazy's handwriting, though I don't see why he should even think of Esterhazy – providing you keep quiet. Try to forget all about this business and I'd ask you not to return to these offices. Your remuneration will be adjusted appropriately."

From then on, Simonini didn't need to rely on confidential information to find out what was happening, since all the newspapers were full of the Dreyfus Affair. Some people, even at military headquarters, were acting with a certain caution, asking for clear proof that the *bordereau* was by Dreyfus. Sandherr sought the opinion of a famous handwriting expert, Bertillon, who confirmed that the calligraphy in the *bordereau* was not exactly the same as Dreyfus's but, he stated, it was a clear case of self-falsification – Dreyfus had altered his own writing (though only partially) so that it would be thought to be the writing of someone else. Despite these tiny details the document was certainly written by Dreyfus.

Who would have dared to doubt it, especially when *La Libre Parole* was now bombarding public opinion every day and even raising the suspicion that the *affaire* would be hushed up, since Dreyfus was a Jew and would be protected by the Jews? "There are forty thousand officers in the army," wrote Drumont. "Why on earth did Mercier entrust national defence secrets to a cosmopolitan Alsatian Jew?" Mercier was a liberal who had been under pressure for some time from both Drumont and the national press, who accused him of being a Jewish sympathiser. He could not be seen as the defender of a Jewish criminal. And so he did nothing to impede the investigation, showing himself, on the contrary, to be most active.

Drumont hammered on: "The Jews had long been kept out of the army, which had maintained its French purity. Now that they've infiltrated even the nation's armed forces they will be masters of France, and Rothschild will direct their mobilisation. . . . And you understand to what ends."

Tension had reached its height. The captain of the dragoons, Crémieu-Foa, wrote to Drumont telling him he was insulting all Jewish officers, and demanded satisfaction. The two of them fought a duel and, to add to the confusion, who did Crémieu-Foa choose as his second? Esterhazy. Then the Marquis de Morès, one of the editors of *La Libre Parole,* issued a challenge to Crémieu-Foa but the captain's superiors refused to allow him to take part in another duel and confined him to barracks, so Captain Mayer took his place, and died of a perforated lung. Heated debates, protests against this rekindling of religious war . . . And Simonini sat back, contemplating with great satisfaction the cataclysmic results of his single hour's work as scribe.

The council of war met in December, and at the same time another document was produced – a letter to the

Germans from Panizzardi, the Italian military attaché, which referred to "that coward D . . ." who had sold the plans of various fortifications. Did the "D" stand for Dreyfus? No one dared doubt it, and only later was it discovered that it was a man called Dubois, an employee at the ministry, who had been selling information at ten francs a piece. Too late. Dreyfus was found guilty on the 22nd of December and stripped of his rank at the École Militaire in early January. In February he would sail for Devil's Island.

Simonini went to watch the degradation ceremony which he describes in his diary as being extraordinarily dramatic: the troops were lined up around the four sides of the courtyard, Dreyfus arrived and had to walk for almost a kilometre between the lines of valiant men who, though impassive, managed to express their contempt for him; General Darras drew his sabre, a fanfare sounded, Dreyfus marched in full uniform towards the general, escorted by four artillerymen under the command of a sergeant; Darras pronounced the sentence of degradation; a giant of a gendarme officer in a plumed helmet approached the captain, ripped off his stripes, buttons and regimental number, removed his sabre and broke it over his knee, throwing the two halves to the ground in front of the traitor.

Dreyfus appeared impassive, and this was taken by many newspapers as a sign of his treachery. Simonini thought he heard him shout, "I am innocent!" at the moment of the degradation, but in a dignified manner, still standing to attention. It was as if, Simonini observed

LE TRAITRE
Dégradation d'Alfred Dreyfus

———

*. . . a giant of a gendarme officer in
a plumed helmet approached the captain,
ripped off his stripes, buttons and regimental
number, removed his sabre and broke it over
his knee, throwing the two halves to the
ground in front of the traitor. . . .*

[PAGE 467]

———

sarcastically, the little Jew identified so closely with the (usurped) dignity of his role as a French officer, that he was unable to question the decisions of his superiors – as if, since they had decided that he was a traitor, he had to accept the matter not allowing any doubt to cross his mind. Perhaps at that moment he really felt he was a traitor, and the declaration of innocence was, for him, just a necessary part of the ritual.

That was how Simonini thought he remembered it, but in one of his boxes he found an article by a certain Brisson in *La République Française*, published the following day, which was quite different:

"At the moment when the General pronounced the sentence of dishonour, he raised his arm and shouted, 'Vive la France, I am innocent!'

"The officer finished his task. The gold which had covered his uniform lay on the ground. Not even the red ribbons, the emblem of the armed forces, were left. With his dolman now completely black, his kepi suddenly dark, Dreyfus appeared already clothed as a convict. . . . He continues to shout, 'I am innocent!' The crowds on the other side of the gates, seeing only his outline, erupt into jeers and catcalls. Dreyfus hears their curses and shows his anger once again.

"As he is passing a group of officers, he hears the words, 'Good riddance, Judas!' Dreyfus turns around furiously and repeats, 'I am innocent, I am innocent!'

"We can now distinguish his features. We study him for several moments, hoping to gain some supreme revelation, some insight into that soul whose deeper recesses only the

judges have until now been able to come at all close to scru-
tinising. But what dominates his face is anger, anger bordering
on paroxysm. His lips are strained into a frightening grimace,
his eyes are bloodshot. And we realise that if he is so resolute
and walks with such a military step, it is because he is so
ravaged by fury that his nerves are strained to breaking
point. . . .

"What is hidden within the soul of this man? Why does
he continue to obey, to protest his innocence with such
desperate energy? Does he perhaps hope to confound public
opinion, to inspire doubt, to raise suspicion about the integ-
rity of the judges who have condemned him? A thought
comes to us, clear as a flash: if he is not guilty, what fearful
torture!"

Simonini appears not to have felt any remorse. Dreyfus's
guilt was certain, given that it was he, Simonini, who had
decided it. But the difference between his recollection
and the newspaper article showed just how much the
affaire had troubled the whole country and each person
had seen what they wanted to see in that sequence of
events.

In the end, though, Dreyfus could just as well go to
the Devil or to his island. It was no longer any concern
of Simonini's.

His remuneration, which reached him in due course
through discreet channels, was indeed much greater than
he had anticipated.

Keeping an eye on Taxil

While these events were taking place, Simonini well remembers that he had not lost touch with what Taxil was doing, especially as Drumont's group had much to say about it. The Taxil affair was seen first of all with amused scepticism, then with scandalised annoyance. Drumont was considered to be an anti-Mason, an anti-Semite and a devout Catholic – and in his own way he was – and could not bear his cause being supported by a charlatan. Drumont had regarded Taxil as a charlatan for some time, and had attacked him in *La France juive*, claiming that all his books had been published by Jews. But during this period their relations had further deteriorated for political reasons.

As we have already heard from Abbé Dalla Piccola, both of them had stood as council candidates in Paris, seeking votes from the same section of voters. Their battle had therefore already begun.

Taxil wrote a pamphlet entitled *Monsieur Drumont, étude psychologique* in which he criticised his rival's anti-Semitism with excessive sarcasm, observing that anti-Semitism was more typical among the socialist and revolutionary press than among Catholics. Drumont replied with *Testament d'un antisémite*, casting doubt on Taxil's conversion, recalling the mud he had thrown on religious issues, and raising disturbing questions about his lack of belligerence towards the Jewish world.

If we consider that 1892 had seen the creation of two publications – *La Libre Parole*, a campaigning political newspaper which succeeded in exposing the Panama scandal, and *Le diable au XIXe siècle* which could hardly be described as a reliable publication – it is understandable that Drumont's editors should treat Taxil with contempt, and that his increasing difficulties should be followed with malevolent sneers.

Taxil's position was being damaged, Drumont observed, not so much by criticism as by unwelcome support. In the case of the mysterious Diana, dozens of dubious opportunists were boasting their familiarity with a woman whom they had probably never even seen.

A certain Domenico Margiotta published *Souvenirs d'un trente-troisième: Adriano Lemmi Chef Suprème des Franc Maçons* and had sent a copy to Diana declaring his support for her campaign. In his letter, Margiotta described himself as Secretary of the Savonarola Lodge in Florence, Venerable of the Giordano Bruno Lodge of Palmi, Sovereign Grand Inspector-General, thirty-third degree of the Ancient and Accepted Scotch Rite, Sovereign Prince of the Rite of Memphis Misraim (ninety-fifth degree), Inspector of the Misraim Lodges in Calabria and Sicily, Honorary Member of the National Grand Orient of Haiti, Acting Member of the Supreme Federal Council of Naples, Inspector General of the Masonic lodges of the Three Calabrias, Grand Master *ad vitam* of the Oriental Masonic Order of Misraim or Egypt (ninetieth degree) of Paris, Commander of the Order of Knight-Defenders of Universal Masonry, Honorary Member *ad vitam* of the Supreme General Council of the Italian Federation of Palermo, Permanent Inspector and Sovereign Delegate of the Grand Central Directory of Naples, and Member of the New

Reformed Palladium. He ought to have been a senior Masonic dignitary, but said that he had recently left Freemasonry. Drumont said that he had converted to Catholicism because the supreme and secret leadership of the sect had not passed to him, as he had hoped, but to a certain Adriano Lemmi.

Margiotta described how this murky character Adriano Lemmi had started his career as a thief in Marseilles when he forged a letter of credit in the name of Falconet & Co. of Naples and stole a bag of pearls and three hundred gold francs from the wife of a doctor friend of his while she was making a tisane in the kitchen. After a period in prison he sailed to Constantinople, where he entered the service of an old Jewish greengrocer, saying that he was ready to repudiate his baptism and be circumcised. With the help of the Jews he was then able to rise up, as we have seen, through the orders of Freemasonry.

This, concluded Margiotta, is how "the damned Jewish race, who are the cause of every human evil, have used all their influence to ensure that one of their own people, the most villainous of them all, is promoted to the Supreme Universal Government of the Masonic order".

These accusations delighted the ecclesiastical world and *Le Palladisme, Culte de Satan-Lucifer dans les triangles maçonniques,* published by Margiotta in 'ninety-five, opened with letters of praise from the bishops of Grenoble, Montauban, Aix, Limoges, Mende, Tarentaise, Pamiers, Oran and Annecy, as well as from Ludovico Piavi, Patriarch of Jerusalem.

The trouble was that Margiotta's information involved

half of the politicians in Italy, and Crispi in particular, who had been Garibaldi's lieutenant and was by that time Italy's prime minister. As long as phantasmagorical stories about Masonic rites were being written and sold, then everyone was reasonably happy, but as soon as they touched upon the real relationships between Freemasonry and political power there was a danger of upsetting certain very vindictive personalities.

Taxil ought to have realised this, but was clearly trying to regain the ground that Margiotta was taking from him, and so he published, in Diana's name, a book of almost four hundred pages entitled *Le 33ème Crispi*, in which he mixed well-known facts, such as the Banca Romana scandal involving Crispi, with news about his pact with the demon Haborym and his participation in a Palladian gathering during which the ubiquitous Sophie Walder had announced that she was pregnant with a daughter whose child would in turn give birth to the Antichrist.

"The stuff of operettas," exclaimed Drumont, scandalised. "That's no way to carry out a political campaign!"

And yet the work was favourably received in the Vatican, which infuriated Drumont even more. The Vatican had a score to settle with Crispi, who had unveiled a monument in a Roman square dedicated to Giordano Bruno, a victim of ecclesiastical intolerance, and Leo XIII had spent that day in prayer of atonement before the statue of St Peter. We can just imagine the Pope's joy at reading the allegations against Crispi: he directed his secretary, Monsignor Sardi, to send Diana not just the usual "apostolic benediction" but also heartfelt thanks and encouragement to continue her meritorious work of unmasking the "iniquitous sect". And the iniquity of the sect was demonstrated by the fact that, in Diana's book, Haborym appeared with three heads, one human with hair aflame, one of a cat and one of a snake – though Diana pointed out with scientific rigour that she had never seen it in that form (on her invocation he had appeared only as a fine old man with a flowing silvery beard).

"They don't even bother to respect plausibility!", spluttered Drumont. "How can an American girl who's only just arrived in France know all the secrets of Italian politics? It's obvious, people don't notice these things and Diana is in the business of selling books, but the Supreme Pontiff . . . the Supreme Pontiff will be accused of believing any old claptrap! The Church must be defended against its own frailty!"

La Libre Parole was the first to openly express doubt about Diana's existence. It was joined immediately afterwards by publications with an avowedly religious viewpoint such as *L'Avenir* and *L'Univers.* Other Catholic groups, though, did everything they could to prove Diana's existence. *Le Rosier de Marie* published a declaration by the President of the Order of Advocates of Saint-Pierre, Lautier, who stated that he had seen Diana in the company of Taxil, Bataille and the artist who had produced her portrait, though it had happened some time ago, when Diana was still a Palladian. Yet her face must already have been radiant with her imminent conversion, since the writer described her as follows: "She is a young lady of twenty-nine, charming, refined, above average height, outgoing, sincere and honest, eyes brimming with intelligence, showing resolution and a commanding disposition. She dresses elegantly and with taste, without affectation and without that abundance of jewellery that so ridiculously characterises the majority of rich foreigners. . . . Unusual eyes, now sea blue, now bright golden yellow." When she was offered a glass of chartreuse she refused out of hatred to everything related to the Church. She drank only cognac.

Taxil had been *magna pars* in organising a large anti-Masonic conference at Trent, in September 1896. But it was here, in fact, that suspicion and criticism from the German Catholics intensified. A certain Father Baumgarten asked for Diana's birth certificate and evidence from the priest to whom she had made the recantation. Taxil claimed to have the evidence in his pocket but didn't produce it.

A month after the Trent congress, a certain Abbé Garnier, writing in *Le Peuple Français*, went so far as to suspect that Diana was a Masonic mystification, a Father Bailly in the highly respectable journal *La Croix* also dissociated himself, and the *Kölnische Volkszeitung* recalled that Bataille-Hacks, in that very same year when the first instalments of *Le Diable* appeared, was blaspheming God and all his saints. Canon Mustel once again came out in support of Diana, along with *La Civiltà Cattolica* and a secretary of Cardinal Parocchi, who wrote to her "to fortify her against the storm of slanderous allegations which would not place in doubt her existence".

Drumont had no lack of good contacts in various circles, or of journalistic intuition. Simonini did not know how he had done it, but Drumont managed to track down Hacks-Bataille, probably surprising him during one of his alcoholic crises, during which he was ever more prone to melancholy and regret. And this is how the dramatic turn of events took place. Hacks confessed he was a fraud, first in the *Kölnische Volkszeitung* and then in *La Libre Parole*. He wrote frankly: "When the encyclical *Humanum Genus* appeared I thought there was some money to be made out of the credulity and unfathomable nonsense of the Catholics. All you need is a Jules Verne to give a terrifying appearance to these tales of brigandry. I was this Verne, and there it is. . . . I described scenes of hocus-pocus, putting them into exotic contexts, feeling sure that no one would go and check them out. . . . And the Catholics swallowed it whole. The stupidity of these people is such that even today, if I were to say I've been fooling them, they won't believe me."

In *Le Rosier de Marie*, Lautier wrote that he had perhaps been misled and the person he had seen was not Diana Vaughan, and then finally the first Jesuit attack appeared, written by a Father Portalié in *Études*, a highly respectable journal. And if this was not enough, certain newspapers wrote that Monsignor Northrop, Bishop of Charleston (where Pike, the Grand Master of Grand Masters was supposed to be living), had gone to Rome to personally assure Pope Leo XIII that the Masons in his city were respectable people and that there was no statue of Satan in their temple.

Drumont was victorious. Taxil had been put in his place. The fight against the Masons and the Jews was back in serious hands.

24

A NIGHT MASS

17th April 1897

Dear Captain,

Your last pages detail an incredible number of events, and it is clear that while you were involved with those matters I was busy with others. And you were obviously informed (inevitably, given the stir that Taxil and Bataille were creating) about what was going on around me, and perhaps you remember more about it than I can piece together.

As we are now in April 1897, my involvement with Taxil and Diana has been going on for about a dozen years, during which time so much has happened. When, for example, did we organise Boullan's disappearance?

It must have been less than a year after we had begun publishing *Le Diable*. Boullan arrived one evening at Auteuil, distraught, continually wiping a whitish froth from his lips with a handkerchief.

"I am dead," he said, "they are killing me."

Dr Bataille decided that a good glass of strong spirits would put him right. Boullan did not say no, and then in broken words he recounted a story of sorcery and witchcraft.

He told us how he was on extremely bad terms with Stanislas de Guaita and his cabalistic Order of the Rose Croix, and with Josephin Péladan who, in a spirit of dissent, had founded the Catholic Order of the Rose Croix – figures whom *Le Diable* had obviously already investigated. There was little difference in my view between Péladan's Rosicrucians and the Vintras sect of which Boullan had become Grand Pontifex, all people who went around in dalmatics covered with cabalistic symbols. It was hard to understand whether they were on the side of God Almighty or the Devil, but perhaps this was why Boullan ended up at daggers drawn with the Péladan camp. They went foraging in the same territory, trying to seduce the same lost souls.

Guaita's closest friends described him as a refined gentleman (he was a marquis) who collected *grimoires* spangled with pentagrams, works by Llull and Paracelsus, manuscripts by his master of black-and-white magic, Eliphas Lévi, and other hermetic works of great rarity. He passed his days, it was said, in a small ground-floor apartment in Avenue Trudaine where he received no one but occultists, and was sometimes there for weeks without going out. Others claimed it was in those very rooms that he fought with a wraith which he held prisoner in a wardrobe and, sodden with alcohol and morphine, gave substance to the phantasms produced by his deliria.

It was clear that he moved among sinister circles from the titles of his "Essays on the Infernal Sciences", where he had denounced Boullan's luciferine or luciferian, satanic or satanesque, diabolic or diabolesque schemes, portraying him as a degenerate who had "raised fornication to a liturgical practice".

The story was an old one. Back in 1887 Guaita and his entourage had assembled an "initiates court" which had condemned Boullan. Was it a moral condemnation? Boullan had long claimed he was being punished physically and he felt continually attacked, struck, wounded by occult fluids, javelins of an

*. . . he fought with a wraith which
he held prisoner in a wardrobe and,
sodden with alcohol and morphine,
gave substance to the phantasms
produced by his deliria. . . .*

[PAGE 480]

impalpable nature that Guaita and others were hurling at him, even from a great distance.

Boullan was now at his wits' end.

"Each evening, as I fall asleep, I feel I am being knocked about, punched, slapped – and it is not a figment of my diseased imagination, believe me, because at the same moment my cat becomes agitated as if an electric shock has been sent through him. I know that Guaita has made a wax figure he pierces with a needle, and I feel stabbing pains. I tried to cast a counter-spell to blind him, but Guaita sensed the trap; he is more powerful than I in these arts, and has cast the spell back at me. My eyes are blurring, my breathing is laboured, I don't know how many more hours I'll be able to keep going."

We were not sure he was telling us the truth, but that was not the point. The poor man was really ill. And then Taxil had one of his flashes of inspiration: "Pass yourself off for dead," he said. "Let your close friends announce that you ceased to be while on a trip to Paris. Do not return to Lyon, find a refuge here in the city, shave your beard and moustache, become someone else. Wake up again, like Diana, in another person . . . . but, unlike Diana, remain there. In that way, Guaita and company will think you're dead and stop tormenting you."

"And if I can't go to Lyon, how do I live?"

"Live here with us at Auteuil, at least until the dust has settled and your opponents have been exposed. After all, Diana needs greater support and you're more useful to us if you can be here each day rather than a passing visitor.

"But," Taxil added, "if you have friends you trust, before passing yourself off for dead, write letters filled with premonitions of death and make clear accusations against Guaita and

*. . . he felt continually attacked, struck,
wounded by occult fluids, javelins of an
impalpable nature that Guaita and
others were hurling at him, even
from a great distance. . . .*

[PAGE 482]

Péladan so that your grieving followers can launch a campaign against your murderers."

And so it was. The only person to know about the subterfuge was Madame Thibault, Boullan's assistant, priestess, confidante (and perhaps something more) who had given his Paris friends a touching description of his dying moments. I don't know how she dealt with his followers in Lyon: perhaps she arranged for the burial of an empty coffin. Shortly afterwards she was employed as a housekeeper by Huysmans, a fashionable writer and one of Boullan's friends and posthumous defenders – and I am convinced that on certain evenings, when I was not at Auteil, she came to visit her old associate.

On news of his death, the journalist Jules Bois attacked Guaita in *Gil Blas*, accusing him of witchlike practices and the murder of Boullan, and *Le Figaro* published an interview with Huysmans explaining in every detail how Guaita's incantations had worked. Bois continued the allegations, again in *Gil Blas*, calling for an autopsy on the body to see whether the liver and heart had actually been damaged by Guaita's fluidic darts, and urging a judicial inquiry.

Guaita replied, also in *Gil Blas,* referring with irony to his deadly powers ("Well, yes, I handle the most subtle poisons with infernal art, I disperse them to send their toxic vapours, a hundred leagues away, into the nostrils of those I do not like, I am the Gilles de Rais of the coming century"), and he challenged both Huysmans and Bois to a duel.

Bataille sneered, observing that with all those magic powers, from one side and the other, no one had managed to harm anyone, but a Toulouse newspaper suggested that someone really had used witchcraft: one of the horses pulling Bois' landau to the duel collapsed without apparent cause, the horse was changed and the second one also dropped to the ground, the landau overturned and Bois arrived on the field of honour covered with bruises and scratches. What is more, he was later to claim that one of his shots was stopped in the barrel of his pistol by a supernatural force.

Boullan's friends sent information to the press that Péladan's Rose Croix had had a mass celebrated at Notre Dame, but at the moment of the elevation they had brandished daggers menacingly at the altar. Who is to know what actually happened. For *Le Diable* this was most intriguing, and not as hard to believe as other news to which its readers were accustomed. Except that Boullan had to be dragged in, and fairly unceremoniously.

"You're dead," Bataille reminded him. "Whatever they say about this disappearance must no longer interest you. Besides, if you should reappear one day, then we'll have created around you an aura of mystery that can only be to your benefit. Don't worry therefore what we write. It won't be about you but about the figure of Boullan who no longer exists."

Boullan agreed and, perhaps in his narcissistic delirium, took pleasure in reading what Bataille continued to dream up about his occult practices. But in reality he now seemed fixed only on Diana. He remained beside her with morbid constancy, and I almost worried for her: she was becoming increasingly hypnotised by his fantasies, as if she didn't already live far enough from reality.

You have described well what then happened. The Catholic world was split in two, and one part doubted the very existence of Diana Vaughan. Hacks had given the game away, and the castle that Taxil had constructed was collapsing. We were now being harassed by our opponents and at the same time by Diana's many impersonators, such as that man Margiotta whom you have already mentioned. We realised we had gone too far; the idea of a three-headed devil who banqueted with the leader of the Italian government was difficult to swallow.

A few meetings with Father Bergamaschi had now convinced me that even if the Roman Jesuits of *Civiltà Cattolica* had decided to continue supporting Diana's cause, the French Jesuits (as apparent from the article by Father Portalié that you referred to) were already determined to drop the whole story. Another brief conversation with Hébuterne had persuaded me that the Masons couldn't wait for the farce to end. The Catholics wanted to end it quietly, so as not to bring further discredit to the hierarchy, but the Masons demanded a dramatic recantation, so that all the years of Taxil's anti-Masonic propaganda would be branded as sheer villainy.

Thus one day I received two messages at the same time. One, from Father Bergamaschi, said, "I authorise you to offer Taxil fifty thousand francs to close the whole business. Fraternally in Xt, Bergamaschi." The other, from Hébuterne, stated, "So let's bring an end to it. Offer Taxil a hundred thousand francs if he publicly admits having invented everything."

I was covered on both sides. All I had to do was proceed – after, of course, cashing the sums promised by my paymasters.

Hacks's defection made my task easier. All I had to do was urge Taxil to convert or perhaps reconvert. Once again I had a hundred and fifty thousand francs, as at the start of this business, and seventy-five thousand was enough for Taxil since I had arguments more persuasive than money.

"Taxil," I said, "we've lost Hacks, and it will be difficult to expose Diana to public examination. I'll think about how to get rid of her, but I'm worried about you. From what I've heard it seems the Masons have decided to end it all with you, and you yourself have written how bloody their revenge can be. First you defended Catholic public opinion, but now you can see that even the Jesuits are creeping away. And that's why they're offering you an extraordinary opportunity: a lodge – don't ask me which as it's highly confidential – is offering you seventy-five thousand francs if you publicly declare that you duped everyone. You understand the advantage it would bring to the Freemasons: they would be cleansed of the mud you've been slinging at them and the Catholics will be covered by it instead; they'll come across as incredibly naive. And so far as you're concerned, with all the publicity from this turn of events, your next works will sell better than your last ones, which were already selling fewer and fewer copies to the Catholics. You'd win back the anti-clerical and the Masonic public. It's worth your while."

He didn't need much persuasion: Taxil's a buffoon and the idea of performing in a new piece of buffoonery brought a sparkle to his eyes.

"Listen, my dear Abbé, I'll rent a room and tell the press that on a certain day Diana Vaughan will appear and present to the public a photograph of the demon Asmodeus which she took with the permission of Lucifer himself! On a handbill, let's say that I'll promise a raffle among those present for a typewriter worth four hundred francs. We won't need to go ahead with the raffle as obviously I'll appear to say that Diana doesn't exist – and if she doesn't exist then of course the typewriter doesn't exist either. I can see it already: I'll end up in all the papers, and on the front page. Magnificent. Give me time to organise the event properly, and (if you don't mind) ask for an advance on those seventy-five thousand francs, for expenses. . . ."

The next day Taxil found a hall at the Société de Géographie but it would only be free on Easter Monday. I remember saying, "That's almost a month away. It's better that you're not seen around during this time, so as to avoid stirring up any more gossip. Meanwhile, I'll think about what to do with Diana."

Taxil hesitated for a moment. His lip trembled, and with it his moustache: "You don't want to . . . eliminate Diana?", he asked.

"Of course not," I replied. "I'm a clergyman, don't forget. I'll return her to the place from whence I took her."

He seemed bereft at the thought of losing Diana, but his fear of Masonic revenge was stronger than his attraction for Diana had ever been. As well as a scoundrel, he's a coward. How would he have reacted if I had said, "Yes, I intend to eliminate Diana"? Perhaps, for fear of the Masons, he would have accepted the idea: as long as he didn't have to do the deed.

Easter Monday will be the 19th of April. If I therefore spoke of a one-month wait on leaving Taxil, this must have taken place around the 19th or 20th of March. Today is the 17th of April. Therefore, in gradually piecing together the events of the last ten years, I have arrived at just under a month ago. And if this diary were to help me, and you, to find out what caused my current loss of memory, nothing at all has happened. Or perhaps the crucial event took place during these last four weeks.

Now it's as if I feel a certain dread about remembering any more.

18th April at dawn

While Taxil was still roaming furiously around the house and having fits of agitation, Diana was entirely unaware of what was going on. In the alternation between her two conditions, she followed our private discussions in a daze, and seemed to revive only when the mention of a person or a place produced a faint flicker in her mind.

She was gradually deteriorating into a vegetable state, with one single animal trait, an increasingly frenzied sensuality, which she directed freely towards Taxil, Bataille when he was still with us, Boullan, of course, and – though I tried not to offer her any pretext – also towards me.

Diana had been barely twenty when she entered our company and was now over thirty-five. Taxil, with an increasingly lubricious smile, said she was becoming ever more attractive as she matured, as if a woman over thirty were still desirable. Perhaps her almost arboreal vitality gave an appearance of enigmatic beauty to her stare.

But these are perversions about which I am not an expert. My God, why do I dwell upon the fleshly form of that woman, who for us was meant to be nothing more than a wretched instrument?

I have said that Diana was unaware of what was going on. Perhaps I am wrong. In March she became frenzied, perhaps because she was no longer seeing Taxil or Bataille. She was in the grip of hysteria, the Devil (she said) was cruelly tormenting her, wounding her, biting her, twisting her legs, slapping her face – and she showed me some bluish marks around her eyes. Marks of wounds similar to stigmata began to appear on her palms. She asked why the infernal powers should act so harshly towards someone who was a Palladian devotee of Lucifer, and she grabbed my cassock, as if to ask for help.

I thought of Boullan, who knew more about devilry than me. In fact, as soon as I called for him, Diana grasped him by the arms and began to shake. He placed his hands round the nape of her neck and calmed her, speaking to her gently, then spat into her mouth.

"And who tells you, my daughter," he said, "that the one who subjects you to these tortures is your lord Lucifer? Do you not think, in contempt and punishment for your Palladian faith, your enemy is the Enemy par excellence, that aeon whom the Christians call Jesus Christ, or one of his supposed saints?"

"But Father," said Diana confused, "if I am Palladian it is because I do not recognise any power in Christ the Tyrant, to such an extent that one day I refused to stab the host because I thought it mad to recognise a real presence in what was only a lump of flour."

"And there you are wrong, my child. See what Christians do, who recognise the sovereignty of their Christ, yet despite this they do not deny the existence of the Devil; indeed they fear his enticements, his enmity, his seductions. And we must do likewise: if we believe in the power of our lord Lucifer it is

because we believe that his enemy Adonai has a spiritual existence, even in the guise of Christ, and manifests himself through
his iniquity. And therefore you must stoop to trample upon the
image of your enemy in the only way that a faithful Luciferian
is permitted to do."

"Which is?"

"The black mass. You will not obtain the benevolence of
Lucifer our lord except by celebrating your rejection of the
Christian God through the black mass."

Diana seemed to be convinced, and Boullan asked my
permission to take her to a gathering of satanist devotees, in
his attempt to persuade her that satanism and luciferianism or
Palladism had the same purposes and the same purifying
function.

I did not like to allow Diana out of the house, but I had to
give her some space to breathe.

I find Abbé Boullan in intimate conversation with Diana, saying,
"You enjoyed yesterday?"

What happened yesterday?

The abbé continues, "Well, tomorrow evening I have to
celebrate another solemn mass in a deconsecrated church at
Passy. A marvellous evening, it is the 21st of March, the spring
equinox, a date full of occult significance. But if you agree to
come I will have to prepare you spiritually, now, alone, in
confession."

I left, and Boullan remained with her for more than an hour.
When he finally called for me again, he said that Diana would

be going to the church at Passy the following day, but would like me to accompany her.

"Yes, Father," Diana said to me with eyes unusually sparkling, and cheeks flushed. "Please do."

I should have refused, but I was curious, and did not want Boullan to think me a prig.

I tremble as I write, my hand runs across the page almost by itself. I'm not recalling but reliving it, as if describing something that is happening at this very instant. . . .

It was the evening of the 21st of March. You, Captain, began your diary on the 24th of March, recounting how I had lost my memory on the morning of the 22nd. If something terrible happened it must have been on the evening of the 21st.

I am trying to piece it together but find it difficult. I have a fever, I fear, my forehead is burning.

Having collected Diana at Auteuil, I give a certain address to the fiacre. The coachman looks at me out of the corner of his eye, as if he mistrusts a customer like me, despite my ecclesiastical dress, but when offered a generous tip he sets off without saying anything. We travel further and further from the centre towards the outskirts, along roads that become darker and darker, until we turn into a lane flanked by abandoned houses which ends abruptly at the almost derelict facade of an old chapel.

We get out, and the coachman seems anxious to be off, to such an extent that when, having paid the fare, I search my pockets for a few extra francs, he shouts, "It doesn't matter,

Father, thanks all the same!" and forgoes the tip in order to be off as soon as possible.

"It's cold, I'm frightened," says Diana, pressing against me. I pull back, but at the same time, though I cannot see her arm, I feel it under the clothes she is wearing, and I realise she is dressed strangely: she is wearing a hooded cloak, covering her entirely from head to foot, so that in the darkness she might be mistaken for a monk, or one of those characters appearing in monastery crypts in those Gothic novels that were much in vogue at the beginning of this century. I had never seen it before, though, there again, it had never crossed my mind to examine the trunk with all the things she had brought with her from Dr Du Maurier's house.

The small door of the chapel is half open. We enter a single nave, illuminated by an array of candles that burn on the altar and by many lighted tripods which form a circle around a small apse. The altar is covered with a dark pall, like those used for funerals. Above, in place of the crucifix or other image, is a statue of the Devil in the form of a he-goat with a dispropor-tionate phallus protruding by at least thirty centimetres. The candles are not white or ivory but black. At the centre, in a tabernacle, are three skulls.

"Abbé Boullan told me about them," Diana whispers to me. "They are the relics of the three Magi, the real ones, Theobens, Menser and Saïr. They received a warning when they saw a falling star burn out, and turned away from Palestine so as not to be witnesses to the birth of Christ."

In front of the altar, arranged in a semicircle, is a row of youngsters, boys to the right and girls to the left. Both groups are so unripe in age that little difference is to be noted between the two sexes, and that charming amphitheatre would seem populated by sweet androgynes, whose differences are all the more concealed by the fact that all wear a crown of dried roses on their heads, except that the boys are naked, and can be distinguished for their member which they flaunt to each other, while the girls are covered with short tunics of almost transparent fabric, which caress their small breasts and the unripe curves of their hips, without hiding anything. They are all very beautiful, even if their faces express more malice than innocence, but this certainly increases their charm – and I have to confess (a curious situation in which I, a member of the clergy, confess to you, Captain!) that while I feel, not terror, but at least fear in front of a woman who is now mature, it is difficult for me to resist the seduction of a prepubescent creature.

Those unusual acolytes hold resinous branches to the tripods, lighting them, and with them they charge the thuribles, from which a dense smoke and an enervating aroma of exotic spices are unleashed. Others among those naked gracile children are distributing small cups and one is also offered to me. "Drink, Monsieur Abbé," says a youth with brazen gaze. "It is to help you enter the spirit of the ritual."

I drink it and now see and hear everything as if in a mist.

Here Boullan enters. He is wearing a white chlamys, and over it a red chasuble embroidered with an upturned crucifix. At the intersection of the two arms of the cross is the image of a black he-goat, rearing up on its hind legs, horns spread. . . . But at the first movement the abbé makes, as if by chance or negligence, but in fact out of brazen depravity, the chlamys opens up to reveal a phallus of notable proportions that I would never have imagined on that flaccid individual, and already erect,

494

due to some drug taken earlier. His thighs are bound by two dark yet transparent stockings, like those worn by Celeste Mogador when she danced the cancan at *Bal Mabille* (now reproduced in *Charivari* and other weekly publications and there, alas, even for priests and abbés to see, whether they wish to or not).

The celebrant has turned his back to the congregation and begins his mass in Latin while the androgynes give the responses:

"In nomine Astaroth et Asmodei et Beelzébuth. Introibo ad altare Satanae."

"Qui laetificat cupiditatem nostram."

"Lucifer omnipotens, emitte tenebram tuam et afflige inimicos nostros."

"Ostende nobis, Domine Satana, potentiam tuam, et exaudi luxuriam meam."

"Et blasphemia mea ad te veniat."

Then Boullan takes a cross from his robe, places it beneath his feet and tramples on it several times: "O Cross, I crush thee in memory of and in vengeance for the ancient Masters of the Temple. I crush thee because thou wert an instrument of false sanctification of the false god Jesus Christ."

At this moment, Diana, without warning, and as if struck by an illumination (but certainly following the instructions that Boullan had given her yesterday in confession), crosses the nave between the two groups of devotees and goes straight to the foot of the altar. Turning towards the faithful (or unfaithful as it were) with a hieratic gesture, she suddenly removes her hood and cloak, appearing stark naked. I cannot describe it, Captain Simonini, but it is as if I see her now, unveiled as Isis, her face covered only by a slender black mask.

I am overcome, as if by a spasm, seeing a woman for the first time in all the unbearable violence of her body stripped bare. Her tawny golden hair that she keeps chastely in a bun is let free, and falls immodestly to caress buttocks of wickedly perfect roundness. The haughty thin neck of this pagan statue rises like a column above shoulders of marble whiteness, while her breasts (and I see the naked bosoms of a woman for the first time) stand out arrogantly and satanically proud. Between them, the only unfleshly remnant, the locket that Diana is never without.

Diana turns and climbs the three steps up to the altar with lubricious ease, then, helped by the celebrant, lies upon it, her head reclining on a black velvet cushion fringed with silver, while her hair flows over the edge of the altar, her belly lightly arched, her legs splayed to show the auburn fleece hiding the entrance to her womanly cavern while her body shines eerily in the reddish glow of the candles. Dear God, I don't know how to describe what I am seeing. It is as if my natural horror of female flesh and the fear it moves within me are melting away to leave just enough space for one new feeling, as if a hitherto unsampled elixir is running through my veins. . . .

Boullan has placed a small ivory phallus on Diana's breast, and on her belly an embroidered cloth on which he has laid a chalice made of dark stone.

From the chalice he takes a host, not one of those already consecrated ones that you trade in, Captain Simonini, but a wafer which Boullan, still a fully fledged priest of the Holy Roman Church, though probably now excommunicated, is about to consecrate on Diana's belly.

And he says, *"Suscipe, Domine Satana, hanc hostiam, quam ego indignus famulus tuus offero tibi. Amen."*

Then he takes the host and, after lowering it twice towards the ground, raising it twice heavenwards, and turning it once to the right and to the left, shows it to the congregation, saying, "From the south I invoke the benevolence of Satan, from the east the benevolence of Lucifer, from the north the benevolence of Belial, from the west the benevolence of Leviathan, open wide the gates of hell, and may the Sentries of the Bottomless Pit, invoked by these names, come unto me. Our Father, who art in hell, accursed be thy name, thy kingdom be annihilated, thy will be scorned, on earth as it is in hell! May the Name of the Beast be praised!"

And the chorus of youngsters, loudly, "Six six six!"

The number of the Beast!

Boullan now cries out, "May Lucifer be glorified, whose Name is Doom. O master of sin, of unnatural loves, of incestuous blessings, of divine sodomy, Satan, it is you whom we adore! And you, O Jesus, I compel to become flesh in this host, so that we can renew your suffering and torment you once again with the nails that crucified you and pierce you with the lance of Longinus!"

"Six six six," the youths repeat.

Boullan raises the host and pronounces, "In the beginning was the flesh, and the flesh was with Lucifer and the flesh was Lucifer. The same was in the beginning with Lucifer: all things were made by him, and without him was not anything made that was. And the flesh was made word and dwelt amongst us, in the darkness, and we beheld the obscure splendour of Lucifer's only begotten daughter, filled with screams and fury, and desire."

He slides the host along Diana's belly then plunges it into

497

her vagina. As he removes it, he raises it towards the nave, crying out loudly, "Take and eat!"

Two of the androgynes prostrate themselves in front of him, raise his chlamys and together kiss his erect member. Then the whole group of adolescents falls at his feet and, while the boys begin to masturbate, the girls pull off each other's veils and roll over each other letting out voluptuous cries. The air is filled with other more unbearably violent scents and all those watching, first with lustful sighs, then gasps of rapture, gradually strip naked and begin to copulate, one with the other, with no distinction as to sex or age, and through the vapours I see a hag, over seventy, her skin heavily wrinkled, her breasts reduced to two lettuce leaves, her legs skeletal, rolling across the floor as an adolescent voraciously kisses what was once her vulva.

I am shaking all over, I look around to see how I might escape from that den of iniquity. The space in which I crouch is so full of poisonous vapour that it is as though I am caught in a thick cloud. What I drank at the beginning has certainly drugged me. I can no longer think straight and see everything now as if through a reddish cloud. And it is through this cloud that I catch sight of Diana, still naked, without her mask, descending from the altar. The demented throng, though continuing their carnal mayhem, help clear a way for her to pass. She comes towards me.

Gripped by the fear of being reduced to the same state as that frenzied mass, I draw back but end up against a pillar. Diana arrives panting over me. Oh, God! My pen shakes, my mind is failing, crying as I am (now as then) with disgust, unable even to scream because she has filled my mouth with something not mine. I feel myself rolling on the ground, the vapours are drugging me. That body trying to merge with mine arouses a death-like excitement within me. I am touching that alien flesh (with my hands, as if I wanted it!) possessed as if I were an hysteric at the Salpêtrière. I penetrate a gash in her with the insane curiosity of a surgeon, I beg that sorceress to leave me, I bite her to defend myself and she cries out for me to do it again. I throw my head back, thinking of Dr Tissot. I know that such abandonment will cause my whole body to waste away, will bring an ashen pallor to my dying face, clouded vision and disturbed dreams, husky voice, pains in my eyeballs, the invasion of pestilent red marks upon my face, the vomiting of calciferous materials, palpitations – and finally, syphilis, blindness.

And though I can no longer see, I suddenly feel the most excruciating and indescribable and unbearable sensation of my life, as if all the blood from throughout my veins were suddenly gushing out from a tear in each of my taut limbs, from my nose, my ears, from my fingertips, from even my anus, help, help, I think I know now what death is, from which every living being recoils, even when he seeks it through an unnatural instinct to multiply his own seed. . . .

I can no longer write, I no longer recall, I am reliving, the experience is unbearable, I wish I could forget it all again. . . .

As if reviving from a state of unconsciousness, I find Boullan beside me holding Diana by the hand, her cloak covering her once again. Boullan tells me there is a carriage at the door: "You had better take Diana home, she looks exhausted." She is trembling, and mumbles unintelligible words.

Boullan is unusually obliging, and at first I think he wants to be forgiven for something – after all, it was he who had dragged me into this disgusting business. But when I tell him he can go and that I will look after Diana, he insists on coming with us, reminding me that he too lives at Auteuil. He seems jealous. To annoy him I say I'm not going to Auteuil but somewhere else, that I am taking Diana to a trusted friend.

He turns pale, as if I were carrying off a trophy that belongs to him.

"Never mind," he says, "I'll come as well, Diana needs help."

Having climbed into the fiacre, I give my rue Maître-Albert address without thinking, as if I had decided that Diana should no longer live at Auteuil. Boullan looks blankly at me, but remains silent, and climbs in, clutching Diana's hand.

We say nothing during the journey. I let them into my apartment. I lay Diana on the bed, grasp her wrist and speak to her, for the first time after all that has happened between us.

"Why, why?" I shout.

Boullan tries to intervene, but I push him violently against the wall, causing him to slide to the floor. Only then do I realise how weak and sickly that demon is – in comparison I am a Hercules.

Diana struggles free, her cloak falling open at her breast. I cannot bear to see her flesh again, I try to cover her up, my hand is caught in the chain of her medallion. In the brief exchange it breaks, the medallion remains in my hand, Diana tries to take it back, I move away to the back of the room and open the small locket.

There is a golden outline depicting, without doubt, Moses' Tablets of the Law, and some Hebrew writing.

"What does it mean?" I ask, approaching Diana on the bed, her eyes staring blankly. "What do these symbols behind your mother's portrait mean?"

"My mother," she murmurs vacantly, "my mother was a Jew . . . she believed in Adonai. . . ."

So that's it. Not only have I had intercourse with a woman of the Devil's stock, but with a Jewess. The line of descent among them, I know, passes on the mother's side and if, in this intercourse, my seed had fertilised that impure belly, I would therefore be giving life to a Jew.

"You cannot do this to me," I shout, and hurl myself at the prostitute, grasping her by the neck; she struggles, I increase my grip, Boullan has regained consciousness and throws himself on me. Once again I push him back, with a kick in the groin, and watch him collapse into a corner of the room. I throw myself on Diana once again (oh, truly have I lost my wits!) and her eyes seem gradually to come out of their sockets, her tongue hangs swollen from her mouth, I hear a last breath, then her body slumps lifeless.

I pull myself together. I think about the enormity of what I have done. Boullan is groaning in a corner, almost emasculated. I try to recover my senses and laugh: whatever happens, at least I won't be father to a Jew.

I pull myself together, telling myself I have to hide the woman's body downstairs in the sewer – it is now becoming even more accommodating than your Prague cemetery, Captain. But it is dark, I need to take a lamp with me, I have to go the whole length of the passageway as far as your house, go down into the shop and from there into the sewer. I need the help of

. . . "My mother," she murmurs vacantly, "my mother was a Jew". . .

[PAGE 501]

Boullan, who is picking himself up from the floor and staring at me with the eyes of a madman.

And in that instant I also realise I cannot let the witness to my murder leave this house. I remember the pistol that Bataille had given me, open the drawer where I had hidden it, and point it at Boullan who continues to stare at me bewildered.

"I am sorry, Abbé," I tell him, "if you want to save yourself, help me dispose of this sweet body."

"Yes, yes," he says, as if in erotic ecstasy. The dead Diana, with her tongue hanging from her mouth and her blank stare, must seem as desirable to him, in his confusion, as the naked Diana who abused me for her pleasure.

But then, I am not entirely lucid either. As if in a dream, I wrap Diana in her cloak, give Boullan a lighted lamp, grasp the dead body by its feet and drag it along the passageway as far as your house, then down the staircase into the shop, and from there to the sewer, the corpse's head banging with a sinister thud on each step, and finally I line it up beside the remains of Dalla Piccola (the other one).

Boullan now seems to have lost his head. He laughs, "Perhaps it's better down here than in the world out there, where Guaita is waiting for me. . . . May I stay here with Diana?"

"By all means, Abbé," I reply, "I could not wish for more."

I draw the pistol, shoot, and hit him in the centre of his forehead.

Boullan falls crookedly, almost over Diana's legs. I have to bend down, pick him up and place him beside her. They lie together like two lovers.

And here, at this very moment, through recounting, I have rediscovered, with troubled mind, what happened an instant before I lost my memory.

The circle is complete. Now I know. Now, at dawn on the 18th of April, Easter Sunday, I have written what happened on the 21st of March, late at night, to the person I thought was Abbé Dalla Piccola. . . .

25

SORTING MATTERS OUT

Diary for 18th and 19th April 1897

At this point, anyone looking over Simonini's shoulder to read what Dalla Piccola had written would have seen the words come to an abrupt halt, as if his hand, no longer able to hold the pen, had of its own accord drawn a long scrawl that continued beyond the paper, marking the green baize of the desk, as the writer's body slumped to the floor. And on the next sheet of paper it appeared that Captain Simonini had resumed writing.

He had woken up dressed as a priest, wearing Dalla Piccola's wig, but now realising, without any shadow of a doubt, that he was Simonini. There, open on the table, he immediately saw those last pages in the handwriting of the supposed Dalla Piccola, written in a hysterical and increasingly confused hand. He sweated, his heart palpitating, as he read and recalled all that had been written to that very moment when the abbé's handwriting stopped and he (the abbé) or rather he (Simonini) were, no . . . *was* struck with panic, and had collapsed.

As he regained consciousness, the cloud of confusion gradually passed and all became clear. Recovering, he realised that he and Dalla Piccola were one and the same. He was now able to recall what Dalla Piccola had written the previous evening – in other words he could now remember that it was he himself, dressed as Abbé Dalla

505

Piccola (not the one with the protruding teeth whom he had killed, but the other he had brought back to life and impersonated for years) who had been through the terrible experience of the black mass.

What happened then? Perhaps Diana had had time to grab his wig during the scuffle, perhaps he had needed to remove his cassock to drag her wretched body as far as the sewer and had returned, by then almost out of his wits, to his own room in rue Maître-Albert, where he had reawoken on the morning of the 22nd of March, unable to find his clothes.

The carnal contact with Diana, the revelation of her vile origins, and her necessary, almost ritual death, had been too much for him, and that same night he had lost his memory, or rather Dalla Piccola and Simonini had both lost their memory, and the two personalities had alternated over the course of that month. In all probability, as had happened to Diana, he must have passed from one state to the other through some form of crisis – an epileptic fit, fainting, who knows – but without being aware of it, so that he awoke each time thinking he had simply fallen asleep.

Dr Froïde's therapy had worked (even though the doctor would never know of its success). By one self recounting to the other self those memories which he had laboriously extracted from the recesses of his mind, as if in a dream, Simonini had reached the critical point, the traumatic event, which had plunged him into a state of amnesia and transformed him into two distinct people, each of whom remembered one part of his past, without either he or that other, who was also him, being able to bring themselves back together as one, and even though each of them tried to conceal from the other the terrible, unthinkable reason for that erasure.

Remembering had left Simonini feeling exhausted of course, and, to reassure himself that he was truly reborn into a new life, he closed his diary and decided to go out, prepared for any encounter, knowing now who he was. He was ready for a good meal, but couldn't yet allow himself any excessive indulgence that day, seeing that his senses had already been so sorely tested. Like a hermit from the Thebaid, he felt a need for penitence. He went to *Flicoteaux*, and for thirteen sous managed to eat badly, but tolerably so.

Returning home, he put down on paper several details which he was still piecing together. There was no reason for him to continue a diary – he had begun it as a way of recalling what he now remembered – but the diary had become a habit. Believing, for just under a month, in the existence of someone called Dalla Piccola, he had created the illusion of someone with whom he could converse, and through this conversation he realised how much he had always been alone, ever since childhood. Perhaps (the Narrator wonders) he had split his personality for that very reason – to create someone to talk to.

It was now time to accept that the Other did not exist. The diary, moreover, is a solitary entertainment. He had, however, become accustomed to this monody and decided to continue. Not that he felt any particular love towards himself, but his dislike of others induced him to make the best of his own company.

He had created Dalla Piccola – his Dalla Piccola, after he had killed the real one – when Lagrange had asked him to deal with Boullan. He thought that for many assignments a priest would arouse less suspicion than a layman. And he rather liked the idea of resurrecting someone he had killed.

When he had first bought the house and shop in impasse Maubert, at a very low price, he had not used the room and its entrance from rue Maître-Albert, preferring to establish his address in impasse Maubert so that he could use the shop. As soon as Dalla Piccola arrived on the scene, he furnished the room cheaply and used it as the illusory abbé's illusory address.

Dalla Piccola had been useful not only for prying into satanist and occultist circles, but also for deathbed appearances, when he was called by the close (or distant) relative who would later be the beneficiary of the will that Simonini had forged – and if anyone were to raise a doubt over that unexpected document, there would be the evidence of a cleric who could swear the will reflected the last wishes expressed to him on the man's dying breath. Then, with the Taxil affair, Dalla Piccola had become essential. It was he who had dealt with practically the whole business for over ten years.

And Simonini's disguise proved so effective that, dressed as Dalla Piccola, he could even meet Father Bergamaschi and Hébuterne. Dalla Piccola was beardless, blondish, with bushy eyebrows and, above all, wore blue-tinted spectacles that concealed his gaze. As if this were not enough, he had managed to devise another style of handwriting which was smaller and almost feminine, and could even alter his voice. And indeed, when he was Dalla Piccola, Simonini not only spoke and wrote differently, but thought differently, so that he fell completely into that role.

It was a shame, then, that Dalla Piccola had to disappear (the destiny of all abbés of that name), but Simonini had to wash his hands of the whole business, not just to erase the memory of those shameful events leading up to the trauma, but also because on Easter Monday, according to the plan, Taxil was to make his public confession and, with Diana now dead, it was better to remove all evidence of the entire plot in case someone began asking difficult questions.

He had only that Sunday and the following morning left. He dressed up once again as Dalla Piccola and went to meet Taxil, who had been visiting Auteuil every two or three days over the last month and had found neither Diana nor him, but just the old lady who told him she knew nothing and feared they had been kidnapped by the Masons. He explained to Taxil that Du Maurier had finally given him the address of Diana's real family in Charleston and he had found a way of sending her back to America – just in time for Taxil to prepare for the public exposure of the fraud. He gave Taxil a five-thousand-franc advance on the seventy-five thousand promised and arranged to meet the following afternoon at the Société de Géographie.

Then, still dressed as Dalla Piccola, he went to Auteuil. He was welcomed with amazement by the old woman. She too had lost sight of him and Diana for almost a month and hadn't known what to say to poor Monsieur Taxil on his frequent visits. He told her the same story. Diana had returned to America and been reunited with her family. The old hag was silenced with a generous pay-off, and she gathered together her paltry rags and left that afternoon.

That evening, Simonini burned all papers and other traces of their occupation during those years, and late that night took a case of Diana's clothes and belongings as a gift to Gaviali – a rag-and-bone man never asks questions about the goods that pass through his hands. The following morning he went to see the landlord to end the lease, pleading a sudden mission to distant lands and even paying another six months' rent to forestall further discussion. The landlord went with him to see that all was in good order, took back the keys and closed up the house.

All that remained was to "kill off" Dalla Piccola (for the second time). It didn't take much. Simonini removed the abbé's make-up, hung the cassock back in the corridor and thus Dalla Piccola disappeared from the face of the earth. As a precaution he removed the prie-dieu and religious books from the apartment, taking them down to his shop as objects to sell to unlikely collectors, after which he had a perfectly normal pied-à-terre ready for use by some other impersonation.

There was no trace of all that had happened, except in the memories of Taxil and Bataille. But Bataille, after his betrayal, would certainly never be seen again, and as for Taxil, the story was due to end that very afternoon.

On the afternoon of the 19th of April, dressed in his normal attire, Simonini went to enjoy the spectacle of Taxil's retraction. Apart from Dalla Piccola, Taxil had known only Maître Fournier, the fake notary, who was beardless with auburn hair and two gold teeth. He had seen the bearded Simonini only once, when he had employed him to falsify the letters of Hugo and Blanc, but that had been fifteen years ago and he had probably forgotten the face of that amanuensis. To cover all eventualities Simonini therefore wore a grey beard and green glasses which made him look like a member of the Institute, so that he could sit amid the audience and enjoy the entertainment.

News of the event had appeared in all the newspapers. The room was crowded, some people there out of mere curiosity, others who were followers of Diana Vaughan, Masons, journalists and even representatives of the archbishop and the apostolic nuncio.

Taxil spoke with typically southern dash and eloquence. Surprising the audience, who were there to see Diana and to hear confirmation of all that Taxil had published over the past fifteen years, he began by attacking the Catholic journalists and introduced the substance of his revelations by saying, "It is better to laugh than to cry, as the wisdom of nations goes." He described his enjoyment of hoaxes ("I wasn't born in Marseilles for nothing," he joked, to the amusement of the audience). He recounted with great delight the story of the sharks at Marseilles and the submerged city in Lake Geneva to convince the audience that he was a prankster. But nothing equalled the greatest prank in his life. And so he began to tell the story of his apparent conversion and how he had misled the confessors and spiritual counsellors appointed to ensure the sincerity of his repentance.

His opening was interrupted first by laughter and then by angry outbursts from several priests who were becoming increasingly outraged. People stood up and began to leave the hall, others took hold of their seats as if to attack him. In short, there was great disorder, over which the voice of Taxil could still be heard, describing how he had decided to attack the Masons in order to please the Church after *Humanum Genus*. "But in the end," he said, "even the Masons ought to be thankful, because my publication of their rituals had a certain bearing upon their decision to suppress outmoded practices which had become ridiculous for every Mason who was a friend of progress. As for the Catholics, I found out in the early days of my conversion that many of them are convinced that the Grand Architect of the Universe – the Supreme Being of the Masons – is the Devil. So all I had to do was embroider upon this conviction."

The commotion continued. When Taxil turned to his conversation with Leo XIII (the Pope had asked him, "My son, what do you wish?" and Taxil had replied, "Holy Father, to die at your feet, right now, that would be my greatest happiness!"), the shouts became a chorus, one

*. . . Diana, he said, was an
ordinary Protestant woman, a copy
typist, the representative of an American
typewriter manufacturer, an intelligent,
active woman of elegant simplicity, as
Protestant women generally are. . . .*

[PAGE 514]

person yelling, "Respect Leo XIII, you have no right to utter his name!", another, "Do we have to listen to this? It's disgusting!", and another, "Ah, the scoundrel! . . . Ah, what orgy of depravity!", while the majority laughed still louder.

"And so," said Taxil, "I allowed the tree of modern luciferianism to grow, introducing a Palladian ritual into it, fabricated entirely by me from beginning to end."

Then he described how an old alcoholic friend had created Dr Bataille, how he had invented Sophie Walder or Sapho, and how finally he himself had written all the works by Diana Vaughan. Diana, he said, was an ordinary Protestant woman, a copy typist, the representative of an American typewriter manufacturer, an intelligent, active woman of elegant simplicity, as Protestant women generally are. He had begun to interest her in devilry, she was amused by it, and became his accomplice. She took a liking to this tomfoolery, writing to bishops and cardinals, receiving letters from the private secretary of the Supreme Pontiff, informing the Vatican about luciferian plots. . . .

"But," continued Taxil, "we saw even certain Freemasons falling for our pretences. When Diana revealed that the Grand Master of Charleston had appointed Adriano Lemmi to be his successor as luciferian Supreme Pontiff, some Italian Masons, including a parliamentary deputy, took the news seriously. They were annoyed that Lemmi had not informed them, and they set up three independent Palladian Supreme Councils in Sicily, Naples and Florence, naming Miss Vaughan as an honorary member. The infamous Monsieur Margiotta wrote that he had met Miss

Vaughan, whereas it was I who spoke to him about a meeting that had never taken place and he either pretended or actually believed he remembered it. The publishers themselves were hoaxed, but they have nothing to complain about since I gave them the opportunity of publishing works which can compete with the *Thousand and One Nights.*

"Gentlemen," he continued, "when you understand you have been fooled, the best thing to do is to laugh with the audience. And you, Monsieur Abbé Garnier," he said, pointing to one of his angriest critics in the hall, "the angrier you get, the more ridiculous you become."

"You're a scoundrel!", shouted Garnier, waving his stick, while his friends tried to calm him.

"There again," continued Taxil with a seraphic smile, "we cannot criticise those who believed in the devils which appeared in our initiation ceremonies. Do good Christians not believe that Satan took Jesus Christ himself to a mountain top, from which he showed him all the kingdoms of the earth. . . . And how did he show him all of them if the earth is round?"

"Quite right!", shouted some.

"No need for blasphemy," shouted others.

Taxil was now reaching his conclusion. "I confess, gentlemen, that I have committed infanticide. Palladism is now dead – its father has murdered it."

The mayhem had reached its climax. Abbé Garnier stood on a seat and tried to address the audience, but his voice was lost in the raucous laughter of some and the angry shouts of others. Taxil remained on the platform where he had been speaking, proudly watching the crowd in uproar. It was his moment of glory. If he had wanted to be crowned king of hoaxers, he had achieved his purpose.

He gazed immovably at those protesting in front of him, waving their fists or canes and shouting, "Shame on you!", looking almost as if he didn't understand. What did he have to feel ashamed of? Of the fact that everyone was talking about him?

Simonini was enjoying himself more than anyone as he thought about what was in store for Taxil over the coming days.

He would seek out Dalla Piccola for his money, but would not know where to find him. If he went to Auteuil he'd find the house empty, or perhaps already occupied by someone else. He knew nothing about Dalla Piccola having an address in rue Maître-Albert. He didn't know how to contact Fournier the notary, nor would he ever think of associating him with that person who, many years earlier, had falsified Hugo's letter. Boullan would be impossible to find. He had no idea that Hébuterne, whom he vaguely knew as a Masonic dignitary, had anything to do with these events and was entirely unaware of the existence of Father Bergamaschi. In short, Taxil wouldn't know whom to ask for his money, so that Simonini could pocket the whole amount (less, unfortunately, the five thousand francs advance) instead of just half.

It was amusing to think of the poor rascal wandering around Paris looking for an abbé and a notary who had never existed, for a satanist and a Palladian whose bodies lay in a forgotten sewer, for a Bataille who, even when sober, would have nothing to tell him, and for a bundle of francs that had ended up in the wrong pocket. Reviled by the Catholics, viewed with suspicion by the Masons who had every right to fear another about-turn, perhaps also heavily in debt to his publishers, not knowing which way to move.

But, thought Simonini, that charlatan from Marseilles deserved it.

26

THE FINAL SOLUTION

10th November 1898

It is now a year and a half since I rid myself of Taxil, Diana and, more importantly, Dalla Piccola. If I was ill, I am recovered. Thanks to auto-hypnosis, or to Dr Froïde. And yet I have been feeling anxious over recent months. If I were religious I'd say it was guilt and that I was being tormented. But remorse for what, and tormented by whom?

The same evening on which I had the pleasure of hoaxing Taxil, I celebrated in happy tranquillity. I was sorry only that there was no one with whom I could share my victory, but I am quite used to my own company. I went to *Brébant-Vachette*, frequented by the diaspora of those who used to eat at *Magny*. With all I had earned from the Taxil debacle, I could afford anything. The maître recognised me, but more importantly I recognised him. He held forth on the *salade Francilion* created after the triumph of the play by Alexandre Dumas *fils* – good God, how old that makes me feel. The potatoes are cooked in stock, cut into slices and, while still warm, dressed with salt, pepper, olive oil and Orléans vinegar, plus half a glass of white wine (Château d'Yquem if possible) and chopped *fines herbes*. At the same time, some very large mussels are cooked in a *court-bouillon* with a stick of celery. It is then all lightly tossed together and covered with thin slices of truffle cooked in champagne. This should be done two hours before serving, so that the dish has cooled to just the right temperature when it arrives at table.

Yet I am not at ease, and feel I must resume this diary to clarify my state of mind, as if I were still under Dr Froïde's care.

Disturbing things continue to occur and I live in a state of continual anxiety. In particular, I'm still anxious to know who the Russian is down there in the sewer. He or they – perhaps there were two – was or were here, in these rooms, on the 12th of April. Has one of them been back since? On several occasions I have been unable to find something – a small object, a pen, a bundle of papers – and then have found it in a place where I could have sworn I had never put it. Has someone been rummaging around here, moving things, looking for something? What?

Russians can only mean Rachkovsky, but the man's a sphinx. He's been here twice, always asking me for what he describes as new, unpublished material inherited from my grandfather. And I have been playing for time, partly so that I can finish putting together a satisfactory dossier, partly to whet his appetite.

Last time he said he wasn't prepared to wait any longer. He wanted to know whether it was simply a question of price. "I'm not greedy," I told him. "The truth is that my grandfather left me some papers which recorded in full what was said that night in the Prague cemetery, but I don't have them here with me. I have to leave Paris to go and collect them from somewhere else."

"Go then," said Rachkovsky, and he made a fairly vague comment about some trouble I might have from developments in the Dreyfus affair. What does he know about it?

The fact that Dreyfus had been packed off to Devil's Island had done nothing to calm the controversy. A campaign had been launched by those who thought he was innocent – the Dreyfusards as they were called – and various graphologists started to challenge Bertillon's evidence.

It all began towards the end of 'ninety-five, when Sandherr retired from service (apparently suffering from progressive paralysis, or something of the kind) and was replaced by someone called Picquart. This Picquart turned out to be a busybody and immediately began re-examining the Dreyfus affair, even though the case had been closed several months earlier. Then, last March, he found in the embassy wastepaper baskets (once again) the draft of a telegram to be sent by the German military attaché to Esterhazy. Nothing compromising, but why was this military attaché in contact with a French officer? Picquart investigated Esterhazy, looked for samples of his handwriting, and realised that the major's writing was similar to that of Dreyfus's *bordereau*.

I came to hear about it when the news was leaked to *La Libre Parole* and Drumont took exception to this meddler who wanted to reopen a case that had been so happily resolved.

"I understand he went to report the matter to Generals Boisdeffre and Gonse, who were fortunately not interested. Our generals are made of sterner stuff."

Around November I met Esterhazy at the newspaper

offices. He was very nervous and asked to speak with me. He came to my house accompanied by a Major Henry.

"It is rumoured, Simonini, that the handwriting on the *bordereau* is mine. You copied from one of Dreyfus's letters or notes, didn't you?"

"But of course. The sample had been given me by Sandherr."

"I know, but why didn't Sandherr call me to that meeting as well? Was it to make sure I couldn't check the sample of Dreyfus's handwriting?"

"I did what I was told to do."

"I know, I know. But it's in your interests to help me sort this mystery out. If, for some obscure reason, you've been used as part of a plot, then someone might think it's a good idea to get rid of a dangerous witness like you. Which means you're involved as well."

I should never have allowed myself to get mixed up with the army. I wasn't at all happy. Then Esterhazy explained what he wanted me to do. He gave me a sample of a letter from Panizzardi, the Italian military attaché, and the text of a letter I had to produce, addressed to the German military attaché, in which Panizzardi referred to Dreyfus's collaboration.

"Major Henry," he explained, "will be responsible for finding this document and passing it on to General Gonse."

I did my job, Esterhazy paid me a thousand francs and then I don't know what happened, but towards the end of 'ninety-six Picquart was transferred to the Fourth Fusiliers in Tunisia.

However, at exactly the same time as I was busy getting

rid of Taxil, it seems that Picquart had managed to pull a few strings, and things became more complicated. It was, of course, unofficial news which somehow reached the press, but the Dreyfusard newspapers (which were few) took it as being certain, while the anti-Dreyfusard press talked of defamation. Some telegrams appeared, addressed to Picquart, from which it seemed as if he was the author of the infamous telegram from the Germans to Esterhazy. So far as I could understand, Esterhazy and Henry were behind it. It was a nice game of tit for tat, where there was no need to invent accusations because all you had to do was throw back at your opponent what he'd sent to you. Heavens above, espionage and counter-espionage are far too serious to be left in the hands of soldiers. Professionals like Lagrange or Hébuterne would never have made such a mess, but what can you expect from people who are good enough for the intelligence service one day and for the Fourth Fusiliers in Tunisia the next, or who pass from the Papal Zouaves to the Foreign Legion?

Most of all, this last move was of little use, and an investigation of Esterhazy was opened. And what if, to put himself above suspicion, he were to say it was I who had written the *bordereau*?

I slept badly for a year. Each night I heard noises in the house. I was tempted to go down to the shop but was worried I might find a Russian there.

In January this year there was a trial behind closed doors, where Esterhazy was acquitted of all charges. Picquart was sentenced to sixty days' imprisonment. But the Dreyfusards are not giving up. A fairly vulgar writer by the name of Zola has published an inflammatory article (*J'accuse!*), a group of scribblers and supposed scientists have joined the campaign, demanding a review of the case. Who are these people . . . Proust, France, Sorel, Monet, Renard, Durkheim? Not the kind who frequent Salon Adam. Proust, I'm told, is a twenty-five-year-old pederast writer whose works are fortunately unpublished, and Monet is a dauber – I've seen one or two of his paintings which look at the world through gummy eyes. What have a writer and a painter to do with the decisions of a military tribunal? Poor France, as Drumont would say. If only these so-called "intellectuals" – as Clemenceau, that defender of lost causes, calls them – kept their minds on the few things they knew something about. . . .

Zola was put on trial and, by good fortune, sentenced to a year's imprisonment. Justice still exists in France, says Drumont, who in May was elected as deputy for Algiers, ensuring that there will be a good anti-Semitic group in parliament, which will help to defend the claims of the anti-Dreyfusards.

Everything seemed to be going in the right direction, Picquart had been sentenced to eight months in prison in July, Zola had fled to London, and I thought that no one would now reopen the case. Then a certain Captain Cuignet appeared, and demonstrated that Panizzardi's letter accusing Dreyfus was a forgery. How could he make such a claim when I had done the job so perfectly? In any event the high command took it seriously and, since the letter had been found and passed on by Major Henry, people began to talk about the "Henry forgery". When put under pressure towards the end of August, Henry admitted everything. He was taken to the prison at Mont-Valérien and slit his throat with a razor the following day. As I said, never leave certain things in the hands of soldiers: what? arrest a suspected traitor and allow him to keep his razor?

"Henry didn't commit suicide," claimed Drumont angrily. "He was forced into it. There are still too many Jews on the General Staff! We shall open a public subscription to fund a campaign to clear Henry's name!"

But four or five days later Esterhazy escaped to Belgium and then to England. Almost an admission of guilt. But I couldn't understand why he hadn't defended himself by throwing the blame on me.

A few nights ago, while I was turning these matters over in my mind, I again heard noises in the house. The next morning I found not only the shop but also the cellar in disarray, and the trapdoor down to the sewer open.

Just as I was wondering whether I too should be making a run for it, like Esterhazy, Rachkovsky rang the bell at the shop door. Without troubling to come upstairs, he sat down in a chair that was for sale, had anyone ever wished to buy it, and began immediately: "What would you say if I told the Sûreté that down in the cellar there are four corpses, one of which happens to be a man of mine I've been searching

. . . *"There are still too many Jews
on the General Staff!"* . . .

[PAGE 524]

for everywhere? I'm tired of waiting. I will give you two days to go and collect the protocols you've told me about and then I'll forget what I've seen down there. That seems a fair deal."

It didn't entirely surprise me that Rachkovsky knew about the sewer. Sooner or later I would have to give him something, so I tried to extract another benefit from the deal he was offering me. "Perhaps," I ventured, "you could help me resolve a problem I have with the military secret service. . . ."

He began to laugh. "You're worried they'll find out it was you who penned the *bordereau*?"

This man clearly knows everything. He put his hands together as if to collect his thoughts, and began to explain.

"You probably have no idea what's going on, and you're frightened that someone's going to blame you. Don't worry. It's important for the whole of France, for reasons of national security, that the *bordereau* is believed to be genuine."

"Why?"

"Because the French artillery is preparing its latest weapon, the 75mm gun, and the Germans must continue to believe the French are still working on the 120mm gun. The Germans had to find out that a spy was trying to sell them secrets about the 120mm gun because they'd then believe this was the sensitive point. You, as a person of good sense, will see that the Germans should have said to themselves, 'Goodness gracious, but if this *bordereau* were genuine, we ought to have known something about it *before* it was tossed into the wastebasket!' And so they should have seen through it. Instead they fell into the trap. That's because no one in the secret service ever tells the whole story. Everyone thinks that the fellow at the next desk is a double agent, and probably each accused the other: 'What? Such an important piece of news had arrived and not even the military attaché knew about it, even though it was addressed to him? Or had he known about it and kept quiet?' Just imagine the torrent of mutual suspicion – someone's head must have rolled for that. It was (and still is) vital for everyone to accept the *bordereau* as genuine. That was why Dreyfus had to be sent to Devil's Island as quickly as possible, to ensure that he wouldn't start defending himself, saying it was impossible that he'd spied on the 120mm gun because, if anything, he'd have spied on the 75mm gun. It seems, in fact, that someone gave him a pistol, offering him a chance to kill himself to avoid the humiliation that awaited him. In that way all risk of a public trial would have been prevented. But Dreyfus was stubborn, he insisted on defending himself because he thought he was innocent. An officer should never think. What's more, I don't believe the wretch knew anything about the 75mm gun. It's hardly likely that certain things end up on the desk of a trainee. But it was always better to be cautious. Understand? If anyone knew the *bordereau* was your handiwork then the whole pack of cards would collapse and the Germans would realise that the 120mm gun is a red herring – these Boche might be slow on the uptake, but they're not completely stupid. You'll tell me it's not just the Germans but also the French secret service who are in the hands of a group of bunglers. That's obvious. Otherwise these men would be working for the Okhrana, which is rather more efficient and, as you see, has informers in both camps."

"But Esterhazy?"

"That fine gentleman of ours is a double agent. He was pretending to spy on Sandherr for the German embassy but in the meantime was spying on the German embassy for Sandherr. He had worked hard in setting up the Dreyfus case, but Sandherr realised his days were numbered and the Germans were beginning to suspect him. Sandherr knew perfectly well he'd given you a sample of Esterhazy's handwriting. The object was to put the blame on Dreyfus but, if things had taken a turn for the worse, it was always possible to put the responsibility for the *bordereau* on Esterhazy. Esterhazy, of course, realised the trap he'd fallen into when it was too late."

"So why then didn't he name me?"

"Because they'd have accused him of lying and he'd have ended up in some fortress, or floating in a canal, whereas this way he can enjoy a life of leisure in London, on a good annuity, at the expense of the secret service. Whether they continue to say it's Dreyfus, or decide that the traitor is Esterhazy, the *bordereau* has to remain genuine. No one will ever put the blame on a forger like you. You're as safe as houses. I, on the other hand, will be causing you a great deal of bother over those corpses down there. So out with that information. You'll receive a visit tomorrow from a young man called Golovinsky who works for me. You don't have to produce the original finished documents – they'll have to be in Russian and he will deal with that. You have to provide him with new, genuine, convincing material, to flesh out that dossier of yours on the Prague cemetery, which by now is *lippis notum et tonsoribus*. What I mean is, it's fine for the revelations to originate from a meeting there, in the cemetery, but it mustn't be clear when the meeting took place, and the discussions must be relevant for today, not medieval fantasies."

I had some work to do.

I had almost two full days and nights to assemble the hundreds of notes and cuttings I'd been gathering during the course of my visits to Drumont over more than a decade. I never imagined using them because they had all been published in *La Libre Parole* but, for the Russians, it was perhaps unfamiliar material. I had to make a choice. Golovinsky and Rachkovsky were certainly not interested in knowing whether or not the Jews were hopeless musicians or explorers. Of more interest, perhaps, was the suspicion that they were preparing the economic downfall of good people.

I checked everything I had already used for the rabbis' earlier speeches. The Jews planned to take over the railways, mines, forests, tax administration and land ownership, to take over the judiciary, the legal profession, education, to infiltrate philosophy, politics, science, art and above all medicine, since a doctor gets even closer to families than the priest. It was necessary to undermine religion, spread free thought, stop the teaching of Christianity in schools, take over the alcohol trade, control the press. Heavens above, was there anything else they could still want?

There was nothing to prevent me recycling all this material. Rachkovsky would have seen the version of the rabbis' speeches I had given to Glinka, which dealt entirely with arguments of a religious and apocalyptic nature. But I certainly had to add something new to my previous versions.

I carefully considered all the issues that might catch the interests of an average reader. I wrote it all out in a fine calligraphy of more than half a century ago, on paper that was appropriately yellowed. And there they were: the documents my grandfather had given me, actually written down during the meetings of the Jews in that ghetto where he had lived as a young man, translated from the protocols which the rabbis had recorded after their meeting in the Prague cemetery.

When Golovinsky came into the shop the next day, I was astonished that Rachkovsky could have given such an important assignment to a flabby, short-sighted, badly dressed young peasant who looked as if he'd always been last in the class. Then, as we talked, I realised he was brighter than he seemed. He spoke very poor French with a heavy Russian accent but he immediately asked how it was that rabbis in the Turin ghetto had written in French. I told him that all educated people in Piedmont spoke French at that time, and he accepted it. Later I wondered whether my rabbis in the cemetery would have spoken Hebrew or Yiddish but since the documents were in French, the question was of no consequence.

"Notice, for example, on this page," I said, "how importance is given to the spreading of ideas by atheist philosophers to demoralise the Gentiles. And listen here: 'We must cancel the concept of God from Christian minds, replacing it with arithmetical calculation and material needs.'"

I had assumed that everybody hates arithmetic. Remembering Drumont's complaints about obscene publications, I decided that, at least for the more orthodox reader, the idea of spreading easy, vapid entertainment for the masses would have seemed excellent for the conspiracy. "Listen to this," I said to Golovinsky: "'To prevent the population from discovering new kinds of political action, we will distract it with novel forms of amusement: athletic games, pastimes, hobbies of various kinds, taverns, and we will invite them to compete in artistic and sporting competitions. . . . We will encourage the unrestrained love of luxury and will increase salaries, but this will bring no benefit to the worker, because we will at the same time increase the price of basic commodities on the pretext of an agricultural crisis. We will undermine the system of production by sowing the seeds of anarchy among workers and encouraging them to abuse alcohol. We will seek to direct public opinion towards any kind of fantastical theory which might seem progressive, or liberal.'"

"Good, good," said Golovinsky. "But is there anything here for students, apart from the arithmetic? Students are important in Russia, they are troublemakers who have to be kept under control."

"Here we are: 'When we are in power, we shall remove from educational programmes all subjects that might harm the spirit of young people, and we shall make them into obedient citizens who love their sovereign. Instead of allowing them to study Classics and ancient history, which contain more bad than good, we shall make them study the problems of the future. We shall cancel from human memory the record of past centuries, which could be unpleasant for us. With a methodical education we will be able to eliminate the remnants of that independence of thought which has served our purposes for a considerable time. . . . We shall double the tax on books of less than three hundred pages, and these measures will force writers to publish works which are so long they will have few readers. We, on the other hand, will publish low-priced works to educate the public mind. Taxation will lead to a reduction in reading for pleasure, and no one who wants to attack us with their pen will find a publisher.' As for the newspapers, the Jewish plan envisages a sham freedom of the press which ensures greater control over opinions. According to our rabbis, as many magazines as possible must be bought up, so that they express apparently different views, to give the impression of a free circulation of ideas, though in reality they will all reflect the ideas of the Jewish rulers. They observe that it won't be difficult to buy up journalists as they are all of the same Masonic brotherhood, and no publisher will have the courage to reveal what they all have in common because no one is allowed into the world of journalism who hasn't been involved in some shady activity in their private life. 'All newspapers will, of course, be prevented from reporting on crime because the people will believe that the new regime has stamped out criminal behaviour. But there is hardly any need to worry about press restrictions since the people, weighed down as they are by work and poverty, won't even notice whether or not the press is free. Why should the proletarian worker be concerned about whether the gossip-mongers have the right to gossip?'"

"This is good," exclaimed Golovinsky. "Our trouble-makers are always complaining about supposed government censorship. They have to understand that a Jewish govern-ment would be worse."

"On this point it gets better: 'We have to beware of the pettiness, inconstancy and lack of common sense of the crowd. The crowd is blind and has no insight; it listens one moment to the Right, one moment to the Left. Is it possible for the masses to administer the affairs of state without confounding them with their own personal interests? Are they able to organise defence against foreign enemies? That is absolutely impossible because any plan, when sub-divided into as many parts as the minds of the mass, loses its value and therefore becomes unintelligible and impractic-able. Only an autocrat is capable of planning on a vast scale, assigning a role to each body in the mechanism of the State machine. . . . Civilisation cannot exist without abso-lute tyranny, because civilisation can only be promoted under the protection of the ruler, whoever he is, and not by the mass.' There we are. And look at this other document: 'Since there has never been such a thing as a constitution which has emerged from the wishes of a population, the plan of command must spring from a single source.' And read this: 'We shall control everything, like a many-armed Vishnu. We will have no need even of the police: one-third of our subjects will control the other two-thirds.'"

"Magnificent."

"And here's another: 'The crowd is barbaric, and behaves barbarically at every opportunity. Look at those terrible alcoholics, reduced to idiocy by their drink, whose consumption is limitless and tolerated by liberty! Should we allow ourselves and our families to do the same? Christians are led astray by alcohol; their young people are rendered mad by premature excess at the instigation of our agents. . . . In politics pure force is the only winner, violence must be the principle; cunning and hypocrisy have to be the rule. Evil is the only way of achieving good. We must not stop at corruption, deception and betrayal: the end justifies the means.'"

"There is much talk about communism in Russia. What do the rabbis of Prague think about it?"

"Read this: 'In politics we must be able to confiscate property without hesitation if, by doing so, we are able to bring down others and gain power for ourselves. For the worker we will appear to be liberators, feigning to love him according to the principles of brotherhood proclaimed by our Freemasonry. We will say we have come to free him from the oppressor, and will invite him to join the ranks of our armies of socialists, anarchists and communists. The aristocracy, who exploited the working classes, were nevertheless interested in ensuring they were well fed, healthy and strong. But our purpose is the opposite: we are interested in the degeneration of Gentiles. Our strength consists in continually keeping the worker in a state of penury and impotence, since, by doing so, we keep him subject to our will and, in his own surroundings, he will never find the power and energy to rise up against us.' And then there's this: 'We shall bring about a universal economic crisis using all secret means possible, with the help of gold, which is all in our hands. We will reduce vast hordes of workers throughout Europe to ruin. These masses will then throw themselves with alacrity upon those who, in their ignorance, have been prudent since their childhood, and will plunder their possessions and spill their blood. They will not harm us since we will be well informed as to the time of the attack and will take the necessary measures to protect our interests.'"

"Do you have anything on Jews and Freemasons?"

"But of course, here we are. It could hardly be clearer: 'Until we have achieved power, we shall establish and increase the number of Masonic lodges throughout the world. These lodges will provide our main source of information; they will also be our propaganda centres. In these lodges we will bring together all socialist and revolutionary classes of society. Almost all international secret police agents will be members of our lodges. Most of those who join secret societies are opportunists who seek to make their own way in one way or another and have no worthy purposes. With such people it will be easy for us to reach our goal. We must, of course, have complete control over Masonic activities.'"

"Excellent!"

"Remember also that wealthy Jews look with interest at anti-Semitism which affects poor Jews, because it induces kinder-hearted Christians to feel compassion towards their entire race. Read this: 'Anti-Semitic demonstrations were also very useful for Jewish leaders, as they stirred compassion in the hearts of certain Gentiles towards a population which was apparently ill-treated. This then served to secure much sympathy among Gentiles for the Zionist cause.

Anti-Semitism, which took the form of persecution of low-class Jews, helped leaders to control them and keep them in servitude. They accepted this persecution because they intervened at the appropriate moment and saved their brethren. Note that during anti-Semitic unrest Jewish leaders never suffer, neither in their ambitions nor in their official positions as administrators. It was these same leaders who set the "Christian mastiffs" against the more lowly Jews. The mastiffs maintained order among their flocks and so helped to strengthen the stability of Zion.'"

I had also found a large number of overly technical pages that Joly had dedicated to loan and interest-rate mechanisms. I didn't understand much about it, nor was I sure whether or not taxation had changed since Joly's time, but I relied on my source and gave Golovinsky pages and pages which would probably have been of interest to an artisan trader who had fallen into debt or indeed into the maw of usury.

Finally, I had been listening recently to discussions at *La Libre Parole* about the metropolitan railway which was to be built in Paris. It was an old story that had been going on for decades, but it was not until July of 'ninety-seven that an official plan had been approved and the first excavation works had just begun for a line between Porte de Vincennes and Porte de Maillot. There was still little to be seen, but a Metro company had been established and *La Libre Parole* had been waging a campaign for more than a year against the large number of Jewish share-holders involved. I thought it was useful, then, to link the

Jewish conspiracy to the metropolitan railways and had therefore written, "All cities will have metropolitan railways and passageways: from here we will blow up all the world's cities, together with their institutions and all their documents."

"But if the meeting in Prague happened such a long time ago," asked Golovinsky, "how could the rabbis have known about metropolitan railways?"

"First of all, if you go and look at the last version of 'the Rabbi's Speech', which had appeared about ten years ago in *Contemporain*, the meeting in the Prague cemetery took place in 1880, when I think there was already a metropolitan railway in London. But anyway, it's quite enough that the plan sounds like a prophecy."

Golovinsky was much taken by this passage which he thought to be, in his words, most promising. Then he observed, "Don't you think that many of the ideas expressed in these documents contradict each other? For example, they want to ban luxuries and superfluous pleasures and punish drunkenness and then, in the next breath, to encourage sport and entertainment, and turn the workers into alcoholics. . . ."

"The Jews are always saying one thing and then the opposite – they are liars by nature. But if you produce a document many pages long, people won't read it all in one go. We have to try to obtain one wave of revulsion after another, and when someone is scandalised by a statement they have read today, they forget the one that had scandalised them yesterday. And then, if you read carefully you will see that the rabbis of Prague want to use luxury, entertainment and alcohol to reduce the common people to slavery *now*, but once they have gained power they will force them to lead far more temperate lives."

"That's quite true, excuse me."

"You see," I concluded with legitimate pride, "I've pondered over these papers for decades and decades, since I was a boy, and know them inside out."

"You are right. But I'd like to end with a very powerful statement, something that will stick in the mind and symbolise the iniquity of the Jews. For example, 'Ours is an ambition that knows no limits, a voracious greed, a desire for ruthless revenge, an intense hatred.'"

"Not bad for a cheap novel. But do you think the Jews, who are anything but stupid, are likely to say such a thing that would condemn them straight away?"

"I wouldn't be so worried about that. The rabbis are talking in their cemetery, sure that no one can hear them. They have no shame. The crowds must feel a sense of outrage."

Golovinsky was a good collaborator. He took, or pretended to take, my papers as genuine but had no hesitation in altering them when it suited him. Rachkovsky had chosen the right man.

"I think," said Golovinsky finally, "I have enough material for what we shall call the Protocols of the Assembly of Rabbis in the Prague Cemetery."

Prague cemetery was slipping out of my control, but I was probably contributing to its success. With a feeling of relief I invited Golovinsky to dinner at *Paillard*, on the corner of rue de la Chaussée-d'Antin and boulevard des Italiens.

... *"But I'd like to end with a very
powerful statement, something that
will stick in the mind and symbolise the
iniquity of the Jews. For example, 'Ours
is an ambition that knows no limits, a
voracious greed, a desire for ruthless
revenge, an intense hatred.'"* ...

[PAGE 538]

Expensive, but superb. Golovinsky clearly appreciated the *poulet archiduc* and the *canard à la presse*. But someone who came from the Steppes may well have tucked into *choucroute* with just the same enthusiasm. It would have cost me less, and I could have avoided the looks of suspicion the waiters were casting at a customer who masticated so noisily.

But he ate with relish, his eyes glinting with excitement, perhaps because of the wine or – I don't know – out of some real religious or political passion.

"It'll be a fine piece of writing," he said, "which reveals their deep hatred as a race and as a religion. Their hatred gushes forth from these pages, it seems to overflow from a vessel full of bile. . . . Many will understand that we have reached the moment of the final solution."

"I've already heard this expression from Osman Bey – you know him?"

"By reputation. But it's obvious. This accursed race has to be rooted out at all cost."

"Rachkovsky doesn't seem to share that view. It's better, he says, to keep the Jews alive as a good enemy."

"A myth. It's always easy to find a good enemy. And don't imagine, just because I work for Rachkovsky, that I share all his views. He taught me himself that while you're working for one master today, you must prepare yourself to serve another one tomorrow. Rachkovsky won't last for ever. In Holy Russia there are those with much more radical ideas than his. The governments of Western Europe are too cowardly to decide upon a final solution. Russia, on the other hand, is a country full of energy and bright hope, thinking always of total revolution. It's from there that we must expect the decisive gesture, not from these Frenchmen who continue to ramble on about *égalité* and *fraternité*, nor from those German boors who are incapable of grand gestures. . . ."

I had already guessed as much after my nocturnal meeting with Osman Bey. Abbé Barruel had decided not to pursue my grandfather's allegations after reading his letter because he feared a general massacre. But what my grandfather had wanted was probably exactly what Osman Bey and Golovinsky were predicting. Perhaps my grandfather had condemned me to making his dream come true. Oh, God! Fortunately it wasn't up to me to eliminate an entire people, but I was making a contribution in my own modest way.

And it was, after all, a profitable business. The Jews would never pay me to exterminate all Christians, I thought, since there are too many Christians and if it were possible they would do it themselves. Wiping out the Jews, when all is said and done, would be possible. Despite their numbers, God Almighty succeeded in drowning all of humanity during the time of the Flood, and the Jews were a minuscule percentage of the earth's inhabitants in Noah's time.

I wouldn't have to destroy them myself – I am (as a rule) a man who recoils from physical violence – but I certainly knew how it had to be done, since I lived through the days of the Commune. Take gangs of men who are well trained and indoctrinated, and anyone you meet with a hooked nose and curly hair, straight up against the wall. You'd end up losing a few Christians but, in the words of the bishop who had to attack Béziers when it was occupied by the Cathars, it is better to be prudent and kill the lot. God will recognise his own.

As it is written in their protocols, the end justifies the means.

27

DIARY CUT SHORT

Having handed over to Golovinsky all the remaining material for those cemetery protocols, I felt an emptiness. "And what now?" I wondered, like a young student after his graduation. Cured of my split consciousness, I no longer even had anyone to tell my story to.

I had completed my life's work, which had begun when I read Dumas' *Balsamo* in the attic in Turin. I think of my grandfather, his eyes staring into the distance, as he described the spectre of Mordechai. Thanks to my work, all the Mordechais in this world are on their way to a tremendous raging pyre. But what about me? There's a certain melancholy when a duty is completed – a melancholy greater and more impalpable than the sadness of a steamship voyage.

I continue to counterfeit wills and sell a few dozen hosts a week, but Hébuterne doesn't come to see me any longer – perhaps he thinks I'm too old – and I might as well forget about the army where my name must have been erased from the minds of those who remembered it, if any of them are still there, now that Sandherr lies paralysed in a hospital bed and Esterhazy is playing baccarat in some smart London brothel.

It's not that I need the money – I've saved up quite enough – but I'm bored. I have gastric upsets and can't even enjoy good food. I make myself broth at home, and if I go to a restaurant I am kept awake all night. Sometimes I vomit. I pass water more often than I would wish.

I still visit the offices of *La Libre Parole*, but Drumont's anti-Semitic ranting no longer interests me. As to what happened in the Prague cemetery, the Russians are now working on that.

The Dreyfus case still simmers away. Today there's a lot of fuss over a surprise article by a Catholic Dreyfusard in *La Croix*, a newspaper which has always been rabidly anti-Dreyfusard (what wonderful times they were when *La Croix* campaigned in support of Diana!) and yesterday the front pages were full of news about a violent anti-Semitic demonstration in place de la Concorde. A satirical newspaper recently published a double cartoon by Caran d'Ache: in the first, a large family is sitting happily at table as the father cautions the others not to discuss the Dreyfus Affair; the caption under the second explains that someone has mentioned it, and we see a furious punch-up.

The affair still divides the French and (from what I've read here and there) the rest of the world. Will they retry the case? Meanwhile Dreyfus is still in Cayenne. Serves him right.

I went to see Father Bergamaschi and found him tired and much aged. Hardly surprising – if I am sixty-eight then he must now be eighty-five.

"Simonino," he said, "I want to say goodbye. I'm returning to Italy, to end my days in one of our houses. I've worked enough for the glory of Our Lord. And you? You're not going to get yourself into any more trouble? I live in fear of trouble. How simple it all used to be in your

*. . . I went to see Father
Bergamaschi and found him
tired and much aged. . . .*

[PAGE 544]

grandfather's day – the Carbonari on one side, we on the other. Everyone knew who and where their enemies were. It's not like that any longer."

He is losing his mind. I gave him a fraternal embrace and left.

Yesterday evening I was passing in front of Saint-Julien le Pauvre. Sitting right by the main door was a human wreck, a blind *cul-de-jatte*, his bald head covered with livid scars. He played a strained melody on a penny whistle which he held to one of his nostrils, while the other produced a dull hissing sound, as his mouth opened to take in breath, like someone who was drowning.

I don't know why, but it frightened me. As if life were a terrible thing.

I cannot sleep. I have restless dreams in which Diana appears, pale and dishevelled.

Often, rising at daybreak, I go out and watch the collectors of cigar stubs. They have always fascinated me. In the early morning I see them going about with their stinking sacks tied with a string to their waists and a stick with a metal spike which they use to harpoon the stub, even from under a table. It's amusing to watch them being thrown out of the open-air cafés by the waiters, who sometimes spray them with a soda-water siphon.

Many have spent the night along the Seine embankment and they can be seen in the morning, sitting on the *quais*, separating the tobacco, still moist with saliva, from the ash, or washing their shirts stained with liquid tobacco and waiting for them to dry in the sun while they continue their work. The bolder ones collect not just cigar butts but also cigarettes, where separating the damp paper from the tobacco is an even more disgusting task.

Then you see them swarming around place Maubert and thereabouts, selling their wares and, as soon as they have earned a few cents, disappearing into a tavern to drink toxic alcohol.

I watch other people's lives as a way of passing the time. I live the life of a pensioner, or a veteran.

It is strange, but I feel a certain nostalgia about the Jews. I miss them. Since my childhood I have constructed my Prague cemetery, stone by stone (you might say), and it is now as if Golovinsky has stolen it from me. Who knows what they are doing with it in Moscow. Perhaps they're putting my protocols together into a dry bureaucratic document entirely devoid of its original setting. No one will want to read it. I'll have wasted my life producing a testimony for no purpose. Or perhaps this is how my rabbis' ideas (they were always *my* rabbis) will spread throughout the world and will accompany the final solution.

I read somewhere that there is a cemetery for Portuguese Jews at the far end of an old courtyard in avenue de Flandre. A town house was built there at the end of the seventeenth century and belonged to someone called Camot who allowed Jews, mostly Germans, to bury their dead there at a cost of fifty francs for adults and twenty for children. The house later passed to a certain Matard, an animal skinner who began burying the remains of his flayed horses and oxen next to the Jews, and the Jews protested. The Portuguese Jews bought an adjoining piece of land for their burials, and Jews from countries to the north found another place at Montrouge.

It closed early this century, but you can still visit. There are about twenty gravestones, some with Hebrew writing and others in French. I saw a strange one which read, "God Almighty has called me in the twenty-third year of my life. I prefer my situation to slavery. Here lies the blessed Samuel Fernandez Patto, died 28th Prairial of the second year of the one and only French Republic." Precisely. Republicans, atheists and Jews.

The place is desolate, but it helped me imagine the Prague cemetery, which I have only seen in illustrations. I was a good narrator, I should have been an artist: from a few details I created a magical place, the sinister moonlit centre of the universal conspiracy. Why did I let my creation slip out of my hands? I could have done so much else with it. . . .

Rachkovsky has returned. He said he still needed me. I was annoyed. "You're not keeping to the agreement," I said. "I thought our score was settled. I gave you material never before seen, and you have kept quiet about the sewer. Indeed, it is I who am still owed something. You don't imagine such valuable material was free."

"It is you who's not keeping to the agreement. The documents paid for my silence. Now you want money as well. Fine then, I won't argue. So the money will pay for the documents. Therefore you still owe me something for my silence over the sewer. But I don't think we should start haggling, Simonini. It is not worth your while. I told you it's essential for France that the *bordereau* is regarded as genuine. But not for Russia. I could easily hand you over to the press. You'd spend the rest of your life in the law courts. Ah, I forgot. Just to get things clear about your past, I spoke to Father Bergamaschi, and to Monsieur Hébuterne. They told me you'd introduced them to an Abbé Dalla Piccola who had been involved in the Taxil affair. I tried to find him. It seems he's vanished into thin air, along with everyone else in the affair who had been living in a house in Auteuil – except for Taxil himself, who's wandering around Paris. He too is trying to find this missing clergyman. I could incriminate you for his murder."

"There's no body."

"There are four of them underneath here. Whoever put four bodies into a sewer could well have disposed of another one somewhere else."

I was in the hands of that wretch. "Very well," I said, "what do you want?"

"There's one passage in the material you gave Golovinsky which I found most fascinating – the plan to use the metropolitan railways to wreak havoc in the great cities. But for the argument to be believed, we need a few bombs to actually go off down there."

"And where? London? There's no metropolitan railway here yet."

"But they've started digging, there are excavations already along the Seine. I don't need you to blow up the whole of Paris. All I need is for two or three support beams to collapse, and even better if it takes away a piece of the roadway. A small explosion, but something that looks like a threat . . . and a confirmation."

"I understand. But where do I come in?"

"You have already worked with explosives and I understand you know a few handy experts. You have to look at things the right way. I'm sure everything will go off without incident – these first excavations are not guarded at night. But let us suppose, for some most unfortunate reason, that the bomber is discovered. If he's a Frenchman, then he risks a few years in prison, but if he's a Russian then it would start off a Franco-Prussian war. It cannot be one of my men."

I was about to become angry. I couldn't be involved in something as crazy as this. I'm a man of peace, a man of a certain age. But then I stopped myself. What had been causing that emptiness I had been feeling for weeks, other than a sense of no longer being a protagonist?

By accepting this assignment I would be back in the front line. I would be helping to bring credit to my Prague cemetery, making it more probable and therefore more real than it had ever been. Once again, alone, I was defeating an entire race.

"I have to talk to the right person," I replied. "I'll let you know in a few days."

I went to search out Gaviali. He still works as a rag-and-bone man but, thanks to my help, his papers are in order and he has some money set aside. Unfortunately, though, in less than five years he has aged badly – Cayenne leaves its mark. His hands shake and he struggles to lift his glass which I generously fill several times. He has difficulty moving around, can hardly bend down and I wonder how he manages to collect his rags.

He greets my proposal with enthusiasm: "It's no longer like it used to be, when you couldn't use certain explosives because they didn't give you the time to get away. Now everything's done with a good time bomb."

"How does it work?"

"Simple. You take any kind of alarm clock and set it to the time you want. When it reaches that hour, the alarm goes off and instead of activating the bell, if you connect it properly, it activates a detonator. The detonator detonates the charge, and bang. By then, you're ten miles away."

The following day he came to see me, bringing a gadget of terrifying simplicity: how could that tiny jumble of wires and that alarm clock, the size of a parish priest's turnip, possibly cause an explosion? And yet it does, Gaviali proudly assured me.

Two days later I went to explore the excavations that are being dug, and asked various questions of the workmen with an air of idle curiosity. I found one point where you could easily climb down from the road to the level immediately below, to the entrance of a tunnel supported by beams. I don't need to know where the tunnel leads, or even whether it goes anywhere: all I have to do is place the bomb at the entrance, and that's it.

I had to be blunt with Gaviali: "I have great respect for your expertise, but your hands shake and your legs can barely support you. You'd never manage to get down to the tunnel, and who knows what you'd end up doing with those wires you tell me about."

His eyes became tearful: "It's true, I'm finished."

"Who could do the job for you?"

"I don't know anyone. All my companions, don't forget, are still in Cayenne. You sent them there. The responsibility for that is yours. You want to explode the bomb? Then you'll have to do it yourself."

"Nonsense, I'm not an expert."

"You don't have to be an expert once you've been taught by an expert. Just look at these things I've put on the table. This is all you need to make a good time bomb. Any kind of alarm clock, like this, provided you understand the mechanism inside that sets the alarm off at the right time. Then a battery which, when activated by the alarm, sets off the detonator. I'm old-fashioned, and so I would use this battery called a Daniell Cell. In this type of battery, unlike the voltaic battery, the elements used are mainly liquid. Half of a small container is filled with copper sulphate and the other half with zinc sulphate. A small copper plate is put into the copper solution and a zinc plate into the zinc. The ends of

*. . . I don't need to know where
the tunnel leads, or even whether
it goes anywhere: all I have to
do is place the bomb at the
entrance, and that's it. . . .*

[PAGE 552]

553

the two plates obviously form the two poles of the battery. You understand?"

"So far, yes."

"Good. The only problem is that with a Daniell Cell you have to be very careful in moving it about, but until it's connected to the detonator and to the explosive, whatever happens there's no problem. When it's connected up it'll be on a flat surface, I hope, otherwise the operator's an idiot. For the detonator, any kind of small charge is sufficient. Finally we come to the charge itself. In the old days, you remember, I used to recommend black gunpowder. But ten years ago they discovered ballistite – ten per cent camphor and equal parts of nitroglycerine and collodion. There was a problem at first over the camphor, which easily evaporates, making the product unstable. But after the Italians began producing it at Avigliana it seems to be reliable. Or I could decide to use cordite, invented by the English, where fifty per cent of the camphor has been replaced by petroleum jelly, and for the rest they've taken fifty-eight per cent nitroglycerine and thirty-seven gun cotton dissolved in acetone, then extruded so that it looks like coarse spaghetti. I'll decide what's best, but there's not much difference. So . . . the first thing to do is set the hands of the clock to the correct time, then connect the clock to the battery, and this to the detonator, and the detonator to the charge, then activate the alarm. And remember, never reverse the order of the operations – it's obvious that if you connect first, then activate the alarm, and then turn the hands of the clock . . . bang! You understand? Then you go home, or to the theatre, or to a restaurant – the bomb goes off by itself. Understand, Captain?"

"I understand."

"I wouldn't go as far as saying that a child could do it, but one of Garibaldi's old captains certainly can. You have a firm hand and a clear eye. Just carry out those small operations as I've told you. All you have to do is follow the right order."

I agreed. If I succeed, it will knock years off me, I'll come back ready to trample underfoot all the Mordechais of this world. And that whore in the Turin ghetto. *Gagnu*, eh? I'll take care of you.

I need to get rid of the smell of Diana in heat, which has been following me through the summer nights for a year and a half. I realise the whole purpose of my life has been to bring down that accursed race. Rachkovsky is right, hatred alone warms the heart.

I must go to complete my task in full attire. I have put on my dress coat and the beard I wore for evenings at Juliette Adam's. Almost by chance, I discovered at the bottom of a cupboard a small supply of the Parke & Davis cocaine I had obtained for Dr Froïde. Who knows how it came to be there. I've never tried it before but, if the doctor is right, it ought to give me a boost. I've also had three small shots of cognac. And I'm feeling as strong as a lion.

Gaviali wants to come with me but I'm not going to let him – he's too slow, he'd get in my way.

I understand perfectly well how it all works. This bomb is going to cause one hell of a stir.

Gaviali's giving me the final instructions: "Watch out here, watch out there."

For heaven's sake, I'm not yet a decrepit old fool.

Dear Readers

The nineteenth century teemed with mysterious and horrible events: the *Protocols of the Elders of Zion*, the notorious forgery that later inspired Hitler; the Dreyfus Case; and numerous intrigues involving the secret services of various nations, Masonic sects, Jesuit conspiracies, as well as other episodes that – were they not documented truths – would be difficult to believe.

The Prague Cemetery is a story in which all the characters except one – the main Character – really existed. Even the hero's grandfather, the author of a mysterious actual letter that triggered modern anti-Semitism, is historical. And the hero himself, though fictional, is a personage who resembles many people we have all known, past and present. In the book, he serves as the author of diverse fabrications and plots against a backdrop of extraordinary *coups de théâtre*: sewers filled with corpses, ships that explode in the region of an erupting volcano, abbots stabbed to death, notaries with fake beards, hysterical female Satanists, the celebrants of black Masses, and so on.

The fact that history can be quite so devious may cause the reader's brow to become lightly beaded with sweat. He will look anxiously behind him, switch on all the lights, and suspect that these things could happen again today. In fact, they may be happening in that very moment. And he will think, as I do: "They are among us . . ."

–Umberto Eco

USELESS LEARNED EXPLANATIONS

HISTORICAL

The only fictitious character in this story is the protagonist, Simone Simonini – his grandfather, Captain Simonini, is not invented, even if he is known to History only as the mysterious author of a letter to Abbé Barruel.

All the others (except for a few incidental minor characters such as Notaio Rebaudengo and Ninuzzo) actually existed, and said and did what they are described as saying and doing in this novel. That is true not only of those characters who appear under their real names (and, though many might find this improbable, even a character like Leo Taxil actually existed) but also of figures who appear under a fictitious name where, for narrative economy, I have made one single (invented) character say and do what was in fact said and done by two (historically real) characters.

But on reflection, even Simone Simonini, although in effect a collage, a character to whom events have been attributed which were actually done by others, did in some sense exist. Indeed, to be frank, he is still among us.

THE STORY AND PLOT

The Narrator is aware that, in the fairly chaotic plot sequence of the diaries reproduced here (moving back and forth, using what cineastes call flashbacks), the reader might have difficulty in following the linear progression of events, from Simonini's birth to the end of his diaries. It is the fatal imbalance between *story* and *plot*, or even worse, as the Russian formalists (all Jewish) used to say, between *fabula* and *sjužet*. The Narrator, to be honest, has often found it difficult finding his own way around, but feels a competent reader need not become lost in the detail and should enjoy the story just the same. However, for the benefit of the overly meticulous reader, or one who is not so quick on the uptake, here is a table which sets out the relationship between the two levels (common in truth to every *well-made* novel, as it used to be called).

CHAPTER	PLOT	STORY
1. A Passerby on that Grey Morning	The Narrator begins to follow Simonini's diary	
2. Who Am I?	Diary 24th March 1897	
3. *Chez Magny*	Diary 25th March 1897 (description of meals *Chez Magny* 1885–1886)	
4. In My Grandfather's Day	Diary 26th March 1897	1830 – 1855 Childhood and adolescence in Turin to death of Simonini's grandfather
5. Simonino the Carbonaro	Diary 27th March 1897	1855–1859 Working for Notaio Rebaudengo and first contact with the secret service
6. Serving the Secret Service	Diary 28th March 1897	1860 Interview with heads of Piedmont secret service
7. With the Thousand	Diary 29th March 1897	1860

		On the *Emma* with Dumas – Arrival at Palermo – Meeting with Nievo – First return to Turin
8. The *Ercole*	Diaries 30th March – 1st April 1897	1861 Disappearance of Nievo – Second return to Turin and exile in Paris
9. Paris	Diary 2nd April 1897	1861 . . . Early years in Paris
10. Dalla Piccola Perplexed	Diary 3rd April 1897	
11. Joly	Diary 3rd April 1897, night	1865 In prison spying on Joly – Trap for the Carbonari
12. A Night in Prague	Diary 4th April 1897	1865–1866 First version of the scene in the Prague cemetery – Meetings with Brafmann and Gougenot
13. Dalla Piccola Says He Is Not Dalla Piccola	Diary 5th April 1897	
14. Biarritz	Diary 5th April 1897	1867–1868 Meeting Goedsche in Munich – Killing of Dalla Piccola
15. Dalla Piccola Redivivus	Diary 6th and 7th April 1897	1869 Lagrange describes Boullan
16. Boullan	Diary 8th April 1897	1869 Dalla Piccola meets Boullan
17. The Days of The Commune	Diary 9th April 1897	1871 The Days of the Commune
18. The Protocols	Diary 10th and 11th April 1897	1871–1879 Return of Father Bergamaschi – Expansion of the Prague cemetery scene – Killing of Joly
19. Osman Bey	Diary 11th April 1897	1881 Meeting with Osman Bey
20. Russians?	Diary 12th April 1897	
21. Taxil	Diary 13th April 1897	1884

		Simonini meets Taxil
22. The Devil in the Nineteenth Century	Diary 14th April 1897	1884–1896 Taxil against the Masons
23. Twelve Years Well Spent	Diary 15th and 16th April 1897	1884–1896 The same years seen by Simonini (during this period Simonini meets the psychiatrists *chez Magny* as described in chapter 3)
24. A Night Mass	Diary 17th April 1897 (which ends at dawn 18th April)	1896–1897 Collapse of the Taxil venture 21st March 1897 – black mass
25. Sorting Matters Out	Diary 18th and 19th April 1897	1897 Simonini understands and eliminates Dalla Piccola
26. The Final Solution	Diary 10th November 1898	1898 The final solution
27. Diary Cut Short	Diary 20th December 1898	1898 Preparation for the bomb attack

Сергѣй Нилусъ.

Великое въ маломъ

и

АНТИХРИСТЪ,

какъ близкая политическая возможность.

ЗАПИСКИ ПРАВОСЛАВНАГО.

(ИЗДАНІЕ ВТОРОЕ, ИСПРАВЛЕННОЕ И ДОПОЛНЕННОЕ).

ЦАРСКОЕ СЕЛО.
Типографія Царскосельскаго Комитета Краснаго Креста.
1905.

First edition of The Protocols of the Elders of Zion, *which appeared in* The Great within the Small, *by Sergei Nilus.*

[PAGE 562]

DATE	LATER EVENTS
1905	*The Great within the Small*, by Sergei Nilus, appears in Russia, with the following introduction: "A personal friend, now dead, gave me a manuscript which, with unusual perfection and clarity, describes the course and development of a sinister world conspiracy. . . . This document came into my hands around four years ago along with the absolute guarantee that it is the genuine translation of (original) documents stolen by a woman from one of the most powerful leaders, and highest initiates, of Freemasonry. . . . The theft was carried out at the end of a secret assembly of 'Initiates' in France – a country which is the nest of the 'Jewish Masonic Conspiracy'. I venture to reveal this manuscript, for those who wish to see and listen, under the title of 'The Protocols of the Elders of Zion'." The *Protocols* are immediately translated into many languages.
1921	*The Times* of London finds similarities with Joly's book and denounces the *Protocols* as false, but they continue to be published as genuine.
1925	Hitler, *Mein Kampf* (I, 11): "How much the whole existence of this people is based on a permanent falsehood is apparent in the famous *Protocols of the Elders of Zion*. Every week the *Frankfurter Zeitung* whines that they are based on a forgery: and here lies the best proof that they are genuine. . . . When this book becomes the common heritage of all people, the Jewish peril can then be considered as stamped out."
1939	In *L'Apocalypse de notre temps*, Henri Rollin writes, "They can be regarded as the most widely circulated work in the world after the Bible."

ILLUSTRATIONS

p.156 – *Victory at Calatafimi*, 1860 © Mary Evans Picture Library / Archivi Alinari.

p.205 – Honoré Daumier, *Un jour où l'on ne paye pas* (Members of the public at the Salon, 10, for *Le Charivari*), 1852 © BnF.

p.438 – Honoré Daumier, *Et dire qu'il y a des personnes qui boivent de l'eau dans un pays qui produit du bon vin comme celui-ci!* (*Croquis parisiens* for *Le journal amusant*), 1864 © BnF.

p.469 – *Le Petit Journal*, 13 Janvier 1895 © Archivi Alinari.

All other illustrations are taken from the Author's collection.